THE HEROES OF SAINTE-MÈRE-ÉGLISE

J.D. KEENE

vinci
BOOKS

Vinci Books

vinci-books.com

Published by Vinci Books Ltd in 2025

1

Copyright © J.D. Keene 2019

The author has asserted their moral right to be identified as the author of this work in accordance with the Copyright, Designs and Patents Act 1988. This work is a work of fiction. Names, characters, places and incidents are the product of the author's imagination or are used fictitiously. Any resemblance to actual persons, living or dead, places and incidents is entirely coincidental.

All rights reserved. No part of this publication may be copied, reproduced, distributed, stored in any retrieval system, or transmitted in any form or by any means, including photocopying, recording, or other electronic or mechanical methods, nor used as a source for any form of machine learning including AI datasets, without the prior written permission of the publisher.

The publisher and the author have made every effort to obtain permissions for any third party material used in this book and to comply with copyright law. Any queries in this respect should be brought to the attention of the publisher and any omissions will be corrected in future editions.

A CIP catalogue record for this book is available from the British Library.

Paperback ISBN: 9781036702373

To Katie, who has always believed.

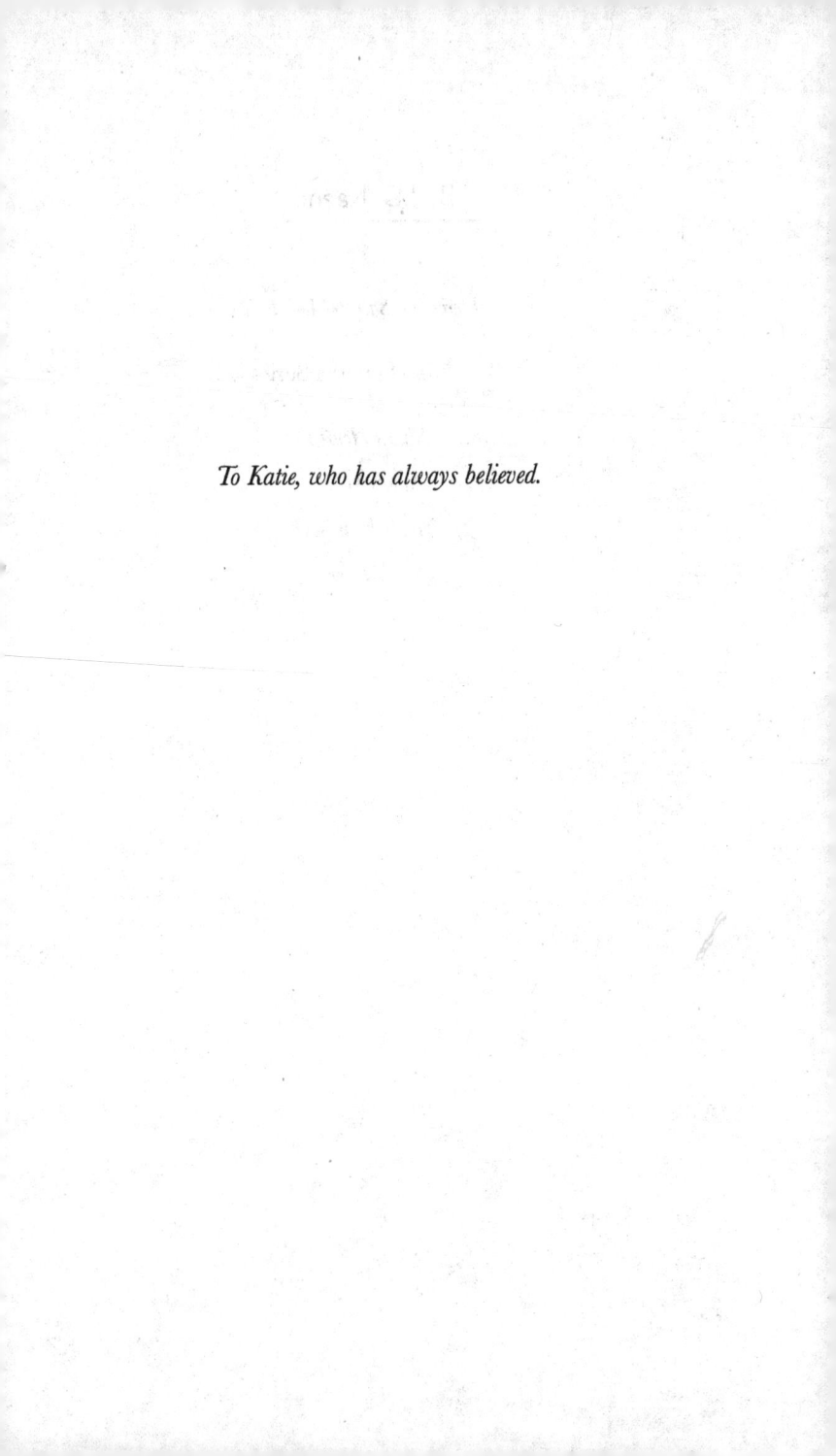

By J.D. Keene

The Heroes of Sainte-Mère-Église

The Nino Servidei Series

Nino's Heart
Nino's War
Nino's Promise
Nino's Blood

Cast of Characters

AMERICAN
Fictional

Jack Wakefield, captain, 82nd Airborne, U.S. Army

Baldwin Hicks, staff sergeant, 82nd Airborne, U.S. Army

Historical

Dwight D. Eisenhower, supreme commander, Allied Expeditionary Force

James (Jumpin' Jim) Gavin, general, 82nd Airborne, U.S. Army

William Lee, major general, 101st Airborne, U.S. Army

Jim Ewens, captain, U.S. Army Air Corps

William Surratt, first lieutenant, 4th Infantry Division, U.S. Army

Wallace Strobel, first lieutenant, 101st Airborne, U.S. Army

John Steele, corporal, 82nd Airborne, U.S. Army

William Shirer, reporter, CBS News

BRITISH
Fictional

Quinn Family

Oliver Quinn, resident of the island of Guernsey, farmer

Margaret Quinn, wife

Claire Quinn, daughter

Mack McVie, sergeant, 51st Highlander Division, BEF

Colin Fradd, sergeant, 51st Highlander Division, BEF

Simon Hancock, sergeant, medic, 51st Highlander Division, BEF

Virgil Pierpont, squadron leader, RAF

Kingsley Dalton, flight lieutenant, RAF

Historical

Winston Churchill, prime minister

Bertram Ramsey, vice admiral, Royal Navy

William Wharton, captain, Royal Navy

William Tennant, captain, Royal Navy

Alan Brooke, chief of the Imperial General Staff

Charles Lightoller, captain of the yacht, Sundowner

Alastair Denniston, commander, Bletchley Park

Stuart Milner-Berry, champion chess player, code breaker

Gordan Welchman, mathematician, code breaker

Frank Nelson, chief, SOE

Kathleen Summersby, General Eisenhower's driver, BMTC

French
Fictional (* Member of the French Resistance)

Legrand Family

René Legrand, farmer*

Cécile Legrand, wife

Philippe Legrand, oldest son

Jean-Pierre, youngest son*

Ganier Family

Pascal Ganier, farmer*

Luke Ganier, son*

Madeleine Ganier, grandmother

Lapierre Family
Brigitte Lapierre, widow
Armand Lapierre, son
Angélique Lapierre, daughter*

Hall Family
Arthur Hall, American/French citizen, thoroughbred horse farmer*
Gabrielle Hall, French wife*

Laurent Family
Martin Laurent, lieutenant, 21st Infantry Division, French Army
Margot Laurent, wife, schoolteacher

Marchand Brothers
André Marchand, grocer
François Marchand, older brother

Garcia Family
Salvador Garcia, hotel owner
Maximina (Max) Garcia, son

Daniel Girard, owner of a tugboat company, resident of Cherbourg*
Antoine Devaux, owner of a marine electrical shop, resident of Cherbourg*
Julien DuBois, dock supervisor*
Domingo Barojas, guide
Maurice Fuquay, student
Marcel Bordeur, corporal, 21st Infantry Division, French Army
Ismaela Abraham, nursing home resident
Hyam Rubin, nursing home resident
Netta Rubin, nursing home resident

Historical

Alexandre Renaud, mayor, Sainte-Mère-Église

Charles de Gaulle, general, French Army

Doctor Pelletier

GERMAN
Fictional

Shapiro Family

Joseph Shapiro, living in France, banker

Ingrid Shapiro, wife

Alfred Shapiro, oldest son

Dreyfus Shapiro, youngest son

German Military

Gunther Dettmer, sturmbannführer, Waffen-SS

Helmut Volk, oberst, Wehrmacht

Wilhelm Ziegler, major, Wehrmacht

Wolfgang Beck, corporal, Wehrmacht

Claus Muller, corporal, Wehrmacht

Historical

Adolf Hitler, chancellor/führer

Hermann Göring, supreme commander of the Luftwaffe

Erwin Rommel, generalfeldmarschall

POLISH
Fictional

Edelman Family

Uri Edelman, professor of music

Miriam Edelman, wife, professor of language

Esther Edelman, daughter

Spanish
Fictional

Uncle Marcos, Spanish revolutionary

Welsh
Historical

Frederick Riddle, seaman, Royal Navy

Contributing Characters**
Colin Fradd

Elizabeth Gassoway

Joe Alvarez

Katie Keene

Kimberly Morrison

*** Contributing characters are neither fictional nor historical. They are actual individuals who made significant contributions to this novel in the form of editing or advanced reading.*

PART I
Invasion

Let us be firm, pure and faithful; at the end of our sorrow, there is the greatest glory of the world, that of the men who did not give in.

Charles de Gaulle

Chapter One

MAY 10, 1940

Tünsdorf, Germany

SS-*Sturmbannführer* Gunther Dettmer had been dreaming of this day since his childhood. When he was seven, his father died in the Great War. He never knew how, only that it happened in a battle against the French army—a thought that never escaped him.

Now, with the early morning sun rising behind him, the tall, broad shouldered *SS* officer stood in knee-high grass on top of a small hill. He represented the classic Nazi image of the master race with his blue eyes and blonde hair.

Through his binoculars he looked west at a column of *Panzer* tanks—their gun turrets pointing toward the French village of Étain. Surrounding him were hundreds of lorry troop-carriers, each with sixteen members of the elite *Waffen-SS*, a unit created to intimidate and control its victims by any means necessary.

"I find the sound of those idling engines exhilarating," he said to a low-ranking foot soldier standing next to him.

"What a beautiful sight. There are more than seven hundred *Panzers* just in this column alone. To the north—two thousand more on the borders of the Netherlands and Belgium."

The Great War ended in 1918, with the surrender of Germany and the signing of the Treaty of Versailles. The treaty forced Germany to pay large reparations to the victors, including the French and British. This became burdensome for the German people, who already struggled in an economic depression.

To pay the obligations forced upon them by the treaty, Germany printed massive amounts of currency. This created inflated prices, causing food, housing, coal, and heating oil to became unaffordable for most Germans. Rampant unemployment left a feeling of helplessness throughout the country.

Now, Gunther Dettmer stands proudly. He is dressed in his green *SS* battle uniform, with the *Totenkopf* skull and crossbones emblem on his cap—his thoughts are focused on his father and mother. His father whom he barely knew, and his mother who had been forced to do unspeakable things to support him and his sister due to the collapse of the German economy.

Not realizing the foot soldier couldn't hear him over the rumble of the engines, Dettmer continued, "Those bastards treated us like common rodents after the war. The day of sweet revenge has arrived. I am proud to be standing here as a witness to history. In just a few moments, our *Führer* will give the order, and the *Blitzkrieg* will begin." *I wish you were here, Mother*, he said to himself. *You deserve to experience this as much as I do.*

In the sky above, the sounds of airplanes roared from behind him. Looking up, he saw the beautiful sight of hundreds of *Luftwaffe* Ju 87 dive bombers headed into France, followed by the accelerated roar of the seven hundred *Panzer* engines that ceased being idle.

"*Es hat begonnen,*" Gunther Dettmer whispered to himself. It has started.

Sainte-Mère-Église, France

Through the poppy fields. That was their favorite path home from school. Their footprints left a wake of red and gold as they leisurely made the journey.

Their friendship, now in its third year, started when Jean-Pierre came to the rescue of Alfred, who was being bullied at school. Several of the other boys, led by the pudgy Maurice Fuquay, had pushed Alfred to the ground, causing him to lose his wire-rimmed glasses. Then they spit on him and shouted "Jew boy" over and over while kicking dirt in his face.

Jean-Pierre, standing several meters away, got a running start, tackled Maurice, and punched him. He landed several blows to his head. After multiple punches to his face, his nose bled, and his lip became cut. With Maurice pleading for him to stop, Jean-Pierre climbed off the defeated tyrant. He then helped Alfred to his feet and handed him his glasses as Maurice and the other boys ran away.

Even though they initially had little in common, Jean-Pierre Legrand and Alfred Shapiro had become the best of friends since Alfred and his family moved to Sainte-Mère-Église from northern France.

Jean-Pierre was Catholic, and Alfred was Jewish. Alfred stood slightly shorter than Jean-Pierre and had black hair.

Jean-Pierre, although only average height, carried himself with a quiet confidence that made him appear taller. He had blue eyes and dark brown hair that he wore a little longer than his parents would have liked. Jean-Pierre's father made his living as a farmer, while Alfred's father was a teller at the only bank in Sainte-Mère-Église.

"You were the best violinist in the recital today, Alfred," Jean-Pierre said.

"Do you really think so, or are you just saying that?"

"Why do you doubt me? Have I ever lied to you before?"

"Only when you think I will get my feelings hurt."

"What is wrong with that? You're my best friend."

"You treat me like a child sometimes, even though we are both thirteen."

Jean-Pierre was getting bored with the conversation. "Did you invite Angélique to your birthday party tomorrow?"

"I was waiting for you to ask me that. Yes, I did, but she has to work at Brécourt Manor."

"Your party isn't until noon. Maybe I'll go help her, so she can finish her chores early and come to your party."

"Jean-Pierre, she barely knows who you are. She is fourteen. She will have nothing to do with you."

"Maybe after your party, you and I can go fishing at Le Grand Vey."

"And to get to Le Grand Vey, we have to ride our bicycles past her farmhouse. You are always working a plan, Jean-Pierre."

"Your bar mitzvah is the following week. You should invite her to that."

"She's Catholic. She won't want to come to my bar mitzvah."

"I'm Catholic, and I'm going. So are my parents. My brother will still be home on military leave. He will come, too, and he is Catholic."

"Okay, I'll ask her. Now stop using the celebrations in my life to spend time with someone who has no interest in you."

"I will marry her one day, Alfred. You will be my best man. The whole town will be there. We are getting married in Notre-dame-de-l'Assomption."

"Okay, Jean-Pierre. Whatever you say."

Home on leave from northern France, Jean-Pierre's brother, Philippe, was a machine gunner on the Maginot Line.

Philippe had explained to Jean-Pierre that the Maginot Line was a long, underground fortress on the border between northern France and southern Germany. It comprised many kilometers of corridors, ammunition storage rooms, and living spaces for French troops. It had large cannons mounted in bunkers pointed toward Germany. The French government built them as a deterrent to prevent Germany from invading France, as they had done twenty-four years earlier during the Great War.

Whenever Philippe discussed his military duties at the family dinner table, Jean-Pierre could see how his father swelled with pride that his oldest son was defending France today, as he himself had done during the Great War. Jean-Pierre's mother did not approve of such talk at the dinner table.

"Prideful tough talk only brings about more war," she would say.

Like every French citizen over the age of thirty, Cécile Legrand had experienced war, and she didn't want her children to live through what she had.

As Jean-Pierre and Alfred stepped out of the poppy field and onto the unpaved road, they looked off into the distance and could see dirt being stirred by a car moving in their direction.

"That is Armand's car," said Jean-Pierre.

"He is really driving fast," replied Alfred.

"I think my brother Philippe is with him."

Armand Lapierre was Philippe's best friend and Angélique's older brother. He, too, was home on leave. Philippe and Armand were both part of the French 3rd Army Division. They were stationed on the Western Flank of the Maginot Line at Fort Jeanne d'Arc at Metz; they were home for the first time in several months.

Jean-Pierre liked it when Armand was around. He would often bring Angélique when he came to visit Philippe. Armand and Angélique lived a few villages to the southeast, in Saint Marie-Du-Mont, with their mother, Brigitte.

Angélique had brown eyes and dark brown hair that she wore pulled back with a ribbon to match one of the two dresses she owned. Jean-Pierre thought it was cute that a few strands of her bangs would always hang down over her beautiful face. Whenever Jean-Pierre was near her, he would get nervous and his mouth would get dry. But he always found the courage to say hello and make her laugh with some silly antic.

Armand's car approached and slowed. Dressed in his battle uniform, Philippe got out and ran up to Jean-Pierre. Philippe, standing much taller than Jean-Pierre, had a strong build and chiseled face like their father. Jean-Pierre could see by Philippe's expression that something was wrong.

"Jean-Pierre," he said. "You need to listen. I must go now. They have called Armand and me back to our garrison. The Germans have moved into France. There are reports of thousands of tanks and infantry troops. Their planes are bombing villages in the Netherlands, Belgium, and northern France. They have already taken control of several villages in the lowlands. We have got to get back. I'm counting on you to take care of Mama and Papa. You will be safe. We won't let them get here. We will fight them off, just like Papa did before."

"When will you be back, Philippe?"

"Only after we have driven them back. But it will be soon. I promise."

He then embraced his little brother, got back into the car with Armand, and off they went at breakneck speed, dirt flying from under the tires.

Alfred said, "I'm scared, Jean-Pierre. My father told me the reason we moved from northern France to Sainte-Mère-Église was because he had heard from relatives in Germany that it was no longer safe to be Jewish and anywhere near Germany. The Nazis were rounding up Jews, taking them away, and they were not returning."

"Don't be afraid, Alfred. You heard my brother. They will never get this far south. Our army is tough and strong and brave. You will see."

Jean-Pierre, looking at Alfred with frustration, said, "I wish I were older. I would go fight with my brother. Together we would fight side by side and push the Germans back."

Alfred said, "I need to get home. I need to tell Papa that the Germans are trying to cross into France."

The boys realized that they still had two kilometers to get home. The walk to and from school every day usually took them an hour. Anxious to see their parents, they both ran. As they did, once again, they looked up and saw the dirt from another speeding vehicle coming in their direction. This time, it was a truck. Alfred recognized it as his papa's truck. In it he saw his papa, his mama, and his five-year-old brother, Dreyfus. Behind the truck was the same trailer they'd used to move all the way from Verdun, France, near the German border, three years earlier.

Just as when they moved to Sainte-Mère-Église, all of their belongings—what little they had—were loaded up in the truck and the trailer. When the old truck got closer, Alfred's papa pumped the brakes hard, causing them to squeak and squeal. Alfred's mother leaped out of the truck and ran to Alfred.

"Alfred, get in the truck. We are leaving for Spain. We have packed all of your things in the trailer."

Alfred looked at his best friend. "I have to go now, Jean-Pierre."

Jean-Pierre tried to be brave and shook Alfred's hand. "You will be back soon—I know you will. I have your birthday present at my house. I will give it to you when you return."

The handshake between the two boys turned into an embrace. Both boys sensed that something evil was happening, and they would probably never see each other again.

As Jean-Pierre made his way through the narrow streets of Sainte-Mère-Église, he approached the centerpiece of the village, the courtyard of the Catholic church, Notre-Dame-de-l'Assomption. Several shops such as Le café Du Quartier, the DuBost bakery, and the pharmacy owned by the town mayor, Alexandre Renaud, surrounded it.

At the other end of the courtyard, lived the town doctor,

Dr. Pelletier. His house was next to the village park, the Park of La Haule. Next to the park was a large barn that stored hay.

Crossing the courtyard on his way home, Jean-Pierre saw many of the townspeople gathering. This was not unusual. The ancient Roman road marker in the church courtyard established itself as a frequent gathering place for impromptu meetings to discuss events, both important and unimportant. Every Thursday since 1889, cattlemen and farmers from all over the region sold their livestock and produce in the courtyard. However, this time the purpose for meeting was different. This time, Jean-Pierre heard both anger and fear in the voices of those who gathered. Some men were carrying shotguns. Those who had fought in the Great War carried Berthiers, the standard issue rifle used by the French army.

Even though it was Friday, a line of people filed into the Catholic church. Some were weeping. All stopped to speak with Father Rousseau as they entered.

In a hurry to get home, Jean-Pierre didn't stop to listen to the details of the discussions. He crossed through the courtyard as he and Alfred had done so many times before. However, he overheard the men planning a strategy to defend Sainte-Mère-Église from the Germans if they ever made it this far south.

He heard Dr. Pelletier ask, "What if Paris falls?"

Mayor Renaud was more optimistic. "The Maginot Line will stop the Germans in their tracks."

This made Jean-Pierre think of Philippe, who would soon arrive at his garrison. The troops may already be under attack, even before he and Armand got there.

Jean-Pierre tried to fight back his emotions, but at that moment he couldn't. He ran home with tears rolling down his cheeks. He was concerned for everyone he cared about. His brother Philippe, his mama and papa, and his beautiful Angélique. He also worried about his closest friend in the world, Alfred.

He asked himself, *What will happen to Alfred? Why do so many people hate the Jews? Why do the Germans treat the Jews so horribly?*

He had overheard conversations between Alfred's parents while visiting Alfred's house. He didn't understand the seriousness of their words. He recalled how upset Alfred's mother was after receiving a letter from her sister in Germany, telling of the arrest of Alfred's uncle.

"They took him away two weeks earlier," her sister wrote, "and nobody would say where he was, or when he would be home."

She added, "This has been happening to Jewish men for weeks, and nobody has been heard from since."

Jean-Pierre hoped that Alfred's family would make it safely to Spain and that Philippe, Armand, and the rest of the French army could push the Germans back into the Rhineland.

Jean-Pierre's family owned a small farm just north of Sainte-Mère-Église. When Jean-Pierre got to the front porch of his farmhouse, he stopped to wipe the tears from his eyes. He wanted his papa to be as proud of him as he was of Philippe. He didn't want either of his parents to see he had been crying. He also knew the time for boyish tears had passed today. He had to stay strong. He had to be brave because he sensed that soon, many people would be counting on him.

Courtils, France

It had been four hours since Alfred and his family drove away from Sainte-Mère-Église. The rain was coming down hard, and the windshield wipers on the old truck only moved at one speed, and that was slow.

"Joseph, please pull over. It isn't safe driving in this rain. We can't even see the road. The rain will subside. Just give it a chance."

Joseph gripped the steering wheel tightly as he tried to find the road through the pouring rain. "Ingrid, you heard the radio broadcast. The Germans are slicing through Belgium, the Netherlands, and northern France. It is only a matter of time before they're at the base of the Pyrénées. We need to get over those mountains and into Spain before they arrive. We have no time to pull over."

As Alfred and Dreyfus were sitting quietly, yet uncomfortably, between their parents on the single bench seat of the old truck, Alfred was thinking of his friend Jean-Pierre.

He felt regret that in the three years since he had become friends with Jean-Pierre, he had not been honest with him. Alfred's father, Joseph Shapiro, had insisted that the family's enormous wealth remain a secret. As an additional precautionary measure, they told everyone they met that they were originally from Verdun, France. Although they lived there for a short time after fleeing Germany, they were in fact German citizens. Also, Mr. Shapiro wasn't just a bank teller, which was his trade in Sainte-Mère-Église, but the president of the largest bank in Berlin.

Joseph and Ingrid Shapiro were only in their early forties, but at first glance, appeared much older. They were both overweight, though they had lost some body mass since their exodus from Germany. Joseph was mostly bald on top with a thick band of black hair that wrapped around the back of his head. He always wore a baggy black suit, black tie, and white shirt. He stood slightly shorter than the average man.

Ingrid could best be described as frumpy. Like Joseph, her wardrobe was sparse, and she could usually be seen in one of the four tattered dresses she wore regularly. Her short dark hair revealed hints of gray, and was often slightly messy, as if she attempted to comb it in the morning, but never got around to finishing. Their disheveled appearance was due in part to their desire to conceal their wealth, and also because the stress of living in hiding had caused the pride they once valued to diminish.

Ingrid said, "Joseph, we will never make it to Spain if we drive over the side of a bridge or hit a tree. Besides, the boys need to stretch their legs."

"Yes, I have to pee, Papa," said Dreyfus.

"You always have to pee, Dreyfus. You must have a bladder the size of a horsefly," said Joseph. "Listen, all of you. We will stop soon, but I will remind you of what I have been telling you since we left Germany. I am a marked man. You know that. Adolf Hitler himself has put a bounty on my head. That means you, my family, have a price on your head, too."

During the rise of Adolf Hitler and the Nazi Party, Joseph Shapiro was the leader of a strong and vocal opposition to Hitler. He also gave large sums of money to any organization that opposed the Nazi Party. Once Hitler became chancellor of Germany in 1933, those who had been vocally against the Nazis were being rounded up by Hitler's "brownshirts" and publicly beaten and imprisoned. Sometimes, they would go missing, taken away in the middle of the night and never seen again. Mr. Shapiro knew

The Heroes of Sainte-Mère Église

if he stayed in Germany long enough, he too, along with his entire family, would be among the missing.

Although it had been four years since he'd spoken to any of his neighbors in Berlin, the last time he had, they informed him that the brownshirts had come by his home looking for him and offered a substantial reward to anyone who could tell them of Mr. Shapiro's whereabouts. They also informed him that the Nazis had raided his home and loaded up trucks with valuable paintings, silver, and furniture. This, Mr. Shapiro had never shared with his wife, Ingrid.

Because he knew the Nazi philosophy was gaining strength throughout the entire European continent, Mr. Shapiro didn't feel his family would be safe if they made it known who they were. So, they used various false names, and everyone thought they were a poor family from northern France who moved to Sainte-Mère-Église because of the Nazi uprising in neighboring Germany.

"It looks like the rain is coming down even harder," said Joseph. "I think now is a good time to pull over until the rain lets up."

As he looked to the right for a safe place to pull over, he didn't notice the large hole on the side of the road where the road bank had been washed away from the rain.

When his left front tire hit the hole, it became submerged below the deep puddle and blew out when it hit the sharp edge on the other side of the hole. As the front wheel hopped out of the deep rift with a violent leap high into the air, slamming down on the asphalt, the rear wheel hit the same hole and suffered an identical fate, causing another violent blowout.

Joseph tried to maintain control of the truck and trailer, but the two blowouts caused the top-heavy vehicle to lean hard to the left and roll over on its side and down the small embankment. The truck turned over multiple times before finally coming to rest on its driver's side, as the wheels of the truck continued to spin freely. The accident caused their belongings to scatter for hundreds of meters throughout the wet field.

Mr. Shapiro lay on his left side, pressed against his door, his family resting on top of him, pinning him to the broken glass of his door.

"Is everyone okay?" asked Joseph.

"I think I am, Joseph. Just a little banged up and sore," replied Ingrid.

"I'm fine, Papa," said Alfred.

"Dreyfus?" Asked Joseph, not hearing a response.

"Dreyfus?" shouted Ingrid. "Oh Dreyfus!"

Ingrid lifted her left arm to find Dreyfus unconscious and bleeding profusely from a severe gash across the left side of his head.

Northern France

Philippe and Armand were just north of Reims when, in the distance, they saw a French military train headed northeast from Paris. Seeing it gave them a sense of pride and confidence. The steam from the stack blew high in the air as the engine pulled flatbed train cars carrying tanks and antiaircraft guns.

Trailing behind the flatbeds were several passenger cars loaded with hundreds of French soldiers heading to the front lines.

"That's right, boys," shouted Philippe. "Those Germans

The Heroes of Sainte-Mère Église

are about to learn their lesson for a second time. We defeated them in the Great War, and we will defeat them again."

In Armand's excitement, he increased the pressure on the accelerator causing his 1932 Peugeot to rattle like an empty oil can filled with bolts.

"We are getting close to Metz, Philippe. God, I hope the Maginot Line holds."

"It will, Armand. Our boys have been training for this moment for years."

Looking in his rearview mirror, Armand noticed three planes approaching from behind. "We have company, Philippe."

Philippe turned his head around and glanced through the rear window. Approaching them rapidly, staying low and parallel to the road, were three planes. With a loud roar and lightning speed, they flew right over their car before gaining altitude.

"Did you see the black crosses on the fuselage?" asked Philippe. "Those are German planes."

They continued to watch them as they headed toward the supply train in the distance. In single file, all three planes quickly gained altitude. They made an abrupt turn to the left and then dove in the train's direction, following a path directly over the tracks.

As they zeroed in on the train, the first plane, a Messerschmitt 109, opened fire on the passenger cars, spraying a ray of bullets into the roof of each car, penetrating the wooden roofs. Philippe and Armand watched as some of the windows were shattered by the strafing bullets and others were sprayed with the blood of French soldiers.

After the first plane veered to the right, the second plane, a Junkers Ju 87, dove sharply over the flatbed train car that was carrying the tanks. It dropped a large bomb directly on the first tank, causing it to explode into a massive fireball. That plane also veered, following the Messerschmitt into the horizon.

Finally, the last plane, also a Junkers Ju 87, followed the same path as the previous two. It flew directly over the steam engine itself. Once again, another massive bomb was released from the bottom of the plane, scoring a direct hit, it created an explosion that was larger than the last.

The train continued to stay on the tracks for several seconds before it tipped over on its right side. A violent shrieking noise could be heard over a kilometer away. Dirt and smoke rose high in the air as the remaining cars slammed together like an accordion, resulting in a third massive explosion.

Armand pulled the car over to the side of the road and slammed on the brakes, causing the car to skid through the dirt.

They sat quietly in disbelief at what they had just witnessed. Philippe felt sick to his stomach as a rush of emotions overcame him. He considered opening the door to vomit but fought the urge. Armand broke the silence. "They didn't stand a chance, Philippe. What the hell are we up against?"

Étain, France

"Don't let them escape," shouted *SS-Sturmbannführer* Gunther Dettmer. "Kill them!"

The small squad receiving the order from Dettmer hesitated. *Had they heard his instructions correctly? Why was he ordering the cold-blooded execution of innocent women and children?*

"What are you waiting for? Did you not hear me? Take them out—now!"

The group of villagers were exiting the little village of Étain, which had the misfortune of being in the path of the advancing German army. It had been set ablaze by air strikes, mortar rounds, and the firepower of dozens of *Panzer* tanks.

The fleeing villagers watched as *SS* soldiers approached and forced them to halt on the edge of the road. Mothers held their crying children closely. The elderly made the sign of the cross and whispered prayers. Moments later— machine gun fire. Then—silence.

Northern France

Though many meters away, the smell of the burning train was pungent—a mixture of wood, oil, and burning flesh.

Armand opened his trunk and removed their weapons. He was slightly shorter than Philippe and looked up as he handed him his MAS-38 submachine gun.

As Philippe inserted the only ammunition clip he had with him, Armand grabbed an ammo box and loaded his bolt-action MAS-36 carbine rifle. "How much petrol do we have, Armand?"

"Not enough. And with all hell breaking loose, it will not be easy to find any."

"Let's find a farm. If we tell the farmer we need to return to the front, he'll give us what we need."

"That's if the Germans haven't already raided all the farms."

After they had traveled another twenty kilometers, cars headed south passed them at speeds that were far too fast for the narrow dirt roads. Tied to their roofs were suitcases and furniture.

Later, they met large numbers of refugees. They were on foot. Some with nothing but the clothes on their backs, others with ox carts loaded with valuables. Their faces reflected exhaustion and defeat. Many had no place to go. They knew from living through the last war that their farms and villages in Belgium and northern France were no place to be during a German assault.

With little room between the two sides of the road, the travelers eased their way to the side to make room for Armand's car. He slowed the vehicle to a crawl, watching each side carefully so he wouldn't hit any of them. There appeared to be few men younger than sixty. The refugees were mainly small children, women, and the elderly. The younger men were already at the front or headed in that direction.

Uncertain of their current location, Armand stopped the vehicle to speak to a man and his wife.

"*Bonjour, monsieur*. We need to get back to our garrison. How far are we from Metz?"

"Metz? Metz is sixty kilometers to the east. You are getting ready to enter Étain. You aren't far from Luxembourg."

Philippe and Armand realized they had taken a wrong turn at Verdun.

"What do you think we should do, Phillipe? We are nowhere near our garrison, and we are almost out of fuel."

"Just keep driving. That's all we can do."

Looking past the open fields, they saw more refugees on the roads. German planes buzzed overhead and would occasionally spray the civilians with machine gun fire, forcing them to dive out of the way.

The sounds of mortar explosions in the distance were getting louder and more frequent. Some were close enough that the concussions caused the ground to shake beneath the car. Puffs of dirt and debris were thrown into the air as the bombs hit the ground. Every village in sight was ablaze.

"Where is our army?" asked Armand. "The only French troops we have seen were on that train."

"Most are manning the Maginot Line east of here. The Germans have outsmarted us. They bypassed the Maginot Line and are making their way through Belgium."

"This is crap, Phillipe. We are screwed. France is screwed."

"You and I have been through many difficulties together, old friend. We have always gotten through them. Just keep driving. If the only thing between France and the German army is Armand Lapierre and Phillippe Legrand, then at least we will give them one hell of a fight. Let's go find some Germans."

As they approached Étain, Philippe saw the carnage and said, "My God, what is that?"

Several meters ahead, bodies lay on the side of the road. Armand pulled over so they could get a closer look. In front of them was the sickening sight of young children mowed down by machine gun fire. Their mothers lay on top of them, the result of a futile attempt to shield them from the spray of bullets. Flies buzzed over the bodies, landing on the dried blood. Philippe and Armand both looked away. After Philippe turned his back to the gruesome sight, he leaned forward, placed his hands on his knees, and vomited from the emotions of the past few hours.

Enraged, Armand said, "I don't know when and I don't know where, but one day the bastards who did this will pay."

As the sun set, it turned the sky a bright orange. Armand looked at his fuel gauge, and it was near empty. He knew it would not be long before he and Philippe would be on foot. Several kilometers farther, they saw a sign for Valleroy.

Armand turned down a side road and headed toward the town to find fuel. After a short distance, they realized that was no longer a possibility. The Peugeot sputtered and choked as the engine rotated its last few turns before completely stalling. Armand tried to start the car, but to no avail.

"Time to walk," said Philippe.

Walking toward Valleroy, they still hoped to find fuel. The sun continued to set, but there was still enough light to see for many kilometers.

Over the hill, they heard several vehicles headed in their direction.

"Do you hear that, Armand? Quick! Over this hedgerow."

The hedgerows stood five meters tall and were mounds of mud and rock. Farmers used them as borders for their property and to fence in their livestock. Over the centuries, they had become overgrown with shrubbery. The roots made the hedgerows firm like concrete.

The engines of the vehicles got louder as they approached the peak of the hill. To their relief, when the vehicles appeared over the horizon, they recognized them as a French artillery unit.

Phillipe and Armand leaped over the hedgerow into the middle of the road, waved their arms, and motioned for them to stop.

The convoy of vehicles applied their brakes, and a lieutenant colonel stuck his head out of the passenger side of the lead vehicle. "Who are you, and what unit do you belong to?"

Philippe spoke first, "*Bonsoir, sir*. I am Sergeant Philippe Legrand, Machine Gunner, 3rd Army Division, stationed at the garrison in Metz."

"I am Sergeant Armand Lapierre, Artillery Specialist, 3rd Army Division, also stationed at the garrison in Metz."

"What are you doing here?" shouted the gruff lieutenant colonel.

Philippe said, "We were home on leave in Sainte-Mère-Église when we heard of the invasion. We have been driving for hours trying to get back to our garrison when we ran out of petrol. Now we find ourselves lost, sir."

The lieutenant colonel barked, "Well, you aren't lost anymore. We came from Metz. There are no Germans anywhere near there. We need you more than the 3rd Army. I will contact your command to let them know you have officially transferred to the 7th Army. Get in."

As Philippe and Armand climbed into the back of the first troop carrier, several hands reached out and pulled them into the canvas-covered seating area just as the wheels turned.

After a few brief introductions, Armand asked, "Where are we going?

A voice from the front shouted, "Dunkirk! We will reinforce the Brits. They are getting crushed."

Courtils, France

Joseph Shapiro kicked out what remained of the windshield, while Alfred scrambled to find his glasses. After putting them on, he climbed out of the wreckage.

Ingrid said, "Alfred, help me with Dreyfus. Be careful; his head is still bleeding."

Kneeling and reaching through the broken windshield, Alfred took his little brother in his arms and carefully pulled him through.

"Careful, Ingrid," said Joseph.

Ingrid slid through the opening slowly, making certain she avoided the sharp edges. Once on her feet, she reached for Dreyfus and carefully laid him on the ground, covering him with her coat for protection from the pouring rain.

"It is your turn, Papa," said Alfred.

After maneuvering around the steering wheel, Joseph climbed over the broken glass on the ground, got to his feet, and hurriedly searched the debris field that was once their family possessions. He found a large canvas cover and some linens. He draped the canvas over the front of the truck, forming a tent that was large enough for all of them.

"Everyone under the tent."

Once under it, he said, "Ingrid, let me have Dreyfus."

Laying him on the ground, he wrapped his head with the linens. He kept checking Dreyfus' pulse and his breathing.

Looking at his sobbing wife, who had already been through so much, he said, "He is still with us, Ingrid. Our baby boy is still with us."

He then placed Dreyfus back in his mother's arms.

The Heroes of Sainte-Mère Église

Looking at Alfred, he said, "Come with me, son. We have to find something."

As the cold downpour continued to soak their saturated clothes, he took Alfred to the middle of the debris field.

"Alfred, we are looking for a large suitcase. It is leather with two brass locks and my initials embossed on both sides. You go look in that direction, and I will be near the road. If you find it, yell. We must find it."

"Yes, Papa," replied Alfred. "We will find it."

Walking in darkness, Alfred circled the field. The rain was cold, and he was shivering.

Searching through their family possessions was heartbreaking. He found everything but the suitcase he looked for. Family photos, his favorite books, Dreyfus's toys, and mama's dresses. All of them ruined by the mud and downpouring rain.

Walking a few more steps, he turned to his right and saw, submerged in a large puddle, his open violin case. It was empty. Continuing, he found himself far away from the truck and his family, yet still found things. He took two more steps and found his violin. It floated in a puddle, the neck broken in two places, and the lower bout shattered.

Alfred felt empty inside. His papa had given it to him when he was just three years old. He couldn't remember a time when he didn't have it. His violin was his escape. His escape from being on the run for so many years. He would sit in his room in Sainte-Mère-Église and play it for hours. Whenever he was sad or scared or both, he would find a quiet place to play. It was his hope. It was his loyal companion. At that moment, he realized he needed it now more than ever.

"Here it is, Alfred," shouted his father. "Here it is—my suitcase. Meet me back at the truck." When Alfred and his father returned to the makeshift tent, Mama was resting with her head on the ground. She was exhausted, as they all were.

Papa checked Dreyfus's wound, and the bleeding appeared to have stopped. His heart rate and breathing were still strong.

Joseph laid the suitcase on the ground. Alfred watched his father open it. Inside were stacks of French *francs*, bundles of large bills. Tucked within the bills was a gun. He was surprised because he was unaware his father owned a gun, or even knew how to fire one. His father removed some *francs and the gun, exposing gold coins and* Mama's most expensive jewelry, some with beautiful colored stones as large as the marbles he and Jean-Pierre used to play with. Mama only wore those pieces on special occasions, like when she and Papa dressed for the opera.

Completing his inventory, Joseph closed and locked the suitcase and looked at Ingrid. "How are you feeling?"

Reaching up to caress his face and looking into his eyes, she said, "I'm fine, dear. We will be okay. We have been through tougher times than this. Our family and friends back in Germany are going through tougher times than this. We will keep moving. We will survive."

Alfred loved his mother with all his heart. She was always calm during the storms of life. Her hugs and her caresses, like the one she just gave to Papa, were always timed perfectly. Just when they were needed most.

Chapter Two

MAY 11, 1940

Courtils, France

The next morning, Alfred woke next to his mama, who was still asleep. She held Dreyfus close.

Looking out from under the tarp, he saw Papa standing on the side of the road. Behind him, the warm sun was rising in the horizon like a long lost friend.

"What are you doing, Papa," shouted Alfred.

"I'm waiting for someone to come by so I can ask them for help. Stay there with Mama and Dreyfus. Keep them safe."

Moments later, he saw his father wave frantically at an approaching flatbed truck. The side of the door read DuPont Farms. It appeared to be hauling turnips, squash, and other vegetables.

After the truck stopped, the driver climbed out of the cab to speak to Papa. The man appeared to be in his fifties, stood taller than average, and his thick belly made his coveralls tight around his midsection.

After two minutes, the driver ran with Papa to the tent.

Papa ripped the tent from the wreckage and said to his wife, "Ingrid, this is Mr. DuPont. He said he is heading to someplace called Mont-Saint-Michel to deliver his produce. There is a doctor there who can help Dreyfus. You, Dreyfus, and Alfred will ride up in the cab with Mr. DuPont. I will ride in the back with the produce."

Mr. DuPont said, "*Bonjour, madame.* We have less than ten kilometers before we will be there. I hope that none of the roads ahead of us are washed out like this one. There is plenty of food and shelter at Mont-Saint-Michel. You can stay there until you figure out how to get back on the road to wherever you are going."

After a few kilometers, Mr. Dupont turned down a road that led into the woods. The farther down the road they drove, the thicker the forest became. Alfred saw a sign that read Mont-Saint-Michel, 6 kilometers. Later, the forest thinned. Alfred could see the ocean in the distance. As they drove a little more, the trees were behind them.

Through the morning fog, Alfred saw the most incredible sight he had ever seen. In the distance was an island with an immense monastery positioned on top. Attached to the monastery was as an abbey. The entire structure gave the appearance of a massive castle resting on top of a large hill. From the base, a narrow, winding road led up to a small village.

Nudging Alfred with his elbow, Mr. Dupont said, "Have you ever seen anything like that?"

"No, sir. But it looks magical."

Chapter Three

MAY 12, 1940

Sainte-Marie-du-Mont, France

As Angélique Lapierre cleaned the cow stalls at Brécourt Manor, she was angry at the world. She had been angry at God for the past year since her father died. She was angry at her mother for easing her own sadness with bottles of wine—one after the other, day after day—until she couldn't get out of bed, causing her to lose her job.

Then she became angry at her brother Armand for volunteering for the French army, causing him to be away from home. Now, she was angry at the Germans for invading France and destroying what little sense of security she had.

Angélique had adored her father. She was always her papa's little girl. When he would come home from his job working in the fields for several of the local farmers, he would always get excited to see her. Returning home to her after work was his favorite part of the day, and he always made certain she knew it.

In the summer, he would smell bad from the perspiration of working in the hot sun all day, but she didn't care. She would sit on the front porch of their old farmhouse every day, waiting impatiently for him to come home. When he arrived, he would kneel, and she would wrap her arms around his neck and give him a kiss, and he would carry her into the house. Her papa was her hero. Her everything.

Then, one day he didn't come home. He was working on Mr. Chevallier's farm that day. She still remembered how Mr. Chevallier drove his truck to the house that evening to tell Mama he had died.

Mr. Chavallier returned to his farm after getting more fuel for the tractor. He found her papa laying on the floor of the barn in a pool of blood. Mr. Chavallier wrapped his head and drove him to Dr. Pelletier. He was dead when he arrived. The cause was a massive head injury. He had been working in the hayloft when he apparently tripped and fell to the concrete floor below.

Angélique now worked at one of the same farms Papa worked at, to try and help Mama make ends meet. She even considered dropping out of school so she could work more. But she knew Papa wouldn't have liked that. He was always so proud of her and her excellent grades.

Although a good student, Angélique didn't enjoy going to school. A bit shy, she was guarded; which led the other students to believe she was unfriendly. Because of her natural beauty, she was popular with the boys, who she wasn't interested in because of their immaturity, and unpopular with the girls because the boys couldn't take their eyes off of her. Her long dark hair, dark eyes, and olive skin were striking.

Her mother, Brigitte, tried to raise extra money by

renting rooms in their three-story farmhouse, but it was nearly one hundred years old, and badly in need of repairs. The roof leaked, the porch was missing boards, and it hadn't received a fresh coat of paint in many years. Worst of all, there was no electricity or indoor plumbing. The few potential renters who came to look at it noticed the outhouse and drove off. Papa never had the time to fix anything. He worked every day of the week and came home exhausted.

The local farmers respected and appreciated the hard work Angélique's father did for them. He was honest, always came to work early, and worked hard all day. After he died, they would take turns leaving fresh dairy and produce on their front porch so they wouldn't be hungry. This had gone on for a year. They would usually leave it in the early morning hours with no note. So, Angélique wasn't even certain which farmers were doing it. And Mama, in her state, never found out.

The next morning, Angélique couldn't sleep. She tossed and turned for hours. Coastal Normandy usually had a cool, temperate climate in May, but that morning it was unusually warm, so she got up to go to sleep on the front porch. She knew there would be a little breeze blowing in from the English Channel.

The sun was on the edge of peeking over the horizon, but it was still dark when she opened the front door of her house. Glancing down, she found the most recent food delivery on her porch. Off in the distance she heard a sound. As her eyes focused through the morning fog, she saw someone on a bicycle peddling away from her house and toward Sainte-Mère-Église. It was Jean-Pierre, Philippe's little brother.

Sainte-Mère-Église, France

Jean-Pierre couldn't concentrate. He kept staring at the empty chair where Alfred once sat. *Where was Alfred? Would he ever see him again? Is Philippe still alive?*

When the school bell rang, his classmates made their way to the door.

His teacher, Mrs. Laurent said, "Jean-Pierre, I need to speak to you. Please stay after class for a moment."

Margot Laurent was in her late twenties with blonde hair and blue eyes. Although her figure was slim, she made it a point to wear dresses that were slightly oversized to hide her figure from the adolescent boys in her class.

Once the other students left, she asked, "Are you okay, Jean-Pierre? You haven't been concentrating."

"I'm sorry, Mrs. Laurent. My brother is fighting up north. I'm worried about him."

"I understand. My husband is also there. I think of him constantly. We must have faith they will survive, and they will win. Your brother doesn't want you to be scared. I'm sure he wants you to keep doing your best in school."

"I'll try and do better."

Looking at Alfred's chair, he said, "I'm worried about Alfred, too. I don't understand why so many people hate the Jews. Alfred and his family have never hurt anyone."

"I don't understand it either, Jean-Pierre. Alfred's parents are resourceful. They will get to Spain safely. Maybe when the war is over, he can return."

Another teacher, Mme Chaput, entered the room. Choking back tears, she said, "I'm sorry to interrupt, Margot, but we were in the principal's office listening to the wireless. The Dutch have surrendered. The Germans are almost to the English Channel. The roads in southern Paris have become clogged with people trying to escape. Principal Séverin is canceling school until further notice."

Chapter Four

MAY 14, 1940

Lille, France

As dusk approached, Philippe and Armand stood behind a chest-high hedgerow. It had been four days since they were picked up by the 7th Army after running out of petrol.

Thousands of Allied soldiers stood with them. Within view were members of the French 21st Infantry Division, as well as the British 20th and 51st Highlander Divisions. Among those units were the Welsh and Irish Guards.

To the northwest was the coastal city of Dunkirk. Beyond that—the English Channel. Their backs were against the wall, and their purpose was to make a last stand.

Artillery shelling was intensifying and getting closer.

German, British, and French airplanes filled the sky. White tracers from antiaircraft guns painted the heavens, occasionally landing a hit, causing black smoke to trail the fuselage of a wounded plane. The luckiest pilots bailed out before their plane spun into a corkscrew pattern and crashed. There was chaos all around them.

The Heroes of Sainte-Mère Église

There were reports of thousands of German *Panzer* tanks to the east and closing fast.

The German infantry was converging on them like a tidal wave over the horizon but were still out of sight.

It was a surreal feeling. They were watching carnage unfold before their eyes but could do nothing about it.

Putting his arm around Armand's shoulder, Philippe said, "I don't know how this day will end. It may be our last. But if this day brings our demise, let it be known we fought like hell."

"I'm with you, Philippe. There is no way in hell those Hun bastards will capture me. I will fight to the death."

"I wish they would get here. I can't stop thinking about those people they murdered outside of Étain. It is time for someone to pay."

Their restless anticipation soon changed to a tense, high-pressure exhilaration.

Looking up, they saw a swarm of planes flying in perfect formation heading in their direction. They were German Ju 52 troop carriers, and they filled the sky.

Passing directly over their heads, their side doors opened simultaneously. German paratroopers dove out headfirst like they were entering a swimming pool. One after the other after the other. There were thousands. They were never-ending. After two minutes, the sky filled with the vision of giant mushrooms. Paratroopers were descending from the sky above and were about to engulf their position.

"This is it, Armand. They will have us surrounded soon. There is no place to run."

"Good luck, my friend."

Chapter Five

MAY 18, 1940

Mont-Saint-Michel, France

It had been only one week since they had arrived at Mont-Saint-Michel, yet the Shapiro family had quickly become familiar with their surroundings.

The village had one narrow and steep cobblestone road that curved to the left as it hugged the base of the mount. On each side of the road were shops, restaurants, and hotels. The most prominent of the hotels was the Hotel Poulard, where the wealthiest guests would stay.

Mont-Saint-Michel had evolved over time. For centuries, visitors made the pilgrimage to the 1,200-year-old monastery at the top of the mount. They came from all over Europe to see the astonishing structure.

"Dreyfus's head injury has healed nicely," said the doctor.

Joseph said, "Thank you for your help. He lost a lot of blood before we got him here."

"He would have lost a lot more had you not wrapped it like you did. You saved his life."

"Doctor, there are many people living here. Where have they all come from?"

"From all over Europe. They are mainly Jews, as I assume you are. They are escaping the Nazis. Word travels fast. It is not good to be a European Jew these days."

"Where are they staying?"

"Some are in the few hotels we have here; most are living in the monastery's basement. It is not good. The monks do their best, but the basement is cold and damp. I treat a lot of sick children. Their parents have no means to pay me."

Joseph was grateful he had the means to take care of his family's needs. This depended on him keeping control of his suitcase. If anyone else found out about the enormous treasure enclosed in the case, their lives would be in danger. People were desperate and would do anything to take it.

Back at their hotel room, Joseph addressed his family. "Be careful who you speak to. As I have told you over and over, nobody can have the slightest hint of who we are or the wealth we have. Trust nobody!"

To keep this appearance, they stayed in the least expensive of the four hotels on the Mount. The four small rooms it rented were on the second floor and all shared the same water closet down the hall. It had one toilet and one small shower that produced only cold water. Even with that, they were still the fortunate ones.

Within a few days of arriving, Alfred made friends with a few of the refugee children who were roaming the streets of the village. Several were around his age.

Most of all, he liked to spend time with Esther Edelman. Although Alfred was small for his age, Esther was even smaller; best described as petite. A physical trait Alfred found to be charming. Her hair was dark, and she wore it short, just below her ears. Like Alfred, she was mature for her age. She loved music and reading classic literature and dressed like an adult, often wearing a white pearl necklace her grandmother gave her.

Esther was one week away from celebrating her thirteenth birthday. Not showing it outwardly, Alfred was disappointed that his birthday had passed without celebration or fanfare because of the events of the day when their truck overturned. He was hoping to find a gift for Esther, so that at least she would have a special birthday.

During the time they knew each other, Esther and Alfred found a secret hiding place under a cluster of trees on the western side of the mount. There, they would look out to the ocean and watch the seagulls circling the water's edge below. Occasionally they would make their way up near them, landing on the side of the castle wall to feed their babies who were nesting in the moss.

"My parents are teachers," said Esther. "My mother teaches language and my father music. Mother has made me learn French, German, and English."

"What about your father? Has he taught you music?"

"Yes, of course. I love music. If I had my piano here, I would play for you. My favorite is Frederic Chopin's 'Nocturne' in B-flat minor. Do you know it?"

"I have tried to play it on my violin, but it wasn't written for a violin."

Esther and Alfred would sit for hours and talk about music and books. Esther showed Alfred a sincere sense of sorrow when she learned of the fate of his violin. Alfred listened intently when Esther discussed Warsaw, Poland, the

The Heroes of Sainte-Mère Église

city where she had spent her life before fleeing to Mont-Saint-Michel.

When German troops amassed on the border of Poland, Esther's parents believed it was time to flee the country. Although it was already filled, they caught a train headed to Paris. Once there, they stayed with a family for several weeks. They then traveled southwest by bus until they arrived at Mont-Saint-Michel.

One afternoon, while at their hiding place, Esther said to Alfred, "I wish I could go home. I miss my school. I wish I could practice my piano again." She then looked into his eyes. "But since I can't be home, I'm glad I am here with you."

Following those words, she leaned forward, and Esther and Alfred both experienced the first kiss of their young lives.

Chapter Six

MAY 20, 1940

Sainte-Mère-Église, France

Jean-Pierre arrived at home after spending the day fishing at his favorite spot, Le Grand Vey.

He knew Mama would be pleased that he caught eight flounder and five large bass for dinner. After removing the fish from the saddlebags of his bicycle, he entered the kitchen. There, he saw Angélique and her mother, Brigitte, standing at the counter helping Mama prepare dinner. They had the radio playing in the background, listening for any hints of what was happening in the war. But for now, there was just music playing.

Cécile said to Jean-Pierre, "Angélique and Mrs. Lapierre stopped by to see if we had heard from Philippe. They haven't heard from Armand either."

Cécile Legrand and Brigitte Lapierre were both forty-two years old. They had become acquainted with each other through the friendship of Philippe and Armand, but a strong bond had never emerged between them.

Cécile was pretty, but not beautiful. Her long sandy blonde hair framed a face that was weathered and prematurely wrinkled. The result of long summers in the field working the family farm with René and her two boys.

Brigitte was an older version of Angélique. Striking, with long dark hair that was starting to show hints of gray. The death of her husband had taken its toll, and the stress of being a widow and her recent bouts of drinking were showing in her face.

"*Bonjour*, Jean-Pierre," said Brigitte.

"*Bonjour*, Mrs. Lapierre."

"Have you been attending school?" asked Brigitte.

"No, we haven't had school since the Germans invaded."

"Angélique hasn't had school either. They will start school again. Things will return to normal one day."

"Let's not talk about that," said Cécile. "I hope you caught a lot of fish because Brigitte and Angélique are joining us for dinner."

"Yes, Mama, I have plenty. They were really biting today."

As he laid the fish down on the countertop for cleaning, he couldn't take his eyes off Angélique. She was more beautiful than ever. Her pretty face and dark features hypnotized him when he was around her. He wanted to start a conversation, but he stood there staring at her until she laughed at the trance he was in.

"*Bonjour*, Jean-Pierre," she said. "It is good to see you,"

"*Bonjour*, Angélique. It is good to see you, too."

Brigitte said, "Jean-Pierre, thank you for bringing us fresh vegetables. Angélique told me you have been the one leaving the food on our doorstep. That is thoughtful of you. I have been sick in bed a lot lately, and it has been helpful. I feel much better now and have even returned to work."

Jean-Pierre said, "I'm glad you are feeling better, Mrs. Lapierre, but I don't mind bringing you food. I know some of the other farmers were making deliveries to you after Mr. Lapierre's accident, but I think they have kind of stopped. I asked Mama and Papa if I could bring you food from our field. They said I could take you as much as I could carry on my bicycle. Sometimes Papa drives me in the truck after we harvest. That way, you'll have a little extra."

"Your family has been so kind," said Brigitte. "Thank you so very much. I like to think Armand and Philippe are taking care of each other, too."

"I'm sure they are," said Cécile.

René Legrand came in the kitchen door, looked at Jean-Pierre's catch on the counter, and said, "Well done, son. I'm hungry. Let's help these ladies get these fish cleaned."

Jean-Pierre laid a sheet of newspaper on the table, grabbed a fish, and sat down to clean it. Before he even grabbed his knife, Angélique also reached for one, sat down next to him, and said, "Do you mind if I help you?"

"No, I don't mind. I would like for you to help."

After several minutes of small talk about school, Angélique said to Jean-Pierre, "Would you mind taking me fishing with you next time? I don't have a bicycle, but I can ride on your handlebars."

"Yes, you can come with me. I am going again tomorrow. Do you want me to pick you up in the morning?"

Frowning and shaking her head, she said, "I have to work at Mr. Linville's tomorrow. I clean the stalls and wash his horses. That will take me most of the day."

"What time will you start?"

"Six a.m. sharp. Mr. Linville likes me to start early."

"I'll pick you up at five. I can ride from your house to Mr. Linville's horse farm in no time. I will help you, and we will finish before lunch. Then we will go fishing. The fish don't bite as well midday, but that's okay. We will still catch some."

"You will do that for me, Jean-Pierre?"

"Of course, I will. I don't care what we are doing."

Angélique grinned at him. She had felt lonely since her papa died. It was nice to have someone else in her life who made her feel special.

The news interrupted the song that was playing.

"We have news from the war front," said the announcer. "There are reports that the Germans have surrounded the western flank of the Maginot Line, and there is fierce fighting near Metz. They have captured several thousand members of the French 3rd Army. Thousands of casualties are reported. The French 7th Army and several units of the British Expeditionary Force are experiencing fierce fighting and are in retreat to Dunkirk. We will report again when we have further information."

As the music played again, the room was silent. Moments later, Jean-Pierre heard sniffles. He turned to see his mama and Mrs. Lapierre embracing in a hug as they both cried. They realized their sons were being overrun in a battle they couldn't win. They may be prisoners by the Germans—or worse. The back door slammed as Papa headed to the barn. Angélique reached for Jean-Pierre's hand and said, "I'm scared, Jean-Pierre."

René Legrand shifted several bales of hay from one side of the loft to the other. He was a large man, but lean. His powerful frame allowed him to toss bales of hay around as if they were empty boxes.

His ancestors migrated to the Cotentin Peninsula from Rome during the time of Julius Caesar. The southern European bloodline is still evident in his dark hair and olive skin.

Using his feet to brush away the loose straw, he exposed four floorboards in the corner.

As he knelt to remove the nails, his mind wandered. He thought about how he had spent the past two decades trying to clear his memory of his days as a younger man. A lifetime ago, it seemed.

Since then, he married the love of his life and fathered two boys. His pride for his two sons was unmatched by anything he ever accomplished. The medals he received were meaningless. He had misplaced his Legion of Honor medal, the highest award a French soldier could earn. It was as if it belonged to another man. In a way it did. He was no longer that soldier. He hadn't been for years.

His family didn't know his secrets. Not the worst of them, anyway. Not even Philippe, who at this very moment may be experiencing the same savagery of war he himself had once known.

René told them he was a mechanic in the war. He cleaned and repaired weapons, he would say modestly.

During the many nights when he woke in a cold sweat, he had no explanation for his wife why he seldom slept through the night. He knew if he told her, she would think no less of him. She loved him. She would understand and support him. But it was his job to protect her from such things. He was determined to shield his family from the horrors he had seen. Most of all, they would never know the horrors he inflicted on others.

The Heroes of Sainte-Mère Église

As the nails came loose and he removed the boards, he looked down into the opening in the floor to see his tools. Not the tools he used as a farmer. Those were in the work shed near the house. But the tools he had used as an assassin—a ghost in the night. A deadly killer trained to perfection.

As he reached in to remove the weapons of his past, he prayed to God he wouldn't need to use them again. But if necessary, he would do the job that needed to be done.

Royal Naval Headquarters
Dover Castle, United Kingdom

The black 1937 Rolls-Royce pulled up to the rear door of Dover Castle. In only his tenth day in office, Prime Minister Winston Churchill had been in a whirlwind of meetings since the resignation of the previous prime minister, Nevil Chamberlin.

As the car came to a stop, he waited patiently for the sharply dressed naval cadet to open his door and stand at attention with a snappy salute. The rotund, sixty-six-year-old prime minister grabbed his cane and slowly rotated his hips toward the open door. Placing his hand on the inside door handle, he eased his way off the bench seat as though it was taking every ounce of energy he had.

The tip of his cane hit the red brick driveway, and he pulled himself to his feet, acknowledged the cadet with a tip of his hat, and in a deep, gruff voice, said, "Thank you, young man. You are looking very dapper today."

Leaning forward, cane in hand, he then walked toward the large, well-polished wooden door.

Vice Admiral Bertram Ramsey donned his formal dress blue uniform with four gold stripes on his sleeves and medals covering his left breast, as he met him with a salute and a handshake. "Good afternoon, Prime Minister. Welcome to Dover Castle."

"Good afternoon, Vice Admiral. Thank you for meeting me here at the rear door. Those thirty-nine steps in the front receiving area are a bit more challenging than I am up for these days. However, when I was a younger man, I could have sprinted up that lot in a rather impressive fashion."

"Indeed, Prime Minister," replied the vice admiral. "I don't particularly care for them these days myself."

The two men entered the castle, strolled through a series of hallways, and entered the massive dining hall. Standing at attention, the Royal Admiralty wait staff—dressed in short coats, tails, and white gloves—had prepared two place settings at the end of an oak table that could seat sixty. The first to be seated was the prime minister, followed by the vice admiral. Moments later, a bowl of clam chowder was placed before each man.

"Well, Vice Admiral, I'm sure you are eager to know why I called this meeting."

"I have my thoughts, Prime Minister, but I have found that speculation is seldom a good companion during times of war."

"Yes—yes indeed," said Churchill. "Let me cut through the fog and get right to it. As we sit here, Brigadier General Whitfield is on his way to Dunkirk, France, to evaluate how bad things are in Western Europe. Preliminary reports appear ominous. Our boys are getting pummeled. They, along with the French and the Belgians, are being shoved to the coast by overwhelming numbers of Germans. The Dutch have already surrendered. The fate of Great Britain may well depend on the success of this impossible task I am about to ask you to take on. We need a plan, and we need it now. A plan that will allow us to evacuate over two hundred thousand British soldiers from Dunkirk in less than a week. Once we get our boys home, we can regroup, defend our homeland, and plan for a future invasion of Western Europe when we are more prepared to deal with an enemy we have underestimated until now."

"Prime Minister, I understand the significance of what you are asking. But let me be clear. This will be a daunting task. Even if every ship in the Royal Navy were available, which they are not, we still would not have enough vessels to evacuate over two hundred thousand men in a week. The *Luftwaffe* is not going to just stand by and let us load our boys onto ships without strafing the piers and bombing our ships as they leave the harbors."

"Vice Admiral, I am asking you to do an impossible task. However, the fate of our nation depends on you doing the impossible. I can assure you; I would not be asking you to do this if I were not prepared to supply you with every resource Great Britain has available. Most of all, I would not be asking you to do this if the difference between success and failure was not also the difference between the Union Jack or a swastika flying over this castle."

After pausing momentarily and staring blankly across the room, Vice Admiral Bertram Ramsey looked at Mr. Churchill. "Prime Minister, thank you for joining me for lunch. But if you will excuse me, I need to call a meeting with my officers. We will have a plan together for you by morning. Somehow, some way, we will not let the people of Great Britain down."

Slapping his hand on the table, Churchill said, "That's the spirit, old boy! I look forward to seeing your plan."

The next morning, Churchill was escorted into the large map room in the basement of Dover Castle. Greeting the prime minister was Vice Admiral Ramsey and two of his officers, Captain William Wharton and Captain William Tennant.

"Gentlemen," said the prime minister. "I would ask you if you slept well last night, but I believe I already know the answer to that question, so let's get on with it. What do you have for me?"

"Prime Minister, as I mentioned yesterday, the Royal Navy does not have enough large vessels to evacuate two hundred thousand British soldiers from Dunkirk in rapid fashion. However, yesterday, I was only thinking of the aerial photographs I had seen of the piers in Dunkirk Harbor, one of which has been destroyed by the *Luftwaffe*. However, Captain Wharton here, who is the commander of our small vessel corps, came up with a brilliant plan. Captain Wharton, it is your plan. Please share it with the prime minister."

"Prime Minister, although we can't possibly evacuate that many soldiers using only large vessels from the piers, I believe we can get them out if we use the piers and the beachhead. The plan is to use small boats to approach the shallow water at the beach. Our lads will wade out from the dunes, and off they go back to England."

"We are talking about two hundred thousand men, Captain. How many boats will this plan require?"

"In addition to the small boats we have in the Royal Navy, which is approximately sixty, there are endless numbers of civilian small craft all throughout England. This morning I counted over forty tied to the piers of the

Thames River. There are rivers and canals all up and down our eastern coast with boats of all sizes. The only risk is that involving our citizens will require a public announcement. We need to inform them that our boys are trapped at Dunkirk and we need their help. You know there are German spies walking among us, and they will notify the Nazi high command with no haste."

Churchill said, "The bloody Germans already know they have us on the run. However, letting them know our evacuation plans will make all our vessels, including the civilians, targets of aerial strafing by the *Luftwaffe*. That is an immense request to ask of our citizens."

"The civilian force will be strictly voluntary," said Ramsey. "They will know what they are up against and I trust they will rise to the challenge."

Churchill pulled a cigar from his inside jacket pocket, struck a match, and lit it. While grabbing his lapel with his left hand, and puffing the cigar in his right, he looked up at the brick ceiling of the small room that was once a prison cell, centuries ago. After exhaling a long drag of smoke, Churchill, still staring at the ceiling, said, "Let's get on with it then. What are we going to call this crazy plan?"

Vice Admiral Ramsey replied, "Operation Dynamo, Prime Minister. Captain Tennant is leaving for Dunkirk within moments to coordinate the logistics from that side of the channel."

"Splendid," replied Churchill. "I will inform King George."

Chapter Seven

MAY 21, 1940

Le Grand Vey, France

Their feet hung over the edge of the fishing pier as they enjoyed the cool breeze blowing in from the English Channel. Angélique watched as Jean-Pierre baited her hook for her.

"Thank you for helping me with Mr. Linville's horses this morning, Jean-Pierre. You are so sweet."

"That's okay. I had fun. I like horses. I wish we had some. Papa says they are expensive to feed and really wouldn't help us on our farm. One day when I have a farm, I will have many. They will be thoroughbreds, like Mr. Linville has. Do you like working for Mr. Linville?"

"Yes, he and his wife have been kind to my mother and me. He pays me more than any of the other farmers. Mrs. Linville sometimes bakes pies and brings them by our house. She and Mama will sit and talk for hours. Mama says her talks with Mrs. Linville have helped her get over her illness. At least Mama says it is an illness. I just think she has been sad a lot since Papa died so she drinks to feel better."

As he handed Angélique her fishing pole, he asked, "Does your mama still drink?"

"No. I haven't seen her drink for a long time. She is doing better now. But I'm worried that she will start again. She is worried about Armand. I am, too. Have you thought about Armand and Philippe, Jean-Pierre? Do you think they are okay?"

"Yes, I know they are. Our brothers have been best friends since the time they were born. You have seen them together. They have always taken care of each other. If one gets into a riff, the other has always been there to help. They will both be home soon. I know it."

"You always know what to say to make me feel better."

After a period of uncomfortable silence, Angélique asked, "Have you ever had a girlfriend?"

"A girlfriend? No, I have never had a girlfriend …. Have you ever had a boyfriend?"

"Yes. Two summers ago, I spent a week at my aunt's apartment in Rouen. There was a boy who lived on the first floor. We spent every day together. The day I was leaving to come home he said he loved me and wanted to marry me. We were only twelve. He was kind of silly."

Afraid he might not get the answer he wanted to hear, Jean-Pierre asked, "Do you ever write to him?"

"I mailed him a letter when I got home, and he never wrote back. I guess he wasn't that much in love with me after all."

"I would have written you."

"I know you would have, Jean-Pierre."

She watched as he reeled in his line, then cast it out again, sending it further than the last.

"Have you ever kissed a girl, Jean-Pierre?"

He wasn't certain how to answer. He didn't want Angélique to view him as an inexperienced little boy. He also didn't want to lie to her either. So, he sat there with his line in the water hoping a fish would suddenly bite and break the tension.

"It's okay if you haven't, Jean-Pierre. I would be honored to be your first. Would you like to kiss me?"

In his dreams, he had already looked into her eyes and kissed her a thousand times. And there, sitting on the edge of the water at Le Grand Vey, his dreams would come true.

Hazebrouck, France

Philippe lay on his belly between a group of large bushes. The sky was pitch black. He rested his head on the ground momentarily. *Stay alert!* he said to himself as he rubbed his face. Surrounding him were thousands of soldiers. Some were friends. Others were Germans who were there to kill him.

Quietly listening for even the slightest sound, he thought about the events of the previous week. He wondered what had happened to Armand.

He remembered that as the German paratroopers were coming down, he and Armand waited for them to drop within firing range. They then pointed their weapons in the air and opened fire with everything they had. Thousands of allies from multiple countries did the same.

The thunder of cannons and incoming artillery combined with the nonstop ripping of machine gun fire was deafening. It was a free-for-all. Chaos of the highest order.

The Heroes of Sainte-Mère Église

He still couldn't forget the face of the first German he killed. As the paratrooper was coming down just meters away from him, the eyes of the soldier were staring at him. Philippe unloaded his MAS-38 submachine gun, and the man was dead before his boots hit the ground. Then there was another and another. It was nonstop. He wasn't certain how many German lives he took that first day. All around him was carnage.

He remembered climbing out of his foxhole and running, all while firing and reloading, firing and reloading, only stopping to take a breath and check his ammunition.

He leaped over bodies—German, French, British, and some so mangled, there was no determining their country of origin. The dead were everywhere. Several times, Philippe dove behind a mound of corpses for cover. Then he leaped to his feet to continue his escape, covered in the blood of the bodies that had just provided him safety. He would never forget those images, or the feeling of the blood of his fellow man coated to him like paint.

Forcing his thoughts back to the present, he realized the sun would rise soon. *Keep moving*, he thought to himself. *Dunkirk should be my destination.* Those were his orders. *"Dunkirk ne doit pas tomber."* Dunkirk must not fall. He needed to get there to link up with his fellow Frenchmen.

Wherever he was, swarming around him were German soldiers. Needing to travel by the cover of night, he grabbed his compass to survey which direction was northwest. Slowly, he crawled forward to peek through the bushes. Stopping, he lay motionless. Just meters away, he heard the breaking of twigs under boots. Footsteps—several of them. Then, in an unmistakable German dialect he heard the words, *"Wir müssen diesen Bereich klaren. Nimm keine Gefangenen."* We need to clear the area. Take no prisoners.

Béthune, France

Armand woke to find himself lying on a dirt floor. The barn was not large and had a second-floor hayloft that spanned only halfway across the second level.

He looked around to see four soldiers and a French officer. Philippe was not among them. Armand's head and right leg were throbbing in pain. He vaguely remembered a mortar landing a few meters from him as he dove into a foxhole during the onslaught.

He looked up at the medic tending to his wounds. "Where am I?"

The medic turned to the French officer on the other side of the barn and said something in English.

French Lieutenant Martin Laurent was intelligent. He graduated first in his class at the University of Paris where he studied chemical engineering. While there, he met his wife Margot, who often told him she was attracted to his handsome face and kind heart.

After graduating, they married and moved to Sainte-Mère-Église, where she became a schoolteacher, and he joined the French army, where he was assigned to a small reserve unit.

Martin Laurent was not a large man, but he was extremely athletic. He was a star footballer for his college soccer team and excelled during physical training in infantry school.

Approaching Armand, Lieutenant Laurent said, "*Bonsoir*, Sergeant. My name is Lieutenant Martin Laurent. How are you feeling?"

"Not good, Lieutenant. I just want to sleep. I feel if I do, I will never wake up."

Rubbing his head, trying to ease the pain, Armand asked, "Where are we?"

"Somewhere near Béthune. We were all separated from our units and pinned down with several others. We decided as a group to run like hell. Those of us who survived, made it here. During our retreat, that large Brit over there, Sergeant McVie, threw you over his shoulder and kept running. He saved your life. Once we arrived here, Sergeant Hancock used his medical bag to work miracles on you. They are both with the British 51st Highlanders."

Pointing across the barn, Laurent said, "So is that Brit over there. His name is Sergeant Fradd. Corporal Bordeur is up in the hayloft keeping an eye out for Germans. He and I are both with the French 21st Infantry Division.

"None of the Brits speak French, but I speak English. So, if you need to communicate with them let me know."

"My name is Sergeant Armand Lapierre. Let them know I am grateful to them for saving my life."

"I will, Sergeant. Now get some rest."

Speaking in English, Laurent asked medic Hancock how Armand was doing, "Our mate here has lost a lot of blood. He shouldn't be buggered out anytime soon. When we move out, he will need a stretcher. I have cleaned and wrapped his wounds, but I'm not giving him morphine. It is difficult to transport the deadweight of an unconscious man."

Lieutenant Laurent yelled up to Corporal Bordeur, "Look around up there for a tarp or blanket. Something large we can carry this man with."

"Yes, sir."

Two minutes later, "Nothing up here but bales of hay, sir."

"Have you seen any movement at the farmhouse?"

"No, sir. It is dark, so I can't see much anymore, but the sun will be coming up soon."

"Okay, Corporal. Stay up there and keep an eye out."

Switching back to English, he addressed the large, blonde Brit who carried Armand to safety.

"Sergeant McVie," he said. "You and I are going out on a little scouting mission. We will make our way to the farmhouse to see if anyone is in there. If so, we will ask them for a blanket to move our wounded soldier. If nobody is there, we will go in and see what we can find. They may have left food behind. Follow me, and stay low and quiet."

"I'm with you, sir. I could use some grub."

Between the barn and the farmhouse were two large trees. They ran from the barn to the first tree in thirty seconds. Pausing, they looked at the house. Seeing no movement, they repeated the process and ran to the second tree. Again, no movement from the house.

Lieutenant Laurent whispered to Sergeant McVie, "Now, this is the tricky part. I will approach the house. You stay here, and wait for my signal before advancing."

"Okay, Lieutenant. Just don't eat all the food before you wave me in."

"I'll keep that in mind, Sergeant."

After a deep breath, Laurent sprinted toward the house until he was under one of the windows. Slowly, he raised his head to peek in. Seeing nothing, he moved to the next window. Again—nothing. After waving to McVie to come forward, they both carefully went into the house through the back door.

Although it was dark, they felt their way around. They found a blanket and two pillowcases on a bed. Taking the pillowcases into the kitchen, they filled them with canned goods from the pantry. As they finished filling the pillow-

The Heroes of Sainte-Mère Église

cases, they heard vehicles from the front of the house. Through the window, they saw a small convoy of motorcycles and German half-tracks. Each half-track carried no less than twelve soldiers. They appeared to be about a kilometer away and headed toward them.

"Time to go, Sergeant," said Lieutenant Laurent.

They sprinted out of the back door, pillowcases and blanket in hand.

Entering the barn door, Laurent yelled to everyone in the group, "*Wehrmacht* are coming! Dozens of them."

Hancock put Sergeant Lapierre on the blanket.

"Corporal Bordeur, grab the other end of the blanket, and help Sergeant Hancock. We are going to the cornfield. The tall cornstalks should provide cover."

"Sergeant McVie, look around and make certain we have left no signs of our existence. You have less than a minute. Then meet us in the cornfield."

"You got it, boss," replied McVie.

As the others left, they closed the barn doors and headed for the cover of the tall cornstalks. McVie looked around and noticed an ammo clip on the ground. He put it in his pocket and then noticed blood stains where Armand had been resting. While kicking dirt over the blood with his boots, he heard a motorcycle racing from the house to the barn.

McVie looked between the boards of the barn and saw it had a sidecar with a second German. They both had MP 38 submachine guns.

No time to make it to the cornfield, he thought.

After climbing the ladder to the hayloft, he hid behind several bales of hay.

His five comrades had made it safely to the cornfield. They, too, heard the oncoming motorcycle.

Lieutenant Laurent told the others to move toward the center of the field, but be as quiet as possible. He stayed behind to straighten the fallen cornstalks at the edge of the field so their entrance would not be obvious.

He then waited and watched the happenings at the barn, knowing Sergeant McVie was still in there. Lying on his belly, he peeked between the stalks as the motorcycle parked a few meters from the barn door.

The Germans stepped forward cautiously, opened the barn doors, and entered.

Hazebrouck, France

Phillipe continued to lay on his belly between a group of bushes wondering what to do. He could hear the German soldiers talking a few meters away but could not see them. *Were there two? Were there eight? Were there more?*

It had been several hours since his last firefight.

Did I change out my magazine? If he switched it like he remembered doing, he had thirty-two nine-millimeter rounds at the ready. If his memory had failed him, the magazine could be nearly empty. His heart was racing. *Control your breathing.* He couldn't let his adrenaline give away his position.

He heard bullfrogs in the distance. *There is water near.* It reminded him of how thirsty he was. He had emptied the last sip from his canteen hours earlier. *If I get out of here alive, I need to find water.*

Voices in the distance reminded him to focus. His thirst was contributing to his exhaustion. He was dehydrated.

He heard what sounded like orders being shouted.

The Heroes of Sainte-Mère Église

Then, the running of boots. A few members of the small German squad headed in different directions. They were on a seek-and-destroy mission looking for the enemy, of which he was one. *Were there still others near?*

Crawling to the edge of the bushes, he heard footsteps. It sounded like just one set. They were getting closer. After one more step, he saw the dirt-covered boots less than a meter from his face.

The German soldier shifted his weight, repositioning his feet. Then, the distinct sound of a cigarette lighter. *How foolish*, Philippe thought. *Everyone knows you never light a cigarette at night, exposing your position to the enemy.*

And then he heard the crack of a single shot in the night as the German dropped to the ground directly in front of him. Philippe saw it was an officer. An *Oberleutnant*.

Seconds later, all hell broke loose. The ripping of machine gun fire was all around him.

He had had enough of this place. *Which way now?*

Remembering his compass reading, he changed out the magazine, got to his feet, and ran northwest. He kept low, taking advantage of the tall bushes and hedgerows.

Incoming mortar rounds now accompanied the machine gun fire. He didn't know if the mortars were incoming from German, French, or British troops, and he knew the death and destruction they brought didn't discriminate.

Running through an open field, looking for cover, he saw a bomb crater.

With the increased frequency of mortar rounds, he ran for the hole. Once there, he leaped through the air and dove in headfirst.

To his surprise, it was already occupied. Scrambling to his feet, he turned toward the young soldier. The German, lying on his stomach, rolled over on his back in an attempt to aim his rifle at Philippe.

Before he could pull the bolt back to load the next round, Phillipe pulled his bayonet from its sleeve and lunged at the soldier.

The boy was much smaller than Philippe, which allowed him to muscle the Mauser out of the way with his left hand. With a firm grip of the bayonet in his right, he watched the fear in the young man's face as his last breath was violently expelled at the hands of Philippe.

Béthune, France

Lieutenant Laurent, peeking between the cornstalks, waited to see what would happen with McVie.

The two Germans had been in the barn for several minutes and there had been no commotion. Laurent assumed that McVie must have heard them coming and climbed up into the hayloft.

Laurent sensed in the short time he had known McVie that he was a fighter with little fear.

Would he try to take them both? He could probably do so easily with his Enfield rifle, but the noise would bring every German at the house in their direction. If McVie then made a dash to the cornfield, he would give away their position. If he stayed, and they found him in the loft, would he surrender, or would they kill him?

Another minute passed. Then another. Then the door opened, and the two soldiers stepped out of the barn. They turned to the right and walked toward the rear of the barn.

Surveying the area, one of them halted and looked toward Laurent. While pointing toward the cornfield, he whispered something to the other man. Laurent realized he must not have completely fixed the cornstalks, and they had spotted their entrance into the field.

As the two men slowly walked toward Laurent, he knew he was in trouble. If he stood to run, they would mow him down with their MP 38s. *If I surrender, maybe I can buy time for the others to escape.*

At that moment, he noticed movement coming around the corner of the barn. It was Sergeant Fradd and Corporal Bordeur. They had circled around through the cornfield and approached the barn from the rear.

The Brit Fradd, like McVie, was a large man. Corporal Bordeur was the smallest in the group, and his baby face made him look like he should be home nursing from his mother's breast, not fighting in a war.

Laurent's heart was racing. *What were they up to?*

The two Germans were only a few meters from his position.

Then, from around the corner of the barn, Fradd and Bordeur sprinted toward them, bayonets in hand. They simultaneously leaped through the air, tackled the two Germans, and quietly ended the threat.

After the deed was done, Sergeant Fradd ran into the barn and retrieved McVie.

McVie, approaching the group, looked at the two bodies that lay in front of him and said, "What took you so long? The entire time I was up in that loft, I had to piss."

"You don't have time to do it here," said Laurent.

As Fradd and Bordeur used the tall grass to wipe the blood from their bayonets, Laurent pointed to the bodies on the ground and said, "When these two don't return, there will be more *Wehrmacht* here than we can handle. Let's go find Hancock and Lapierre. We need to get Lapierre to a doctor."

With the sun rising, they stepped into the cornfield. Following the path created by their previous journey, Sergeant Fradd and Corporal Bordeur led the way.

Once there, Lieutenant Laurent asked Hancock, "How is Sergeant Lapierre doing?"

"He is stable, but he needs plasma. He has lost a lot of blood. I have changed his bandages multiple times, but I have run out, so these will need to stay in place until we get him to a doctor."

Laurent, switching back to French, instructed Corporal Bordeur to help Sergeant Hancock transport Armand on the blanket.

Continuing through the cornfield, they could see woods in the distance. They estimated one hundred meters. The tall, stiff cornstalks were providing cover while simultaneously causing fatigue as they fought their way through.

McVie and Fradd, the largest men of the group, led the way, using their forearms to knock the stalks out of the way for Hancock and Bordeur, who were carrying the makeshift stretcher.

Hoping the woods would provide sanctuary, they stayed focused on the treetops in the distance. When they were about thirty meters from the forest, they heard shouting from the barn they had just left. It was the distinct sound of the German language. *"Sie sind im Maisfeld. Schnappt sie. Bringe mindestens einen von ihnen leband zuruck. Schnell. Geh, Geh, Geh!"* They are in the cornfield. Get them. Bring at least one of them back alive. Quickly. Go, go, go!

The group went from hurrying to the closest thing to a sprint they could manage under the circumstances.

The Heroes of Sainte-Mère Église

Could they make it to the woods? wondered Laurent. *If so, then what?*

They kept running behind the two lead men until they were fifteen meters, then ten, then out of the cornfield they went.

Running through an open area between the cornfield and the woods, Laurent surveyed the edge of the forest and saw a large, fallen tree about twenty meters ahead.

In English, he shouted to McVie and Fradd, "Head for that fallen tree. That will be our cover."

They leaped over the tree, then turned to assist in transferring Armand over the chest-high tree trunk. He was unconscious, so they laid him on the ground behind them.

"Lock and load," shouted Laurent. "We don't know how many will come out of the cornfield, but when they appear, wait for my command. I will fire first, then let them have it."

They took cover behind the tree and pointed their weapons at the edge of the cornfield. Their position was on the base of a hill, so there was a slight elevation behind them. They could see the cornstalks moving in the distance. Laurent's heart pounded. There appeared to be about thirty. They outnumbered Laurent's small squad five to one.

When their pursuers were about thirty meters away, they spread out. Laurent knew that would make survival even more difficult.

Laurent had a MAS-38 submachine gun, and Fradd had the most potent weapon, a British Bren gun, which could fire five hundred .30-caliber rounds per minute. The others had bolt-action rifles. They were accurate but had limited firepower.

Laurent positioned himself and Fradd at each end of the tree. That allowed them to spray automatic fire from the outside in. He instructed the others to stay on the inside and take out the closest targets available.

As the German soldiers approached the edge of the cornfield, they hesitated, sensing that exiting might be risky.

Soon, the first one stepped out cautiously like a sacrificial lamb. Then the second and third. After about a minute, they were all out and walking toward the woods.

Laurent counted to himself, *one, two, three*, then stood to fire.

As he did, a barrage of heavy machine gun fire came ripping down from the hill behind them.

Stunned, Laurent and his squad ducked behind the tree, then turned to see where the firing was coming from.

Exiting the forest on the hill were dozens of French soldiers. They had a mixture of submachine guns and long rifles. They kept coming down the hill.

As Laurent's small force continued to stay low behind the log, they heard the zipping of automatic weapons ripping through the air like a buzz saw.

After realizing they had unexpected help, Laurent and his men turned around and shot toward the cornfield. But by the time they did, the few Germans who were still alive had scrambled back into the thick corn as French soldiers continued to unload on them. Their shots tore through the stalks that were mowed down by the barrage.

After the gunfire ceased, with smoke settling but still in the air, Laurent and his crew looked around at French soldiers who were still coming down from the hill. There were hundreds. *An entire company,* thought Laurent.

He approached a *capitaine*, saluted, and introduced himself. I am "Lieutenant Laurent, 21st Infantry Division."

Returning the salute, he introduced himself. "*Capitaine*

The Heroes of Sainte-Mère Église

Caron, with the 106th Line Infantry Division," said the tall, bearded, battle-hardened officer.

Laurent said, "There is a platoon of Germans at the house. They were in half-tracks and motorcycles, but no tanks I could see. They were on the other side of the cornfield."

"Approaching the enemy by cover of cornfield is not a good strategy. Those *Wehrmacht* soldiers lying dead over there are clear evidence of that. We will leave them be for now," said the *capitaine*.

Pointing toward Armand, Laurent said, "I have a man in bad shape. He needs medical attention."

Turning to two of his men, the *captaine* shouted, "Go get a stretcher."

Laurent walked over to where Hancock was tending to Armand.

Hancock said, "Lieutenant, we need to get him to a doctor as soon as possible. His blood pressure has dropped, and his heart rate has slowed. He is looking pale."

In French, Laurent relayed the information to the *capitaine*, who said, "When the stretcher gets here, we will take him over the hill to our vehicles. They will rush him to our headquarters in Dunkirk. There is a hospital tent there. You and the rest of your men will accompany him. They will give you food and allow a short rest."

"How are things going everywhere else?" asked Laurent. "Are we pushing them back?"

"Far from it, Lieutenant. They have ordered us to retreat to Dunkirk," said the *capitaine*.

Pointing toward McVie, Fradd and Hancock, the *captaine* said, "I see you have a few Brits with you."

"Yes, sir," replied Laurent. "After a heavy firefight, we all hunkered down in the barn across the cornfield. We have been together since. They are great soldiers, sir. I would fight with them anytime."

"I don't doubt that, Lieutenant. I have seen the Brits in action myself. When you get to Dunkirk, Lieutenant, they need to head to the beach and report in. The Brits are being evacuated home."

"Home, sir?"

"That's right. They have already evacuated thousands. It hasn't been easy. I hear the *Luftwaffe* has been strafing the beach. It has been a bloodbath. They have sunk several ships. The Brits are also using civilian small watercraft. They have sunk several of them. We have been instructed to cover their flank as they continue the evacuation. That's why we are headed to the Lys River. It is marshy in that region, and the German tanks will never make it through there. We hope to pounce on them while they are bogged down."

"Sir, do you want me and my men to go with you?"

"No, proceed to Dunkirk. You will find plenty of fighting there to keep you busy."

Saluting, the two men parted ways.

Laurent turned toward the injured Armand as the two French soldiers returned from over the hill. They knelt to transfer Armand from the ground to the stretcher, pausing momentarily to wait for Hancock. He checked his blood pressure and pulse.

After placing his ear to Armand's chest, Hancock looked up at Laurent, and with hesitation he said, "Lieutenant, I regret to inform you that Sergeant Lapierre is dead."

Chapter Eight

MAY 22, 1940

Hazebrouck, France

Phillipe had been in the foxhole for fourteen hours. He spent the time resting and trying to get his bearings. Much of the artillery barrage had ceased, and all he heard was an occasional firefight in the distance.

In the air was the sour smell of exploded artillery and death. *War has a unique smell*, he thought. *Not only does the odor of its victims permeate the air, but so does the aftermath of the explosions used to kill them.*

The sun had come up but hid behind the haze of a darkening sky.

Looking up at the gray clouds, Philippe thought it might rain. Mud was not something he wanted to contend with, but he also realized he could use a shower. It had been days since he'd bathed. *It might be refreshing*, he thought. Maybe the unpleasant aroma he couldn't get away from was himself.

With the cover of darkness no longer available, *everyone must lie low*, he thought.

Like himself, they realized that no matter which army they were fighting for, there was probably an enemy not far with an itchy trigger finger, waiting for the first sign of movement.

He felt alone. He had not seen an Allied soldier for days. Not since Armand was next to him in the bunker, and the parachutes had come down all around them.

His only companion in the world was his latest victim who lay just and arm's length away from him. He had already closed the dead soldier's eyes and rolled him on his stomach, so he would not be reminded of the boy's youth. He looked to be fifteen or sixteen. Not much older than his little brother, Jean-Pierre, he thought. Philippe hoped he was older and only appeared to be young. But what did it matter? If he hadn't killed him, the German would be in this foxhole rummaging through his pockets, as he himself was doing with the boy.

He searched him to see if he had anything usable.

First, his canteen. The several sips of water it held restored energy to his exhausted body. He pocketed a pack of cigarettes, even though he didn't smoke. Cigarettes were always the next best thing to cash. Strangely enough, they were American Lucky Strikes which would command even more in a trade. He also found his identification papers and wallet. The wallet held German *Reichsmarks*, but just a few. Phillipe left the money alone. He knew if he were captured, and they found it, they would shoot him.

The identification papers read Klaus Birkhofer. He had the rank of *Schutz*, which was the equivalent of a private.

Philippe realized that with such a low rank, he had not

The Heroes of Sainte-Mère Église

been in the army long. This may have been his first combat action ever.

Phillipe thought to himself, *Hell, I had seen no action myself until a few days ago.*

Yet, he had been through so much. He felt like a veteran. *An exhausted warrior,* he thought to himself.

How far have I traveled over the past few days? Where am I? How am I going to get out of this foxhole?

He placed his helmet over the end of his MAS-38 and raised it above the edge to see if it would get shot at. Nothing happened. He then took a deep breath and raised his head over and looked around. Other than death, he saw nothing.

Around him lay the carcasses of both cows and soldiers, all of whom appeared to be the victims of mortar fire.

What do I do now? he thought.

He could stay in the foxhole until the sun went down, but he had heard the rumble of German tanks during the night and knew they would continue to pass by as the Germans advanced toward Dunkirk.

It would only be a matter of time before they would cut through this field and find him. Getting caught in this hole with a dead German and a bloody bayonet would not end well for him.

The closest hedgerow was to the east about forty meters. But he needed to go west. To the west, the hedgerow was seventy meters.

That is too far during the middle of the day, he thought. *I would be target practice.*

Looking at his lifeless companion, he said, "Don't take it personally, *Shutz* Birkhofer, but I've had enough of you. I'll take my chances."

He checked the magazine of his weapon, confirmed he

had plenty of ammunition, climbed out of the hole, and away he went. He kept as low as possible without sacrificing his speed.

When he'd made it to the other side of the field, he leaped over the hedgerow. As he flew over the top, he caught his foot in a shrub growing out of the top, and when he hit the road on the other side, he landed on his back, knocking the wind out of him.

He stood up and leaned against the hedgerow for several minutes to catch his breath. Moments later, he heard a motorcycle coming from the south. He pushed himself against the hedgerow, taking advantage of the cover provided by the thick foliage growing out of the mound. He glanced left waiting for the bike to get closer. He wanted to confirm it was a German.

As the lone *Wehrmacht* soldier approached, Philippe stepped in front of him, aimed his MAS-38 sub-machine gun at his head, and opened fire.

After taking direct hits to his chest and face, the soldier flipped off of the back, causing Philippe to dive out of the way of the riderless motor bike speeding toward him.

Leaping to his feet, he looked first at the lifeless body lying in the road, then to the motorcycle that had traveled several meters before settling in a ditch.

Philippe guessed that the lone cyclist was a messenger.

He ran over to the body and turned it over. It was a ghoulish sight. Several machine gun shots to his face and chest, followed by a violent landing on the road created a significant amount of blood and loose flesh.

There was a leather satchel around his shoulder. As Philippe searched it, he realized he was becoming anesthetized to killing his fellow man. He found his own callousness both surprising and disturbing.

How could he have gotten so numb so soon?

Within the bag he found several documents. Orders of some type, he assumed. They looked like codes. It was an odd series of numbers and letters jumbled together.

Because they wrote the document in German, he did not understand what it said. He put the papers back into the satchel.

Placing the strap around his neck and shoulder, he pulled the dead soldier into the woods.

Trying to avoid evidence of his existence, he returned to the middle of the road to cover the pool of blood with dirt. He did the best he could, but doing a thorough job would require more time than he had.

He then ran over to the motorcycle to assess the damage. Other than a slight bend in the handlebars, everything appeared to be in working order.

After pushing the bike back onto the road, he threw his leg over the seat and checked the tank for fuel. It was nearly full.

He pumped the kick-start several times. At first, he had no luck. Then, suddenly the engine came to life. Philippe gripped the throttle, twisting it back several times, as the engine roared.

Before leaving, he checked his compass one last time, then said to himself, "Next stop, Dunkirk."

Mont-Saint-Michel, France

Alfred sat in the corner of their hotel room with his legs crossed, putting the final touches on Esther's birthday present. Mama and Dreyfus were asleep on the bed. They were resting before Esther's birthday party later in the evening.

Papa had stepped out to go to the only market in the village. It was at the end the cobblestone street at the top of the village. He hoped to get bread and meat. Meat was both scarce and expensive.

The widow who owned the hotel, Mrs. Raux, agreed to cook any meat the guests brought back if they would share some with her.

"Yes, I will cook your supper, but only if I get to keep a portion for myself," she would say.

"What kind of hotel is this where the guests buy the food and the proprietor charges a portion of the meal to cook it?" Papa would say angrily.

Tonight's meal was extra special because he would also feed Esther and her parents for Esther's birthday.

As Alfred used the end of his shirt to polish the music note he had carved from the shattered pieces of his violin, he felt happy that his mama and papa had met Esther's parents. They had become close friends in the short time they had been on the mount and had been by the hotel twice in the past week. As small as the room was, they said they enjoyed being there rather than the cold, damp basement of the monastery.

During their visits, Alfred, Esther, and Dreyfus sat on the floor and played games. Their parents sat on the bed and discussed the future of Europe. There was fear for their families back home. It had been weeks since anyone had access to a telephone to call them.

Like the Shapiro's, Uri and Miriam Edelman were in their forties. They had fled Warsaw, Poland, in September of 1939, just as the Germans were invading. They'd spent time in Paris with relatives before making their way to

The Heroes of Sainte-Mère Église

Mont-Saint-Michel.

Uri was tall and thin, and like Joseph Shapiro, had lost much of his hair in recent years. He was a professor of music and looked the part with his conservative brown suit, well-groomed beard, and little round glasses.

Miriam was short but had some girth to her frame with broad shoulders and a thick waistline.

Alfred had made a mental note that she was always easy to spot in the crowded single street of Mont-Saint-Michel because she usually wore a bright floral dress.

Papa and Mr. Edelman discussed ways to get a radio, but Mont-Saint-Michel was hundreds of kilometers from the nearest radio station, so even if they'd had one, there would be no signal.

The only news they had received was from travelers passing through the village. The news shared was not encouraging. The previous day, there was a man heading to Portugal on horseback.

Mr. Edelman said to the man, "Have you heard any news about the war?"

"When I was in Vire, there was a radio report that the Dutch had surrendered, and the western flank of the Maginot Line had been under attack. German units are moving toward Paris."

"Have you heard anything about Warsaw? What is life like there under the German occupation?"

The man replied, "I have only heard rumors. But what I have heard is not good. The parts of the city not destroyed during the invasion are under the control of the Germans. Like much of eastern Europe, entire families are being deported to work camps."

Papa liked Mr. Edelman but was cautious of not revealing too much. Mama and Mrs. Edelman discussed their childhoods and laughed at the silly things they'd done as little girls.

One night after Esther and her parents left, Papa was angrier at Mama than Alfred had ever seen him. Mama had slipped and mentioned an art museum she would frequent in Berlin. Papa overheard the conversation, interrupted, and told the Edelmans that Mama had a rich cousin in Berlin who she visited. They took her to the museum. That was how she'd gone so often.

After they left, Papa said to Mama, "If that ever happens again, we can no longer visit with the Edelmans."

Alfred removed that thought from his mind and went back to polishing the music note he had carved for Esther. He'd created a little hole in the top and inserted a long, red ribbon his mother had saved from their belongings at the truck accident.

After tying the two ends of the ribbon together, he picked up the excess wood he'd carved from the music note, opened the case of his damaged violin, and placed the scrap wood back in with the other pieces.

My violin will always be with Esther, no matter what happens.

Cherbourg, France

After a one-hour drive, René Legrand drove through the narrow streets of Cherbourg. He exited the western side of the city and approached the pier in his 1936 Berliet delivery truck.

In the truck and the trailer behind it, he hauled an excellent spring harvest of turnips and cauliflower. He expected to get a good return per bushel.

The Heroes of Sainte-Mère Église

Where are all the ships? he asked himself.

He had been delivering his produce to the pier at the Cherbourg docks for many years. It was always bustling with activity created by the excitement of British cargo ships and ferries carrying Brits, Frenchmen, and freight back and forth between the two countries.

On the pier, food brokers bought produce and beef from French farmers, then promptly resold it to British merchants who were eager to load the fresh product onto the ships.

Except for a few Portuguese and French trawlers, along with a few personal pleasure craft, there were no vessels tied to the docks.

Baffled, René climbed out of his truck and walked over to a maintenance shop to find someone who could explain the nearly uninhabited pier.

Approaching a dockworker who stood at a workbench, the man was around René's age, with a husky build that left little room in his coveralls.

René saw that the man had an entire arsenal of weapons laid out on the bench. He was dismantling and cleaning the firearms with the efficiency of an expert, just as René himself had done a few days prior.

René said to the man, "Where is everyone? If I didn't know better, I would think today was Sunday."

"Haven't you heard? The British are trying to evacuate Dunkirk. Prime Minister Churchill has made a call out to all available civilian watercraft to aid in their escape. Everything owned by a Brit that floats is making its way to Dunkirk."

"What about our French boys?" asked René. "Are they going to be left there to be slaughtered?"

"That appears to be the situation, my friend. My son is

there right now. He is with the 7th Army. If he is still alive, he is probably covering their flank while the Brits bail out like cowards."

"My boy is there, too. He is with the 3rd Army near Metz. I haven't heard from him in weeks. My name is René Legrand."

"I am Julien Dubois."

"It looks, by the status of your workbench, that you don't plan on sitting around and letting the Germans have their way when and if they get down here."

"You're damn right, Legrand. I have a wife and two beautiful daughters. There is no way I'm letting a single German soldier get anywhere near them. I fought them in the Great War. I saw what they did. They are bastards. They help themselves to anything they wish."

René asked, "What unit were you in?"

"I was in the 7th Infantry, just like my son," said DuBois. "And you, Legrand?"

Out of habit, always trying to keep his secret, René hesitated before answering. "I was in the *Chasseurs*."

Julien DuBois stopped what he was doing, wiped his hands on a cloth, and turned toward René. "That was an elite bunch. You boys were experts at sneaking out of the trenches in the dark of night, never making a sound, and returning with your knives covered in German blood. The *Chasseurs* are legendary."

Putting his hand out to shake René's, he said, "I'm pleased to know you. Where did you say you live?"

"I didn't. But I own a farm in Sainte-Mère-Église. I'm here because I need to get rid of these two hundred bushels while they are still fresh."

"Monday, there is a dry cargo ship scheduled to arrive

from Portugal. I'm sure they will be happy to take your harvest off your hands."

"I'm sure they will, but for a small fraction of what the Brits will pay. But what choice do I have?"

"None, my friend, and soon getting top *franc* per bushel will be the least of your worries. What are you doing this afternoon, Legrand?" asked DuBois.

"Why do you ask?"

"There is a group," replied DuBois. "We are made up of veterans of the Great War. There is a handful of us. Five or six, I would say. We could use more. Many more. There is one other like you. A member of the *Chasseurs*."

"His name?" asked René.

"No names for now. Our group must remain as secretive as possible. You will meet the others tonight."

Although already sensing the answer, René asked anyway, "What is the purpose of this group?"

DuBois said sharply, "You will learn more this afternoon. Meet me at 4:00 p.m. in Saint-Cyr. There is a crossroad at L'Ancien Presbytère and La Mabillé. Tucked back into the woods, you will see a double gate. It is old and rusty and stands twice as tall as you. It is overgrown with shrubs and looks impossible to open. That is by design. Make certain nobody is around, open the gate, and drive through. When you close the gate behind you, be certain you have left no evidence you entered. Then, follow the narrow drive for half a kilometer. It will lead you to an abandoned *château*. We call it *Liberté*. It is overgrown with vegetation and surrounded by tall trees, and impossible to see from a distance. Drive around to the back. You will see our vehicles and several doors. Enter through the door on the far left. Climb the winding staircase until you get to the third floor of the turret. There you will find us. We will hear you coming long before you make it down the road, so don't worry about knocking. Just come in."

"I will be there," replied René.

Mont-Saint-Michel, France

Joseph Shapiro had become a regular at the local market since arriving on the mount. He had been there nearly daily, since he had no means of storing the food he purchased for his family.

After paying for his most recent purchase, the owner asked, "Where are you from?"

"Sainte-Mère-Église. Why do you ask?"

"How long do you plan on staying here?"

"Why are you asking me these questions?"

"Sir, I don't care who you are, or where you are going. It makes no difference to me. However, you have been in here multiple times since arriving to the mount. You have spent more money on meat than most people here can afford in a year. You obviously are a man of means."

"I do not appreciate nor have time for your questioning. *Au revoir, monsieur,*" replied Joseph as he turned toward the door.

"Would you like a way to make it to Spain, *monsieur*?" shouted the man.

Joseph stopped and stood for a moment. He stared out at the street; his instincts told him to return to his family at the hotel.

Turning back, he said to the man, "I have no vehicle. The bus only stops here once per month and with the war

The Heroes of Sainte-Mère Église

and fuel shortages, even that is questionable. So, what makes you think I have any intention of going to Spain?"

Stepping out from behind the counter and walking over to the front of his market, the owner closed and locked the door and turned to Joseph. "Follow me, please."

With hesitation, Joseph followed him down a spiral stairwell to the basement of the store. When they arrived, he saw another man sitting at a table.

The owner introduced him. "This is my older brother, François Marchand, and I am André."

The Marchand brothers were raised on their family winery in Bordeaux, France. It had been in the family for six generations, and as the only males in the family, they expected to inherit the massive estate when their parents passed.

However, their parents had a work ethic that François and André didn't share.

The two brothers were both tall and handsome and flaunted their wealth as they traveled Europe together, wining and dining beautiful women in the finest of establishments.

After the death of their parents, they discovered that their sister, Liliane, who ran the business in their parents' later years, inherited the winery. François and André each received a few thousand francs, but nothing else.

Shortly after, André purchased the market at Mont-Saint-Michel, and François moved there with him where they share a little apartment adjacent to the market.

Both men waited for Joseph to tell them his name, but he stood there stone-faced, offering no information about himself.

After a moment, François said, "You are Jewish, no?"

"That is unimportant. You either tell me why I am down in this basement or I am leaving."

"Have a seat and we will explain," replied François.

After standing motionless for a moment, Joseph pulled out a chair and sat down at the table.

André pulled up a chair next to him and said, "You are clearly a man of few words, so let me be brief with mine. We think we can help you and we think you can help us."

"I doubt that, but I am listening."

François said, "The battle up north is not going well—you surely must have heard by now."

"I've heard rumors, but trapped here with no radio, nobody can be certain."

François said, "The Nazi Party has taken control of Germany. They have captured Poland and the Netherlands. In a matter of days, Belgium and northern France will also fall. It is only a matter of time before they take Paris and continue south to the Spanish border and the Mediterranean Sea. They will most certainly stop here. You are looking at a matter of weeks—maybe even days. You are a Jew, and you are on the run. The same with the dozens of other Jew families that are here. The difference is, they don't have money. You do."

"You know nothing about me. You are guessing, gentlemen. If you will excuse me, I am leaving, and will not be returning."

Joseph stood and headed toward the same set of stairs he had just come down.

André shouted, "*Monsieur*, you are living in a world where Jews cannot stay in one place nor move to another. You are not in a position to turn down offers to help you."

Stopping and turning around, Joseph asked, "What are you proposing?"

The Heroes of Sainte-Mère Église

François said, "Have you ever heard of the Canfranc Railroad?"

"Everyone has—it is no secret. What is your plan?"

"We can get you and your family there. We have a truck parked at La Caserne. Once per week, we bring it here to restock our store. We will use it to take you and your family safely to Pau, France. There you catch the Canfranc Railroad. It will take you through the tunnels of the Pyrénées mountains and safely to Spain. We can have you to Pau in a week. At the pace the Nazis are advancing, that may be all the time you have."

"What is your price?"

"Forty thousand *francs*," replied François.

"That is preposterous. If I had that kind of money, I would not be stuck in this hole, talking to you two scoundrels. I could have purchased my way to the United States by now with that kind of money."

"We don't believe you," said André. "And in a matter of days, the Nazis will be on their way here, and you, my little Jew friend, will see the price for your freedom go way up."

Saying nothing, Joseph stood and stared. First at André, then at François. He glared into their eyes until they looked away. Then he marched up the stairs, unlocked the door, and let himself out.

Dunkirk, France

As Philippe approached the outskirts of Dunkirk on the BMW motorcycle, he slowed to an idle.

There was a bottleneck caused by a caravan of British

and French troops lining the roads. They were making their way to the sanctuary of the city.

Most were on foot—many in trucks overflowing with soldiers. They all looked like he felt—exhausted. They moved slowly. There was a traffic jam caused by the narrow bridges crossing the canals that surrounded the city.

Placed beside those bridges were sandbags stacked chest high with French soldiers behind them. Guns resting on top, waiting for the imminent onrush of German tanks and infantry who were just kilometers away.

In the air, Philippe noticed dozens of *Luftwaffe* planes. Some were Messerschmitt 109 fighters, others were Junker dive-bombers dropping their payloads on the city. Direct hits caused plumes of dark smoke to swell from the ground. Many were in the city's center, but most looked to be near the beachfront.

Along with the German planes, he saw dozens of British and French planes battling them with varying degrees of success.

On his journey from Hazebrouck, Philippe had seen columns of German *Panzer* and Tiger tanks sitting idle in open fields. Most were getting maintenance performed on them before the charge on Dunkirk.

Philippe felt helpless. On the drive up from Sainte-Mère-Église, he and Armand were boasting about how they would shove the Germans back into the Rhineland.

Now, it is all slipping away, he thought.

The Germans had his French army, the British, and Belgians all on the run. They were shoved forcefully into Dunkirk with no place else to go.

Our defeat is imminent, he realized.

Philippe had resolved himself to accept that it was only a matter of time. How would it end?

The Heroes of Sainte-Mère Église

Will we fight to our death or will we surrender?

Philippe had heard the stories of how the Germans had behaved in the Great War.

What would Germany demand in victory? How will they treat my family in Sainte-Mère-Église?

Restless and frustrated at the idleness of his advance into Dunkirk, Philippe opened up the throttle of the motorcycle and bypassed the caravan of soldiers. He cut through the field, leaping over ruts and little hills along the side of the road, frequently becoming airborne.

As he made it to the first bridge over the exterior canal around the city, he approached the two sentries.

"Arrêtez!" shouted one of the French soldiers. Stop!

Initially he slowed, but then realized they may question and detain him after seeing he was on a German, *Wehrmacht* motorcycle.

When he was alongside them, he twisted the throttle back, spinning the rear wheel on the cobblestone bridge, and quickly accelerated to the other side before they could react.

Not knowing where he was going, he rode through the streets of Dunkirk looking for any signs of his previous units —either the 3rd or the 7th Army, his last assignment with Armand. He would settle for any leadership at all.

Who is in charge here? he thought.

It looked like a free-for-all. French soldiers scattered throughout the city, huddled behind sandbags that were positioned with no rhyme or reason. Scores of British soldiers hurriedly headed toward the beach, all while the skies filled with airplanes.

The *Luftwaffe* planes were dropping payloads of bombs all around him, some landing close enough that the shaking ground nearly made him lose control of the bike.

There were square blocks demolished, intermingled with others that still stood in their entirety. Rubble blocked streets with debris from structures that were no longer standing.

Once in the center of town, Philippe pulled over to the side of a road. He noticed a makeshift hospital tent. It was French. Injured with multiple wounds from the previous days, he parked and walked to the tent.

With the sound of aerial bombardment in the distance, he entered the hospital.

Upon entering, he saw dozens of wounded soldiers. There was limited medical staff who spent their time tending to soldiers with life-threatening injuries. The severely wounded were laying on stretchers. Others on the dirt floor.

Those less severe, like himself, sat on benches along the perimeter of the tent. One man, a corporal, moved over and made room for Philippe to sit.

"*Bonjour*, Sergeant. My name is Corporal Bordeur. I'm with the 7th Army."

"I'm Sergeant Legrand. Two weeks ago, I was with the 3rd Army, but circumstances found me with the 7th."

"I spent the last few days with another guy from the 3rd. I thought it was strange he was this far west. I thought you guys were at the Maginot Line."

"We were. But we ended up lost and hopped on a troop carrier headed west."

Philippe then said, "This guy from the 3rd you were with, do you remember his name?"

"I remember he was a sergeant. But his last name escapes me," said Bordeur.

"Lapierre? Was his name Sergeant Lapierre?"

The Heroes of Sainte-Mère Église

"Yes, that's it," replied Corporal Bordeur. "Our lieutenant kept referring to him as Sergeant Lapierre."

Philippe then asked, "Where is he now? When is the last time you saw him?"

With hesitation in his voice, Bordeur quietly said, "Sergeant, I hope he wasn't a close friend of yours. I hate to tell you this, but Sergeant Lapierre is dead. He died of shrapnel wounds he received several days ago."

Philippe said nothing. He paused for a moment, stood, and walked out of the tent. Walking across the street, he noticed a series of knocked-over tables and chairs. They were laying in front of what was once a bustling café. Now, the glass from the front window laid shattered on the sidewalk. Philippe was in a daze. He had been through enough. What more was he going to endure? When he got to the first chair on the sidewalk, he turned it upright, sat down, and stared at the debris on the cobblestone street in front of him.

He thought about his years with Armand. Growing up together from the time they were small boys. School, sports, working on farms together to raise money. Double dates with girls from Saint-Lô. Then the army.

Training and being stationed together made the lifelong bond even stronger. He then thought of Armand's mother, Brigitte, and his little sister, Angélique. They still struggled with the death of Mr. Lapierre; whose accident was only a year ago. Now Armand's death. It would devastate them.

How were they going to find out about Armand? A letter?

Philippe believed he should be the one to tell Armand's mother and sister. Not a letter from Paris. The way the war was going, they may never know the truth. The French government may not even exist in a few days once Paris falls. He then realized that Paris may already be in the control of the Germans.

Dunkirk, which must be held at all costs, was about to fall. He saw the massive columns of German tanks himself. It was only a matter of time.

Philippe looked over at the motorcycle that brought him to Dunkirk. He thought about hopping on and heading home. Back to Sainte-Mère-Église.

Do I really want to be a deserter? What would Papa think if I showed up at home, knowing there were still French boys fighting?

As the sound of artillery fire and aerial bombardment increased throughout the city, he looked over at the BWM still parked where he'd left it. He then stood up. "I'm going home."

As he walked across the street to the motorcycle, suddenly he heard the unmistakable sound of an incoming mortar round. A sound he had become all too familiar with.

He sprinted back to the café and dove through the opening in the front that once held a plate glass window. Just as he landed on the café floor, a massive explosion landed behind him. He stood up and looked toward the direction of the blast.

The hospital tent he was just in took a direct hit.

He thought about the corporal who had informed him of the death of Armand. *There is no way anybody survived that.*

Off to the side was the disintegrated motorcycle that would no longer be taking him home.

What next?

Moments later a French troop carrier came zipping down the street. It stopped in front of him.

The driver shouted to Philippe, "Get in. The British have evacuated two hundred thousand troops. The boats are still coming from England. Now it is our turn. We are going to the beach. Then England."

As the troop carrier rolled onto shore, the entire beach was covered with large craters from the German aerial bombardment.

In and around the craters lay the body parts of British soldiers. There must have been thousands massacred by the bombings and strafing of *Luftwaffe* machine gun fire. They were *Luftwaffe* target practice while they waited for the next wave of rescue vessels to arrive.

In the English Channel, Philippe saw a large assembly of small boats landing on the beach. They were intermingled with larger ships tied to the piers. Those that were still afloat were being loaded with British and French soldiers. Dozens had sunk.

In the distance, he saw a large destroyer resting on the bottom of the channel, listing on its port side. The hull name was visible: HMS *Basilisk*.

Around the *Basilisk*, black smoke and flames rose as fuel oil burned on the surface of the water. Dead bodies floated in the water along with a few survivors.

As the organized chaos of evacuating soldiers continued, the fighting in the air was intense.

Philippe looked directly overhead and saw British and French planes chasing German planes. Then the reverse would happen, causing the Allied planes to be on the run. Aerial dogfights were everywhere.

Occasionally a German Messerschmitt 109 would break free long enough to fly directly along the length of the beach, strafing the evacuees, causing them to dive out of the way as the Messerschmitt machine guns sprayed sand and debris in every direction. Most soldiers were fortunate enough to get out of the way, yet some were not—adding to the death toll.

Philippe suddenly heard orders being shouted from a French lieutenant to head toward the edge of the water.

The lieutenant gathered a small company of men, about twelve, Philippe being one.

The lieutenant then shouted, "Men, my name is Lieutenant Laurent. My orders are to lead as many men as possible off this beach. Stick with me and follow my orders."

As the men gathered closer, Laurent yelled, "Do you see that motor yacht headed our way? When it gets near the beach, head out to it. Keep your weapons dry. When we are in the middle of the channel, we will be sitting ducks for the *Luftwaffe*. If they come after us, we will shoot back at the bastards."

As the boat approached, Philippe and the other men waded into the chest-deep water. He held his MAS-38 and the leather satchel high over his head to keep them dry. In the midst of the onslaught around him, Philippe felt strangely at peace. The cool water was refreshing, and for the first time since leaving Sainte-Mère-Église, he sensed he had a chance to survive the day.

Saint-Cyr, France

Before leaving for Saint-Cyr, René went to his farm, had lunch with his family, and traded his delivery truck for a 1934 Ariel 600cc motorcycle.

The Heroes of Sainte-Mère Église

The trip to Saint-Cyr took him thirty-five minutes. The directions Julien DuBois gave were exact.

The rusty old gate DuBois referred to was tucked back into the woods. The late afternoon sun was blocked by a tall, thick tree line which casted a dark shadow, making the gate hard to see from the road unless someone were looking for it.

Letting his bike idle, he lowered the kickstand and shined the headlight directly on the latch. It was difficult to operate due to the lack of maintenance over the years. After breaking the latch free, he wrestled with the weight of the unwieldy gate, whose hinges hadn't seen oil in decades. He then pushed his motorcycle through the opening.

The driveway leading to the chateau had seen so little traffic over the years that there was little exposed surface dirt. After closing the gate, he did as Julien instructed and looked around to confirm there was nobody around.

Climbing back on his motorcycle, René made his way down the narrow drive leading to the chateau. The Cotentin Peninsula was peppered with ancient chateaus. Except for the Great War, René had lived in the region his entire life and thought he knew of all of them. However, this one was a mystery. It was well hidden, deep in the remote forest. The large walls around the perimeter were covered by ten centuries of thick overgrowth.

When the structure came into view, it looked more like a castle than a chateau. He rode around to the back and saw the other vehicles. There were four trucks and a car. Five—just as Julien had said.

He parked his motorcycle, and as he turned to head toward the last door on the left, Julien stood in the open doorway. Next to him was a sight that made René stop and do a double take. He couldn't believe his eyes. Before him stood Pascal Ganier, his closest comrade from the trenches of the Great War.

Pascal, like René, was a large, powerful man who always kept himself fit. Even though they were both in their forties, the youngest of men were no match for either of them in a brawl.

When they were together in the French army, they were inseparable. Their relationship started in their late teens, while in infantry school together. During the Great War, their skills and instincts on the battlefield became legendary, and they were soon recruited for the *Chasseurs*, the most elite unit in the French army.

After training in the *Chasseurs*, they were assigned together, as a team of two, where they were unleashed on the German army. Once the sun went down, no German was safe in his foxhole. They had snuck out at night, knives in hand, took care of business, and returned to their own trenches, leaving a wake of death to be found the next morning.

Those who knew them well joked that when René and Pascal joined the *Chasseurs*, that was the beginning of the end of the Great War. The Germans never stood a chance after that.

Both men smiled as they approached each other and embraced, each excited to see their long-lost friend.

"Damn, it is good to see you, Pascal," said René. "Where have you been for the past twenty years?"

"I have been living in Paris. I owned a restaurant there. It was right on the Champs-Élysées. I have been in Fresville for the past year. It was a rather sad series of circumstances, my friend. My wife passed away two years ago. Then my father passed this year. I couldn't run my restaurant by myself, and my mother couldn't run the family farm by

The Heroes of Sainte-Mère Église

herself. So, I sold the restaurant, and my son Luke and I moved here. The three of us are managing the farm rather nicely."

"Son? You have a son?" asked René.

"Yes. His name is Luke. Let's go upstairs, old friend. I'll introduce you to him."

At the top of the stairs, they entered a room where Julien made the introductions. Looking around the room, besides Pascal and Julien DuBois, from the dock, there were three other men, a woman, and Pascal's son, Luke.

As DuBois had said, the men in the group were all in their forties and veterans of the Great War.

"Luke," said Pascal. "I want to introduce you to one of the finest men I have ever known. This is Mr. René Legrand. If it were not for him, neither you nor I would be here today. Long before you were ever born, he saved my life more times than I could count."

"Don't let him fool you, Luke. We are both here because we had each other's backs. Your father is like a brother to me. I have a son about your age. His name is Jean-Pierre. You will meet him soon; I am sure of it."

"Yes, sir," replied Luke. "I would like to. There is nobody my age near our farm. Papa makes me work all day, so I don't get bored."

"Well, soon you and your papa will be at my house for dinner. Bring your grand mama too, okay?"

"Yes, sir," said Luke.

René then made his way around the rest of the room to get to know the others.

In addition to DuBois, there was Antoine Devaux, who owned a marine electrical repair shop in Cherbourg. Then there was Daniel Girard, who lived in Cherbourg and owned a handful of tugboats he hired out to shipping companies when their boats arrived. He was a master tugboat captain and was an expert at guiding the ships to the dock safely. Then there was his old buddy Pascal, former Paris restaurateur and now farmer who served with René in the *Chasseurs*.

The last two members of the group were the most intriguing to René. They were Gabrielle and Arthur Hall.

Arthur was rather plain looking, not unattractive, but not handsome either. He was a man of moderate height and was physically unimpressive but left an impression of being extremely intelligent.

Gabrielle was breathtaking. The type of woman who turned heads when she entered a room. She had long auburn hair, hazel eyes, and a body she wasn't afraid to flaunt. She was a little younger than the men in the group, including her husband. However, she, too, came across as extremely intelligent and was a master of multiple languages, a skill the group may need in the near future.

Arthur was an American who had married Gabrielle at the end of the last war. Hall had been a major in the US 13th Infantry Division. After the Armistice on November 11, 1918, he was tasked to stay in France and help manage the logistics of transporting men and supplies back to the United States. The job was massive. It took over a year for the process to be completed fully.

To assist him in his efforts, he contracted a group of French civilians to operate vehicles and load ships at the docks. This required him to also hire a translator to communicate his instructions to the workers. The translator assigned to him just happened to be the beautiful Gabrielle.

She was perfect for the job since she had recently earned her degree in language from the University of Paris.

The Heroes of Sainte-Mère Église

Their professional relationship soon evolved into a romantic one, and they married soon after.

Arthur and Gabrielle Hall have been married for the past twenty-three years. They own a thoroughbred race horse farm in Picauville, just outside of Sainte-Mère-Église.

Gabrielle taught Arthur her language skills, and except for a slight American accent, his French and German were both flawless.

"Gentlemen," said DuBois. "Let's get this meeting started. The clock is ticking, and the Germans will be here in a matter of weeks. We have little time to figure out how the six of us will defend the entire region of Normandy, France, from the Nazis."

English Channel

In addition to Philippe Legrand and the twelve Frenchmen on the beach, Lieutenant Martin Laurent took command of fourteen Brits when they boarded the yacht. Also on the vessel were the captain and the crew.

The name of the yacht was the *Sundowner*, and the sixty-six-year-old captain was Charles Lightoller, a former second officer on the *Titanic*.

After making his way from the beach, Lightoller was forced to maneuver the yacht around the HMS *Basilisk*, which was surrounded by burning fuel. There were other boats in the vicinity looking for survivors.

The men in the water waved their hands over their heads, desperate to be rescued. Most were within the burning perimeter of the oil slick. The heat was intense.

Laurent said to Lightoller, "We can't let them die. We

must try to save them. Can't you just throttle through that blaze?"

Lightoller agreed, found a small opening in the inferno, and shoved the throttle forward.

Once inside the burning ring, Lightoller threw it in reverse to stop the momentum.

Everyone on the *Sundowner* who was physically able to do so, reached into the water and pulled men in. Most were severely burned.

One was missing both legs yet was still conscious.

"Medic!" shouted several of the men.

As the medic knelt, he needed to know the man's state of consciousness, so he asked, "What is your name, sailor?"

"My name is Seaman Frederick Riddle. I am a gunner from Wales."

As the medic applied a tourniquet to both legs, he wanted to keep Riddle awake. He didn't want him to pass out.

"What happened to you?"

"The torpedo hit right below the seat of my antiaircraft gun, and I was thrown in the air."

One of the Brits standing near said, "It figures he is from Wales. Only a Welshman could get both legs blown off and live to tell about it."

The medic said to Laurent, "Tell Lightoller we need to get him to a medical boat. He will never make it to England with us. He will lose too much blood."

Although there were still men in the water, the *Sundowner* was overcapacity.

"This boat wasn't designed for this many men," said Lightoller. "We have to leave the rest behind."

He opened the throttle and shot through the same opening of the inferno he entered.

Chapter Nine

MAY 24, 1940

Saint-Cyr, France

René pulled up to *Liberté* just as he had done two days before. This time, he drove his pickup truck and had Jean-Pierre with him.

When he parked at the gate before getting out to open it, Jean-Pierre said, "Where are we, Papa?"

"I'll explain that in a minute, son. Let's get inside first."

René parked the truck in the back of the chateau. He made certain they arrived before the other members of the group. He wanted to be certain he had plenty of time to explain to Jean-Pierre what was about to happen.

René shut off the engine and turned toward Jean-Pierre. "Son, I need to share something with you. But what I share with you tonight must never be shared with anyone. Not your mother, not Angélique, none of your friends from school, nobody. If you do, you will put the lives of many people at risk, particularly the people you tell. Do you understand me? Do you promise that you will tell nobody?"

"Yes, Papa. I promise."

"When this evening is over, you will be a different person. You will no longer be a boy. I know you are only thirteen, but some things will happen soon that I will need your help with. What I need your help with is not a job for a boy, but for a man. I need for you to be a man. Can you do that, Jean-Pierre?"

"Yes, Papa."

"Jean-Pierre, the Germans are winning the war up north. The British have been evacuating by the tens of thousands from Dunkirk. The fighting is fierce. Our soldiers are getting hit hard. I want you to be brave when I tell you this, but I'm not certain where Philippe is. It doesn't look good. Many of the 3rd Army have been captured or killed."

"Do you think they have captured Philippe?"

"I don't know, Jean-Pierre. The Dutch have surrendered, and the Belgians are about to. With the Brits bailing out at Dunkirk, soon it will only be our French boys doing the fighting. They can't possibly hold their ground. Our boys are fighting hard, but the Germans are moving aggressively toward Paris. It will soon fall. Once Paris falls, it will only be a matter of time before they arrive here. Do you understand me so far, Jean-Pierre?"

"What are we going to do when they get here, Papa?"

"That is why we are here, Jean-Pierre. In a few moments some other men will arrive. Like me, they are veterans of the Great War. We have already fought the Germans once—twenty years ago. We are preparing to fight them again."

"Is Mama going to be safe? What about Angélique and Mrs. Lapierre?"

"We will protect them. I promise."

"Are we going to fight them as soon as they get here?"

"We will let them settle in. Let's see what they have planned for us. If they let us live in peace, we may do nothing. But if they behave like they did during the last time we fought; we will unleash a secret hell on them like they have never seen."

"What are we going to do?"

At that moment, the other vehicles arrived. Arthur and Gabrielle Hall, Devaux, Girard, followed by Julien DuBois and Pascal Ganier. Luke was with him.

"Come, Jean-Pierre. Let me introduce you to everyone."

Chapter Ten

JUNE 4, 1940

Dunkirk, France

The trio looked out a broken window of an apartment at 13 Avenue de la Mer.

"The *Wehrmacht* are everywhere," said the husky McVie.

"This is my fault," said Hancock. "I should have listened to you. We should be on a boat to England right now."

"Don't blame yourself," said Fradd. "Nothing forced us to stay with you. You kept finding wounded. You're a medic. You were just doing your job. We hung back because we are a team."

"He's right, Hancock," added McVie. "We could have hauled ass to the beach at any time. You didn't stop us."

"We got in this together, and we'll get out of this together," said Fradd. "Just like we got out of that barn and the cornfield."

The French army had surrendered three days earlier. The last rescue ship left Dunkirk two days before that. Now sergeants, McVie, Fradd, and Hancock were trapped in the middle of Dunkirk.

They had seen dozens of enemy soldiers patrolling the streets, entering buildings and clearing them out, occasionally finding a lone British or French soldier and marching them down the street with their hands over their heads.

The two buildings across the street had been searched, along with one building next to them, but so far, random luck had kept them from being found.

They were hungry and thirsty. Two weeks of aerial bombardment had left the city's utilities, including the water and sewage systems, in ruins. They had consumed their last drop of fresh water twenty-four hours earlier. They hadn't had food in twice that time.

Hancock said, "There is a café at the end of the street. The windows are blown out, but the building is still standing. Maybe we can find food and water."

"I'd settle for stale bread," said McVie.

"The sun will be down soon. Once it's dark, we should head down there," said Fradd.

"I'm willing to give it a go," said Hancock.

As they waited impatiently for nightfall, they noticed several vehicles coming down the street.

"Brace yourselves, boys," said McVie. "Those aren't *Wehrmacht*. Those are *SS*."

The column of vehicles—one car followed by three lorry troop carriers—simultaneously applied their squealing breaks. They came to a stop in front of their apartment building. The *SS* soldiers leaped from the back of the trucks and at once entered every building on the street.

"Out the back door," said Hancock.

As the three Brits pushed open the back door and ran,

they were intercepted by six *SS* soldiers. There were MP 38 sub-machine guns pointed at them.

Although they spoke no German, they knew the order to halt. With the other five pointing their guns at them, one of the *SS* soldiers forcibly ripped their weapons away from their grasp. Then they ordered the Brits to put their hands above their heads.

They were marched back through the apartment that was once their sanctuary and escorted out the front door. As they stepped out, they saw four more British soldiers and six Frenchmen with their hands up. Two of the Frenchmen appeared to be civilians.

They all stood in the street for several minutes—hands resting on top of their heads as the rest of the apartment buildings were searched.

After they cleared the last few buildings, two more French soldiers were found in the last building at the end of the street.

They then marched the fifteen prisoners toward the beach. The journey was three kilometers.

As they approached the beach, in the distance was a beautiful sunset. For McVie, Fradd, and Hancock, the thought of home just over the horizon of the English Channel gave them a sense of serenity. Even though they had been captured, they took solace in knowing that hundreds of thousands of British and French soldiers had made it to England to fight another day.

After stepping onto the beach, they were marched to an old truck. A large canvas covered the back. It was parked next to one of the largest bomb craters on the beach. Standing next to the truck was *SS Sturmbannführer* Gunther Dettmer. He raised his hand and motioned for an *SS* corporal to come over.

Looking at the truck, Hancock said to McVie and Fradd, "It will be a long ride to a German prison camp in that old thing."

McVie replied, "Wherever they take us, I hope there is a beautiful *Fraulein* who knows how to cook, because I'm starving."

As the three Brits were chuckling at the comment, Fradd turned around and looked down into the crater. Before he could warn the other two of the pile of bloody bodies stacked up in the hole, the *SS* soldier summoned by Major Dettmer climbed onto the back of the truck. He removed the large canvas tarp exposing two MG 34 machine guns pointed directly at them, and with the deafening sound of ripping machine gun fire, fifteen more lifeless bodies fell into the crater.

Chapter Eleven

JUNE 14, 1940

Sainte-Mère-Église, France

Standing in an open field at the Legrand family farm, the two boys were in disbelief at what they were witnessing. Their fathers, laying on their bellies one hundred meters away from the targets, were not missing a shot. On the fence posts were dozens of metal cans that because of the distance, the boys could barely see themselves. Yet their fathers were sending them flying into the air, shot after shot after shot with the Berthier rifles they had used in the war. Then they both switched to MAS-36 single-bolt action rifles and were just as deadly accurate.

Where did they learn to do that? the boys asked themselves. *And why did we never know they had these skills?*

Mesmerized and in awe of their father's abilities, the boys continued to look on.

René Legrand and Pascal Garnier held the same philosophy after the war. They were not ashamed of what they

The Heroes of Sainte-Mère Église

did, but they didn't want to talk about it. Particularly with their families.

For them, that was a different time and, in some respects, a different life. They both battled their emotional and psychological demons, but they learned to cope. They learned to cope with the memories of taking another man's life. Of watching him fall in the distance after slowly squeezing the trigger. Of listening to him gasp his last breath after sneaking up behind him in the dark of night, knife in hand. It was a job. A job that needed to be done, and they accepted it. For the past twenty years, they tried to forget. Push it out of their minds—sometimes successfully.

Now, the same enemy they fought before was about to return, and this time they appeared to be stronger, faster, and more prepared.

After about thirty minutes of shooting, they walked over to René Legrand's pickup truck, opened another box of ammunition, and reloaded.

Both men handed the rifles to their sons. "Boys, now it is your turn."

Cécile Legrand, back at the farmhouse frantically clanged the large bell on the back porch. René knew that it was too early in the afternoon for dinner to be ready.

"Something is wrong. Everyone in the truck."

With René and Pascal in the front, and Jean-Pierre and Luke in the back, they raced back to the house.

Arriving in the backyard, René parked the truck, and they ran through the backdoor into the kitchen.

René asked, "What's wro—"

Before he finished the sentence, Cécile cut him off and said, "Listen!" while pointing to the radio.

Moving closer to the radio and intently focusing, the

voice of the announcer said, "Paris has fallen. The *Wehrmacht* has taken the city. The German Army is now in the streets of Paris. They have instructed all Parisian citizens not to resist. An 9:00 p.m. curfew has been in imposed. All residents must be in their homes before the night turns dark. You will turn all firearms and radios in to the nearest police station within one week. Those who don't comply will be arrested."

A visibly shaken Cécile Legrand, looked at her husband and asked, "What if they come to Sainte-Mère-Église? What will we do?"

René walked over and embraced his wife as she tucked her head into his shoulder.

Looking across the room at Pascal, he replied to his wife, "How we respond depends on what they do when they get here. At that time, we will respond accordingly."

Pascal said, "Boys, let's get back at it. It's time for you to learn how to shoot."

Chapter Twelve

JUNE 16, 1940

Mont-Saint-Michel, France

Out of necessity, Joseph continued to return to André Marchand's market. Other than visiting one of the two cafés on the mount, he had no place else to go to feed his family.

When he went, he refused to speak to André or his brother François. He ignored their taunting and their reminders that their offer of freedom still stood but would remain at the extraordinarily high price of forty thousand *francs*.

Each visit, André would raise his market prices slightly. He was sending a message that as time passed, and the Germans experienced more success in the war up north, times would get more desperate.

At the market, Joseph laid his meat and produce on the counter.

François laughed as André said, "That will be one hundred *francs*."

"My price was half that last time, and I purchased more," said Joseph. "You two are pigs."

"Maybe we are," said André. "But we plan on being fat pigs. We plan on becoming fat pigs from wealthy Jews like you who are desperate. You Jew swine have all the money. The rest of us have to figure out some way to pry it from your clutches."

"By the way," said François. "Have you heard the latest news?"

With a tone of continued disgust, Joseph said, "What news is that?"

"So, you haven't heard. We were wondering why you haven't been begging for our help," said François. "Paris has fallen. It fell two days ago. Your time is about up, my Jew friend."

Realizing the fear that was suddenly showing in Joseph's eyes from François's news, André said, "Your price for freedom is now fifty thousand *francs*."

Joseph paused and said nothing. He was feeling sick to his stomach. *I should have taken them up on their first offer*, he thought to himself. *If I had, my family would already have been in Spain by now.*

Sensing that the news he shared with Joseph was like a body blow, André said, "Each day you postpone the decision, we will raise the offer by five thousand *francs*. I suggest we complete this deal right now, or soon it will be the Nazis spending your precious wealth while you and your family are taken away and never seen again."

Joseph had been thinking about an alternate plan for several days. However, that plan was a desperate alternative. A plan that, until now, he had immediately removed from his mind.

The Heroes of Sainte-Mère Église

Standing there in silence as the two thugs stared at him, he said, "I'll be back this evening. I need to figure out where I will get that much money. Despite what you two fools think, I don't have fifty thousand *francs*."

The two brothers grinned. They were elated. Soon their lives would change forever.

André said, "Give us until 6:00 p.m. It will take us that long to go get our truck and bring it up the hill. You made a smart decision for you and your little Jew family, my friend."

As Joseph left the store, his mind raced. He did, in fact, have fifty thousand *francs*. He estimated that with the cash, the gold coins, and Ingrid's jewelry, he had the equivalent of sixty thousand *francs*.

But he would still need money for protection from the many dangers ahead. The Pyrénées Mountains had a nasty reputation. In addition to the Nazis patrolling the French side, the Spanish side had its share of thieves, crooks, and *bandidos*—leftovers from the Spanish Civil War. The communists and fascists could also be a brutal bunch. Sad as it was, money could buy protection from the evils of the world. He couldn't afford to give all his wealth to the two barbarians he had just left.

Most of all, he didn't trust them. Once he handed over the cash, they could drive them out into the woods and execute them, just like the Nazis would probably do.

When Joseph returned to the hotel, he handed the groceries to Mrs. Roux and asked her to have dinner ready for his family around 4:00 p.m.

"I can do that," she said. "But why so early?"

He had sprinted up the stairs before he heard the question.

Entering the room, he said to his wife, "Ingrid, Alfred is on his way here. I found him with the Edelmans. I told him to return here, but I didn't tell him why. But I am telling you. In a few hours we will be leaving. It is 2:00 p.m. right now. At 6:00 p.m., you, Alfred, and Dreyfus will meet me at the other end of the village, at the bottom of the hill. Stand at the bridge we crossed over to get here. When you arrive there, wait for me. Miriam Edelman and Esther will be there, too."

"What is all of this about, Joseph?"

Without answering her question directly, he said, "Before you leave, go down to the kitchen around 4:00 p.m. Mrs. Roux promised to prepare an early dinner. Don't miss it. It might be the last meal you and the boys eat for a while."

"Joseph, you are talking crazy. What has happened?"

"I have no time to explain, Ingrid. Please! Just do as I ask." He then grabbed his suitcase and headed down the stairs.

Sainte-Mère-Église, France

Under the supervision of their fathers, Jean-Pierre and Luke had spent much of the previous two days practicing their shooting. Although nowhere near their fathers' skill levels, they had rapidly made great progress.

Today, instead of walking out to the middle of the field, as they had been doing, their fathers took them into the

The Heroes of Sainte-Mère Église

barn. Once there, the boys noticed four hogs in one of the pens.

"Where did the hogs come from, Papa?" asked Jean-Pierre.

"We purchased them from Mr. Belanger."

"What are they for? Are we going to raise hogs? I thought you said you chose to be a vegetable farmer because you didn't want to slaughter animals."

"You are correct, Jean-Pierre. That is what I said."

René looked at Pascal and asked, "Do you want to tell them or should I?"

Hesitating, Pascal said, "Boys, the reason these hogs are here is that we are going to kill them. There is a hog for each of us. You will watch us slaughter the first two, then each of you will slaughter the other two."

"No, Papa!" said Jean-Pierre. "I won't do it. There is no reason for me to kill one of those hogs."

"Jean-Pierre, you eat ham. Where do you think ham comes from?"

"I know where it comes from. But someone else kills those hogs. I'm not killing one of those hogs."

"Yes, you are, Jean-Pierre."

"But, Papa, I've never killed anything. You always said because of what you saw in the war, you didn't want to kill anything either. Why are you making me do this?"

"Jean-Pierre, this isn't just about killing a hog. This is about supplying food for others. This is about doing difficult things. It is about teaching you that sometimes for there to be life, there sometimes must be death."

Jean-Pierre felt sick. He looked at Luke and could see he didn't feel any better. Neither boy wanted to disappoint his father. But the act of killing an animal was not something they were prepared for.

The barn was silent for nearly a minute. Neither father spoke up. They stared at their sons, waiting for a response.

"Can I give the meat from my hog to Angélique and her mother?"

"Yes, you may, Jean-Pierre, if that is your wish."

"I'll do it, Papa."

Looking up at his father, Luke reluctantly said, "I'll do it too, Papa."

René walked to the workbench and removed a cloth exposing four newly sharpened knives.

Mont-Saint-Michel, France

After descending the stairs and entering the basement of the monastery, Uri Edelman walked past a group of refugee families resting on cots in the damp passageway. The monks had assigned the Edelman family an area in the back corner. Uri had found some nails and spare blankets to hang from the wooden beams on the ceiling. Although the hanging blankets gave them privacy most of the other families didn't have, the air in the corner was damp and cold, and their little cubby hole smelled of mildew. This had caused Uri, Miriam, and Esther to experience occasional bouts of coughing.

When he arrived at his family's makeshift home, Uri repeated the same instructions to Miriam and Esther that Joseph Shapiro had given to his family. He told them to meet him at 6:00 p.m. at the bridge at the bottom of the mount. He informed them that Ingrid, Alfred, and Dreyfus Shapiro would be there, too. They were all to wait for him and Joseph to arrive. He then sprinted back up the stairs,

The Heroes of Sainte-Mère Église

exited the basement of the monastery, and stepped onto the steep road that would take him to the Marchand market at the top of the hill.

As he walked to the top of the narrow street, the truck was parked in front of the market, just as Joseph had said. It was parallel to the building but backed up to the front door of the market so they could load and unload it easily.

Uri went to the opposite side of the truck and walked up the narrow stone stairs that led up to the top of the monastery. A few steps up, he found a spot behind a row of bushes where he could look down through the plate glass window of the store.

He positioned himself so that he was well hidden but could still see into the storefront. From his vantage point, he had a good view of both the front counter and the top of the stairway leading down to the basement.

It was about 5:10 p.m. He was concerned he wouldn't have enough time. Another thirty minutes passed—time was running out. Joseph would be there in less than ten minutes.

At that moment, François showed up and entered the front of the store.

That wasn't part of the plan, Uri thought. *François was supposed to already have been in the basement.*

Another five minutes passed. André and François both still stood at the counter having a conversation.

Uri looked down the narrow street and saw Joseph at the bottom making his way to the market.

Looking back into the store, he realized now was the time. Both André and François were out of sight. He assumed they had gone down the stairs together.

Uri quickly ran down the stone steps of the monastery, around the truck, and into the store. He looked around and saw nobody. He then went to the back of the store and hid behind some shelves.

After a few minutes had passed, both André and François came up the stairs.

Uri saw that François had a gun and placed it behind the counter.

Moments later, Joseph walked through the front door.

"We were wondering if you would show up," said André.

"Yes, I'm here—what choice did I have?" said Joseph.

André walked over to the front door and locked it. Then François, who was standing behind the counter, pulled out the Barretta he had placed under the counter and pointed it at Joseph.

"Put the case on the counter," said François.

"What is that for?" asked Joseph.

André said, "We learned a long time ago that when you deal with Jews and large sums of money, you can never be too safe."

Joseph laid the case on the countertop.

"Now, put your hands up," said François.

"This isn't necessary," said Joseph.

After Joseph put his hands up, André walked over and patted him down. Other than a small pocketknife, he found nothing.

André laid the pocketknife on the counter next to the suitcase and said, "He has nothing. Just that pocketknife."

Still pointing the gun at Joseph, François said, "Open the case."

Pulling the key from his pocket, Joseph inserted it into the lock and the case opened.

"Look at that, André. Have you ever seen that much money in your life?"

The Heroes of Sainte-Mère Église

"My God," said André. "Stacks of *francs*, beautiful jewelry, and gold coins."

The two brothers looked each other and smiled.

"Life will never be the same, François."

Joseph said, "When do we get out of here? My family is at the bottom of the hill near the bridge. I don't want to keep them waiting."

François asked, "Other than your family, who else knows you are here?"

"What kind of question is that? What difference does it make who knows I am here?"

"He has told no one," said André. "You know the way this Jew is. He tells no one anything. We are safe."

"I don't like the way you two are talking. What are you up to?" asked Joseph.

"Get down the stairs," said François, while holding the gun on him.

Joseph did as they told him and marched down the spiral staircase. André grabbed the bag and followed the other two.

Once in the basement, François ordered Joseph up against the wall and said, "You really didn't think we would drive you all the way to the Canfranc Railroad, did you?"

"So, what are you going to do with me?"

André replied, "You will take a ride in our truck, all right. But you will be in the back, and you will be dead."

François followed with, "Then your little Jew family will be stuck here with no money with all the other Jews who are here. They will sit and wait and wait, wondering whatever happened to you. Then the Nazis will show up and rid the mount of all of your kind."

"You can't shoot me down here. Someone will hear the shot."

"No, they won't," replied André. "They cut this basement out of the core of the mountain. These walls are too thick for any sound to travel through them."

As André finished those words, he heard a crack so loud it sounded like a massive explosion. The confines of the enclosed basement caused the gunshot from Uri to be deafening.

After getting over the shock of seeing Uri behind him at the bottom of the stairs, André saw his brother lying on the floor, gasping for air. The bullet had penetrated his right lung, causing it to fill with blood.

André then dove for François's Berretta that laid on the floor. Just as his hand grabbed it, Uri fired two more shots, both hit André squarely in the chest and killed him instantly.

With François still on the floor, grabbing his chest and gasping, trying to suck in more air, Uri stood there holding the Luger that Joseph had given him. He was in shock, realizing he had just shot two men.

Joseph walked over, took the gun out of Uri's hand, pointed it at François's head and pulled the trigger, ending the torment that the two maggots had put him through.

Grabbing Uri by his lapels and shaking him, Joseph said, "Snap out of it. It is done. Our families are waiting at the bottom of the hill. Let's go. Now!"

After grabbing his case that laid next to André, Joseph Shapiro led the way to the top of the spiral staircase, through the front door, and into the 1935 Citroën Cargo van.

Pushing the ignition button, he released the parking brake. The gravity of the steep hill caused the vehicle to roll before he hit the accelerator.

Joseph held his foot on the brake most of the way down

The Heroes of Sainte-Mère Église

the hill. He was careful not to hit anyone that stepped out onto the only street in the tiny village.

He rolled past Mrs. Roux's hotel that had been their home for several weeks, then the two restaurants, then two more hotels, and through the arch that was the entrance to the village.

Once he hit flat land, he put the little truck in gear and stepped on the accelerator, then headed toward the bridge that was forty meters away.

Joseph and Uri saw their families at the end of the bridge, just as instructed.

After Joseph pulled up next to them, Uri opened the back doors of the van.

"Get in!" shouted Uri.

One by one, Uri helped all five into the van and said to Ingrid, "Go sit in the passenger seat next to your husband. We will be fine back here sitting on the floor."

Once all suitcases and passengers were in place, Joseph stepped on the accelerator.

Driving over the bridge, the passengers in the back all looked through the two rear windows and watched as the beautiful mount that had been their home got smaller in the distance.

When Joseph got to the end of the bridge, he continued straight, drove through the town of La Caserne, and continued to the main road near Pontorson.

When he turned right and headed south, Joseph felt liberated, as though he had just been let out of prison. As he continued down the road, he saw a hill off to the left. On the hill was a dirt road that headed toward Mont-Saint-Michel.

Noticing the cloud of dirt that was being generated

from the road, Ingrid said to her husband, "What is that, Joseph? What are those vehicles?"

On the road were a series of vehicles: two open-top cars and a truck with a large antenna protruding from the top, followed by two troop carriers.

"Those are German soldiers, Ingrid. *Wehrmacht*. And they appear to be headed in the direction of Mont-Saint-Michel."

Chapter Thirteen

JUNE 17, 1940

Sainte Mère-Église, France

Jean-Pierre, Angélique, and Luke were at the DuBost bakery, sitting at a table sharing two large cherry pastries.

Angélique and Jean-Pierre were curious what it was like to live in Paris, and Luke was eager to tell them.

"It was fun," said Luke. "There are people everywhere. There is always something to do, and your friends all live in the same building—not several farms away like they do here."

"What do you think it is like now that the Germans are there?" asked Angélique.

"I don't know," said Luke. "Papa said he is glad we sold the restaurant last year. He would not like serving German soldiers who had just invaded the city. He said he would probably poison their food. But I think he was joking."

Moments later, a crowd of about twenty people gathered outside the bakery. Among them was Mayor Renaud.

Jean-Pierre said, "What is going on out there?"

The crowd was looking toward the east entrance of town. Some appeared angry—others concerned. A few just had looks of disbelief at what they were watching.

Then the three teenagers heard it. The sound of machinery. Large machinery, and it had become louder by the moment. They couldn't make out what it was from their vantage point at the table, so they got up and stepped out on the curb.

Looking east—a column of German *Panzer* tanks entered the village. Three of them. Led by four motorcycles and two open-top *Kübelwagens*.

Bringing up the rear were three half-tracks, each carrying twelve to fifteen *Wehrmacht* soldiers.

It was a stunning sight for all who witnessed it. The peace and innocence of Sainte-Mère-Église, their hometown, the place that most of them had known as their only home since birth, had been invaded by a foreign government. A government that had already proven itself to be led by tyrants.

"What should we do, Mayor?" asked a voice from the crowd.

"There is nothing we can do," said the mayor.

As the intimidating sight continued to roll in their direction, Jean-Pierre said to Luke, "Let's get out of here. We need to tell our fathers."

They ran to the center of the courtyard where their bicycles were leaning against a tree. Jean-Pierre and Luke climbed onto their bikes, then Jean-Pierre held his steady for Angélique to climb upon the handlebars. Then off they went, peddling swiftly back to Jean-Pierre's farm.

Continuing to watch the enemy invade his town, Alexandre Renaud said, "Nothing will ever be the same."

PART II
Occupation

…I am hurt but I am not slain.
    I will lay me down and bleed a while,
    And then I'll rise and fight again…

Sir Andrew Barton

Part II
Occupation

Chapter Fourteen

JUNE 18, 1940

London, England

After entering the building of the British Broadcasting Corporation (BBC), he passed through multiple administrative offices. He was a towering figure, which drew the attention of curious onlookers, who had no idea who he was.

He entered the broadcast booth in studio B2 and received instructions on how the radio cast would take place. Once seated, he removed his hat, cleared his throat, and positioned himself in front of a desktop microphone. Picking up the typed statement he had written himself, he waited patiently for the green light to illuminate, indicating it was time to speak.

The man at the microphone was French General Charles de Gaulle. He had just arrived in Great Britain the previous day on board a small airplane provided by the British.

The exiled general hoped his words would be the start

of the fight to return France to a condition of sovereignty. To a condition of liberty and freedom.

When the green light came on, de Gaulle summarized the events of the previous few weeks.

He then shifted his tone to that of inspiration, saying, "But has the last word been said? Must hope disappear? Is defeat final? No! Believe me, I who am speaking to you with full knowledge of the facts, and who will tell you that nothing is lost for France. The same means that overcame us can bring us to victory one day. For France is not alone! She has a vast empire behind her. She can align with the British Empire that holds the sea and continues to fight. She can, like England, use the immense industry of the United States."

He then called to arms all French citizens who were available to fight, whether they were in France or Great Britain. He closed by saying, "Whatever happens, the flame of the French resistance must not be extinguished and *will* not be extinguished."

Although his words that day were heard by few, they were echoed throughout France and among the one hundred thousand French soldiers in Great Britain who had escaped from Dunkirk. They were, in fact, the words that ignited the flame that started the Free French Forces and the French Resistance.

Sainte-Mère-Église, France

Leading a group of *Kübelwagen*, the Mercedes staff car pulled up to City Hall.

Exiting their vehicles, the group of officers made their

The Heroes of Sainte-Mère Église

way up the stairway and through the courtyard in the front of the building.

Standing at the doorway, dressed in a tweed three-piece suit, was fifty-nine-year-old Mayor Renaud.

Reaching his hand out to the mayor, the *Wehrmacht* officer in charge said in excellent French, "Good afternoon. I am *Oberst* Helmut Volk. Whom do I have the pleasure of speaking to?"

"I am the mayor of Sainte-Mère-Église, Alexandre Renaud."

"It is a pleasure to meet you, Mayor," said Volk. "I hate to inform you of the inconvenience I am about to impose on you, but my men and I will be commandeering your City Hall building. This will be our new headquarters."

"Under what authority will you be doing this?"

"The authority of the German Third Reich. Please show me around so I may assign administrative quarters to my officers."

"And if I refuse?"

Grinning. "It really doesn't matter if you refuse. I have dozens of lorries filled with armed men and a half a dozen *Panzer* tanks within a few kilometers of here. Refuse all you wish, it really doesn't matter. We will get what we want one way or the other."

Forty-eight-year-old Helmut Volk was a career military officer. During the Great War, he managed to stay out of the trenches with the help of his father, who was an adviser to Kaiser Wilhelm II. His father used his considerable clout to keep his son busy with administrative assignments, and Helmut Volk never fired a shot.

When Adolf Hitler became Chancellor of Germany in 1933, Helmut used the political skills he learned from his father to climb the ranks of the German regular army, eventually gaining the rank of *Oberst*. Holstered to his side was a Luger that had never been fired in battle.

Stepping past Mayor Renaud and into the City Hall building, *Oberst* Volk led the way, as several of his officers trailed behind him. The mayor's two staff employees looked on, uncertain how to respond.

Mayor Renaud stood helplessly as *Oberst* Volk pointed into the few small offices on the first floor, assigning each room to a member of his staff.

Volk then sprinted up the stairs to the second floor, with his two remaining aides behind him. He found the largest office, which belonged to the mayor. It was in the front of the building and overlooked the courtyard. Once in, he looked around and made his way behind the desk and looked out the window to see several civilian onlookers, curious as to what was happening.

Following Volk into his office, Renaud said, "*Oberst* Volk, I resent this intrusion. You have no right to help yourself to my office, or the offices of my staff."

"Mayor, I resent that we are still having this discussion. Let's put an end to it right now. It will save us both a lot of headache, especially you. I am not an unreasonable man. I will leave and go eat lunch. I am starving. I will be gone for an hour. That should give you enough time to remove your personal items from my office, will it not?"

"What are your plans for Sainte-Mère-Église, *Oberst*?"

Volk was losing patience with the mayor. He stepped around the desk and approached Renaud, who stood in the center of the room.

"Mayor, I understand your resentment. I'm sure if I were in your position I, too, would harbor the same resentment for an invading force. Maybe if France would have offered some compassion to Germany after the last war, we would be more inclined to offer you some in this one. But of course, as France will soon learn, the German people have a good memory.

"Let me add, Mayor, and when I say this, you need to listen carefully. I need you. But much more important is that the people of Sainte-Mère-Église need you. I say to you humbly: I now have supreme authority over this town. I say what happens. I determine the level of force my soldiers use on your people. I hope that level of force remains low. My men have been instructed to handle your people with a velvet glove rather than an iron fist. However, that can change in an instant. You, Mayor, will play a key role in this relationship. My door is always open to you, but you only. If your people have a complaint about my men, they are free to take it up with you. At that point, you can bring it to my attention. If appropriate, I will punish my men. However, let this be clear. I will not tolerate insubordination from your citizens, and I will not tolerate threats to the safety of my men. If that were to ever happen, the rules will change dramatically.

"Finally, and this may well be the most important piece of information of all, I am a member of the *Wehrmacht*. I am regular German Army. I am not the *Waffen-SS*. Be grateful you are dealing with me, Mayor. Because if the time ever comes where you see the uniforms of the *Waffen-SS* roaming your streets, you will wish I were still around.

"By the end of today, we will post the rules of our occupation throughout Sainte-Mère-Église. The best thing you can do for your citizenry is to be certain they are aware of them. Is all of this understood, Mayor?"

"I understand completely, *Oberst*."

"Very good, Mayor. If I need to contact you, where can you be located?"

"In addition to my duties as mayor, I am also the town pharmacist. My pharmacy is in the center of town across the street from the church courtyard. You passed it on your way here."

"I will come see you. I have severe pain. Conquering a country in the passenger seat of a *Kübelwagen* can be bad on one's back. Maybe you could recommend an antidote."

With disdain in his tone, he said, "I will see what I can do for you."

Exiting the office door, Volk turned and asked the mayor, "Can you recommend a restaurant, Mayor?"

"Le Café du Quartier. It is across the courtyard from my pharmacy."

La Rochelle, France

Running low on fuel, Joseph Shapiro pulled the stolen delivery van into the village of La Rochelle.

"I'm hungry, Papa," said Esther.

Alfred, who was sitting next to Esther, pulled a small piece of bread from his pocket and gave it to her. "This was left over from my breakfast. You can have it."

Esther replied, "*Merci*, Alfred, but I don't want to take your food. You will need it."

"I'm not hungry. You are. Take it."

Although Esther did not like taking Alfred's bread, she had not eaten since dinner the previous evening.

Darkness was setting in, and by the time they found a petrol station it was closed.

"What should we do?" asked Ingrid.

Down the street was a sign that read Covered Market,

The Heroes of Sainte-Mère Église

with an arrow to the left. Next to the market was a café with no patrons. Joseph parked the van and said, "Let's see if we can get food at that café."

As they got out of the van, Uri Edelman grabbed Joseph by the arm and pulled him aside as the others crossed the street to the café.

"Joseph, I have to tell you something."

"What is it, Uri?"

Choked up and in tears, he said, "I am not a rich man. I have so little. I can't feed my family in that café. I can't feed my family anywhere. When the Germans invaded Poland, I hastily locked the door to our house, and we walked to the bank. It was closed. I had to get to the train station, so I couldn't wait. I had to leave much of my money behind. I should have taken it out sooner, but the German invasion caught me by surprise. Getting this far has taken everything we had. I don't know what to do."

Placing his hand on Uri's shoulder, Joseph replied, "Uri, my friend, don't worry. If it were not for your courage back at Mont-Saint-Michel, I wouldn't be here myself. I approached you with my problem, handed you a gun, and said I needed your help. Without hesitation you showed up just in time to save my life. I will always be grateful."

"Thank you, Joseph."

"Uri, there are things about me I have not shared with you. When the time is right, I will tell you. As for now, you are better off not knowing. Don't worry about feeding your family. We will stick together. We will survive together—your family and mine. Do you understand?"

"Yes, my friend. I understand. I will repay you one day."

"You already have. Now let's go feed our families."

The two men walked over to the café and joined the

others. The children at one table and the adults next to them.

The waiter approached, "At this time of night, all I can offer you are omelets. Will that be fine for you?"

"Bring us seven omelets, four coffees, and plenty of water," replied Joseph.

"Oui, monsieur."

As they sat at the tables discussing a hotel, a German staff car came around the corner and parked behind their van. It was a convertible Mercedes with the top down. There were two *Wehrmacht* officers in the back, and a low-ranking driver.

All three men walked over to the café and took the table next to the children. The adults continued their conversation, occasionally glancing at their children and the officers.

Any sense of security they felt had suddenly vanished. There were German soldiers scattered all throughout Europe. They realized that this feeling of terror every time they encountered one was permanent. Everywhere they went, they could be arrested simply for being Jewish.

The Germans who sat next to the children started a playful conversation with them.

First to Alfred, "What is your name, young man?"

Remembering his father's instructions to never reveal his Jewish heritage, he replied, "Adrian Salvatore, sir."

"It is nice to meet you, Adrian."

Looking at Dreyfus, he asked the same question, who followed his brother's lead. "Demetrius Salvatore, sir."

Finally, the German looked to Esther and asked a third time. Esther, understanding the deception, replied, "Emma, sir. My name is Emma Salvatore, and I am their sister."

After the exchange between the German officer and

their children, the four parents hoped their sigh of relief was not obvious.

Looking at Joseph and Ingrid, he said, "Are these your children?"

"Yes," replied Joseph. "They are our children."

"They are beautiful and very polite."

"Thank you," replied Joseph. "We are very proud of them."

Chapter Fifteen

JUNE 19, 1940

Portsmouth, England

After being briefed by the French military leadership who had evacuated to Britain, Lieutenant Laurent entered the barracks of the small squad assigned to him.

One hundred and twenty thousand French troops had been evacuated from Dunkirk. Many had returned to France by order of the French government. Others still waited in England for their orders.

For those who had returned, their plan was to land at remote ports throughout the coastal regions of France and regroup. They would then continue the fight against the Germans. Those who remained in England were scattered throughout British military facilities along coastal England.

"Gather around, men," shouted Lieutenant Laurent. "I know we all want to get home to the fight, but we must be patient.

"French soldiers have been returning to France en masse for the past several days. Reports are that their return has

The Heroes of Sainte-Mère Église

been a disaster. With the impending surrender of the French government, they arrived on French soil with no military leadership. Most of the soldiers tried to create their own makeshift units. They were poorly organized and ineffective against the massive German army. Many have been killed, captured, and some executed. General Charles de Gaulle has requested we stay in Great Britain and become part of the Free French Forces. However, he has no authority to give us that order. We are still officially under the control of the French government.

"Let me make this clear. As members of the French army, you are being ordered to return to France. If you stay here in England, you will do so as a deserter. If you return, you will be asked to surrender. The German army is unpredictable. As a member of the French army, they may consider you a threat and imprison you. If you fight and they capture you, they may execute you. Finally, you can stay here in England and join General de Gaulle and the Free French Forces. Whatever you do, you will not receive judgment from me. I, for one, will return to my wife in Sainte-Mère-Église."

After listening to Lieutenant Laurent's speech, Philippe approached him. "Lieutenant, my name is Sergeant Philippe Legrand. I, too, am from Sainte-Mère-Église. Is your wife a schoolteacher?"

"Yes, that's right. She teaches at the school east of town. Do you know her?"

"No, but my little brother, Jean-Pierre, is in her class."

"Sergeant, I'm sure you are as concerned for your family as I am for my wife, Margot. I have heard reports that the Germans have advanced rapidly. If they aren't already in Sainte-Mère-Église, they will be soon."

"How do you plan on getting back home, Lieutenant?"

"There is a light cruiser leaving tomorrow, named the *Jean De Marseillaise*. It is scheduled to take us to Cherbourg, provided the port isn't already occupied by the Germans."

"I'll be on it with you, Lieutenant."

Laurent said, "When we get to Cherbourg, find me. We will make our way home together."

Sainte-Mère-Église, France

"What are they nailing to the tree?" asked Angélique.

"Let's go see," said Jean-Pierre.

With Angélique in her usual spot on Jean-Pierre's handlebars, and Luke on his own bicycle, they peddled across the church courtyard and arrived as the soldier had finished driving the nail.

A notice was attached to the tree;

By order of the Kommandant, 216th Infantry Division, German Army
"Let it be known, Sainte-Mère-Église is now under the occupation of the Third Reich. All firearms and wireless devices are to be turned into the Constable or German Command office. Your homes are to be made available for billeting German soldiers as requested. All citizens are expected to cooperate. We will try to make our occupation as pleasant as possible. However, any attempt to threaten the security of your occupiers will be met with harsh reprisals."

"Are they going to move into our homes?" asked Angélique.

"I don't think it would be a good idea for them to move in with my papa," said Jean-Pierre.

Chapter Sixteen

JUNE 20, 1940

**His Majesty's Naval Base
Portsmouth, England**

Philippe Legrand stood in a single file line with hundreds of French soldiers. They waited to board the French light cruiser *Jean De Marseillaise* for the six-hour trip across the English Channel that would return them home. He kept an eye out for Lieutenant Laurent but couldn't locate him.

After boarding the ship, Philippe was directed down a stairwell and into a berthing area where he stowed his gear for the voyage across the channel. Returning from below deck, he watched the ship pull away from the pier and into Portsmouth Bay.

He was eager to get home yet concerned for what awaited him.

Had the Germans arrived in Sainte-Mère-Église? What should I do when I get home—fight? It will devastate Mrs. Lapierre and Angélique when I tell them of Armand's death.

Thirty minutes later, as the sun was setting, Great

Britain disappeared into the horizon. The mood among the soldiers and crew of the ship was that of exhilaration.

The *Jean De Marseillaise* had made several return trips to Cherbourg, repatriating French soldiers with each return. However, the Germans had recently arrived on the Cotentin Peninsula, and the reports said they were moving quickly toward Cherbourg. This trip was a race. A race to get this final group of soldiers to Cherbourg before the Germans arrived at the port city.

Pau, France

"This town is crawling with Nazis, Joseph," said Uri Edelman. "They aren't going to just let seven Jews board a train to Spain. We don't even have documents."

Parked at an intersection in the center of Pau, France, Joseph realized that Uri's pessimism was justified. However, he knew the group looked to him for leadership. He couldn't express the feelings of defeat he experienced as he stared at the throngs of people from all over Europe bustling in the streets. They consisted of political refugees, Gypsies, homosexuals, and the disabled. But they were mostly Jews who tried desperately to conceal their heritage. They all wanted the same thing, and that was to get to Spain. The emerging Nazi oppression had already become unpleasant in France.

Intermingled on several street corners, *SS* officers checked papers and glanced at their lists of fleeing political refugees. Joseph knew he was near the top of that list because of his anti-Nazi activity in Berlin. Just his presence in the van put his family and the Edelmans in jeopardy.

The Heroes of Sainte-Mère Église

Towering over the town of Pau, were the massive Pyrénées Mountains. They were both rugged and deadly. They held the bones of many a traveler who never made it to the other side.

"We will figure something out, Uri. We have made it this far. We will find a way to Spain even if we have to walk through those mountains," said Joseph.

"We have no papers," replied Miriam Edelman. "What will we do if they ask for them?"

"We have false papers," replied Ingrid. "We had them made before leaving Berlin."

"That was in 1936," said Joseph. "I don't trust the Nazis would consider them valid. We have to find a way to get false papers before attempting to board the train."

"How will we do that, Joseph?" replied Ingrid. "You knew people in Berlin, but we know nobody here. You can't just walk up to perfect strangers and ask them where we get false papers."

"Papa, what are we going to do?" asked Alfred. "Esther and I are hungry. I don't think she is feeling well. I'm worried about her."

Although she was ill from lack of food, Esther said, "I'll be all right, Alfred. But thank you for caring about me."

"Let's park the van and find a hotel, then a café for dinner. But be careful. Remember what happened in La Rochelle," said Joseph. "There are even more Germans here, and these are *SS*, not *Wehrmacht*."

After parking the van, they walked around the corner looking for a hotel not infested with German officers.

"There's one, Papa," said Alfred.

They all glanced down the alley that Alfred had found.

"Fine job, Alfred," said Joseph. "That one may work."

The cold, damp breeze that blew through the shaded

passageway was refreshing after the long ride in the van. They entered the small lobby and looked around at the unkept, dusty surroundings.

"This is the perfect place," said Uri. "No Nazi *SS* snob would ever check into this fleabag."

Joseph rang the bell on the front desk. Stepping out of the office was a man in his sixties. He wore a ragged black suit that carried as much dust as the rest of the lobby.

Also entering the room was a younger man in his thirties. He was wearing an apron and came from the other side of the hotel where there was an adjacent café.

"We need two rooms. Can we get them on the third floor?" asked Joseph. "We would prefer to have them in the back if that is possible."

"I have one available room on the third floor, and another on the second. They both overlook the street in the rear of the hotel."

"Those will work fine."

Joseph felt uneasy as the two men looked at him and his group with curiosity.

As Joseph finished the room arrangements, the others looked at the posters that covered the alley walls. They were all disturbing with images of intimidating Nazi propaganda. Much of it anti-Semitic, depicting Jews as rats and other disgusting creatures.

After getting the keys for the rooms, Joseph stepped out into the alley to join them.

Alfred and Esther sat close on a bench laughing at Dreyfus who made funny faces to ease his boredom.

The adults stared intently at one poster specifically. Joseph approached to read it. It was a wanted poster written in German, French, and Spanish.

The Heroes of Sainte-Mère Église

Wanted

*For the Murder of André and François Marchand
The crime took place at Mont-Saint-Michel.
The suspects are two Jewish men in their forties.
One of the men is tall, has a beard and wears glasses.
The other man is significantly shorter.
They were last seen driving a stolen 1935, dark green Citroën
cargo van.*

The poster depicted two poorly drawn sketches of Joseph and Uri.

"At least they don't look like either of you," said Miriam.

"No, but if Uri and I are seen together, it might give us away," said Joseph.

"What should we do, Joseph?" asked Ingrid.

"We need to find somewhere else to stay. The van is right around the corner. We can't take a chance that someone saw us come down this alley."

"Where are we going to go?" asked Miriam. "I'm tired, and so is Esther."

Uri barked at his wife, "That's enough, Miriam. We can't stay here any longer."

As they stepped out of the alley, they looked down the street toward the van. It was surrounded by French police and *Waffen-SS* soldiers.

They turned left and headed in the other direction, passing in front of the café of the hotel. As they did, the young man from the front desk approached them. He glanced around to be certain nobody could hear him, then whispered, "Don't go. I can help you. Please follow me."

Thinking of his experience with the Marchand brothers

at Mont-Saint-Michel, Joseph reluctantly instructed the others to follow the young man into the café.

Bletchley Park
Buckinghamshire, Great Britain

Hut 6 of Bletchley Park was a nondescript, one-story wooden building. The white paint had peeled, and the only door of the one-room laboratory was warped and wouldn't close completely. It was frigidly cold in the winter and stifling hot in the summer.

Not the environment a champion chess player and a brilliant mathematician expected to be working in. But Stuart Milner-Barry and Gordon Welchman realized the future of Great Britain was at stake, and now was not the time to be focused on the luxuries of life.

Both men were thirty-four years old, and although still eligible to join the military, the British government believed their intellect could be best used to decipher German communication codes.

Hut 8 had made great strides in decoding German naval Enigma codes.

Hut 6 was responsible for decoding *Wehrmacht* Enigma Codes. Unlike the *Kriegsmarine* and *Luftwaffe*, the *Wehrmacht* codes could be transferred by ground, making them more difficult to intercept.

The codes were typed on paper and given to a messenger who would escort them to the front lines. The messenger often traveled by motorcycle. Once at the field headquarters, the messenger would personally hand deliver the codes to the commanders, reducing the chance of interception.

"If only we could get our hands on a few bloody *Wehrmacht* codes, we would be in business," said Milner-Barry. "Somehow, someway, we need to figure a way to capture those codes."

Welchman replied, "We have what we have, Stuart. We must work with it. The *Wehrmacht* codes can't possibly be that much different from the *Kriegsmarine* codes. Let's go talk to the boys in Hut 8 and see if we can get clues from them."

Milner-Barry replied, "We've been down that road dozens of times, Gordon. It is a dead-end."

After a full day of painstaking and pointless brainstorming, the two men grabbed their hats and stepped toward the door of the hut to go home.

As they reached for the knob, the door opened and in walked the head of the entire Bletchley Park decoding operation, Commander Alastair Denniston.

"Commander," Milner-Barry said. "What gives us the pleasure of your visit?"

"Good evening, gentlemen. Brace yourselves. I am here because I am about to present you with what I believe to be one of the most significant breakthroughs since Bletchley opened."

He placed a leather satchel on the drafting table in front of them. After Denniston removed the contents and laid the documents on the table, Milner-Barry and Welshman looked at each other in jubilation.

Welchman said, "This is astonishing, Commander. There must be three weeks' worth of *Wehrmacht* codes here. These documents just saved us a year of research."

"Where did you get these, Commander?" asked Milner-Barry.

"They were given to our boys at the naval base in Portsmouth. They were just casually handed over by a French soldier who escaped from Dunkirk. I believe they said his name was Legrand. Yes, that's it. Sergeant Philippe Legrand."

Liberté
Saint-Cyr, France

René parked the truck behind the chateau that had become to be known as *Liberté* by the small group of resistors. On the bench seat between Mayor Renaud and René sat Jean-Pierre.

"Well, this is an interesting place," said Mayor Renaud. "I have driven past these woods more times than I can count and never had any idea this was tucked back here."

"That's what makes it so perfect for our operation," replied René.

"So, who is in this group you've told me about, René?"

"Follow me in, Mayor, and I will introduce you."

The mayor followed René and Jean-Pierre up to the third floor. When they entered the room, the others were sitting around a large oak table that looked as old as the ancient castle itself.

Besides René and Jean-Pierre, every member of the core group was there—Pascal and Luke; Arthur and Gabrielle Hall; Julien DuBois, the dock foreman at Cherbourg; Daniel Girard, the owner of the tugboat company at Cherbourg; and Antoine Devaux, the owner of the marine electrical shop and builder of the wireless devices they communicated with.

The Heroes of Sainte-Mère Église

After the introductions, René said, "Mayor, we are a small group, but we all play our own roles. Even though we work as a team, we operate as two branches of the same tree. DuBois, Girard, and Devaux handle the western half of the peninsula. They are based out of Cherbourg. The rest of us cover the east out of Sainte-Mère-Église. That is another reason *Liberté* is ideal—it is halfway between our two teams."

The mayor asked, "What is your purpose?"

"That depends on the Germans," replied DuBois. "If they behave themselves, we hope to play the role of being observers. We will watch what happens and relay the information to the Brits with the hope they can use it to help us liberate France."

"And if they don't behave themselves?" asked the mayor.

"We will keep you out of that discussion, Mayor," replied Pascal. "Let's just say, occasionally our occupiers might require a little pushback."

"So how can I assist you?" asked the mayor.

"Fill us in, Mayor. What are we up against? What did this Volk tell you?" asked René.

"There are two main points he drove home. First, the German *Wehrmacht* is running the show. They are overseeing the entire Cotentin Peninsula. They will try to be 'good neighbors,' but they are also not going to hesitate to take what they need. What that means remains to be seen."

"And the other main point?" asked René.

Mayor Renaud replied, "The other point Volk emphasized is that we are fortunate that we are dealing with the Wehrmacht and not the *Waffen-SS*."

DuBois spoke up, "I know of them. I have met people catching boats out of Cherbourg to England who have crossed paths with the Waffen-SS. I met a man who was missing three fingers on his left hand. He said the SS snipped them off while they were interrogating him. He said he was one of the lucky ones because he was released. The SS are considered an elite force and allowed to play by their own evil rules."

"That's right," replied the mayor. "Apparently they are sent to places they consider strategically important areas where security is a problem. Volk said if we cooperate with their 'limited' demands, we will continue to have the *Wehrmacht* here. However, if they feel the safety of their soldiers is threatened, they won't hesitate to bring in the *SS*."

"So, they are threatening us?" asked Arthur Hall.

"I believe Volk would refer to it as a warning," replied the mayor.

"How often will you meet with Volk?" asked René.

"I requested at least twice per week, which Volk agreed to. He also said his door is always open for me and only me. If any citizen has a complaint, they are to bring it to me, and I will address it with him."

Glancing at his watch, Daniel Girard said, "I need to get back to Cherbourg. I have my crew preparing four tugboats to dock another ship bringing in French soldiers. The *Jean De Marseillaise is scheduled to arrive soon.*"

The mayor said, "Hopefully, you can dock her, disembark the soldiers, and get her back out to sea before the Germans get to Cherbourg. So far, they have been stalled east of the peninsula performing maintenance on their vehicles."

As he left the room, DuBois said, "Thank you for telling me, Mayor. That's exactly the kind of information we need."

Pau, France

Alfred held Esther's hand as they sat on the attic floor above the hotel. She rested her head on his shoulder as she slept. Even though they had the window open, the heat was unbearable. The emotional stress of the past few days had left them all exhausted.

The waiter from the café had brought them to the attic to hide. They knew little of the young man or his father, other than they owned the dingy little hotel and the adjoining café.

"How long will we need to stay here, Papa?" asked Alfred.

"I don't know, son."

"Do you believe them, Joseph?" asked Ingrid. "Do you really believe they are interested in helping two Jewish families? Why would they risk their own lives for us? They haven't even told us their names."

"And they haven't asked us for ours," replied Joseph. "Maybe it is best if both parties keep it that way. We must trust them. We are not in a position not to. We have no vehicle, and we have no papers to board the train."

"If they were going to turn us in, they would have done so by now," added Uri.

"I say we demand they tell us what they have in store for us," said Miriam. "We can't just sit here in this attic indefinitely. We haven't bathed in days, and I resent that we can't go down the stairs to use the toilet without their permission."

"I'll talk to them," said Joseph. "He said he would bring some food to us soon."

Another hour passed before the attic door opened. The

young man entered. He brought a large pot of beef stew and porcelain bowls.

"I'm sorry dinner is so late," said the young man. "There have been *SS* officer's downstairs. They were asking questions. Then they lingered in the café eating dinner and sipping brandy."

"We understand," said Joseph. "We appreciate you helping us. You and your father have been exceedingly kind. What should we call you? What are your names?"

"Our last name is Garcia. My father is Salvador. I am Maximino. But everyone calls me Max. This hotel and café have been in our family for three generations."

Salvador was fifty-seven years old and was thick around the middle causing his white shirt to be in a constant state of being half tucked. His life had been hard, and it showed on his face as the sweat from his bald head dripped over his brow.

Max was twenty-nine and appeared too young to be Salvador's son. Like his father, he was average size, and his Spanish heritage was evident in his thick dark hair and olive complexion. Unlike his father, the white shirt and black pants he wore were crisp and sharp.

"Are you originally from Spain?" asked Miriam.

"My grandfather moved here from Spain in 1873. His brother was killed in the Third Carlist War, and he made his way over the Pyrénées to avoid the conflict himself. Shortly after his arrival, he met my grandmother. Then my father arrived."

"Where is your mother?" asked Ingrid.

"She died giving birth to my sister, who also didn't survive the birth. It has just been my father and me for the past twenty-three years."

"I'm so sorry," said Ingrid.

"Life isn't fair," said Max. "I lost my mother, and you people are hiding in our attic to avoid whatever miserable fate the Nazis have in store for you."

"How long do you think we will be here?" asked Miriam.

"I'm afraid you will be here for a while. I know someone I can trust to create your documents, but he is in Paris. I've been trying to telephone him, but he never answers. I'm concerned they've discovered him."

At that moment, the attic door opened, and Salvador entered. "We have trouble. The Germans are insisting on billeting six soldiers here. They will occupy four of our six rooms. We must find another place to hide you. Until then, you can't make a sound."

French light cruiser Jean De Marseillaise
English Channel

With two hours before their scheduled arrival in Cherbourg, the French soldiers gathered on the mess deck for their final briefing.

The captain announced over the main communication system, "Attention, passengers and crew. Reports indicate the German army has advanced through the Cotentin Peninsula with no resistance. They are within an hour of taking the city of Cherbourg. We have changed course, and our new heading is for the port of Brest—one of the few pieces of French soil the Germans haven't reached. We will be there in eight hours. As we receive further information, we will pass it on."

Addressing the soldier next to him, Philippe said, "That means they must be in Sainte-Mère-Église."

"Is that where you are from?" asked the soldier.

"Yes. My family is there. My parents and my little brother."

The soldier said, "I am from Paris. The Germans have arrived there, too. My wife is pregnant. She lives with my parents above our family bakery."

Not paying attention to the personal concerns of the soldier, he said, "Brest? If we must travel all the way to Brest to dock safely, it is over. They have conquered France."

"What should we do when we get to Brest?" asked the soldier.

"I'm going home to Sainte-Mère-Église," said Philippe.

"What if our orders are to fight? Or surrender? What will you do then?"

"If they wanted us to surrender, we could have docked at Cherbourg. This uncertainty is because France has no leadership. The French government has given up, and the only members of the French army with the will to fight are in England."

Interrupting their conversation, the sound of the ship's emergency horn blared throughout the vessel.

"Alerte d'urgence. Tout l'équipage à vos postes de combat." Emergency Alert. All crew, man your battle stations.

The horn and announcement went on continuously while the soldiers watched the ship's crew race through the vessel in all directions.

They ran to storage cabinets to retrieve firefighting equipment. Others grabbed helmets and .50-caliber machine guns before climbing the stairs to the surface deck. Some went below decks to prepare for damage control if a torpedo hit.

The Heroes of Sainte-Mère Église

They operate with precision.

The soldiers retrieved their own weapons and made their way to the top deck.

The evening sky was filled with German J 87 dive bombers circling the vessel.

With thundering explosions, the crew unleashed large antiaircraft guns. Cannon shots exploded in the sky, creating dark plumes of smoke as they sprayed shrapnel.

Philippe stood at the stern of the ship just above the two propellers. They turned so rapidly, ocean water sprayed him.

The bombers broke into different formations.

The first set dove to the surface of the water and dropped several torpedoes.

Phillipe followed their path as they traveled under the surface of the water. Moments later, two hits squarely on the port side caused a massive explosion, lifting the ship out of the water as an enormous wave crashed over the deck.

The force of the explosion threw dozens of men overboard. Others became engulfed in flames as the penetration of the hull ignited fuel.

As flames reached high into the air, crew members raced to the port side with fire hoses, tying to take control of the spreading blaze.

In the sky, four more dive bombers were closing in—this time from the starboard side.

I feel like I'm riding on the back of an injured animal as the buzzards above circle their prey.

In sets of two, the planes skimmed the ocean, each releasing a torpedo.

Phillipe watched as two of the four torpedoes missed the fantail directly behind him. The third and fourth were on target.

"Brace for impact!" someone shouted.

The two torpedoes hit the starboard side simultaneously, causing the ship to explode in a mass of flames. The force threw Phillippe high into the air and over the railing, where he splashed deep under the surface.

After getting his bearings, he looked up to see the surface above him coated in fuel oil and orange with fire.

I can't go to the surface. It's too hot.

Continuing to hold his breath, he swam away from the wreckage.

Ten meters below the surface, he kicked his legs and paddled his arms frantically—kicking and paddling, kicking and paddling until he could no longer hold his breath. Above—a small hole between the flames.

He stuck his head above the surface, sucking in as much fresh air as he could. The immense heat and the smell of burning fuel stung his lungs as he inhaled.

I must get away from the ship.

He dove back down and repeated the process multiple times until he was several hundred meters away. Once he was a safe distance, he rested and treaded water.

The wreckage of the sinking ship and the surrounding fire was even more glaring as the sun began to drop below the curved horizon of the English Channel.

After what seemed like an hour, Philippe looked on as he watched a series of explosions, followed by the *Jean De Marseillaise* vanishing below the English Channel.

Even at a distance, the heat was intense.

Philippe heard the popping of flames, intermingled with the screams of men.

There were hundreds of victims of the attack calling out for help.

Phillipe's legs were cramping, and he was losing the

feeling in his toes and fingers from the cold current of the English Channel.

Morning will come. Help will arrive …. Will it? What if it is only the Germans who know we are here? If they return in the morning, it won't be to save us.

Cherbourg, France

The 7th *Panzer* division, led by General Erwin Rommel, was the most elite tank unit of the German army. Since crossing into France on May 10, the division had spent the past six weeks rolling through the French countryside and plowing through what remained of the French army.

After traveling down the coast of France, then through the length of the Cotentin Peninsula with little resistance, Rommel had halted his column on the outskirts of Cherbourg to allow the tanks in the rear to get into position.

Cherbourg was one of the few deep-water ports on the western coast of France. It was in a perfect strategic location to launch an amphibious assault on Great Britain when the time came.

With the thundering sound of idling tanks around him, General Rommel stood up in his *Kübelwagen* and looked out at his trophy before him.

He was not a tall man, but the forty-nine-year-old Rommel was physically fit, and always looked like a proud and distinguished leader, even in the filthiest of battle uniforms.

Looking toward the city, he saw no signs of French troops. If that remained the same during his entrance into the city, his planned assault would turn into an intimidating parade of mechanized warfare through the streets of Cherbourg.

With victory at hand, he raised his arm and waved it forward, unleashing the power of 56 *Panzer* tanks on the awaiting city.

Cherbourg, France

German *Panzer* tanks were scattered throughout the city. They presented a ghastly sight, made even more intimidating in the darkness of the early evening. In addition to the tanks, there were heavily armed *Wehrmacht* soldiers patrolling the streets.

As Daniel Girard approached the city, he was astonished at the lightning speed of their advancement. When he left for Saint-Cyr in the morning, he had seen no evidence of the invaders on road N-13. They must have rolled halfway down the Cotentin Peninsula in a matter of hours.

Daniel knew he had to get to the wireless shack at his tugboat office. The *Jean De Marseillaise* was scheduled to arrive, and he had to warn them to turn back. If the German troops in Cherbourg knew of their imminent arrival, they would contact the *Luftwaffe* to intercept them. They would be sitting ducks once they came over the horizon of the English Channel. He hoped that one of his crew members had already contacted the ship.

Arriving at the north end of the docks where his tugboat company was located, he sprinted up the exterior stairs to his third-floor control tower. It was located at the end of the pier and allowed the controller to use a wireless to direct the tugboats around the docks as they positioned the ships.

The Heroes of Sainte-Mère Église

Daniel Girard served in the French Navy during the Great War. He received the *Croix de guerre* for valorous service during the Dardanelles Campaign.

A massive man, Girard's shoulders typically aligned even with the top of most other men's heads. His shoulders were so wide that his oversized coveralls had to be custom made at a tailor.

When he entered the control room, he was greeted by his three tugboat captains. Besides monitoring the wireless, they were peering out of the windows, watching the movement of the German army in the city.

Speaking to his senior captain, Gregory Augustin, who was on the wireless, Daniel asked, "Have you contacted them, Gregory?"

"No, Mr. Girard."

"Try three hundred megahertz," said Girard.

"I already did. I have tried every frequency on the dial multiple times. Maybe they have already received word of the German arrival from another source."

"If that is true, something isn't right. They would still be on their wireless even if they have turned back."

The door to the control tower burst open. Panting heavily from a long run, a dock worker entered.

"Have you heard?" said the man.

"Heard what?" asked Daniel.

"A fishing boat just arrived. They have several injured French soldiers and sailors on board. They pulled them out of the water. They are from the *Jean De Marseillaise*. It has been sunk. The water is ablaze from the engine oil, and there are still hundreds of men floating in the water."

Daniel turned and said, "All right, men, fire up your tugboats. We have some Frenchmen to save."

After untying the vessels from the pier, Daniel and his

three captains, each in their own boats, opened the throttles of the four massive diesel engines. With a roar, they pulled away from the docks.

Daniel turned around to glance at the pier, where he saw a convoy of German troop carriers pulling up next to his control tower.

Chapter Seventeen

JUNE 21, 1940

English Channel

It was just after midnight when Daniel Girard and his crew found what remained of the *Jean De Marseillaise*. The weather and sea were both calm, but the westerly wind carried the smell of burning fuel oil for several kilometers, making it easier to locate the wreckage.

Using his wireless, Daniel called the pilots of his other three tugboats. "Circle the perimeter of the debris field. We will create four quadrants. Patrol the outer sections and work your way in. Only retrieve the living."

Daniel took the northwest quadrant and moved toward the center, being careful not to pass any survivors.

The corpses he found were French soldiers and were floating face down. As he moved inward, he heard cries for help. Advancing toward the voices, he found several French sailors who had stayed together by locking arms. Unlike the dead soldiers, they were wearing life jackets.

Two hours after discovering the wreckage, Daniel had

rescued over thirty soldiers and thirty-five of the ship's crew. Many of them were burned, sick, or both.

Using his wireless, Daniel asked, "How many men have you found?"

"I have sixty-two, Mr. Girard."

"Fifty-nine with me."

"Sixty-eight here, boss."

Girard considered his options.

If we abandon the search now, we may leave men out here who are still alive. But we can't stay out here all night. Where should we go? We can't return to Cherbourg with 250 French soldiers and sailors. The Germans will arrest us and throw us in work camps.

Over the wireless he asked, "Men, how much fuel do you have?"

"I still have several hours if I cut back on my throttle."

"Same here, boss."

"Me too."

"Okay, this is what we will do. Set your heading to 225 degrees southwest. We are going to the island of Saint Anne. Once there, we will refuel, then head to the British island of Guernsey. There is a hospital there where the injured men can receive care."

"Roger, boss."

As Daniel throttled forward, one sailor standing at the stern of the tugboat shouted, "Look! Over there. I think I see a man in the water. He is hanging on to that wooden bulkhead. He is still alive."

Daniel slowly moved in that direction. As he got closer, he cut back on the throttle and shoved it in reverse to slow his momentum. Floating on top of the debris was a soldier.

As the tug moved next to him, several sets of hands reached over and pulled him aboard. He was alert but exhausted. They placed him on the deck next to the injured.

Sitting up he asked, "My name is Sergeant Philippe Legrand. Is there a Lieutenant Laurent on this boat?"

A voice from the back asked, "Are you sure he was on the *Jean De Marseillaise*, Sergeant? I was the duty officer. I oversaw the mustering of every officer on that ship. There was no Lieutenant Laurent on my muster sheet."

"I spoke with him last night. He should have been onboard. We are both from Sainte-Mère-Église and were going to travel there together once we arrived in Cherbourg."

After hearing the discussion, Daniel Girard approached Philippe and asked, "Legrand? Your last name is Legrand, and you are from Sainte-Mère-Église?"

"Yes, sir, that's right."

"Your father—is your father's first name René?"

"Yes, that's right. My father is René Legrand. He is a farmer in Sainte-Mère-Église."

"Well, I'll be damned," replied Daniel.

The Island of Guernsey

Under the cover of darkness, Daniel Girard and his fleet of tugboats approached the southwest seacoast of Guernsey. They had stayed several kilometers off the shore, setting their course south until the coastal lights disappeared.

Noticing a cove being protected by a high cliff, Daniel directed his three tugboat pilots toward the beach.

His next concern was what to do with the nearly 250 French soldiers and sailors he escorted. Even though he knew none of them personally, he was a veteran of the

Great War. It was probable that like Philippe Legrand, many of the young men on his four tugboats were the sons of other veterans. There was a natural bond, and he felt an obligation to care for them as though they were his own sons.

If his instincts about Guernsey were correct, the island would be free of German soldiers, and he could get them to a hospital. If his instincts were wrong, they would all be shipped back to France and transferred to German prison camps.

Using his wireless, Daniel instructed his tug boat pilots. "Anchor here while I move in to check the depth."

Slowly opening the throttle, he creeped his tug toward the beach. He soon felt the bottom of his tug graze the sand on of the shallow cove.

Shutting down the engine, he said, "Make your way to the beach. Those who are able, assist the injured."

Through the wireless, Daniel instructed the other tugs, "Head on in."

Philippe helped a corporal over the side and into the water. "I'm here with you, Corporal. I'm not going anywhere," said Phillipe.

On the beach, a few of the ship's medical staff had put together a makeshift triage infirmary. With no medical supplies, they were limited to wrapping wounds with torn shirts.

With the corporal's arm around his shoulder, Philippe walked through the cool shallow water and over the sand until he could hand him to the medical staff.

From the time they were small boys, Philippe and Jean-Pierre had been taught by their father to be problem solvers.

"When you find yourself in a jam, don't waste time feeling sorry for yourself. Look for a solution and get

The Heroes of Sainte-Mère Église

moving," his father would say. This was a lesson that had served Philippe well in recent days.

With the other men taking refuge in the soft sand, Philippe looked up at the steep cliff. He wasted no time searching for a path to the top. It was still dark outside, but the moonlight offered enough light to guide him to the base. He calculated the height to be about sixty meters. As he made his way up, the thick vegetation provided a firm handhold as he carefully ascended.

Halfway up, he glanced down to see the other three tugs in the shallow bay of the cove unloading the other injured men.

He continued the journey, hand over hand, foot over foot; he would grab a branch and give it a yank to be certain the roots would hold his weight. After what seemed like an eternity, he reached the top, grabbed a thick bush, and pulled himself over the edge.

The cool breeze blowing off the Atlantic Ocean was refreshing after the exhilarating climb. Looking landward, he saw a farmhouse about a kilometer away. There were no lights, which was to be expected at this early hour of the morning. Below him, the men from the four tugboats lay on the beach, resting from the ordeal of the past twenty-four hours.

Philippe stood motionless, looking out at the ocean. His mind wandered to the events of the past few weeks. He thought of his family. With a sense of remorse, he thought about his old friend Armand, thinking they should have stayed together. He thought of the countless German soldiers he had killed. His body told him to lie down in the tall grass and sleep. His mind forced him to turn and walk toward the farmhouse.

Pau, France

Everyone was sleeping comfortably except for Dreyfus. Against his father's wishes, he had consumed too much water.

"Dreyfus, you can't drink so much," Joseph told him often. "It will cause you to use the toilet. You must wait for the German soldiers to leave in the morning before going to the WC."

If I don't pee soon, I'll wet myself, thought Dreyfus.

After sitting up and putting his shoes on, he stepped onto the top stair landing.

As he made his way down the steps, his leather-soled shoes thumped softly with each careful step. At the bottom of the stairs he opened the door, causing the hinges to make a creaking sound.

Dreyfus stared at the two doors on the third floor, knowing behind both were German soldiers.

Walking the length of the hall, he made it safely to the bathroom and closed the door.

At the toilet, he felt relieved that he made it. He thought to himself, *I should have listened to Papa and not drank so much.*

Then a noise in the hallway—a door shutting. Uncertain what to do, he finished, zipped his trousers, and stood quietly.

At first, he heard nothing. Then the sound of footsteps coming his way. The doorknob turned, and the door opened. Standing in front of him was a tall *Wehrmacht* officer who asked, "Where did you come from?"

Pleinmont, Guernsey Island

Philippe approached the farm cautiously. Near the farmhouse were two barns to the north. The first was thirty meters from the house and the second about fifty.

He positioned himself between them so he could scope out his surroundings. Peeking between the wooden planks of the first barn, he saw what appeared to be a tractor and a plow, although it was difficult to be certain in the dark. He also noticed the white outline of several ropes hanging from the overhead loft.

I could use those to pull the wounded men up the cliff.

Around the corner of the barn was a horse carriage. It looked like something out of an American Western movie. Next to the house, a pickup truck.

Moving to the next barn, he found several stalls. They contained eight cows and two horses.

Fresh milk.

Around the corner of the second barn was a chicken coop. Philippe made his way over to it. Starving, he reached in and found several eggs. As he pulled them out, he disturbed the chickens and they made a cackle that interrupted the otherwise silent morning.

Moments later, he heard the barking of a large dog coming from the house. Then the lights came on.

He dropped the eggs and opened the door of the second barn, where he hid in one of the cow stalls.

The screen door of the house opened and then slammed shut.

Someone set the barking dog free and it headed his way.

Philippe hoped that the cow shit he was standing in would hide his scent.

In the deep gruff voice of an Englishman he heard, "Angus! Angus! Get back here!"

Then the voice of a girl. "What is it, Papa?"

"I don't know, Claire. Stay in the house."

Philippe, not knowing English, was uncertain what they were saying. *At least they aren't speaking German.*

Outside of the barn, the dog sniffed around the chicken coop. Then it went around to the barn door Philippe had closed behind himself. The man trailed behind the dog, opened the door, and followed him in.

Philippe watched as a man in his mid-fifties entered the barn, leaving the door behind him open. He was a gentleman of considerable heft and armed with a shotgun. He was taller than Philippe and outweighed him considerably.

Crouching down behind the wooden stall, Philippe peeked over to watch the man who wore blue coveralls as he stepped cautiously, not knowing what or whom was hiding in his barn.

Philippe squatted motionless. The dog, sniffing his trail, soon spotted him, barked, then lunged at him.

Standing, Philippe shouted, *"Ne tire pas! Ne tire pas!"* Don't shoot! Don't shoot!

The dog bit at his legs repeatedly as the man held the gun on him.

"Down, Angus! Down, Angus! Release him and come here."

Escaping from the dog, Philippe climbed the wooden barrier between the stalls, and over to the other side he went, separating himself from the large Irish wolfhound.

"I am a French soldier!" he shouted. "The Germans sank my ship!"

The Heroes of Sainte-Mère Église

He repeated those words over and over, hoping the large Brit would understand him.

To his relief, the girl, who was about Philippe's age, and a woman who appeared to be her mother entered the barn in time to hear Philippe's pleads.

"Don't shoot, Papa!" said the girl. "He says he is a French soldier, and the Germans sank his ship."

Her papa then motioned with his shotgun for Philippe to exit the stall but continued to aim the weapon in his direction.

In flawless French, the girl said, "My name is Claire, and these are my parents, Oliver and Margaret. Our last name is Quinn."

Claire wore a white night shirt that seemed too large for her, and the bottom hem hovered just above her bare feet. Having been awoken abruptly in the early morning, her long dark hair was a mess.

Like much of the property on the island of Guernsey, the Quinn farm had been in the family for multiple generations. In their circumstance, it was an inheritance from Margaret's parents.

Oliver had met Margaret while working as a laborer for her father. They married soon after and lived in the large farmhouse with her parents until their passing.

Oliver was also raised on the island in the little village of Le Foulon, just outside of the capital city of Saint Peter Port.

Unlike Margaret, who spent her youth isolated on the family farm, Oliver had been well known on the island throughout his lifetime. Loved by all, everyone he met instantly became his friend. If he found someone suffering from a hardship, he would find a way to help them.

Responding to Claire's introduction, "My name is

Philippe Legrand. I am a French soldier. We were traveling from Great Britain back to France when German planes sank our ship. A group of French tugboats rescued us. They are anchored in the cove below the cliff. There are injured men on the beach. We came here to get them to a hospital."

Claire turned to her parents and in English explained Philippe's story.

"Those German bastards," replied Oliver. Lowering the shotgun, he said, "Ask him how many of his mates are down there."

After Claire's translation, he replied, "There are about two-hundred-fifty men in total. I would guess about one-third of them need medical attention. About half of those have severe wounds."

Claire relayed the message to her parents.

"Good God," her mother, Margaret, said. "What are we to do with two-hundred-fifty men?"

Oliver said, "Claire, let him know we have a problem. Let him know a small force of Germans came on the island two days ago. There will be many more coming in the days ahead. Let him know we have no military defenses here. The Germans will soon have free run of the entire island."

She relayed her father's comments to Philippe.

"I need to get down the cliff and warn everyone. We need a different plan. We can't hide two-hundred-fifty men in plain sight on this island."

After Claire translated Philippe's words, her father instructed them to get in the truck. He would drive them to the cove.

Margaret and Angus went back to the house as Philippe, Claire, and Oliver drove toward the edge of the overlook. Behind them, the sun was rising over the horizon.

As they neared the edge, they heard what sounded like

The Heroes of Sainte-Mère Église

machine gun fire. Oliver stopped the truck, and the three ran to the overlook.

What they saw was beyond belief. Four German patrol boats had converged on the enclosed cove.

Through the cool morning mist, Philippe, Claire, and Oliver were horrified as they listened to the ripping sound of MG 32 machine guns affixed to the bow of each boat. They were mowing down the dozens of Frenchmen who were trying to escape up the side of the cliff.

As they were hit, they dropped back down below. Those who didn't escape either lay wounded on the beach or stood with their hands up, hoping they would not suffer the same fate as those scaling the side of the cove.

Philippe watched as the men he had just crossed the channel with were slaughtered.

Looking at Claire, he said, "We can't let them see us up here. If they do, they will be here in an instant. You mustn't get caught with me or they will arrest you."

"Oh, God, Philippe! Your friends. They were just murdered before our eyes."

"Let's get back to the house," said Phillipe. "I need to find a new place to hide. I can't stay with you, Claire. I don't want to put your family at risk."

The three climbed back into the truck and drove to the house. Once they arrived, Oliver informed Margaret of the travesty of what they had just witnessed.

"I thought I heard a loud noise, but I wasn't certain what it was," said Margaret.

As she peeked through the curtains toward the cliff, Margaret's face was red. "Will they come up here next?"

"I don't know, Margaret," said Oliver. "They might visit us to see if anyone escaped."

Claire said, "Philippe wants to leave. He is concerned what will happen to us if they catch him here."

"Where would he go?" asked Margaret. "This is a small island that will soon have thousands of German soldiers patrolling it. He wouldn't stand a chance."

"I agree, Mama," said Claire. "He should stay with us. He can hide in our attic or in a barn."

Oliver said, "I agree with Philippe. He is right. If it were just me here, I would let him stay, you know that. But I am not willing to put you two at risk. If we get caught with him, we may suffer the same fate as those men down there."

"I'm willing to take that chance, Papa. You raised me to help people in need. Philippe is in need, and we must help him."

"I agree with Claire," replied Margaret. "We have never been a family who turned our backs on others, and we are not going to start now."

Philippe stood silent. The discussion taking place among his English hosts confused him.

The only thing he was certain of was that the conversation was intense, and that when Claire raised her voice she pointed in his direction. He wasn't certain if that was good or bad. He only knew her intensity made her look beautiful. Although her figure was hidden under her baggy night shirt, he did manage to get a glimpse or two of her well-toned body when the night shirt laid against her.

"I guess I am outnumbered," replied Oliver.

"It's settled then," said Claire.

Switching to French, she informed Philippe of their decision. He would stay with them.

The Heroes of Sainte-Mère Église

Pau, France

"He is my nephew," shouted Max, as he saw the *Wehrmacht* officer—dressed only in trousers, T-shirt, and socks—questioning Dreyfus.

"He is here visiting us from Paris. My sister just had another child, and she wanted him to stay with me until she recovered. It is difficult for a widowed mother to care for two children. Her husband was killed at Dunkirk."

The German soldier replied in excellent French, "Does he speak? I have been trying to talk to him and he just stares at me."

"You scare him. He saw your tanks roll into Paris on the same day he found out his father was killed. Men like you drove their tanks down his street."

At that moment, the door from the attic swung open and into the hallway stepped Ingrid Shapiro.

"Dreyfus!" she said quietly but firmly. "Why are you down here?"

"I had to pee, Mama."

"Mama?" asked the soldier. "You are the boy's mother?"

As Max stood there thinking of something to say, the soldier grabbed both Mrs. Shapiro and Dreyfus by their arms and calmly guided them up the stairs. At the top, he saw the entire group laying on the floor. He knew who they were and why they were there.

Back down the stairs, he instructed Max to join them at the top, then closed the attic door behind them.

While he was gone, the group in the attic stood and Uri whispered to Joseph, "Maybe we can jump him. With Max's help, we can tie him up and escape."

When the soldier returned to the attic with Max, there

was a momentary silence as he stared at the terrified group gathering against the wall.

The soldier stood in the middle of the room. In German, he addressed Ingrid, "Mrs. Shapiro, you don't remember me. My name is Wilhelm Ziegler. You were friends with my mother, Meta Ziegler. You belonged to many of the same social clubs. You and my mother worked together to raise money to build the library."

"Wilhelm? Yes, I remember you."

Walking over and embracing him, she said, "It is so good to see you. How is your mother? I miss her so. She is such a lovely woman."

"She is doing fine. But Germany is not. What is happening there is unspeakable. I am ashamed of what our country has become. The last few years have been a nightmare for anyone who is not Aryan and a loyal German. People are disappearing at alarming rates. Especially Jews. It is good you left when you did. We never knew what happened to you. We were afraid they had arrested you."

Ingrid said, "We couldn't tell anyone we were leaving. Not even your mother. I always regretted that."

"She will be glad to know you are safe."

Ingrid looked up at Wilhelm, who was much taller than her, and said, "Wilhelm, we are trapped here. Joseph and Uri are the two men on the wanted poster. They killed those two men, but it was self-defense. They were going to shoot Joseph and Uri shot them first. You must believe us."

Wilhelm rested his hands on Ingrid's shoulders and looked into her eyes. "Of course, I believe you, Mrs. Shapiro. But guilt or innocence doesn't matter. You are Jews, and therefore they have already found you guilty."

Joseph asked, "Wilhelm, is there any way you can help us? We have no vehicle, we have no papers, and we have no

The Heroes of Sainte-Mère Église

place to go but Spain. Your comrades are guarding the train station and are checking everyone."

"I'll try and help you, Mr. Shapiro. But I'm uncertain I can. The good news is that I hold the rank of major. I am responsible for the entire *Wehrmacht* garrison on this side of the city. Unfortunately, I have no authority at the train station. That is controlled by the *Waffen-SS*. They are a different breed entirely. They are bastards. What I will do is this. I will billet my men someplace other than this hotel. However, I will stay here myself. That will provide you with a small level of protection until we can think of a way to get you to Spain."

Switching back to French and addressing Max, Wilhelm said, "They will explain to you what we discussed. Let me tell you, I am no threat to you, your father, or these fine people. Thank you for what you are doing for them. Let me know what I can do to help keep them safe. Until then, you all need to continue to be as quiet as possible until I can find another home for my men. I will have them out of here by the end of today."

Glancing down at Dreyfus, he said, "Once they are gone you can come use the water closet without fear. I'll try to keep it clean for you."

Chapter Eighteen

JUNE 22, 1940

Compiegne Forest, France

From a distance, American journalist William Shirer stared intently at what had become known as the "Wagon of Compiegne."

Formerly a railroad dining car, it had been converted to an office by the French army for Marshal Ferdinand Foch. After Germany's defeat in the Great War, France forced members of the German delegation to sign their official surrender onboard.

Twenty-two years later, the location for the official French surrender was not by accident. Adolf Hitler deliberately chose the Wagon of Compiegne as the site to sign the Armistice. He ordered the railcar parked in the exact location as the German surrender on November 11, 1918. He wanted to humiliate the French as he believed they had humiliated Germany.

Shirer waited as the occupants of the carriage conducted their business inside the tiny compartment. After several minutes, he saw movement through the windows. A small group prepared to leave.

Watching as they exited the railcar, the first to step down was Hitler himself. He was followed by a series of German generals, among them Hermann Göring.

As a witness to the event, Shirer reported to CBS radio in New York, "I am but fifty yards from Hitler. I have seen that face many times at the great moments of his life. But today! It is afire with scorn, anger, hate, revenge, and triumph."

After exiting the train car, they departed in an open-topped Mercedes 770. The next day, Adolf Hitler would make his first and only visit to Paris.

Pleinmont, Guernsey Island

"I think I should stay in the barn," said Philippe as he sat with Claire on the parlor sofa. "If they catch me in the barn, you and your parents could pretend you didn't know I was there. If I'm caught in the house, they will arrest you."

"But you are more likely to get caught out there. If they show up here, the barn will be the first place they will look. They will climb the lofts just to be certain. In the house, we can hide you in the attic."

"No. I am already putting your family at risk. I insist on staying in the barn."

"Okay, I won't argue with you. The barn it is. We will put you in with the animals. They could use the company. But I hope you don't snore. Our best milk cow, Betty, needs her beauty rest."

"I'll try not to disturb her."

"Let me go get dressed, and I will take you out there."

On the way, Philippe asked, "Where did you learn to speak such flawless French?"

"In my early years, my parents sent me to school in Saint-Germain-sur-Ay. My aunt and uncle live there. I lived with them during the week and rode the ferry back here to Guernsey during the weekends and holidays."

"Saint-Germain-sur-Ay? Do they still live there?"

"Yes, but we are worried for them. We have had no contact since the Germans invaded France. We don't have a telephone, and the closest postal telephone exchange is in Grange."

"How far is Grange from here?"

"We can get there from here in thirty minutes. We can get anywhere on the island in less than an hour in the truck. Why do you ask?"

"I have a crazy idea. I was hoping I could contact my parents by telegraph or wireless. The Germans are in Sainte-Mère-Église by now. I'm concerned for their safety."

"That would be risky, Philippe. Grange is near Saint Peter Port, our capital. It will be swarming with Germans."

"Are there any other exchanges?"

"Not that I know of, but let me ask my father. He is tending to the animals."

They continued their walk until they arrived at the livestock barn.

"Good morning, Papa."

"Good morning, Claire."

Although Oliver was not fluent in French, like most Europeans, he was familiar with cordialities. "*Bonjour*, Philippe," he said.

Acknowledging his effort, and respecting his presence on British soil, he replied, "Good Morning, Mr. Quinn."

The Heroes of Sainte-Mère Église

"Papa, Philippe would like to contact his family in Sainte-Mère-Église. He hasn't spoken to them since the German invasion. He is concerned for their safety."

"Too risky. Tell him I'm sorry, but the Germans have taken control of the postal exchanges. There is no way we could safely get a message out."

Claire relayed the information to Philippe.

"Let your father know that I understand and agree with him."

After listening to Claire's translation, Oliver said, "There might be a way. Although we must keep him away from Grange, there are two communication huts the Germans may not be aware of. One is in Jerbourg and another in Saints. I have an old friend who works for the division of utilities. He once told me that these huts are along the northeast coast and are the closest points to France. They have both wireless transceivers and telegraph connections.

"So, what are you saying, Papa? Will you contact your friend?"

"Yes, I will. I also think it is time to find out where they are holding Philippe's mates from the ship. Tell him to stay put for now. Once I find my mate Ben and snoop about the Jerrys, I'll be back. While I'm gone, take him into the house, and see if any of my clothes fit him."

On his way to Jerbourg, Oliver drove past the airfield. As he drew near, he saw German cargo planes positioned on the runway. They were unloading crates.

Past the airport, he was behind a convoy of troop carriers. He kept his distance, so he wouldn't draw attention to himself, but kept them in sight.

They merged onto Forrest Road, then turned left onto Les Muilpieds toward the center of the island. He waited for them to turn and get out of sight before following their path.

Accelerating, he soon had them in sight again. They turned left, then right, then right again until they approached the little village of Camptréhard, where they turned into a field. In the middle was a makeshift prison camp surrounded by barbed wire and guard towers.

Oliver parked behind a thick row of trees two hundred meters away.

The uniforms of the prisoners indicated they were French soldiers and sailors.

Those must be Philippe's mates.

The troop carriers he was following entered the gate, then drove next to one of the huts.

Several *Wehrmacht* soldiers leaped out, followed by a group of civilians dressed in gray uniforms. Most were young men but there were a few women and even young children.

Where did these people come from?

Guernsey was not a large island, and he had lived there his entire life. He came across few people he had not previously crossed paths with. He recognized none of them.

Why were their children in a prison camp?

Returning to the main road, he continued his journey to Jerbourg at the tip of a peninsula.

He had not been down this desolate road since he was dating and needed a remote destination that would inspire romance. While daydreaming, a smile came to his face, as his thoughts wandered.

The Heroes of Sainte-Mère Église

At the end of the road were a series of huts. The one on the end had a utility truck parked next to it.

There was a beautiful view of the sea, much like the cliff overlooking the cove on his own property. The wind was blowing hard, and the salty smell of the ocean and the sound of the crashing waves was something he never tired of.

Entering the little building, he saw his old friend Benedict Beaulieu.

Like Oliver, he was thick around the middle, but considerably shorter and slightly balding on top. His coveralls had smatterings of dirt and grease.

"Ben, you old bloke, how are you?"

"Oliver! It is good to see you. What brings you to the end of the world?"

"I am isolated on my property. You travel this island more than anyone, and I was hoping you could tell me what the hell is going on. What do the Jerrys have in store for us?"

"That is why I am here, Oliver. The *Wehrmacht Kommandant* told me to disconnect all wireless and telegraph on the island."

"So, we can't communicate to France?"

"Nobody will be able to once I finish here."

"What is it like elsewhere on the island?" asked Oliver.

Ben said, "I just came from Saint Peter Port. They have posters everywhere. All citizens of Guernsey are to turn in their firearms and wireless devices. They have prohibited listening to the BBC."

"And if we don't adhere to their absurd requests?"

"They will arrest you. The good thing is, they only have about five hundred soldiers on the island. Many of them are at the work camp in Camptréhard."

"I drove past it on my way here. Do you know who is there, Ben?"

"I'm surprised you don't already know with the hell that broke loose at your cove early this morning. What was that like? Did you hear all the firing?"

"I heard it."

Ben said, "The estimate is that they slaughtered about forty men. There are still about two hundred at the camp. Some are in bad shape. They have let a few doctors and nurses in to treat them. Some need surgery, but the German bastards won't let them leave. The docs will go back and do what they need to do at the camp, but the sanitary conditions are atrocious."

"I saw others there, too. They were in odd gray uniforms. They looked like night clothes. They were all ages. Men, women, and children. They didn't look well."

"They are called Todts. Nothing more than slave labor from Eastern Europe. Mainly Jews. They will be building antiaircraft bunkers."

"What are your thoughts on the Germans being here?" asked Oliver.

"What the hell kind of question is that? I'm so mad I could spit nails. What concerns me is that Churchill appears to be writing us off the blotter because we are just a little island. The Jerrys could be here forever."

"I didn't mean to offend you, Ben. I needed to get a feel for where your loyalties lie."

"You didn't just come here to get general information, did you?"

"No, Ben, I didn't. You asked me if I heard the firing at my cove this morning. One bloke made it up the cliff—a French soldier. He is at my farm."

"Good God, man, are you mad? If the Germans find him at your house, they will put you in front of a firing squad."

"I'm well aware of that."

"So, where do I come in? And I ask that knowing I will not like the answer."

"He has been away from his family for a long time. He was at Dunkirk, then Britain, then his ship was sunk on its way back to France. His parents probably assume he is dead. He would like to call them."

"And you want me to help him from this hut. Am I reading you right, mate?"

"Will you do it?"

"So, you're asking me to put my life at risk so that some French kid I have never met can call his mum and dad?"

"Yes, that's right. That's what I am asking you."

"Why should I do this? I have a family, too, you know."

"I am asking a lot of you, Ben. There will be no hard feelings if you say no."

Benedict Beaulieu put his tools back in his toolbox, wiped his hands on a rag, and the two men walked to the cliff and listened to the peaceful sound of waves crashing ashore.

"I have disconnected the lines from the hut inland to Guernsey. But the lines from the hut to France are still in working order."

"Are you telling me you'll do it?"

"That's right, Oliver. I'll do it. Go get the lad. But remember, curfew is nightfall. So, you must get him here, we do the linkup, then you get him back to your farm before dark. I'll give you an hour to return. If you're not back, I'll sod off, mate."

Guernsey Island, Jerbourg

Dressed in coveralls, Philippe followed Oliver and Claire into the communication hut.

"This is the lad, Ben. He doesn't speak much English, so we will bypass the introductions and get right to business. Claire will translate any instructions you may have for him."

"How are you, Claire?" asked Ben.

"I'm fine, Mr. Beaulieu. Thank you for helping Philippe. We know you are taking a risk."

"It's okay. Anything to screw with the Jerrys is a jolly good show in my book. There isn't much to it. I just need to know which town to contact."

"Sainte-Mère-Église," said Claire.

"While I hook everything up, have him tell you who the message is for and what he wants to tell them."

Ben connected the wires to a board on the wall of the hut. He then connected the transmitting key to the wires.

"Okay, we're ready, Claire. What is his message?"

Sainte-Mère-Église, France

Wearing a white shirt, blue waist coat, and dark pants—the uniform of the French postal service—the slender Henri Fontaine was stuffing letters into mail slots.

He had been the postmaster in Sainte-Mère-Église for twenty-four years. It was his first and only job after getting out of the army.

When the Germans arrived, they stationed a *Wehrmacht*

The Heroes of Sainte-Mère Église

officer in the building to monitor all correspondence both written and telegraphically.

Although *Oberstleutnant* Claus Ritter read French adequately, he did not understand the international Morse code system and relied on Mr. Fontaine to be honest with the translations.

If the message were general information, Henri Fontaine would translate it accurately. However, if it had the slightest hint of helping the German war effort, he would jot down a phony message for *Oberstleutnant* Ritter while memorizing the actual message. His challenge was getting the real message to the intended recipient. Over time, he had learned who he could trust and who he couldn't.

Click-click—click—click-click-click-click was the sound coming in at the telegraph receiver.

Henri grabbed his notepad and pencil.

The message read:

Guernsey Island:
From: Philippe Legrand
To: René Legrand
Message:
I am safe on Guernsey Island—stop.
Your friend, Daniel Girard, rescued me—stop.
Girard may be in a prison camp—stop.
Armand Lapierre killed in northern France—stop.
Message for Jean-Pierre's teacher, Mrs. Laurent—stop.
I spoke to Martin Laurent in England—stop.
Love to you, Mama and Jean-Pierre—stop.

When the message had finished, Henri handed a slip of paper to *Oberstleutnant* Ritter:

From the Guernsey Weather Bureau;
The weather in Guernsey has been hot this summer and if it doesn't rain soon there will be a dreadful corn harvest.

Reaching for the doorknob, Henri said to Ritter, "I'm going to the pharmacy."

Chapter Nineteen

JUNE 23, 1940

Sainte-Marie-du-Mont, France

After hearing the knock, Brigitte wiped her hands on her apron and swept the loose strands of her long dark hair out of her face before making her way to the front door.

"This is a pleasant surprise, Cécile. It is good to see you. Please come in. If you are looking for Jean-Pierre, he is helping Angélique finish her work at Brécourt manor. I'm expecting them soon. I was hoping Jean-Pierre would stay for dinner. Would you like to join us?"

"No, but thank you, Brigitte, I need to get back and make dinner for René, however I appreciate the offer."

"Come in, and have a seat in the parlor. Would you care for a glass of water?"

"That would be lovely—thank you."

Brigitte returned to the parlor and sat a tray on the coffee table before filling two glasses with water. As she sat on the sofa next to Cécile, she realized her look had turned solemn.

Brigitte asked, "What is wrong, Cécile. You look troubled."

Cécile looked down, unable to look Brigitte the eyes.

Brigitte raised her hand to her mouth as her lip quivered. "You have heard something about Armand, haven't you?"

Cécile paused and reached for Brigitte's hand. She held it tightly as she told her, "We received a cable from Philippe. Somehow, he ended up on the island of Guernsey. He said Armand was killed in northern France. The cable was brief. That is all we know."

Chapter Twenty

JULY 7, 1940

**10 Downing Street
London, England**

"Send him in," said Prime Minister Winston Churchill.

Sir Frank Nelson had recently returned to Britain from Switzerland. His job there was council to Basel—a position that had been eliminated after the German invasion of France.

The fifty-seven-year-old Nelson served with distinction during the Great War. He was a member of the all-volunteer Bombay Light Horse regiment and spent the war in India. He later served for a brief time as a member of the British Parliament, before becoming a diplomat.

He was tall and thin, and clearly a man whose appearance was important to him. He usually wore a freshly pressed three-piece suit, and a heavily starched shirt; the knot of his necktie resting on a gold collar pin.

Churchill met him in the center of the office with his

hand extended. "Thank you for coming, Nelson. I trust my abrupt request did not ruin your plans for the day."

"It is not every day when one is summoned by the British prime minister. Rearranging my schedule was something I was glad to do."

Returning to his chair behind the desk, Churchill said, "Yes, well I thank you for that. I also appreciate your work in Basel. I have heard good things about your accomplishments in maintaining our relationship with the Swiss. I hope they understand why the war forced us to dismantle our office there."

"They understand fully, sir."

"Splendid."

"So why are you here, Nelson? That is the question you are surely asking yourself."

Grabbing a cigar from an oak box on his desk, Churchill struck a match and took a series of tokes to confirm it was well lit.

"Nelson, you know as well as anyone that the Germans are on a mission to blanket mainland Europe with their evil. Many here in Britain are still of the belief we should just sit back, protect our homeland, and have no concern for what is taking place on the continent. I say poppycock to that. We can't just sit here and let them ravage mainland Europe like an out-of-control firestorm, then hope they will leave the UK alone after they have done so."

"I tend to agree with you, Prime Minister. It is only a matter of time before Hitler sets his sights on invading Great Britain. Anyone who believes otherwise isn't paying attention.

"I was hoping we would be in agreement. Now Nelson, the reason you are here: There are resistance forces throughout Europe. They are everyday citizens who agree with you and me that now is not the time to just lay down and die. Their forces are small, their weapons are few, but their determination is unmatched. Right now, they are all we have, and we want to help them."

"Help them how, sir?"

"We will insert our people among them. They will deliver wireless communication devices, weapons, explosives, training, food, anything they may need. We will have our people on the ground side by side with them harassing the Jerrys and giving them hell at every turn."

"Do you think that will work, sir?"

"It won't hurt, and at this point, it is all we have."

"What exactly is the plan, Prime Minister?"

"The ultimate plan is to persuade the Americans to join the fight. I have been on the phone with Roosevelt nonstop since the Germans invaded France. In spirit, he is with us. I think if it were solely up to him, the Americans would already be here with us planning an invasion. But America hasn't been a monarchy since we graciously gave them their independence in 1776. FDR must answer to the American people; they don't consider Europe to be their fight. Until that time comes when they do, it is just us and a ragtag group of citizens in France, Belgium, and the Netherlands. That is where you come in, Nelson."

"Me, sir? What role do you see me playing?"

"We are starting an organization. It will be called the Special Operational Executive, which is an absurd mouthful, I know. We will refer to it as the SOE. You will be its chief. You will get it started. You will recruit, train, come up with and execute the plan. You will work directly under me."

"Why me, sir?"

"Why not you? Are you telling me you don't want the job? I admit it will be a challenge."

"Prime Minister, the first question that comes to mind is the recruiting. Where am I supposed to find qualified volunteers? First, they will need to be bilingual. They will need to be experts in weapons and explosives. They will need to be familiar with the countryside. People with that package of qualifications are not just running in from the street, volunteering to put their life at risk."

"I was hoping you would be more optimistic, Nelson. But I understand. I have asked those same questions. That's why I already have one of my best people working on it."

"What is his name, sir?"

"'His?'" responded the prime minister, with a chuckle. "It isn't 'his,' Nelson. It is her. Her name is Katie Keene, and she is the best damn recruiter the world has ever seen. Every time I have ever needed to find the right person for the right job, I have given the assignment to her. She has never let me down. You will meet with her tomorrow, assuming you want the job. You do want the job, don't you, Nelson?"

"Yes, sir. I want the job."

Chapter Twenty-One

JULY 22, 1940

Fort Benning, Georgia

"Have you seen the reports, General?" asked Captain James Gavin as he entered Major William Lee's office. "The Germans did it again. Italy and North Africa were just practice jumps compared to Western Europe. They dropped thousands of troops in a near-flawless attack. The time has long passed for us to start a parachute battalion."

General Lee replied, "Say no more, Jim. They have approved it. They want to see our plan put into action. Training, strategy, where we pull the soldiers from. They want to see everything."

"What made them cave?" asked Gavin.

"The fall of France! The writing is on the wall. It will only be a matter of time before we are over there fighting again, and those in charge of the defense budget are waking up to that fact.

"Jim, I need you to put a staff together. We need someone in charge of finding volunteers, building our facility, and procuring equipment. We don't have much time to build the U.S. Army's first parachute battalion."

"I'll get right on it, General."

SOE Headquarters
24 Baker Street, London, England

There is nothing exceptional about this place, Nelson thought to himself as he walked in the front door of his new office building. *That was intentional by someone—probably Churchill himself. The work within these walls should be known to nobody but a few. It's not a place for curious onlookers.*

Climbing the stairs, he noticed the second floor had only a handful of offices and they were unoccupied. The same with the first.

Nobody in sight—odd at this hour on a Monday morning.

Arriving at the third floor, he found one door at the top of the landing.

Locked.

After knocking, a Royal Navy officer opened the door.

"Nelson, I presume?"

Extending his hand, he replied, "Yes, that's right. Chief Frank Nelson."

"I'm pleased to meet you. My name is Lieutenant Commander Wally Cress."

"Yes, it is a pleasure to meet you, Cress. Can you direct me to my office? Then I need an introduction to Katie Keene. Can you send her to me?"

"By all means, Chief. But first let me introduce you to another member of our team."

Nelson followed Cress to a small room on the left side of

the hallway. When Nelson entered, there was a desk facing an open window, and two rows of filing cabinets located at opposite ends of the room. Sitting at the desk and typing what appeared to be agent profiles was a young woman in her thirties who Cress introduced as Kimberly Morrison. Morrison had blonde, shoulder length hair and was smartly dressed in a conservative gray dress.

Morrison stood and said, "Good morning Chief, I am looking forward to working with you."

"It is my pleasure to meet you, Morrison. I hope you are prepared to work long hours. We have enormously important work to do."

Morrison replied, "I understand that, sir. I am willing to do whatever I need to do for the war effort."

"That's the attitude, Morrison. Carry on."

After stepping out of the office, Cress said, "If you will follow me, sir. I will show you to your office."

Cress was a slim chap, but energetic. Every movement was made at a sharp pace, as though he was in a race to get as many things accomplished as possible before the clock ran out. Nelson, too, kept an internal sense of urgency, but never appeared to be in a rush. He fell several steps behind Cress who was darting toward the large office down the narrow hallway.

Once in his office, Nelson laid his briefcase on the desk and said, "Thank you, Lieutenant Commander. Please let Keene know I need to see her urgently."

He sat down in the wooden chair, realizing he would need an upgrade since he would spend a significant amount of time in it as he built the organization from the ground up.

After a few minutes of getting organized, he looked up to see a woman in her fifties standing at the threshold of his office door. She was attractive, thin, and had long sandy-blonde hair. Although sharply dressed in a dark blue dress with a white collar, the observant Nelson noticed a few stray cat hairs on her sleeve.

"Chief Nelson," she said. "My name is Katie Keene. Lieutenant Commander Cress said you wanted to see me."

"Yes, come in. Please have a seat. Churchill said you were the absolute best at recruiting personnel. That is high praise from the prime minister. I am putting together a list of qualifications I want you to look for. We will need to review them."

"Sir, I would be happy to review your list, but I have worked with Mr. Churchill for many years. I have recruited and vetted resources for him to do everything from cut his hair to date his daughter Mary. But don't tell her that. It is a family secret between Mr. Churchill, his wife Clementine, and me. My assumption is that since he put you in charge of the SOE, he trusts that you can keep that secret."

"I'll keep your matchmaking for the Churchill family close to the vest, Keene."

Keene said, "I have been briefed by the prime minister. I am aware of the unique skills required of the candidates. I already have several in the pipeline, Chief. Most should have their clearances vetted within the week. However, I have one candidate who has already cleared and is eager to get started. He is a Frenchman. A French lieutenant from the Cotentin Peninsula named Laurent. He was preparing to board a ship for home when I tracked him down."

"Where did you hear about this Laurent chap?"

"General Cummings of the 51st Highlander Division recommended Lieutenant Laurent. He led a small group of Brits and Frenchmen to Dunkirk. They considered his leadership to be extraordinary. In addition to French, he also

The Heroes of Sainte-Mère Église

speaks English and enough German to interpret a conversation."

"Does he have any family in France?"

"No children, but he is married. His wife is a schoolteacher in the little village of Sainte-Mère-Église. When I intercepted him an hour before boarding, he wasn't pleased to be missing the ship for home. But when I told him our plan was to get him home at a later date after we trained him, he was on our team."

"That is rather splendid work, Keene. You don't waste time, do you?"

"No, sir. I believe the sooner we get our assets in place on the continent, the sooner we can win this war."

Nelson said, "We also need someone to lead our training program. We want our people well prepared before entering the war zone. Their work is too valuable to allow them to get killed due to carelessness."

"Sir, I've already recruited someone to head up the training program. His name is Colonel Dawson."

"Is it Colonel Mark Dawson?"

"Yes, sir."

"I know Dawson. He is a brilliant choice. Great work, Keene. When you can, get me Laurent's personnel file. I'll also need the files of the others you are vetting."

Chapter Twenty-Two

AUGUST 19, 1940

**SOE Training Facility, STS 1
Brock Hall, Flore
Northamptonshire, England**

Along with fourteen other operatives, Martin Laurent was escorted to a classroom by a colonel with the British Army. Like himself, the other volunteers were all wearing civilian clothes.

Once in the room, the colonel said, "I am your instructor. Find a seat. Stay silent, and do not speak to each other at any time."

Although none of them knew it, the group was comprised of eleven Brits, a Norwegian, a Pole, and two Frenchmen, including Laurent.

There were eight men and seven women.

"We are sorry to have kept you in the dark. I trust your accommodations have been adequately comfortable.

Approaching the front of the room, the thin man with the thin mustache made no introduction of himself. The

The Heroes of Sainte-Mère Église

only hint of who was leading them was his collar device indicating his rank.

He looked hardened as though he had been through the very worst of what a war can bring. His age and rank would indicate he was a veteran of the Great War.

Martin Laurent thought to himself, *Whatever these Brits have in store for us, they are taking it seriously. They wouldn't send a colonel to address a ragtag group of volunteers unless there was something big planned.*

The colonel crossed his arms and sat down on the front desk.

"I know this is the first time you have been together as a group. While here, you may speak only to aid in the training process. At no time are you to share your identities with each other. You are not to spend time together away from this facility. When on the continent, you will work independently, so there is no need to know specific details of anyone else in this room. If you are captured, you will be harshly interrogated, so the information we provide you will be limited to what you need to know, and nothing else. Is this understood?"

"Yes, Colonel," replied the group in unison.

"During the next level of training, you will go your separate ways to learn the details of your specific missions."

Standing and pacing the room, he said, "We will discuss communications, weapons techniques, and document forgery. Over time, you will learn every minor detail required to keep yourself alive. When I say every detail, that is exactly what I mean. For example, you Brits have been taught since you could walk to look to the right before crossing the street. On the Continent, if a Nazi officer sees you do that, he will arrest you. This is not a game—this is serious business. One minor mistake could cost you your life and, at the very least, jeopardize your entire mission.

"Over the next several months, we will drive you hard. Sometimes we will deprive you of sleep and food. We will make you walk and sometimes run for many kilometers. Then we will bring you into a room like this and interrogate you until you slip up. We will test you constantly. We will mistreat you regularly, not because we don't like you, but because we want you to make your mistakes here and not over there. Are there any questions?"

Laurent asked, "How long will this training last? I want to get home to my wife in Sainte-Mère-Église."

The colonel replied, "As punishment, you will miss dinner this evening, agent. You foolishly informed a room full of potential captives you have a wife in Sainte-Mère-Église. And to answer your question, based on your obvious stupidity, you may never finish."

Chapter Twenty-Three

APRIL 12, 1941

Sainte-Mère-Église, France

"My wish is that Armand and Papa are together in Heaven," said Angélique as she blew out the fifteen candles on her birthday cake.

Brigitte was grateful that Cécile Legrand had agreed to host Angélique's birthday party. The past few years had been difficult. The frequent kindness offered by the Legrand family had lifted the spirits of both Angélique and Brigitte.

Besides Mr. and Mrs. Legrand, they invited Pascal and Luke as well as Arthur and Gabrielle Hall. However, Brigitte knew the person that made Angélique the happiest was Jean-Pierre. He cherished her daughter. Unless they were at school or working, they were together. They had become inseparable. Even though they were both young, everyone who knew them assumed they would one day be married.

"Are you ready for your present, Angélique?" asked Jean-Pierre.

"You know I am, Jean-Pierre."

Before leaving, Jean-Pierre said, "Wait here. I'll be right back."

As they waited for him to return, Cécile cut the cake and passed out the plates.

Brigitte said, "It is so nice of you to bake the cake, Cécile. It is getting harder and harder to find flour and butter. Next month will mark a year since the Germans invaded. They have confiscated everything they have gotten their hands on. Even the things they pay for create shortages for the rest of us."

René said, "At first they were just taking enough to feed the troops here locally. Now with war expanding, they are shipping food back to Germany. One advantage of living on a working farm is that we can hide more than we give to the Germans."

At that moment, the kitchen door opened and in walked Jean-Pierre pushing a bicycle.

"Is that for me, Jean-Pierre?"

Cécile Legrand said, "He has been saving his money for over a year to get that for you, Angélique. Every opportunity he had to work extra in the fields for his papa, he would. He also sold tomatoes to the German soldiers in town."

Angélique ran over to Jean-Pierre and gave him a hug, then took the bicycle back out of the kitchen door and rode it in the backyard.

She yelled back to everyone standing on the porch, "Now I don't have to walk everywhere I go. And Jean-Pierre, I won't have to ride on your handlebars. We can ride together."

Returning to the house, they finished eating cake, and Brigitte said to Angélique, "We need to get home. It will be

The Heroes of Sainte-Mère Église

dark soon. My ration card for fuel is all used up. I can't get another one for two weeks. I don't have much petrol in the car, and I don't want to run out in the dark."

René said, "I have petrol in the barn. They let farmers have more than what you get because we need it to operate our equipment."

"We can't take your petrol, René. You have already been too kind to us. I'm sure I have enough to get home. I have a small can stowed in my shed. I'll use it to get to work until I can get more."

Jean-Pierre put Angélique's bicycle in the back seat of the car, and they all waved as they drove off.

Brigitte wished they had left sooner. Within a few minutes of leaving, the sun had receded over the horizon and the narrow roads were hard to see. The petrol gauge on the old Citroën hadn't worked in years. Brigitte had a feel for how long she could drive on a tank of petrol. She knew it was about empty.

Just a little farther. We are almost there.

Then her fears became a reality.

Why didn't I take the petrol from René when he offered?

The engine sputtered and spit.

"Oh, no, Mama. Are we out of petrol?" asked Angélique as the car's engine shut off.

"It looks like it, Angélique. We will have to walk home. Tomorrow, I'll get the little container of petrol from the shed and walk back here to get the car started."

"We are almost home, Mama. Our house is on the other side of that field. We can cut through. Jean-Pierre and I do it all the time."

"Okay. Let's remove your bike out of the back seat. We will take it home with us."

They walked through an opening in the tall hedgerow.

"We will need to take our shoes off before entering the house, Angélique. This mud is sticky."

Halfway across, a vehicle drove through the opening of the hedgerow and headed in their direction. It was a *Wehrmacht* troop carrier.

"What are they doing, Mama?"

"I don't know, honey. Just stay here close. We have done nothing wrong. The curfew doesn't start for two hours."

The truck approached, and the squeaky brakes brought the vehicle to a stop.

Two soldiers got out of the cab, and two more leaped from the back. Their uniforms were disheveled, and they reeked of alcohol.

Brigitte guessed the two from the cab were in their thirties, but the other two were just boys. Probably three years older than Angélique.

"Is that your car back there?" asked the driver in broken French.

Brigitte replied, "Yes, that's our car. We ran out of petrol. We are walking home."

"Where do you live?" he asked.

"I know where they live," said one of the soldiers from the back. His French was much better. "They live in that house on the other side of the field. They live alone. She has no husband."

"How do you know so much about us?" asked Angélique.

"Because I have been watching you. I patrol these roads every day. I know everything that goes on around here."

Brigitte said, "Please, just let us go home. We haven't missed curfew. We have done nothing wrong."

"I like that bicycle," said the one from the back. "It would be nice to have a bicycle to get around with."

The Heroes of Sainte-Mère Église

"No, this is my bicycle," shouted Angélique. "It is my birthday present."

"Oh, it is your birthday, is it? Well, my birthday was last month, and I didn't get a present. Maybe you should give me your bicycle as a present."

"Please leave us alone," said Angélique.

For a moment nobody said anything. Then the driver nodded to the others and they all approached Brigitte and Angélique.

"What are you doing?" shouted Brigitte. "Leave us alone."

Two of the soldiers grabbed Brigitte, and the other two grabbed Angélique.

"Leave us alone!" shouted Brigitte.

"Mama!" shouted Angélique.

"Please! Leave her alone. I beg you!" shouted Brigitte.

The two soldiers who had Brigitte dragged her to the other side of the truck before her assault began. The two who had Angélique threw her to the ground where she stood.

For the next thirty minutes, Brigitte Lapierre lived through a nightmarish hell. Not just from what she was experiencing, but most of all from hearing the terror in her daughter's screams on the other side of the truck.

Chapter Twenty-Four

APRIL 13, 1941

Sainte-Mère-Église, France

The parlor of Dr. Pelletier's home also served as a waiting room for his medical practice. The antique furniture was from the Victorian era, with two chairs, a sofa and a bookcase that covered an entire wall from floor to ceiling. The fireplace mantel held photos of the Doctor's wife who passed away seven years earlier.

Cécile Legrand and Gabrielle Hall sat on the sofa, Jean-Pierre and Luke sat in the chairs. René, Pascal, and Arthur Hall stood and discussed their options as they waited for the doctor to exit the examining room.

René said, "What happened to Brigitte and Angélique last night is intolerable. Our citizens have endured much over the past year. Our homes have been taken over. They have confiscated our crops and livestock. Many of our Jewish friends have disappeared into hiding—or sometimes worse. Now this. When is this nightmare going to end?"

"Mayor Renaud is at Volk's office right now demanding answers," said Pascal.

René said, "What if we don't get the answers we want? What if they ignore this as a minor incident? I don't know about you, Pascal, but I'm losing patience."

"You know you aren't alone, René," replied Pascal.

"We all need to keep our heads," said Arthur. "As angry as we all are, we are still dealing with a German army that is well armed and has threatened to bring in the *Waffen-SS* units if they feel threatened."

Entering the parlor from the examining room, Dr. Pelletier said to the group, "They both suffered a significant amount of trauma last evening. Brigitte is very strong and is comforting Angélique. They will both need our support. They are scared. May they stay with one of you for a while? They shouldn't spend the night in their home right now. It is too isolated and too close to their attackers."

"They can stay with us," said Cécile. "As long as they need."

"May I go see Angélique?" asked Jean-Pierre.

The Doctor said, "Yes, Jean-Pierre. She specifically asked for you."

As Jean-Pierre and the women entered the examining room, René, Pascal, Arthur Hall, and Luke spoke to the doctor.

"Were they able to describe them, Doc?" asked René.

"Yes. They provided detailed descriptions of all four."

"Four?" asked René.

"Yes. There were four. Angélique said her attackers referred to each other as Beck and Muller, and she described them in detail. Brigitte didn't get their names, but she knows what they look like. Angélique said their garrison is near their home at Sainte-Marie-du-Mont. They apparently patrol the area often."

"I know where they are," said Luke. "We have ridden our bicycles past their camp many times."

"How many are at the camp, Luke?" asked Pascal

"Not many—maybe six or seven."

"Can you show us, Luke?" asked his father.

"Yes. It is easy to find."

René said, "The mayor should finish with Volk soon. I think we should let Jean-Pierre and the ladies stay here with Brigitte and Angélique. We will go to the mayor's pharmacy and wait for him to finish his meeting with *Oberst* Volk."

Pascal said, "Luke, stay here with the others. We will be back after we speak to Mayor Renaud."

"Yes, Papa."

As Mayor Renaud approached his pharmacy, he saw his three friends at the door.

"I know why you are here, gentlemen. I wish I had good news for you. Volk said he'd investigate it. When I asked him what that meant, he said he will ask his men if they assaulted anyone, but it is not likely they will confess. Without a confession, there is no evidence it ever happened. I'm sorry I don't have more information."

René, Pascal, and Arthur Hall stared at each other in silence as though they were reading each other's minds.

"Thank you, Mayor. We have all the information we need," said René.

Chapter Twenty-Five

APRIL 16, 1941

**Camp Claiborne
Forest Hill, Louisiana**

Twenty-six-year-old Second Lieutenant Jack Wakefield sat in the back of a crowded bus as it entered the gates of Camp Claiborne. Although a man of average height, he had broad shoulders and an athletic build that made the small seat cramped. He had removed his cap and the breeze from the open window felt good on his short brown hair that he wore in a near buzz cut.

Born in the little town of Bedford, Virginia, the always adventurous Wakefield requested a transfer from the 29th Infantry Division to the recently formed, all-volunteer First Paratroop Battalion.

"You are crazy," his buddies from the 29th told him. "You will get killed jumping out of airplanes. What if your chute doesn't open?"

"We will all die of something, won't we? It might as well be a thrill when it happens," Wakefield told them.

As the bus drove down a series of roads, Wakefield saw several groups of soldiers marching in perfect formation through side streets and open fields

"Jesus, this is like basic training all over again," he said to the soldier next to him. But he also felt a rush of excitement.

The 29th was a reserve unit he had joined after graduating from the University of Virginia.

With the 29th, he was only away from home during drill. When he wasn't drilling, he was living on his family's farm and teaching literature at the Bedford County school. Now he was no longer in a reserve unit, but active duty. Serving in one of the most elite units of the U.S. Army.

As the bus stopped, a drill instructor climbed onboard. In a series of profanity laced instructions, he ordered the men to get off the bus and line up in formation.

What the hell have I gotten myself into?

Chapter Twenty-Six

APRIL 18, 1941

Sainte-Marie-du-Mont, France

Corporal Wolfgang Beck was on motorcycle patrol on the backroads of Sainte-Marie-du-Mont.

Making his daily run past the Lapierre farmhouse, he was aware they hadn't been home since the incident.

If they ever return, maybe I'll pay the girl another visit.

Oberst Volk had questioned all four of the attackers three days after the assault.

Nothing will happen to us. We will never confess. Volk doesn't care what we do to these people.

With his patrol duties for the day about to end, he turned left down the side road to his camp, he thought about the ration of hot beef and potatoes that waited for him.

The road narrowed between two large hedgerows. Ahead of him, a single figure stood in the road.

Beck slowed the BMW, expecting the individual to move to the side. But before he could react, a Berthier rifle was raised, and with a single shot through the chest, Jean-Pierre sentenced Angélique's first attacker to death.

The camp was comprised of four small tents. Each tent housed two soldiers. In the middle was a table and firepit.

During the day, the small squad of *Wehrmacht* soldiers patrolled the Normandy coast, with one lone soldier on motorcycle patrolling the roads near Sainte-Marie-du-Mont. That duty belonged to Corporal Beck.

"Where the hell is Beck?" asked *Oberleutnant* Bierman. "He should have been back four hours ago."

"Maybe he stopped to pay a visit to our two *Frauleins* from the other night," a voice from a tent shouted. Laughter among the squad followed the comment.

"You bastards are lucky *Oberst* Volk didn't hang your asses," responded Bierman. "The only reason he didn't is he knows I am already short of men. I can't afford to lose four more. It is too dark now, but in the morning, we need to find Beck. Now get in your tents and get some sleep."

Corporal Claus Muller woke in the middle of the night. He sat up in his bunk, lit a cigarette, and stared at the empty bunk assigned to Beck.

Hearing a noise, he called out, "Beck, is that you? Who is there?"

As he opened his mouth to ask again, a left hand reached around and covered his mouth. His muffled words turned into a gasp as a serrated knife plunged into his throat.

The next morning, the remaining six soldiers woke with the sun. The camp was between a group of trees, with their motorcycles and a troop carrier behind the tents.

"Konig, go wake up Muller," said Bierman.

As he grabbed the flap of Muller's tent and pulled it open, he said, "Muller, we need to…"

Before finishing his words, he back-peddled and tripped over a tent stake. "Muller is covered in blood. He is dead."

Bierman investigated Muller's tent and confirmed Konig's assessment.

"Get on the wireless. Tell Volk we have a problem."

"The wireless is gone, *Oberleutnant*," shouted one soldier.

"And all of our tires are flat," shouted another.

"Everyone grab your weapons," yelled Bierman.

"We have no weapons, sir. Everything is gone."

"How could this have happened?" asked Bierman. "Who could have done all of this in the dark of night?"

In the distance, a Citroën pickup truck approached.

As the vehicle came closer, they noticed a driver and two men standing in the back hanging on to the roof. One was armed with an MP 40 machine gun, and the other man a Mauser rifle. The weapons stolen from their camp.

The truck came to rest a few meters from the first tent.

The broad shoulders and powerful appearance of Pascal and René were intimidating as they leaped from the back of the truck. Arthur Hall, although not physically intimidating, was confident, and spoke flawless German, which caught the soldiers by surprise. All three men noticed Angélique's bicycle leaning against a tree.

Arthur looked at the collar devices on the uniforms and

in German said to Bierman, "*Oberleutnant*, I'm assuming you are in charge of these barbarians?"

"I don't know who you are, but you will pay dearly for what you have done here," replied Bierman.

Without responding directly to Bierman, Arthur translated his comments to René and Pascal. They stared at Bierman, laughing at his expense.

Switching back to German, "That's a stupid statement coming from an unarmed man. But how bright can you be, seeing how you allowed your camp to be raped and pillaged in the middle of the night? Speaking of rape, tell us who was involved the other night?"

"Is that what this is about?" asked Bierman.

Arthur replied, "Justice has already been served on two of the culprits. It is time for the other two to pay."

"Two of the culprits?" asked Bierman.

"You mean you didn't notice one of your men missing last night? I believe his name was Corporal Beck."

The two remaining soldiers who attacked Angélique and Brigitte stood to the side listening. They felt ill hoping Bierman would not turn them over.

"The *Wehrmacht* has its own justice," said Bierman. "We will punish them appropriately."

Without responding, Arthur walked over to the bicycle and asked, "Who owns this?"

After receiving silence from the group, Arthur walked up to Bierman and pointed a gun in his face, nearly touching his nose.

"I believe this happens to be your Luger. I hear one of the greatest humiliations for a soldier is to be executed with his own weapon. Is that true, *Oberleutnant*? Is it humiliating to be staring down the barrel of your own gun?"

Taking a deep breath, Bierman turned and pointed to the two guilty soldiers standing next to the tents.

The first one turned and ran. Pascal stepped around the tents and through the trees, giving himself a clear shot.

When the soldier was sixty meters away, Pascal raised the Mauser and fired. They all watched as the back of the soldier's head exploded in a spray of red.

Then the last of the attackers stood alone with terror in his eyes. Arthur motioned for Bierman and the other three to stand to the side.

René laid the MP 40 machine gun in the bed of the truck and turned toward the cowering soldier, now on his knees pleading for his life. Approaching him, René held the serrated knife that was still stained with Muller's blood.

Two of the other four Germans vomited uncontrollably as they watched the punishment René inflicted on the fourth attacker.

They were slow to notice Pascal, who had reached in the truck bed to pick up René's machine gun. By the time they did, it was too late to run, and Pascal unloaded the entire clip of ammunition on what remained of the small squad.

Chapter Twenty-Seven

APRIL 25, 1941

Saint-Marie-du-Mont, France

"Who do you think killed those men, Mama?"

"I don't know, Angélique. I'm just glad we are home now, and those evil soldiers are no longer living down the road."

"There is a rumor that Jean-Pierre's papa was involved. Do you think he was?"

Brigitte closed her empty suitcase. She had just finished unpacking it after spending two weeks at the Legrand farm. She then asked Angélique to sit with her on the bed.

"Angélique, I have no idea who did it. I have my ideas, but no certainties. I know that in spite of everything, we have been blessed to have good friends in our lives who look after us."

"Mama, how old were you when you fell in love with Papa?"

"A little older than you are now. Why do you ask?"

"Because I love Jean-Pierre, and although he has never told me, I know he loves me, too. I have this feeling he would do anything for me."

"Yes, Angélique, I believe he would."

Chapter Twenty-Eight

MAY 9, 1941

Sainte-Mère-Église, France

As Mayor Renaud entered the courtyard of the City Hall building, he realized this was the first time *Oberst* Volk had requested a meeting with him. Their earlier meetings had been at his own request. Those meetings had been frequent enough that the sentries no longer questioned him as he entered the building.

An annoyance of the mayor's was being directed to the waiting area. From his point of view this was his office, and he shouldn't have to wait to enter. Adding to his irritation, Volk always made him wait for at least thirty minutes before he agreed to see him.

However, this time was different. Just moments after Mayor Renaud sat down, an aide came down the stairs and said, "The *Oberst* will see you now, Mayor."

As he climbed the stairs, he could see into the offices on the first floor. The *Wehrmacht* officers who were occupying them appeared to be packing boxes as though they were moving.

Upon entering the office, he saw that Volk too was having his contents packed.

"Good afternoon, *Oberst*. You asked to see me?"

"I warned you, Mayor. I told you I would take care of disciplining my men. You and your citizens chose to take matters into your own hands. That did not sit well with Berlin."

"What are you talking about, *Oberst*?"

"I informed you the first time we met that Sainte-Mère-Église was fortunate it would be the *Wehrmacht* in command here and not the *Waffen-SS*. Thanks to whoever murdered my men that will change as of tomorrow. I am getting transferred, and the *Waffen-SS* will now occupy your town. About half of my men will remain, but they will be under the command of the *SS*. I wish you and your citizens the best of luck. You will need it."

"So, who will I be communicating with?"

Volk laughed and said, "Communicating? There is no communicating with the *SS*. They don't care what your opinion is. They do what they want. Your experience with the *Wehrmacht* will be looked upon as a minor inconvenience compared to what you and your town are in for with the *SS*."

Chapter Twenty-Nine

MAY 12, 1941

Sainte-Mère-Église, France

The sight of it made them enraged. As René approached the center of Sainte-Mère-Église, he pulled his truck to the side of the road in front of City Hall. Pascal was in the passenger seat.

Draped over the front of the two-story mayor's office was a large red flag with a swastika in the middle. The *Wehrmacht* hung them, but not like this. Now, they were hanging everywhere. On flag poles, light poles, and over the front of every third business.

Under the flag in front of City Hall were four guards dressed in gray—*Waffen-SS* soldiers. In addition to MP 38s and Mauser rifles, they had an MG 32 machine gun mounted on a tripod.

Soldiers dressed in gray were everywhere.

Across the courtyard they saw a German staff car parked in front of Dr. Pelletier's home, with two *SS* sentries at the front door.

The Heroes of Sainte-Mère Église

They walked across the courtyard and toward the doctor's home. They were stared at by several *Waffen-SS* soldiers who were congregating in the church square.

Halfway across, René and Pascal stopped and stared back at them.

Continuing their journey, they got closer to the doctor's house and saw Doctor Pelletier and Alexandre Renaud come out of the front door.

The doctor was carrying his medical case, and Mayor Renaud had a large suitcase that contained the doctor's personal possessions.

"What is going on here?" asked René.

The doctor said, "It's nothing, René. They have informed me they will use my home to billet the new *Kommandant*."

"But your medical office is in there. How are you going to see patients?"

"The mayor is kind enough to let me move my medical practice to the rear of his pharmacy. I will manage, René."

"I don't think so," replied René.

In a quick pace, he walked past the doctor and mayor toward the house.

Mayor Renaud shouted, "No, René. Stop!"

Ignoring the call, he marched to the front door and tried to enter the house. One sentry raised his Mauser and brought the butt into René's groin, causing him to hunch over and fall to the ground.

Pascal made his way toward the house, but the other sentry pointed his Mauser at Pascal, causing him to stop in his tracks. The other pointed his rifle at René, who was still on the ground reeling in pain.

From the house stepped *SS-Sturmbannführer* Gunther Dettmer.

In rudimentary French, he asked, "What is going on here?"

Pascal said, "Your two goons here don't know how to treat their hosts."

Dettmer stood on the front step with his hands resting on his belt. He looked at René laying on the ground and laughed. "No, it's you and your friend on the ground here who don't know how to treat your guests." Looking at Pascal, he demanded, "Who are you, and who is your friend on the ground here?"

Before Pascal could answer, René rose to his feet. "We are your worst nightmare."

Pointing at René, Dettmer shouted, "Arrest this man!"

Chapter Thirty

MAY 13, 1941

**Liberté
Saint-Cyr, France**

With a map of the Cotentin Peninsula spread out on the table, Pascal addressed the group.

"The mayor has confirmed René is being held in the jail. We have little time. The Germans have been using the rail system to transfer prisoners to German munitions factories—they need the slave labor. It won't be long before René is put on one of those trains."

"How are we going to stall them?" asked Arthur.

"We need to sabotage the train," said Pascal.

"They have too many troops at the railyards," said Arthur.

"I say we blow up the tracks," said DuBois.

"Where are we going to find the explosives?" asked Pascal.

"Don't worry about the explosives," replied DuBois. "I've been working the docks for twenty-two years. You make a lot of friends and receive a lot of strange gifts when your job is to decide who leaves the docks first. I have a warehouse filled with interesting things."

"I know just the place to take out the tracks," replied Arthur. "They will probably take him to the train station at Chef-du-Pont. About halfway between Chef-du-Pont and Pommenaque is the Le Douve canal. The train passes over the canal on a wooden bridge near La Croix. If we blow that bridge, it will take weeks to fix it."

"Point it out on the map," said Pascal.

"This is the canal—the bridge is here."

"Where can we park the truck without getting seen?" asked Pascal.

Arthur said, "There is a farm here. A road wraps around the back. It has hedgerows and thick trees on both sides. The truck will be safe tucked in there."

"We'll go tomorrow night."

"Who do you want with you, Pascal?" asked DuBois.

"It is only a two-man job. Arthur, you are familiar with this bridge—

will you go with me?"

"I'm in."

"I'll have the explosives here in the morning," replied DuBois.

"I'm assuming dynamite, DuBois?" asked Pascal.

"That's right."

Looking to Devaux, the smallest man of the group, an excellent technician, but quiet, Pascal asked, "Antoine, will you have our wireless devices built by tomorrow? The Germans are cutting more phone lines. We will need to communicate."

"I have two more to build. I'll finish them tonight, and they will be here tomorrow."

The Heroes of Sainte-Mère Église

Pascal reached in a cabinet and pulled out a bottle of Cognac and several glasses.

After pouring, he made a toast. "Here's to our friends René and Captain Girard, who is somewhere in Guernsey. May they both return home safely."

Chapter Thirty-One

MAY 14, 1941

La Douve Canal

"That should do it," said Pascal after climbing down from the wooden crossbeams that were supporting the tracks above. "I placed about twenty sticks of dynamite up there. Most of them directly under the tracks. Even if the entire structure doesn't come down, the tracks will get blown to smithereens. They won't be using this rail system anytime soon."

Arthur Hall replied, "We only have about twenty meters of wire left to connect to the detonator. Make certain you keep your head down, because those beams will fly in every direction, including ours. Once you twist that detonator, our window of escape is less than ten minutes."

Pascal looked to confirm their escape route was clear, then said, "Do it."

Arthur Hall twisted the knob of the detonator.

The massive explosion lit up the night sky and could be

heard for several kilometers. The train rail and crossbeams were jettisoned into the air in every direction—debris falling all around them as they covered their heads.

Jumping to their feet, they sprinted to the truck.

Chapter Thirty-Two

MAY 15, 1941

La Croix, France

Rodolphe Bonnel's family sat at the breakfast table. He stood at the kitchen window watching the German soldiers at the scene of the bridge explosion.

Rodolphe was a docile man—small in stature and could fit into the clothes of his unusually large eleven-year-old adopted son Marcel.

A devout Catholic, he and his wife, Paulette, were active in the church and frequently volunteered their time in the orphanage in Carentan. Both of their children, eleven-year-old Marcel and eight-year-old Jacqueline, were adopted from there.

The blast from the previous night shook the house. They hadn't been back to sleep since.

Their farm was three hundred meters from La Douve Canal, and four hundred meters from the scattered field of debris that was once the railroad bridge.

"Children, don't worry about your chores today. Just stay in the house until they leave."

"Yes, Papa."

"Who do you think did it?" asked his petite wife, Paulette.

"I don't know, dear. The Germans have angered many people since their arrival."

As they cleared the table, there was pounding on the front door.

"Go upstairs, children. Don't come down until we tell you," said Paulette.

After Rodolphe opened the door, Dettmer and two *Wehrmacht* soldiers entered without an invitation. Both soldiers carried a Mauser rifle.

"Have a seat," said Dettmer, as he pointed to the sofa in the parlor. Looking to Paulette, he said, "You may sit next to your husband."

Dettmer's knee high black boots thumped on the floor as he paced the room, before stopping at the fireplace mantel. There, he picked up photos of their children before glancing up the stairs. Rodolphe knew it was an intimidation tactic, and it worked. The Bonnels experienced terror like they had never known. Their hearts raced, wondering why the *SS* officer who had entered their home wasn't speaking.

Returning the children's photos to the mantel, he turned and stared at them.

He then removed his cap and ran his black gloves through his blonde hair to remove the perspiration.

Stepping toward them, he knew his large physical presence would add to the intimidation. He stood directly in front of Rodolphe, staring down at him. "You will tell me everything you know about this sabotage, and you will tell me now. Do you understand?"

Staring directly up at the towering figure before him, Rodolphe said, "I know nothing of the explosion other than it woke my family up. Why would I blow up a bridge within sight of my house? That would be insane," replied Rodolphe.

Turning and walking away from Rodolphe, Dettmer said, "Maybe, but we are living during insane times, are we not?"

"I know nothing of the bridge. I am just a simple farmer trying to keep my crop plentiful and my cows fed."

"Speaking of your cows, we will commandeer them this afternoon. Along with your chickens, your goats, and that truckload of turnips you are getting ready to take to market. I must feed my men."

Rodolphe stood and said, "You can't do that. How will I provide for my family?"

"Take him outside," said Dettmer.

The two soldiers grabbed him by the arms and dragged him to the center of the dirt courtyard as chickens clucked and scattered in all directions.

Paulette Bonnel followed them out as their children watched from the second-floor window.

"On your knees," shouted Dettmer.

After Bonnel refused, the two soldiers knocked him down with their rifle butts.

As Rodolphe knelt in the dirt, Dettmer withdrew his Luger from the holster and pressed the muzzle to the back of Rodolphe's head.

"No!" shouted Paulette, as their children looked on.

Dettmer shouted out, "Let this message ring out to the entire Cotentin Peninsula that I will not tolerate sabotage."

He then squeezed the trigger.

Chapter Thirty-Three

MAY 16, 1941

Le Café du Quartier
Sainte-Mère-Église, France

"Can you start tomorrow?" asked Mr. Visage, the owner of Le Café du Quartier. "Since the Germans arrived, my business has been more than I can handle. I wish they would get driven into the sea and drowned, but until that happens, they are here, I will take their money, and donate it to the resistance."

"Yes, I can start tomorrow," replied Gabrielle Hall.

"I'll need you here before they arrive in the evening."

Gabrielle knew Arthur would be angry at her. He had told her not to do it. "It is too dangerous," he said. But she wanted to do her part. Her country needed her, and she had seen people she had known for years mistreated.

First, the confiscation of property, followed by the rationing of food and fuel, then the assault on Angélique and Brigitte. It was all intolerable.

Her plan was simple but brilliant. Le Café du Quartier

was open until the early morning hours, and a favorite gathering place for top-ranking German officers. It was always a full house, with wine and cognac consumed by the liter.

Gabrielle was a master of the German language. Working as a waitress, she would ask them to speak French, pretending not to understand. She would make them comfortable. Once she had their guard down, they might discuss important operational information. She would in turn pass it to Arthur and the other members of the resistance.

Gabrielle Hall was a strikingly beautiful woman. She caught the attention of men of all ages. They stared and flirted endlessly, even when she wore her wedding ring—something she would not have on at the café.

Chapter Thirty-Four

MAY 19, 1941

Sainte-Mère-Église, France

As the guard opened his cell door, René hoped it was to bring him food. He had been in this cell for a week, and they had only fed him once per day since his arrival, each meal comprising a half baguette and uncooked squash. He had already tightened his belt to the last hole.

If I lose more weight, my pants will fall down to my ankles.

The guard, unable to speak French, motioned with his Mauser for René to exit the cell, then pushed him toward the back door of the jail.

The rain fell hard, and his clothes became drenched during the short walk to the lorry. He climbed in the back, followed by the two guards.

In a futile attempt at intimidation, René stared at them until they eventually looked away to light their cigarettes.

Assuming they didn't speak French, René asked, "Are you two baboons as dumb as you are ugly?"

The Heroes of Sainte-Mère Église

They ignored his comment and continued to smoke and make small talk as the rain bounced off the canvas cover.

Ending the idleness, the driver walked past the lorry and beat on the side, then climbed into the driver's seat. After the engine roared to life, they headed west.

Where are they taking me? What is west? Cherbourg?

After twenty minutes of driving, the truck came to a stop and the two sentries leaped out.

They aren't stupid enough to leave me unattended, are they?

He made his way to the back of the truck, then peeked around the canvas.

He saw they were at the nursing home outside of Neuville-au-Plain.

Why are we here? This makes no sense. There is nobody here who threatens them.

Pulling back the canvas flap, he saw there were three other troop carriers and a van.

In the front yard stood every resident of the nursing home. Some were dressed in civilian clothes, with the frailest among them still in their nightclothes. They had their suitcases as though they were leaving permanently.

Some were in wheelchairs, others in stretchers as the rain poured down on them. Nursing home staff tended to those in the most need.

How can they treat people like this? They'll get sick in this rain.

René wanted to do something, but there were dozens of *Wehrmacht* around.

Soldiers went into the building and removed hospital beds and other furniture. It was all piled across the street in an open field where they set fire to it. The orange flames and dark smoke reached high into the air.

They forced the residents into troop carriers along with the nursing staff. They ordered everyone to climb into the vehicles regardless of their ability. Those who could not climb in by themselves received aid from the nursing home staff.

A doctor approached the *Wehrmacht* major who appeared to be in charge and shouted something at him. Before the doctor was anywhere near the major, a guard grabbed him and threw him to the ground, muddying his white coat. They lifted him to his feet and shoved him into the back of a van.

René noticed three elderly residents being forced in his direction. Two women and a man. They were all in their nightshirts. They were ambling, prodded along with rifle muzzles.

That is Mrs. Abraham.

Mr. and Mrs. Abraham lived on the farm next to his parents when he was a boy. Mrs. Abraham would care for him when his parents took their produce to market. Now here she was, elderly, in the pouring rain being shoved along by German soldiers.

She is Jewish. I bet the other two with her are also Jewish.

As they struggled to climb into the back of the truck, one by one, René reached a hand out to help them. The last to climb onboard was the only man in the group.

As he pulled himself up, with a scowl on his face, he said something in German to a sentry. The young guard just laughed and replied with sarcasm. They continued to exchange words for several minutes. The elderly man raised his voice, with the guard continuing to smirk.

Settling in, the frail Mrs. Abraham sat next to René, not recognizing him at first. She was slightly hunched over, but agile for a woman in her eighties. The others sat across from them.

Mrs. Abraham said, "René Legrand. Is that you? It has been so long. Why are you here?"

"They arrested me. My mouth got me in trouble."

Introducing the couple on the opposite bench, she said, "René, this is Hyam and Netta Rubin."

"Bonjour."

Mrs. Abraham said, "Where do you think they are taking us, René?"

"I'm not certain, Mrs. Abraham. Did they give you any hints?"

Hyam Rubin said, "They said they were transferring us to another facility. But I don't trust them. We have all heard the rumors. Netta wanted to leave weeks ago. I insisted we stay. This is my fault."

Mrs. Rubin said, "I am sick. I need my medication. They wouldn't let me bring it."

"We will get your medication, Netta. Just a little longer," Hyam said, even though he knew she might never take her medication again.

The two sentries climbed into the back of the truck and both doors of the front cab slammed shut. René's mind raced.

This will not continue. I've seen enough.

Sainte-Mère-Église, France

Cécile Legrand parked the truck in front of the jail and stepped out into the rain. Her sandy blonde hair was drenched and sticking to her forehead by the time she made it to the jailhouse door.

She approached the sentries guarding the jail, and for

the sixth day in a row, she made the same request. "I'm here to visit my husband."

The two guards, not familiar with the French language, said nothing and escorted her in where she was greeted by the same *Oberstleutnant* she had spoken to the previous days.

"I'm here to see my husband," she repeated.

With his limited French vocabulary, the overweight *Oberstleutnant* told her, "I know why you are here. I am tiring of being summoned from my office to tell you the same thing. No! You can't see your husband. Furthermore, you can stop coming here to harass me, because your husband is no longer here. He was transferred this morning."

"Transferred? Where did you take him?"

"That is not information I am at liberty to provide."

With her finger pointing at the *Oberstleutnant's* face, she said, "Now you listen. You have wreaked havoc on our peaceful community. We have had enough of you. Now where have you taken my husband?"

Looking toward the sentries, he ordered, "Escort her from the building. Never let her in here again."

Leaving the jail, she noticed Gabrielle Hall down the street. With umbrella in hand, she motioned for Cécile to approach her.

When Cécile was near, Gabrielle whispered, "Meet me at Mayor Renaud's pharmacy in thirty minutes."

She then stepped away with no further conversation.

When Cécile entered the front door of the pharmacy, there was a *Wehrmacht* officer at the counter making a purchase.

Gabrielle was already in the pharmacy—Cécile caught a glimpse of her distinctive auburn hair appearing above a shelf. She was standing in the far aisle, out of the view of the officer.

The Heroes of Sainte-Mère Église

After handing him his change, the mayor escorted the officer to the door and locked it behind him. He then gathered with the two women at the counter.

Gabrielle said, "Cécile, I think I know where they are taking René. It was the only topic of conversation among the officers at the café last evening. They are angry about the bridge getting blown. Able-bodied civilians throughout the region are being rounded up to rebuild it—forced labor, they said."

The mayor said, "Cécile, tell Jean-Pierre to be careful. If they find out he is René's son, he will have a target on his back."

Gabrielle continued, "The mayor is correct. They have orders to arrest young men for any reason until there is enough labor. There is a work camp outside La Croix. They have a makeshift prison there. My guess is that is where they are taking René."

"Do you think he is there now?" asked Cécile.

"It depends on when he left the jail," said the mayor.

Gabrielle said, "I was on my way home to tell Arthur. Maybe he and Pascal can do something. Then I need to return for the lunch rush at the café."

"What will Arthur and Pascal do?" asked Cécile.

"I don't ask those questions," said Gabrielle.

She then said, "There is one more thing. They have taken revenge for the bombing—an execution. They shot a farmer in La Croix. Bonnel was his name. They shot him in front of his wife and children. It was *SS Sturmbannführer* Dettmer. He pulled the trigger. The same scoundrel who arrested René."

Neuville-au-Plain, France

René sat between the guards and the three elderly passengers. He noticed when they hit a bump, Mrs. Rubin winced in pain from the wooden benches. The guard who sat opposite from René was small in stature and held the rank of *Obergrenadier*. He was the junior of the two.

This baby-faced kid is no older than Jean-Pierre.

The guard next to René was massive.

He outweighs me by thirty pounds. That uniform has been through hell. He may have been involved in the invasion. Maybe against Philippe.

The rain had stopped, and the back canvas was open. This gave René a good view of their surroundings. They turned off Rue Le Val and onto Rue Le Bourg. He was familiar with the road and knew it was narrow and desolate and had tall hedgerows on both sides. The young soldier across from him had his Luger holstered on his left side. The big guy next to him kept his bayonet in his right boot, which was closest to René.

Which do I go for first? What about the two goons in the front cab—the driver and his passenger? I'm outnumbered four to one. Twenty years ago, this would be easy. Now I'm old and slow.

René's mind raced as he weighed several attack scenarios in his head. He felt the truck slow as the brakes squealed in a high-pitched tone before stopping completely.

The guard sitting in the front passenger seat opened his door and got out. René heard the soldier yell something in German.

Mr. Rubin—fluent in the German language—whispered to René, "There is debris in the road. They are getting out to move it."

Moments later—the crack of rifle shots. Several in quick

secession. The large sentry next to René told the junior soldier to stay put, then threw his legs over the tailgate.

After landing on the ground, he turned the corner of the truck—another shot. He fell back on the ground as blood spurted from his neck.

Within a second, René had the other soldier's Luger. He pressed the muzzle to the boy's chest and pulled the trigger.

Leaping from the back, he glanced around the side, stepping cautiously as he made his way to the front.

Lying in the road were the lifeless bodies of the two *Wehrmacht* soldiers. Standing over them holding bolt-action rifles were Pascal, Arthur, and Jean-Pierre.

Le Café du Quartier
Sainte-Mère-Église, France

SS-Sturmbannführer Gunther Dettmer, with two of his lieutenants trailing behind, approached the sidewalk tables at Le Café du Quartier and seated themselves.

In broken French, he snapped his fingers at Gabrielle Hall and shouted, "*Mademoiselle*, we are ready to order."

Gabrielle made her way to the table—her stiletto heels clicking on the sidewalk as a few strands of her long auburn hair danced in the light breeze.

With one hand on her hip and displaying a playful smile —accentuating her bright red lipstick—she asked, "*Bonjour messieurs*, what can I get for you?"

After listening to the question, their eyes moved from her beautiful face to the fullness of her white blouse and slim, knee length black skirt.

Although her uniform was intended to be conservative,

the three officers snickered and laughed like adolescent boys, discussing in their German language how it fit her snug in all right places.

Dettmer said, "As you can see by their response, my two officers are pleased that our waitress is so beautiful."

"You are being kind so I'll give you better service."

"Do you not provide good service without being complimented?"

Laughing, "Typically not. Compliments and great tips always result in better service."

"I'm sure you get plenty."

"Which do you mean, tips or compliments?" she asked.

"Both."

"I prefer tips. Compliments don't pay the rent."

He laughed, looked to his officers, and in German explained what she said.

Not letting on that she was fluent in German, she said, "It's rude to talk about a girl in a language she doesn't understand."

"Maybe I can teach you our language."

Not wanting her flirtatious bait to go too far, she replied, "That is kind of you, but not necessary. What may I bring you?"

"A bottle of Brandy and three glasses, *mademoiselle*," said Dettmer.

Gabrielle returned with their order. As she placed the bottle on the table and a glass in front of each officer, an open-top *Kübelwagen* zipped around the corner and came to an abrupt stop next to their table.

A *Wehrmacht* sergeant was driving, and the officer sitting in the passenger seat got out and saluted Dettmer.

In German, he said to Dettmer. "We have a missing vehicle, *Sturmbannführer*."

The Heroes of Sainte-Mère Église

"What do you mean by missing?"

"It's gone. It was transporting a prisoner from the jail to the work camp in La Croix. Three Jews who were being transported to Germany are also missing."

"What is happening around here? First a bridge gets blown up, now four soldiers, a prisoner, and three stinking Jews are missing. Who is the prisoner?"

"Legrand, sir. He was the Frenchman you arrested last week."

"Get me everything you know about this Legrand. Start with the pharmacist. Renaud is his name. They are friends. His pharmacy is right over there on the other side of the church courtyard. I'll go with you. We will sort this out."

There were four customers at the counter when Dettmer kicked open the front door. Mayor Renaud, standing behind the counter, said nothing.

"Mayor, I need to speak with you and the good doctor. Is he here?"

"He is in the back with a patient."

"Go get him—now!"

As the mayor made his way to the back room, Dettmer looked around at the scant shelves. Addressing the customers, he said, "I will have to ask you to leave. I have business to tend to with the mayor."

After setting their items down, the customers made their way past the armed soldiers and exited the store.

Entering from the back room, Dr. Pelletier said, "What is the meaning of this? Is it not enough you have kicked me out of my home? Now you are preventing me from seeing my patients?"

"Tell me about this Legrand. Who is he and where does he live?"

Mayor Renaud said, "The last I knew he was living in the jail. You should know that. You put him there."

Dettmer grabbed the mayor by the lapel of his suit and shoved him against the wall—their faces close enough that Mayor Renaud could smell brandy on Dettmer's breath.

"Let me make something clear, Mayor. You are no longer dealing with *Oberst* Volk. I am not a patient man. Your friend Legrand is wreaking havoc. I've been briefed on the death of the eight *Wehrmacht* soldiers at Sainte-Marie-du-Mont. I know it was done in retaliation for an attack on a mother and daughter. I am aware the daughter is the whore of Legrand's son. After I arrested Legrand, a bridge mysteriously blew up. Now I have a truck and four men missing with Legrand nowhere to be found. I am not stupid. Legrand is in the middle of this chaos. You will tell me where he lives, and you will tell me now."

Dr. Pelletier said, "Please, *Sturmbannführer* Dettmer. You have it all wrong. We are a peaceful little village. None of our citizens know anything about these things you speak of."

Dettmer released the mayor and backhanded the doctor across his face. The doctor lost his balance and fell back into a row of shelving. Pulling his Luger from its holster, he pointed it at Doctor Pelletier's head.

"Mayor, unless you want your citizens to be without a doctor, I suggest you tell me where Legrand lives."

Liberté
Saint-Cyr, France

Behind the wheel of the stolen troop carrier, René waited as Arthur leaped out of the passenger seat to open the rusty old gate to *Liberté*.

Pascal followed behind in his pickup. He had Mrs. Abraham and her friends with him.

When they arrived at the chateau, Arthur said, "I'll bury the bodies while you three make our guests comfortable."

"I'll help you," said Jean-Pierre.

René and Pascal escorted Mrs. Abraham and her friends inside.

"We are sorry, this is the best we have for you," said René.

"Where are we?" asked Mrs. Abraham.

"It is best you don't know, Mrs. Abraham," said René. "You are safe. We will find you a permanent hiding place in due time."

"It is only a matter of time before they realize their truck and four goons are missing," said Pascal. "Then they will look for you, René. They will go to your farm. You must stay away."

"Cécile is there right now. She is by herself."

Pascal said, "I'll grab Jean-Pierre. We will bring her here until the dust settles."

Whispering so they wouldn't hear, René said to Pascal, "We need to figure out what to do with Mrs. Abraham and her friends. They can't stay here. We don't have beds, blankets, or even running water. They can't stay at my farm. I can't even stay there."

"I'm afraid my farm is a target too," said Pascal. The

Wehrmacht have already searched my property twice looking for God knows what."

Pausing for a moment to think, Pascal then said, "I think I have a solution. But we will need to recruit help. Stay here with our guests. I'll take Jean-Pierre to get Cécile. We will be back in a few hours."

René was helping Arthur return the dirt over the buried bodies.

"How is Gabrielle, Arthur?" asked René.

"She is still working that dreadful job at the café."

"Is her plan working?"

"She is the reason we found you. Once those bastards get a few drinks in them and she wiggles past, they tell her everything. Hell, they'd tell her where Hitler is hiding if they knew."

"Does it bother you she flirts with them?"

"Hell yes, it bothers me. But I'm proud of her. I'm proud of her courage, and I'm proud that my Gabrielle is outsmarting the German army. Last week she learned that their plan is to have the rail bridge repaired by next month. Then they will increase the number of slave laborers they send to Germany."

"We will need to blow up another section of the track," said René.

"No, René. We understand the risks and accept them. But I must live with the fact that because of me, Dettmer murdered that farmer—Bonnel was his name. He left behind a wife and two children. I can't do that again."

René raised the shovel over his head and threw it to the ground. "Where the hell are the Brits? What about the

The Heroes of Sainte-Mère Église

Americans? Innocent people get murdered and they do nothing. Why aren't they helping us?"

Arthur said, "I can't answer that, René. But we must have faith they will arrive. But until then, all we can do is fight the Germans with what we have."

After a period of silence, Arthur asked, "What are we going to do with Mrs. Abraham and her friends?"

"I don't know yet. When you were out here digging, Pascal said he had a plan but needed to recruit help. It will be dark soon and he can't break curfew. That is all we need, for him and Jean-Pierre to get arrested."

While they continued to replace the dirt on the graves, Pascal drove around the back of the chateau. Behind him were Brigitte and Angélique in her Citroën. In the cab of the truck with Pascal was Cécile. Jean-Pierre and Luke were in the back.

Cécile leaped out of the truck, ran to René, and they embraced.

"I thought I'd never see you again."

"You know me better than that, don't you?"

Looking over at Pascal, Arthur, and Jean-Pierre, René replied, "Those three, right there, came to my rescue."

"We have your back, Papa."

"I know you do, Jean-Pierre. And I'm very proud of the man you have become."

Pascal said, "Let's go inside—we have some planning to do."

When they entered the second floor, Mrs. Abraham and the Rubins were sitting at the table.

With Brigitte and Angélique at his side, Pascal said, "I

want to introduce you to Brigitte and Angélique Lapierre. They are going to hide you. Their farmhouse is away from town. They are isolated and see far fewer German patrols than the rest of us."

Arthur added, "And unlike the rest of us, they aren't being watched by the *Wehrmacht*."

Mrs. Abraham stood and approached Brigitte. Grabbing her hands, she formed them into a cup. She then reached up and undid the large bun in her hair. In the bun was a pouch. She opened it and dumped the contents into Brigitte's hands.

Brigitte looked down and saw several diamonds and a few large jewels. Their colors were beautiful and sparkled in the light.

"What is this for, Mrs. Abraham?"

"I am an old woman. I have lived a good life, but I am not ready to die. Neither are my friends. Not at the hands of the Nazis. These jewels are all I have. You and your daughter are putting your lives at risk to save ours. It is the least I can do."

Brigitte grabbed the empty bag from Mrs. Abraham and returned the contents.

Caressing Mrs. Abraham's hands, she gave the bag back to her.

"You keep your jewels, Mrs. Abraham. They are yours, not mine. My home is open to you and your friends as long as you need. Together we will sit out the war until someone comes to save us. But I must warn you. My home is no palace. It is old and in need of repair. There is no running water or indoor plumbing. We have a well and an outhouse. But you and the Rubins are welcome to stay."

Sainte-Marie-du-Mont, France

"We will be home soon," said Brigitte.

Angélique was in the front seat with her mother. In the back were Mr. and Mrs. Rubin along with Mrs. Abraham.

"I'm not feeling well," said Mrs. Rubin.

"Tomorrow, I'll get Dr. Pelletier to come by the house."

"She needs her medication. It's for nausea," said Mr. Rubin.

"Let me know what she needs when we get home. In the morning, I'll go see Mayor Renaud at the pharmacy."

As they drove past Mr. Linville's horse farm, Angélique said, "What are they doing at Mr. Linville's, Mama?"

There were several *Wehrmacht* lorries parked next to a barn. They had hooked Mr. Lineville's horse trailers to them and were loading his prized thoroughbreds.

"Are they taking his horses?" asked Mr. Rubin.

"Where are Mr. and Mrs. Linville?" asked Angélique.

"I don't know, honey," replied Brigitte as she pulled the car over to the side of the road.

Thick trees and shrubbery surrounded the Linville farm. Brigitte parked the car behind a cluster of bushes, hoping the soldiers wouldn't notice it.

"What is that on the ground?" asked Angélique as she raised herself off the seat to get a better view. "Do you see it near the side of the house?"

The house was far enough away that it was difficult to make out the image, but it appeared to be two objects. Brigitte didn't want to believe what she saw, but she felt sick. She hoped that she was wrong.

"Stay here with the others, Angélique," said Brigitte.

Cautiously she opened the car door, but not close it for

fear of making a noise. She made her way to a single row of trees to get a better look.

She watched as the soldiers loaded the horses.

Softly stepping through the trees, she got a closer look.

Oh, God, no.

Lying next to the house like two disposed-of piles of debris were the lifeless bodies of Mr. and Mrs. Linville.

How can they murder fine people like the Linville's in cold blood? Who is that heartless?

Her breathing became heavy, and she was hyperventilating. She ducked behind a large tree, rested her back against it and looked up at the branches, taking deep breaths to regain her composure.

She heard German voices. They were laughing.

They are getting closer.

She listened as boots approached—then more laughter. They sounded as though they were just a few meters away.

Glancing toward her car, she was comforted knowing her car was well hidden from their view.

The jovial conversation stopped, and she heard fluid falling on the ground. Then the smell of urine.

They are pissing.

It seemed like an eternity.

Will they ever stop?

When they finished, their conversation continued as their voices faded, and they returned to their work.

Chapter Thirty-Five

JULY 15, 1941

Le Grand Vey, France

The water was choppy, and Lieutenant Laurent had already vomited twice during the voyage across the English Channel.

It had taken eleven hours in the fifty-four-foot fishing trawler. The hull was painted deep blue to keep it hidden in the night crossing. On four different occasions German patrol boats passed by them, scanning the water with spotlights, yet never shining the beam in their direction.

"We are nearly there, Lieutenant," said the captain of the boat. "I will get you as close to the beach as I can, but you may get a little wet."

"Just do what you can. I need to get ashore and find a place to hide before the sun comes up."

The captain said, "And I need to get out to sea and get my nets in the water to keep from getting shot at by the *Luftwaffe*. The Germans love fresh fish. If they think I am a French fisherman, they may leave me alone."

Laurent said, "Once I contact the Resistance, we will find a good spot for a night airfield. You won't need to take this risk anymore."

"There is the shoreline, Lieutenant."

The captain moved as close to the beach as he could.

Laurent grabbed two large canvas bags, thanked the captain for getting him home, then leaped over the side, fighting hard to keep the bags above the surface of the water.

Fearing he would run aground, the captain dropped him seventy meters off shore, so he had to swim much of the way to the beach He strained to keep the two bags over his head and out of the surf.

I'm glad the Brits trained me so hard.

Once on the beach, he found a large dune with an indentation in the middle. Tall grass grew around the perimeter.

I should be safe in here for a while.

After resting, he threw the heavy gear over his shoulder and walked inward several kilometers.

Behind an old farmhouse, he found a wooded area, and positioned himself between a group of tall trees and rested. He opened the first bag and removed a folding stock Sterling submachine gun and pushed in the clip until he heard a click. Then he removed a Walther PPK handgun, loaded that clip also, then tucked it into his belt.

There were also apples and dried beef, but his stomach was still turning from the trip across the channel, so he put the food back in the first bag.

He opened the second bag and pulled out a Hummerland shortwave wireless. The leather suitcase it was in was cumbersome. His plan was to find a safe place to stow it, so he could be more agile.

The Heroes of Sainte-Mère Église

For now, he needed it to call Dover.

Turning on the switch and adjusting the dial to the prearranged frequency, he grabbed the microphone and in English said, "Nighthawk to Beehive, Nighthawk to Beehive, can you hear me?"

After a few seconds he repeated the call, and a female voice with a British accent replied, "This is Beehive. Come in, Nighthawk."

"This is Nighthawk. I am nesting safely."

Chapter Thirty-Six

JULY 16, 1941

Sainte-Marie-du-Mont, France

As the sun rose, Laurent remained hidden in the trees. He had been awake for three hours and had only seen one lorry and a German motorcycle on patrol.

Watching the farmhouse, there was little movement except for an elderly man who used the outhouse and a female who appeared to be a teenager. She used the hand pump at the well to fill two buckets of water.

As the day passed, he became sleepy, but was concerned he may snore if he dozed off, giving away his position.

I must sleep so I can travel by night.

The Brits were masters at making false documents, but he was a French male of military age. That always brought added scrutiny, regardless of how perfectly forged his papers might be.

The Germans liked to arrest French males and ship them off to work camps. There were two benefits to doing

The Heroes of Sainte-Mère Église

this. It kept them from joining the Resistance, and it provided German manufacturing with strong backs.

After waking from a light sleep, it was late in the afternoon. Once again, he saw the teenage girl in the backyard. This time she was with a woman in her forties whom he assumed was her mother.

They had the hood up on a little four-door Citroën and were trying to start it.

Leaving his gear in the woods, he walked toward them. He was within twenty meters before they noticed him.

"*Bonjour*, may we help you?" asked Brigitte.

"*Bonjour*, I'm hoping you can. My name is Lieutenant Martin Laurent. I am a Frenchman from Sainte-Mère-Église. Although I am in the French army, I am currently working with the British. May we go inside? It isn't safe out here with the German patrols passing by."

Brigitte and Angélique looked at each other. They shared an unspoken look of caution.

Sensing their hesitation, he said, "I can prove I am who I say. My wife is Margot Laurent. She is a schoolteacher in Sainte-Mère-Église. I need to contact her. She will confirm my identity."

Angélique spoke up. "I know who she is, Mama. She is Jean-Pierre's schoolteacher. He speaks of her often."

"My name is Brigitte Lapierre. And this is my daughter, Angélique. Come in."

"*Merci*. Wait here. *S'il-vous-plaît*," said Laurent. "My gear is in the woods."

Sainte-Mère-Église, France

As they turned off N-13 to head to their farm, they saw a *Waffen-SS* staff car and two lorries coming from the opposite direction with road dust climbing high into the air. The dirt road was narrow, and Jean-Pierre had to edge the passenger side tires into the tall grass as the three vehicles zipped past.

"That looked like Dettmer's Mercedes, Mama," said Jean-Pierre, as he stepped on the clutch and shifted into third gear.

"What is he doing on this side of town?" asked Cécile, turning to watch them pass.

"I bet he drove past our farm looking for Papa."

Cécile said, "He is safe at Pascal's. It may be a long time before your papa can come home, Jean-Pierre. I want you to be prepared for that. Dettmer has him marked. You and I will have to work the farm by ourselves."

"We can do it, Mama. Maybe Philippe can make his way home from Guernsey soon to help us."

After a brief moment of silence, Jean-Pierre looked over to the passenger seat to see his mama crying. "I'm sorry, Mama. Did I upset you?"

"I'm just tired, Jean-Pierre. I'm tired of worrying about the fate of my family. I think about Philippe all of the time. Now your papa. It won't be long before the Germans will have a mark on your head, too, Jean-Pierre."

"Don't worry about me, Mama. Papa taught me how to take care of myself. And Philippe is smart and tough. Whatever he is going through, he will find his way home. I know he will."

"I hope you are right, Jean-Pierre. I'm just afraid none of this will ever end, and the Germans will always be here making our life hell."

"It will end one day, Mama. I have heard rumors that eventually the British and Americans will come and help us. When they do, we will fight alongside them. You must have hope."

"You and Philippe are so much like your papa—always ready to fight. It scares me. Jean-Pierre, when we get to the house, I'll go upstairs and pack your father's clothes. You go to the barn and get his motorcycle. When we leave, follow me back to Pascal's farm."

"I love to ride Papa's motorcycle," said Jean-Pierre.

With less than a kilometer away, they saw smoke rising above a small wooded area.

"Mama, that smoke is coming from our farm."

Pressing his foot to the accelerator, Jean-Pierre raced down the dirt road, then weaved around a cluster of trees.

When they arrived, orange flames from the second-floor windows reached into the sky.

"Oh, God, no!" said Cécile.

The roaring blaze engulfed their home.

Their furniture lay in the front courtyard—smashed to pieces.

Cécile's two-hundred-year-old piano was in the middle of the debris. She was the fourth generation of her family to own it. It appeared as though it had been run over by a lorry.

They stepped out of their truck, and Jean-Pierre embraced his mother as they watched their life go up in flames.

Fresville, France

Pascal Ganier's family farm was located twelve kilometers north of Sainte-Mère-Église. Although it was away from the main roads, German patrols could be seen in the area often because they had placed an ammunition storage facility nearby.

Pascal was the third generation in his family to own the farm. His widowed mother—who still lived there with Pascal and Luke—had sold him the property for a few francs knowing that as an only child, he would inherit it anyway. Pascal and Luke had closed their restaurant in Paris and moved to the farm a year earlier after Pascal's father passed away. Pascal's wife, Luke's mother, had passed away shortly before his father.

René, Cécile, and Jean-Pierre sat on the sofa in the parlor of the Ganier farmhouse. "I'm so sorry about the fire," said Madeleine Ganier. "Pascal told me what the Germans did to your farmhouse. Those people are dreadful."

"We will survive," said Cécile "We try and remind ourselves that they have mistreated people far worse than us."

"You are welcome to stay here as long as you need. It has been pleasant having René staying with us for the past few days. I know it has been difficult for him since he has been in hiding. As unpleasant as the circumstances are, at least you will be staying here together as a family."

"We are more grateful than you know, Madeleine," said René.

"Nonsense, René," said Madeleine. "Pascal has always told me that even though he had no natural siblings, you were, in fact, his brother. Therefore, you are family.

"Cécile, it will be nice to have a female around. I love my son and grandson, but the constant talk of guns and revenge is rather boring for an old woman."

Pascal, René, Luke, and Jean-Pierre stepped out of the house and went to one of the barns. Cécile stayed with Mrs. Ganier.

Madeleine Ganier was seventy-one years old. She had Pascal later in life. She and her husband, Pascal Senior, had been extremely active. With the aid of hired help, they managed to work the farm together. One day, she tried to wake her husband, but she couldn't. He had died in his sleep. Shortly after that, her health declined—physically and mentally. She now spent her days in a winged back chair in her night clothes, quilt over her lap.

Cécile said, "I know René has said this more times than you care to hear, but thank you for letting us stay here. I'm uncertain when we can rebuild. The Germans are looking for René. I'm sure Jean-Pierre and I are also on whatever list they use for their enemies."

"You are safe here. Although the German patrols around our farm have increased significantly as of late, we have hiding places as long as you are nimble. I hope you can run fast. My late husband became paranoid after the Great War. He built secret hiding places under both barns." Laughing, she added, "There is even a tunnel connecting them."

"Have you hidden in them, Mrs. Ganier?"

Leaning her head back with a chuckle, Madeleine said, "Gracious, no. I'm too old to run, so whenever the Germans arrive, I charm them."

"Have they come here before?"

"Oh yes, many times. That's why you need to be on the alert. Fortunately, it is a long drive from the road to the farm, and their vehicles make a ghastly sound coming down the driveway, so you should have ample warning."

"I hope we aren't putting you at risk by being here, Mrs. Ganier?"

"Please, call me Madeleine."

"Madeleine it is."

"Cécile, don't worry about me. I've had a wonderful life. What happens, will happen. I just hope to live long enough to see France free again."

Sainte-Marie-du-Mont, France

At the kitchen table, Brigitte, Angélique, and their three guests from the nursing home listened intently to Laurent's stories—the battles in northern France, his training in England, and his journey by boat across the channel.

"We are glad you made it home," said Brigitte. "My son was killed in the battle up north."

"I'm very sorry to hear that," said Martin.

Brigitte said, "It has been difficult the past few years for many reasons. But we will survive, won't we, Angélique?"

"Yes, Mama. Papa and Armand would want us to be strong."

"I know Margot will be excited to see you. We can take you to her this evening," said Brigitte. "But first, we must get my car started."

"I can help you with that. I'm handy with motors," said Martin.

As the conversation continued, they told him what life had been like since the Germans arrived. The confiscation of property. The food and fuel rations. The police state, and why there were three elderly Jews hiding in their house. They also told him of the horror at the Linville farm.

"This place is a nightmare," he said. "I need to get to Margot. She must be terrified living through this by herself."

"We will get you there. But we must be back before curfew."

"There is one other thing," he said. "My purpose here is not just to return home. I also have a job to do. I need to connect with the Resistance. Do you know if they are active on the peninsula?"

"Yes," said Brigitte. "Angélique's friend Jean-Pierre—the one who's in Margot's class—his father is involved in the Resistance, but he is in hiding. We can connect you to him."

"When?"

"Maybe tomorrow. But first, let's get the car running so we can get you home to Margot."

As they left the table, he noticed a family photo hanging on the wall.

He recognized Brigitte; she was seated. Standing behind her was her late husband. Sitting on the floor in front of Brigitte was Angélique. Next to her husband was her son.

Laurent paused.

She said their last name was Lapierre. Her son was Sergeant Lapierre. My Sergeant Lapierre from the barn.

Sainte-Mère-Église, France

With Laurent in the passenger seat and Angélique in the back, Brigitte drove to Sainte-Mère-Église.

"I'm a little nervous, Brigitte. She hasn't seen me in over a year. She doesn't even know I am alive."

"It will thrill her to see you," said Brigitte

As they approached the town, German lorries and motorcycles appeared on the back roads.

"It gets worse," said Brigitte. "Wait until we get to the center of town."

Brigitte drove past City Hall. Laurent noticed the large swastika hanging from the second floor, and the smaller swastika flags hanging from the light poles and on buildings.

When she approached the church courtyard, he asked her to pull over to the side of the road.

"They have taken over our town," said Laurent.

"The *Kommandant* has even confiscated Dr. Pelletier's house. The doctor is now seeing patients in the back of Mayor Renaud's pharmacy."

Closing his eyes and clenching his teeth, Laurent was furious. "We have to win this war. This cannot stand."

"We are all doing our part," said Brigitte.

She pointed across the courtyard. "Do you see over there? Le Café du Quartier?"

"Yes, I remember it. Margot and I have eaten there many times," said Martin.

"It is popular with the German officers. Do you see that pretty waitress there? The one with the long auburn hair?"

"Yes, what about her?"

"That is Gabrielle Hall. She and her husband Arthur are with the Resistance. They work with René Legrand. There are others, too. You will meet them."

"I look forward to working with them," said Martin Laurent. "I've seen enough. Please take me to Margot."

Sainte-Mère-Église, France

Margot and Martin Laurent lived two kilometers south of the courtyard.

Their house had three small rooms and was located in an open field. They bought it because of its close proximity to the school, allowing Margot to walk to work.

As they approached the house, Laurent said, "Stop, Brigitte."

The car jerked as Brigitte applied the brake. "What do you think it means?" asked Brigitte.

"I don't know," replied Laurent, as they looked at a black Mercedes in front of his home.

Why is there a Nazi vehicle in front of my house? How many are in there with Margot?

"We can't stay here, Brigitte. We look suspicious," said Laurent. "Go behind that hedgerow."

Brigitte put the car in gear and continued down the road, hoping nobody had seen them stop.

Once out of sight, she turned around and parked behind a hedgerow seventy meters away.

Laurent went to the trunk and removed his submachine gun. He inserted the clip and pulled the bolt back until he heard the first round enter the chamber.

"Brigitte, it will be dark soon. I don't know what will happen tonight. I'm staying here until I know Margot is not in danger. But I'm not comfortable putting you and Angélique at risk. You need to go. I'll be fine here by myself."

"What are you going to do?"

"Once it's dark, I'll crawl on my belly to the house and

look in the windows. What happens after that depends on what I see."

Brigitte and Angélique had left two hours earlier, and the sky had turned dark.

Laurent crawled over the hedgerow and through the open field. The weeds and tall grass provided cover.

The blinds of the house were closed, a common practice throughout Europe because of air raids. A silhouette of light surrounded the edge of the windows.

When he was within thirty meters, the back door opened and slammed shut. Laurent raised his head slightly while lying motionless.

A *Wehrmacht* officer stepped out, lit a cigarette, and took a deep drag. Taking a few more steps away from the house, he unzipped his fly and urinated in the backyard.

Laurent had a clear shot if he wanted to take it, but there was too much uncertainty.

How many are in there? Which room is Margot in? Is she even there?

The officer flipped his cigarette into the field and went back in.

Laurent continued his crawl until he was at the side of the house. Once there, he pressed his ear to the wall.

Male voices—at least three. Two in the kitchen, one more in the parlor, raising his voice, but not angrily.

Although not a master of the German language, he had learned a few words over the years.

Intermingled with conversation and laughter he heard, *Lehrer*—teacher, *Frau*—Mrs., *laufen*—running, and *entkam*—escaped.

Entkam! She escaped. What was she escaping from, and where did she escape to?

Chapter Thirty-Seven

JULY 14, 1941

Sainte-Mère-Église, France

Large trees encircled the school. Laurent found a position behind one that gave him a clear view of both the school and his house.

The three German soldiers occupying his home had left before sunup. Now, he waited for the teachers to arrive.

In the distance, a four-wheeled ox cart pulled by two mules approached.

At the reins, he recognized the school principal, Mr. Séverin. There were four or five women in the back. He couldn't see all of them, however, he recognized Anastasie Lebeau. She taught mathematics and was Margot's closest friend. Her long brown hair was in a bun on top of her head. Her green dress was worn and tattered. As with many of the townspeople Martin had seen since his arrival, Anastasie appeared thin and tired. Principal Séverin stopped the cart at the rear of the school, and they all leaped out.

Laurent looked closely at each of the teachers. *I don't see my Margot.*

Stepping out from behind the tree, Laurent approached the group.

"Martin!" shouted Anastasie. "You are home. Margot will be so excited to see you."

"*Bonjour*, Anastasie. Where is Margot? Is she okay?"

"She is fine."

Addressing the others, Anastasie said, "You all go in. I will be in shortly."

She grabbed Laurent by the arm and pulled him behind the tree. "Margot is safe. Nobody knows but me, but she is living with a couple in Picauville. Their names are Arthur and Gabrielle Hall."

"Why is she there? What do you mean by she is safe? What does she need to be safe from? Why are those Germans in my home?"

"I'll let Margot explain that. For now, let me tell you how to find her."

Picauville, France

Traveling by day without getting discovered was easier than he thought. Laurent hugged tree lines and hedgerows and found side roads with no German patrols.

Approaching the property from the rear, he saw several corrals but no horses.

The property had a large home and three barns. The barndoors were opened, and he entered the one farthest from the house. The stalls were empty.

"May I help you?"

Laurent turned to see a male in his forties.

"Are you Arthur Hall?"

"Yes, that's right. What can I do for you?"

"I believe my wife Margot is here. My name is Martin Laurent."

Before they got to the house, Margot ran out of the back door with her arms open and embraced her husband.

"I have missed you so much. I heard you were alive. A soldier sent his parents a wire from Guernsey mentioning he spoke to you in England. Since receiving that message, my heart has been filled with hope."

Martin lifted Margot into the air. He held her tightly, never wanting to let her go. He smelled her hair, taking in the fragrance he remembered before looking into her eyes, "I have missed you so, my beautiful Margot. You don't know how much I have wanted to return home to you."

Arthur Hall said, "Let's go inside."

Gabrielle made dinner while Margot and Martin held hands at the kitchen table. Arthur sat across from them.

"Why are you here, Margot? Why are there three *Wehrmacht* officers living in our home?"

The room was quiet for a moment. Margot was hesitant to tell him.

"We will step out so you two can be alone," said Gabrielle.

As Arthur and Gabrielle left, Margot said, "Martin, when the *Wehrmacht* arrived, they requisitioned homes to quarter soldiers. I asked them not to take ours, but they said it was located in a central location and they needed it. I explained I had no place to go. They said I could stay, but they would be using our home. Initially there was only one officer. He was rude, but not unbearable. Between my teaching and his work, we were seldom there together. They reassigned the *Wehrmacht* officer, and a few days later, three *SS* officers showed up at the door."

The tears started to flow down her face as Martin embraced her.

"Again, they told me I could stay. But our home is small. Where would I sleep? I knew it would not work, so I decided that the next day, I would find someplace else. But that first night I stayed at the house. I shouldn't have. They brought several bottles of wine home. I went into our room and locked the door. But they were getting rowdy. They beat on my door demanding that I come out. I got scared and climbed out of the window, but one of them was there waiting for me. He dragged me back into the house. And ... I'm so sorry, Martin."

She buried her face in his shoulder, weeping uncontrollably. He wept with her and said, "Why are you apologizing? I should apologize to you for not being here to protect you. Don't worry, Margot, I'm here now."

As they held each other close, Martin was enraged. He wished he would have known this the previous evening when he was there. He would have firebombed his own house while they were in it; mowed them down with his machine gun as they tried to escape the blaze.

During dinner, Arthur explained that he and Gabrielle were part of the Resistance. He told him about René and Pascal, as well as the others in their small group and what roles they played.

Martin explained where he had been over the past two years, including his training with the SOE and that his primary role on the Cotentin Peninsula was to help the Resistance.

Then Martin said, "Margot, you said a soldier in

Guernsey sent a cable to his parents that he knew me from England. What was his name?"

Arthur spoke up, "It is René Legrand's son, Philippe."

"Sergeant Philippe Legrand?" asked Martin

"Yes, that's right," said Arthur.

"How did he end up in Guernsey?" asked Martin

"Apparently his ship was sunk," said Arthur.

Martin said, "I was supposed to be on that ship before I got recruited by the SOE. It's a long story."

Then he asked, "Margot, the three who attacked you, are they the same three who are at our house now?"

"I don't know. That was last school year. I haven't been back since. The Hall's heard my story and let me stay here."

Arthur spoke up. "Yes, they are the same three. A group of us have been watching them. We have plans for them."

"Who is 'we,' and what kind of plans are you talking about?" asked Martin.

Arthur said, "When we are alone, I will explain it to you, Martin. Maybe you would like to join us when we pay them a visit."

"I wouldn't miss it."

"What are you talking about?" asked Margot.

The room was silent.

Margot asked Gabrielle, "What are they talking about?"

More silence.

"Margot, will you help me with the dishes?" asked Gabrielle.

Chapter Thirty-Eight

JULY 15, 1941

**Liberté
Saint-Cyr, France**

After entering the third floor of the ancient chateau known to the group as *Liberté*, Arthur introduced Martin Laurent to everyone.

René spoke first. "I understand you were with my son, Philippe, in England."

Martin said, "Yes. I met him before his ship departed. He's in Guernsey now, I hear."

René said, "Yes, along with another member of our group, Daniel Girard. He went out with his fleet of tugboats. He saved a couple hundred men."

"Any additional communication with him?" asked Martin.

"No. The Germans cut the phone lines to the island. They have done the same thing here in Normandy."

Since establishing *Liberté*, the group had furnished it

with a blackboard from an abandoned school, and several maps of Normandy and the Cotentin Peninsula.

They spent the afternoon planning strategy, with Laurent running the meeting. He informed them of what the SOE was working on.

"We need to find a safe place to land a single-engine airplane. Preferably a smooth, open field. It should be located where the Germans seldom patrol."

"I know a field," said Jean-Pierre. "It is south of here. There are no major towns or roads. The roads are narrow and overgrown with trees. It would be difficult to get a lorry down them." Pointing to the map, he said, "It's here. Between Le Vrétot and Quettetot."

"Can you get me there tonight? I need to get the coordinates. I will use the wireless to send them to London, and they will make arrangements for the first landing. They will pick me up, take me back to England, where I'll brief them."

"What happens after that?" asked René.

"You will see a lot of me. I will travel back and forth from London. Each time, I will bring weapons, explosives, food—whatever you need."

"That is great news," said Pascal. "We need to get the Germans the hell out of France."

"That day will come, my friend. Be patient," said Laurent.

Chapter Thirty-Nine

JULY 21, 1941

Sainte-Mère-Église, France

"They are missing, *Sturmbannführer*," said Dettmer's aide. "They were the three officers staying at the little house near the school."

"How can this happen again?" Dettmer shouted while pounding his fist on the desk. "Three *SS* officers, four *Wehrmacht* soldiers, one staff car, and a troop carrier have simply vanished into thin air. Add the eight who were executed when that girl was raped, and that makes fifteen of our men killed or missing since our arrival in Sainte-Mère-Église. This is Legrand and his bunch again. I am sure of it. Find them!" Dettmer shouted. "Find them at once—do you hear me?"

Chapter Forty

JULY 29, 1941

Le Vrétot, France

Angélique stood at one end of the field, Luke at the other, with Jean-Pierre in the middle. Each held a torch and a lighter.

It was quiet, initially. Nothing but a slight wind in the trees, and a few crickets in the woods. Then, they heard the sound they'd waited for. The hum of a small engine in the sky.

"There it is. Set the torches," Laurent yelled.

Once lit, the circling pilot came around and guided the plane to the three lights in the open field.

As the little plane descended, Laurent knew the first of many landings was about to take place, and they were one step closer to ending the war.

Chapter Forty-One

OCTOBER 23, 1941

Pleinmont, Guernsey Island

The temperature on Guernsey had dropped, and a cold October wind blew in from the Atlantic. Philippe prepared to spend his second winter in the barn since arriving on the island after his ship was sunk by the *Luftwaffe*.

Although he wanted to help Claire and her parents on their farm, his options were limited since it was important that he remain out of sight as much as possible. The *Wehrmacht* patrolled the island frequently, even though they seldom visited their isolated end of Guernsey.

Philippe's father had taught him many skills, and he was a capable mechanic, which enabled him to work in the barn maintaining farm equipment.

He had made a comfortable place for himself in the hayloft, but the barn was not airtight and the space between the old planks allowed the wind to slice through.

Claire and her mother had lobbied for Philippe to stay in the house during the winter, just as they had the previous two winters, but Oliver stood fast. He wanted the alibi of ignorance if the Germans ever found Philippe. Although that was true in part, it also concerned Oliver that a handsome Frenchman would sleep under the same roof as his daughter.

"I brought you more blankets, Philippe," Claire shouted as she climbed up the ladder of the loft.

"Thank you. You are always so thoughtful."

"I'm just trying to be a good host."

"You certainly are that. I owe so much to you and your parents."

"Nonsense. You owe us nothing," said Claire. "It won't be long, and Mother and I will break Father. Soon he will allow you to sleep in the house next to the fireplace."

"I'll be fine here, Claire. I understand your father's concerns."

"I'm trying to find information about your friends from the ship," said Claire. "The Germans have agreed to allow local volunteers into the prison camp to give care packages to the prisoners. I have volunteered. We go in next week."

"That is perfect, Claire. Some boys had severe injuries. I hope they all survived."

"I'll see what I can find out."

Claire laid the blankets flat on the hay in the little bed Philippe had made for himself. First one blanket, then the next.

"There. That should help keep you warm," she said.

"I always love to see you, Claire. Even when you are out in the field helping your father, I watch you between the boards of the barn."

"You do, do you? There are names for men like you. I believe they are called Peeping Toms."

"No. A Peeping Tom is someone who looks into a

building to spy on a beautiful woman. I, on the other hand, am looking out of a building. Therefore, I believe they would find me innocent in a court of law."

"Maybe in a French court of law, but I am not so certain here on Guernsey."

"I see your point."

Philippe stepped toward Claire and took her in his arms and said, "What if Mr. Peeping Tom were standing in a hayloft of a barn and he tried to kiss a beautiful woman? Would that get him into trouble?"

"Well, I don't know, I'm not a lawyer." Moving her lips to his and feeling his warm breath on her face, she said, "Let's try it and see what happens."

Chapter Forty-Two

DECEMBER 4, 1941

Decryption Station HYPO
Pearl Harbor, Hawaii

Lieutenant Rex Randolph was on the last hour of his shift.

The twenty-four-year-old had been stationed in Hawaii for two years and was having the time of his life. His hometown in Wisconsin had experienced subzero temperatures for three straight days while he recovered from a sunburn he had gotten frolicking in Hanauma Bay, an activity not ideal for a young man with red hair and pale skin.

He had met a girl from California who served as a nurse at the Naval Hospital. He had recently proposed to her, and they were to be married in May.

Just three weeks earlier, he had deciphered a Japanese message that read, If Japanese-American relations continue to be in danger, we predict an east-west rain.

Randolph sent that message up the chain of command, unaware if it was significant, or if any action had been taken.

The Heroes of Sainte-Mère Église

Glancing at the clock, he realized only seventeen minutes remained before he could leave.

He considered slipping out early. His fiancée wanted him to come to her apartment for dinner to meet her parents who had just arrived on the island from their home in San Francisco.

They can wait. This next one is short.

After pulling the final message of the day, he checked the chart of known indicators from previously decoded messages. Upon completion of the decipher he jotted it down, Prepare the eastern rain.

Picking up the telephone, he dialed the apartment of his fiancée. "Honey, my apologies to you and your parents. I will be a little late. I have a message I need to hand deliver to HQ."

Chapter Forty-Three

MARCH 25, 1942

**Le Café du Quartier
Sainte-Mère-Église, France**

The cool air blew into the café as they entered.

"*Bonjour, Mademoiselle* Gabrielle," said Dettmer as he and three junior officers sat down at one of her tables.

Gabrielle had been busy all evening. She weaved her way between her five tables, taking drink orders while ignoring the catcalls and groping. The conversations she overheard were of one topic.

Die Atlantische Festung—The Atlantic Fortress.

"I must say, Gabrielle, you look exhausted. But still beautiful," said Dettmer.

Brushing the bangs of her disheveled auburn hair from her eyes, "It has been a busy day, *Sturmbannführer*. I have had no time to freshen up. Would you like your usual brandy and four glasses?"

"*Oui.*"

"I'll bring it right out."

The Heroes of Sainte-Mère Église

When she returned, Dettmer was speaking in German to the other officers at the table. "We will use our own men and French civilians. They can either volunteer, or they will be harshly persuaded. Either way, the French will help us build the Atlantic wall. We will also receive a trainload of prisoners from Germany."

Setting the brandy on their table and looking down at the seated Dettmer, she asked, "May I get you anything else?"

Putting his arm around her waist—his hand on her hip—staring up into her hazel eyes, he replied, "Do you know what I would really like?"

Grinning at him, she said, "*Oui*, I do. You have told me many times, but we only provide food and drink at Le Café du Quartier. You will never get the other from me."

"Never, *mademoiselle*? You underestimate me. I am a man who always gets his way, eventually."

Breaking his grasp and turning away to clean the table next to him, she said, "And you underestimate me, *Sturmbannführer*."

"What is the timeline, *Sturmbannführer*?" asked one of the junior officers.

Dettmer replied, "They will start building north of here first—Norway to Calais. However, the *Führer*'s plan is to have an indestructible barrier along the entire western coast of Europe. From Norway to the border with Spain. They are reinforcing the deep-water ports first. Then the focus will be on the other coastal regions"

Gabrielle took an order from a table next to Dettmer's, keeping an ear toward his table.

"Do you think the Brits and Americans will invade this far south, *Sturmbannführer*?"

"No. Neither does the *Führer*. He believes there is a low

probability of a Normandy invasion. He is concentrating most of our resources further north at Calais. But we must also be prepared here in Normandy."

Before leaving, Dettmer approached Gabrielle and placed several *francs* in her hand. "One day, I hope to offer you more than a gratuity."

As he walked away, she thought to herself, *You already have.*

Chapter Forty-Four

MARCH 27, 1942

**10 Downing Street
London, England**

Removing a cigar from his mouth, Prime Minister Winston Churchill answered his desk phone. "Yes, Elizabeth, what is it?"

"SOE Chief Frank Nelson is here to see you, sir."

"Nelson? Yes, by all means send him in."

"Prime Minister, forgive me for arriving unannounced. However, we received information from one of our agents in Normandy. It is of immediate concern."

Churchill returned the cigar to his mouth and reached for the sheet of paper Nelson presented to him, then sat down as he studied the message.

Nighthawk Calling
Resistance agent has reported the following information;
It is considered to be Highly Reliable.
Germany to build Atlantic wall from Norway to Spain.

*German Fuhrer believes Invasion will take place in northern Europe. Resources to be concentrated at Calais.
German Fuhrer believes Normandy invasion is unlikely.
End of message.*

Still staring at the paper intently, he asked, "How reliable is this resource, Nelson?"

"Prime Minister, this agent has been providing us with intelligence for over a year. He has always proven to be both valuable and dead-on accurate. I would consider Nighthawk to be one of our best agents."

Churchill said, "Contact this Nighthawk chap. We need him to return to London for a debriefing."

Picking up the telephone, Churchill said, "Elizabeth, ring Chief of the General Staff, Alan Brooke."

Chapter Forty-Five

APRIL 30, 1942

Le Vrétot, France

Laurent was the first to spot the torches on the ground. "There they are, over there to the right."

The airplane banked right and descended toward the three sets of flames, landing in the bumpy field as it had done for the seventh time in the past year.

Shaking the pilot's hand, Martin Laurent climbed out, exiting to the rear to avoid the propeller.

He grabbed four large canvas bags from the storage compartment located under the plane and then pounded the side, signaling to the pilot it was all clear to taxi back down the field.

As the plane turned around, René, Jean-Pierre, and Angélique met Laurent.

"*Bonjour. Good to see you,* Martin. How was the flight?" asked René.

"Smoothest so far. The Brits and Americans have given

the *Luftwaffe* hell. There seem to be fewer German planes in the air than there were a year ago. However, the Germans are still managing to sneak bombers over England."

Everyone grabbed one of Martin's bags and headed for the tree line.

"What is in here, Mr. Laurent?" asked Angélique. "It is heavier than I am."

"Let me swap with you, Angélique. You took the heaviest one. I packed it with American M1A1 machine guns. The ammo is in your bag, Jean-Pierre. René, your bag has plastic explosives, so be careful."

"Jesus, what do they want us to do with this arsenal?" asked René.

"I'll fill you in when we get to Arthur's house."

At the pickup, they buried the bags under a pile of hay René had in his truck and headed to Arthur's farm. During the drive, Jean-Pierre and Angélique rode in the back of the truck. Martin Laurent rode in the cab with René.

During the drive, René asked, "What is the latest from Britain?"

"It is beautiful. The Americans have been pouring in since January, and they are everywhere. Every little village I passed through had American GIs. On the backroads and open fields were tanks, jeeps, trucks, and planes as far as I could see. Something big will happen. When and where, I don't know. But René, I have a feeling we only need to hold on a little longer and France will be ours again."

"Will they be coming here—to Normandy?"

"No details have been released yet. But rumor has it there is a badass American general by the name of Patton building forces across the channel from Calais."

"So, what role will we play?"

"Don't worry, my friend. We won't be left out of the action. They have big plans for us, too. We need to call a meeting at *Liberté* so I can fill everyone in."

Chapter Forty-Six

JULY 23, 1942

**Pleinmont
Guernsey Island**

It had been nine months since Philippe and Claire shared a cool, cozy afternoon in the hayloft.

After their initial disappointment in Claire and Philippe's irresponsible behavior, Oliver and Margaret were now excited that their daughter was on the verge of giving birth to their first grandchild.

Margaret sat on the bed between Claire's legs.

"I can't wait for the doctor. The baby is coming now," Claire said to her mother.

Philippe paced in their upstairs bedroom, frustrated he couldn't help his wife, or understand their conversation, which was in English. They had been married in a secret wedding eight months earlier. Oliver had driven into town and retrieved a Catholic vicar to perform the ceremony, making him promise a vow of silence that Philippe was living with them.

Speaking to Claire in French, he said, "What can I do to help?"

"Go downstairs and wait for my father to return with the doctor. Mother and I can handle this. Once he gets here, bring him up."

Philippe, relieved at his wife's suggestion to leave the room, made his way down the steps and transferred his nervous pacing to the front porch.

I hope the doctor gets here before the baby comes.

After twenty minutes on the porch, he went back into the kitchen and stared out of the window, still on the lookout for Oliver and the doctor.

"Push!" he heard from Margaret as he kept his ear toward the upstairs bedroom.

With another glance out of the window, he saw dust flying from the rear of the truck as Oliver sped down the dirt road to the house.

"They are here!" shouted Philippe.

As they reached the house, he heard it. The wail of a baby crying from the top of the stairs.

Philippe greeted them on the front porch.

While entering the house, the doctor spoke to Philippe in French, "Bonjour, you must be Phillipe."

Philippe replied, "Bonjour, Doctor, thank you for coming so quickly. The baby was just born. I can hear it crying."

"That's a good sign," said the doctor. "Babies are supposed to cry when they are born."

As he held the door open for Oliver and the doctor, he glanced behind them to see another vehicle coming.

"We have company," said Philippe.

As the other two men turned around, Dr. Martin said, "What is that?"

Philippe replied, "It is a *Kübelwagen—Wehrmacht*."

Philippe laid in the third-floor attic with his ear pressed to the floor.

He heard Angus barking ferociously, followed by a gunshot, a yelp, then silence.

It was difficult to hear the conversation taking place in the kitchen two floors below.

He listened to the muffled sounds of Germans trying to speak English and the responses from Claire's parents. Their voices were loud.

Then up the stairs—boots of a single soldier.

He entered the bedroom with Claire and the doctor.

"Where is he?" shouted the soldier.

More yelling followed by the cries of the baby.

Dr. Martin said, "I don't know who you're looking for, but he isn't here. This young lady just gave birth. She and the baby need to rest."

"Whose baby is this?"

"It is my baby," said Claire.

"Where is the father?"

"He was killed."

"We were told there's a French soldier living here. Where is he?"

"Your information is false," said the doctor.

Philippe heard the thud of Doc Martin being shoved to the ground.

"We will find him," said the soldier.

He yelled something in German to the other soldier guarding Oliver and Margaret.

Philippe lay motionless on the floor. Over in the corner

was an Enfield rifle and a box of ammunition Oliver had hidden in the attic.

The German walked down the hallway, passing directly below the hatch, checking the other third-floor rooms.

I must get to the Enfield.

The soldier walking below Philippe headed back down the hall, never noticing the hatch above his head.

He's going back in with Claire.

"No!" screamed Claire.

The doctor shouted, "Leave her alone!"

Philippe leaped from the attic and made his way down the hall, Enfield rifle in hand.

Entering the room, he saw the soldier trying to take the baby from Claire—the doctor and Claire struggling with the large man.

Philippe raised the butt of the Enfield and with one blow brought the butt of the rifle down on his neck, dropping him to the ground.

Downstairs—he heard the sound of a single shot.

Philippe made his way down the steps with the muzzle of the Enfield leading the way.

When he entered the kitchen, the other soldier lay on the floor with blood flowing from his chest. Margaret stood next to an open drawer with a revolver in her hand.

"Margaret is a bit shaken up after killing that boy, but the sedatives I gave her will allow her to sleep," said Doc Martin.

"You need to tell the doctor he needs to leave before the Germans get here," said Philippe. "Nobody knows he was here but us."

In English, Claire translated Philippe's statement.

"He's right, Doc," said Oliver. "This isn't your problem."

"What are you going to do with the bodies?" asked the Doc.

"I have a plan for them," said Oliver.

"They are right," said Claire. "Mama is resting, and the baby is healthy. It's only a matter of time before the *Wehrmacht* come looking for their missing soldiers. They could be here any minute. This island needs you. You can't allow yourself to get arrested."

"What are you going to do when they arrive?" asked the doc.

"We will figure that out when they get here," said Oliver. "Let's just get you in the truck, so I can get you out of here.

Oliver said, "Claire, ask Philippe to help me get the bodies in the truck. I will find a place to hide them."

After she relayed the information to Philippe, he put the bodies in the back of Oliver's pickup and covered them in a tarp.

Turning to Claire, Philippe said, "I'm going with your father. I'll turn myself in and say I killed them."

"No, Philippe. They'll shoot you."

"Listen to me, Claire. They will punish someone for this. If I don't turn myself in, they will arrest all of us, including you and your parents. What will happen to our son if we are all executed? That is no option and you know it."

With tears flowing down her face, Claire embraced Philippe. "No, I won't let you go."

"Tell your father what I'm doing. I'll go in the house and kiss my baby boy goodbye."

Phillipe stood in the second-floor bedroom holding his

The Heroes of Sainte-Mère Église

sleeping son close to his chest, hoping he would remember his beating heart.

"You are beautiful like your mama. Grow up and make her proud. One day you will meet your grandmama, grandpapa, and your Uncle Jean-Pierre in Sainte-Mère-Église. They will love you like I do, my precious son."

Philippe kissed him on his forehead. "I love you," he said, then nestled him between the two pillows on the bed.

Before returning downstairs, he glanced out of the window to see Claire on her knees, weeping loud enough that she could be heard from the house. In the distance, Oliver and Doc Martin were driving away.

Chapter Forty-Seven

JULY 24, 1942

Pleinmont
Guernsey Island

Claire and Margaret sat on the front porch watching as the people of Guernsey came to give their condolences. Claire was holding Baby Oliver.

The line of cars, trucks, and horse carriages stretched further than they could see.

Oliver Quinn had been well respected on the island. He grew up there and seldom went anywhere he didn't see a friend.

"He was well loved, Mama," said Claire.

"Yes, he was, dear."

Philippe knew he must remain out of sight. Even though the *Wehrmacht* had publicly executed Oliver for the murder of the two soldiers, they still suspected a French soldier was living on the farm.

Oliver's execution had created unrest throughout the

island. The Germans would stay away for a while to let the anger subside. But they would return.

Philippe watched the crowd gather as he peered through the planks of the barn. As he witnessed the love flowing from the people of Guernsey toward Claire and her mother, he cleaned Oliver Quinn's Enfield rifle.

Chapter Forty-Eight

JANUARY 9, 1943

Pau, France

"We have lived in this attic for over three years," said Miriam Edelman. "Will it ever end, or will we die here?"

"Stop, Miriam. Just stop," replied Uri. "We are alive. That's more than can be said for the Jews in Warsaw who could not escape. We will get out of this. You must have faith."

Joseph said, "Miriam, just think where we would be without the help of Max and Salvador. They are putting their lives at risk by letting us hide here in their hotel attic."

Ingrid added, "Wilhelm is using his authority as a *Wehrmacht* officer to keep our existence here a secret."

Joseph said, "Miriam, when you feel a sense of despair, read the stack of newspapers Max has been bringing us. The Americans are in the fight now. They, along with the Brits are giving the Nazis hell in north Africa. They are also bombing Germany around the clock, and the Russians are starting to turn the tide to the east."

The Heroes of Sainte-Mère Église

It was late in the afternoon, and Wilhelm would be home soon, and Max would bring their dinner in a few hours.

"I'm cold, Papa," said Dreyfus, bundled in his overcoat and flat hat, both of which he had outgrown since they had arrived.

"We are all cold, Dreyfus," said Joseph. "You, too, need to remember to count your blessings. We all do."

"Come here, Dreyfus. Cuddle with your mama."

"This winter has been even colder than the last two," said Miriam.

As they lay on the floor, they could hear boots on the third floor. They sounded like Wilhelm's and Max's, but there was always a sense of fear until confirmed.

The attic door opened, and Wilhelm and Max made their way to the top of the stairs and entered the attic.

With no greeting, Wilhelm spoke first, "I need you all to brace yourselves. I have learned that by the end of the week, I will be transferred to the eastern front to fight the Russians. Our forces have been in a brutal battle in the Caucasus. We are pulling reinforcements from other regions of Europe to try and keep the Russians from gaining ground. You can't stay here. I will be gone in six days, and they will assign another officer to this command. He is a member of the *SS*, and just like I have done, he will make this hotel his command post."

"Oh, God," Mrs. Edelman said while covering her mouth with her hand.

"Well, Miriam, you wanted out of here," said Ingrid Shapiro. "Now you have your wish."

The seven of them waited for Max to arrive. They were used to waiting. They had waited for over three years. They had waited for their meals. They had waited for nighttime when they were free to roam around without creaking the floorboards. They had waited for the opportunity to escape. However, this was not the opportunity they were looking for. They had hoped to have a safe passage with perfectly prepared documents. Now, they were waiting for Max to arrive with whatever risky scheme he had derived.

The day was exceptionally cold for southern France. They all had winter coats and gloves, which they were grateful for, but their shoes were not designed for the winter cold.

The attic door opened and shut at the bottom of the stairs. When Max entered the room, he had a young man with him who appeared to be in his late teens.

Max said, "This is my cousin Domingo. His mother was my mother's sister. His father is from Spain. He has contacts there and believes he can help us. It is going to be risky, but you must trust him."

Domingo was average height, and his Spanish heritage was obvious with his thick dark hair and beginnings of a five-o'clock shadow, on what otherwise could be described as a babyface. He was not large, but clearly in excellent physical condition. His waist was thin, and his strong arms and legs were evident even in his thick winter coat, which was a size too small.

"But he is just a boy," said Miriam Edelman. "How is he going to get us to Spain?"

Without taking offense, Domingo said, "I have an uncle in Spain. He was a military general and worked directly under Prime Minister Manuel Azaña before his overthrow by Franco. Now my uncle is a revolutionary. He lives in the mountains with a group of other revolutionaries. They have a network of remote outposts that are hidden. Some are cabins deep in the woods—others are caves. I have contacted my Uncle Marcos. He has arranged for one of his men to meet us at an outpost in Astun, at the peak of the Pyrénées. From there, the escort will take you down the other side of the mountain and into Spain. The main challenge is getting you up there."

"Forgive me for questioning you, but why would your uncle do this?" asked Joseph. "Why would your uncle risk everything to help seven Jews he doesn't even know?"

"Why have Max and Salvador put their lives at risk by letting you stay here?" replied Domingo. "Why am I putting my life at risk to escort you out of Pau? Why have I put my life at risk to help dozens of other Jews out of France?"

Surprised by the comment, Max looked at Domingo and said, "Dozens of other Jews? What other Jews?

"For over two years I have been working with my uncle and his rebels to escort Jews out of France. Not just Jews. We have also escorted downed British pilots and political prisoners who escape the Nazis. Now that the Americans have entered the war, we are escorting their downed airmen too."

"Why am I just learning of this?" asked Max.

"You have never approached me about helping Jews before, cousin. You had no need to know until now. You must promise me you will tell no one."

"Of course not," replied Max.

"Our challenge is this," said Domingo. "In the past, I have been able to get papers from a contact in the Spanish diplomatic office here in Pau. However, my contact is in Budapest, and I have no way of contacting him. I don't trust anyone else in his office."

"So, without documentation, how do we get to the top of the mountain?" asked Joseph.

"There are two ways," replied Domingo. "One is by truck, which is dangerous. The German's have patrols scattered all over the French side of the mountain face. Some in vehicles—others on skis. They also have checkpoints on all of the main roads going up to the peak. The side roads are patrolled from the air by *Luftwaffe* planes. If they were to spot us, they would contact the ground patrols who would swarm us.

"The Spanish side of the mountain is only slightly safer. Franco has made it clear that Spain will remain neutral, so you won't see *Wehrmacht* or *Waffen-SS* on the southern face. However, Franco looks the other way at *Gestapo* agents dressed in civilian clothes. They, too, patrol in vehicles and on skis. They even roam the streets of Madrid looking for escaped Jews and pilots. Their pockets are stuffed with Spanish pesetas and gold they use to pay off Spanish soldiers, policemen, and other opportunistic informants.

"Then of course there are the *bandidos*, who will cut your throat for a warm coat. If we are fortunate enough to avoid all of them, the Spanish army may arrest us for being in their country with no papers. They are always on the lookout for rebel organizations like my uncle's."

"This all sounds frightening," said Miriam.

"It will be a daunting task. But keep in mind, I have done this many times before. However never in the dead of winter," said Domingo.

"You said there were two ways to get us to Spain. What is the other way?" asked Uri.

"I smuggle you on the train," replied Domingo. "I work for the French railroad agency. I manage cargo. I'll put you in crates and load you up in a freight car. The French train only travels from Pau to the top. Then it unloads the passengers and freight at the Confranc rail station at the peak of the mountain. Everyone and everything gets transferred to the other side of the station and loaded on the Spanish train for the remainder of the journey down the southern face."

"We are going to be boarded up in crates?" complained Miriam Edelman.

"Miriam, we have had enough of you," said Ingrid. "This young man is putting his life at risk to try and save us. Stop complaining."

"But won't it be cold in the freight car?" asked Miriam.

Max said, "You may not be aware of this, madame, because you have been in this attic for so long. But there are Jews all over Europe being loaded up in cattle cars and shipped to work camps in Germany. Sometimes those trips take days, and they receive no food, water, or blankets. I have seen it with my own eyes."

"As have I," said Domingo.

"So, what happens to us at the top?" asked Joseph.

"After loading you up, I will climb in the freight car with you. When the train starts to move, I will let you out of the crates."

"Then what, Domingo?" said Joseph.

"The Confranc station at the peak of the mountain is heavily guarded by *Waffen-SS*. They perform thorough inspections of everyone and everything before it is transferred to the Spanish side of the station."

"So how do we get through the inspections?" asked Joseph.

Domingo said, "We don't. Shortly before the train arrives at the Confranc station, it travels through a long, dark tunnel. It slows considerably before entering. By the time it reaches the other side, it is at a crawl. We will jump into the darkness of the tunnel right before it exits."

"I am a forty-two-year-old woman," said Miriam. "I can't jump from a moving train. And we have three children with us. What about them?"

"We will be fine," said Alfred. "I will jump with Esther and Dreyfus. I will take care of them."

Joseph asked, "What happens after we jump?"

"When we land, everyone will roll to the outer edge of the tunnel and stay there until the train passes. We will then run to the other end of the tunnel, then to the woods and hope we are not spotted."

"When do we execute this plan?" asked Joseph.

"Tomorrow morning," replied Max. "Wilhelm is going to help us. I will bring your breakfast at 4:00 a.m. We will leave at 4:30 a.m. I will take you by truck to the warehouse at the rail yard where Domingo will put you in the crates and load you on the train."

Domingo said, "The sentries here in Pau also perform inspections. However, before they get a chance, Wilhelm is going to arrive and pull rank on them, sending them away to do something else. At that moment, I will use a hand truck to load you on the train."

"What if it doesn't work?" asked Miriam.

"Then we will all get shot, madame," replied Domingo.

As they stepped out of the hotel and into the early morning darkness, a light snow greeted them. Even though it was cold, the freedom of being out of the hotel attic after thirty months was exhilarating.

They hesitated when Max asked them to climb into the back of the truck.

They looked into the sky at the falling snow and enjoyed the cool breeze blowing across their faces. The three children opened their mouths and caught snowflakes on their tongues as they spun around and laughed, trying to momentarily forget that their lives would soon be in jeopardy.

"We must go now," demanded Max, as he helped them in.

Max drove through the streets of Pau, with the seven in the back taking turns looking through the two small windows in the door.

There were few people out at that early hour, but they noticed *Wehrmacht* soldiers guarding a small group of men dressed in what looked like gray pajamas. They were unloading a truck in front of an office building with a large red swastika flag draped over the front.

"Who are those men, Alfred?" asked Esther.

"I don't know."

"Why don't they have coats on? They must be terribly cold."

"And they look so thin," said Alfred. "They look like they are sick."

Max purposely found side roads and back alleys to limit the chance of a sudden inspection.

After several more turns, they approached the train station and noticed two sentries at the main gate.

He drove around to the back, hoping to find another entrance to the rail yard, but the only ones he found had locked gates or sentries like the main gate.

Max knew time was critical. There was only a small

window of opportunity to get to the warehouse so Domingo and Wilhelm could do what they needed to do.

Driving to another locked entrance, he turned off his lights and parked the truck. He reached under his seat and pulled out a set of bolt cutters.

We will get in here one way or the other.

He leaped out, looked around to confirm nobody was in sight, then with one quick squeeze had the chain cut and the gate opened.

As he drove through the warehouse section of the railyard, the large quantity of buildings surprised him.

Number eight is what Domingo said. There are no numbers on these buildings. How do I find number eight?

As his frustration mounted, he saw Domingo waving his hands.

"What took you so long?" shouted Domingo.

"You didn't tell me there would be sentries at the main gate," replied Max.

"There never have been before," said Domingo.

"Why do they have increased security? Hopefully not because of us," said Max.

"Don't worry about it. Let's just do what we need to do," said Domingo.

The seven passengers jumped out of the back with the help of Domingo and Max. Joseph held on to his suitcase as though it were a newborn baby.

"I'll take them from here, Max," said Domingo. "You go on. There is no reason for you to put your life at risk any more than you already have."

The seven approached Max.

"You saved our lives," said Ingrid. "We can never repay you and your father."

"You can thank us by getting safely to Spain," said Max.

"Then, when the war is over, come back and stay at the hotel. We will charge you full price."

Ingrid and Miriam embraced Max, and they each kissed him on his cheek.

"Be safe, young man," said Ingrid.

Once in the warehouse, Domingo sealed the four crates just as Wilhelm entered. The first crate contained Joseph and Dreyfus. The second Ingrid and Alfred. In the third Miriam and Esther, with Uri occupying the final crate by himself.

"It is chilly in here. Will they be okay in those crates?" asked Wilhelm.

"They are warmer than we are," replied Domingo.

"What time do the inspectors usually arrive?"

"Not until 0700 hours. We still have over an hour. What excuse are you going to give to order them away, Wilhelm?"

"Something that will scare the hell out of them. I will tell them that Heinrich Himmler is arriving in an hour and that *Sturmbannführer* Krieger has ordered them to guard gate nine."

"There is no gate nine."

"Even better. By the time they figure it out, you should have all four crates on board, and hopefully, the wheels of the train will be rolling up the mountain."

Wilhelm said, "I better get out of here and come back in an hour. It looks a little suspicious having a *Wehrmacht* major hanging around with a French warehouse worker."

"I agree. I'll see you in an hour."

Before leaving, Wilhelm leaned down to each crate and whispered, "Keep your faith. Everything will be fine."

The two *Waffen-SS* sentries inspecting the freight arrived twenty minutes later than usual. Wilhelm hid inconspicuously in the back of the warehouse. He watched them enter, then started the inspection.

Because of the language barrier, there was never any communication between Domingo and the sentries. They entered the warehouse, grabbed their pry bars, flashlights, and inspection mirrors, and got to work.

Wilhelm could see that it was routine for them. Without speaking, they began by first climbing into a truck at the opposite end of the warehouse, then to a series of crates on the floor. They took the pry bars, ripped off the tops, and glanced at the contents, before replacing the tops.

When they were close to the seven stowaways, Wilhelm emerged from behind a truck and shouted, "You two. Come here."

They stared at him with puzzled looks, then walked in his direction.

"Yes, Major," asked one of the sentries.

"I have received orders from *Sturmbannführer* Krieger to send you to guard gate nine. Heinrich Himmler will arrive here at noon. Let no one in, do you understand?"

One of the *SS* sentries looked at Wilhelm and said, "Major, we have been instructed by *Sturmbannführer* Krieger to inspect these crates before they are loaded on the train. Do you mind if I call *Sturmbannführer* Krieger to confirm these orders, Major?"

"Are you questioning my authority, Sergeant?"

"No, Major. I want clarification why our orders have been changed."

"That will be fine, Sergeant. There is a telephone on

that wall. We will call *Sturmbannführer* Krieger together. After he confirms he has indeed instructed you to guard gate nine, I will tell him how insubordinate you have been, and recommend that you get transferred to the eastern front. It is my understanding they are looking for soldiers to replace the ones who are freezing to death in the brutal Russian winter."

"That won't be necessary, Major. We will go to gate nine right now," said the sergeant. "Come on, Schutze, let's go find gate nine."

After the confrontation, the two sentries grabbed their weapons, climbed back into their *Kübelwagen*, and drove off.

Domingo, not understanding the discussion, said to Wilhelm in French, "That sounded more challenging than you had expected."

"Yes, it was. Load them up. I'll stay here and watch your back. It may not be long before they return."

The sun was up by the time Domingo had the four crates placed on the loading platform. He purposely positioned them between other crates to block the seven stowaways from the crisp wind, and to make them less noticeable.

Wilhelm hid behind the sliding door of the warehouse and watched as Domingo slid the door of the freight car open and loaded the containers.

SS guards were checking the documents of everyone before they entered the passenger cars. They were diligent. Besides looking closely at the papers, they were also asking questions, looking for any hint of something being out of place, like a British accent.

Because Domingo purposely intermingled the Jews with

the other crates, he had lost track of which ones held the stowaways. Using the hand truck, he kept loading the crates one by one, eventually getting all of them on the freight car.

At that moment, *Sturmbannführer* Krieger stepped on board the loading dock with an *SS* sentry and two men who appeared to be Jewish prisoners dressed in gray work suits. He approached Domingo and said something to him, but Wilhelm couldn't make out what it was. Domingo looked confused, since Krieger was barking out orders in German.

Krieger pointed to one of the crates and ordered Domingo to remove it from the freight car. He then ordered the two Jewish prisoners and the sentry in to replace it, while grabbing Domingo and pulling him out before closing the door.

Domingo stood on the dock, watching the *Sturmbannführer* leave the platform. He then knelt, knocked on the crate, and spoke, trying to hear if anyone was in it.

Approaching Domingo on the dock, Wilhelm asked, "Is there anyone in there, Domingo?"

As the steam from the train intensified and the whistle on the engine blew to indicate it was time for final boarding, Domingo said, "Yes, Uri is in there."

"We need to get both you and him back in that car," said Wilhelm.

"What about the sentry?" asked Domingo.

Without hesitating, Wilhelm opened the door and addressed the guard. "You are not needed in the railcar, *Oberschütze*. Get out now."

"I received my orders from *Sturmbannführer* Krieger, Major. If you want me to leave, take it up with him."

Wilhelm stepped into the freight car so others on the platform couldn't see him. He then pulled his Luger from its

The Heroes of Sainte-Mère Église

holster and pointed it in the *Oberschütze's* face and said, "Get out of this freight car now, but leave your Mauser."

The sentry set his rifle down as instructed and stepped out onto the platform.

Wilhelm switched back to French and said, "Domingo, load Uri back on the train." Then turning to the two prisoners, he added, "You stay here with us. You will be safer."

The whistle blew two more times, and the train rolled. Wilhelm pulled the door shut as the train pulled away, leaving the sentry on the dock by himself.

They felt the vibration of the accelerating train as Domingo grabbed a pry bar and ripped open the tops of the crates. One by one, the two families appeared.

"Wilhelm, why are you here?" asked Ingrid. "I didn't know you were coming with us."

"Until a few moments ago, Mrs. Shapiro, neither did I. In just a split second my life just changed forever."

"He saved your lives," said Domingo. "Had it not been for Wilhelm, there would be an *SS* soldier on this train, and you would be discovered and arrested."

"Actually, I probably just saved my own life," replied Wilhelm. "I was scheduled to be transferred to the Russian front in a few days. If I am going to die, I would rather die trying to free all of you than freezing to death for Hitler."

One of the prisoners spoke up and asked, "What is going on here?"

Joseph explained their plan to escape over the Pyrénées Mountains and into Spain.

"You are welcome to join us," added Domingo. "Otherwise, who knows what your fate will be at the Canfranc station."

"I am sick," said the other prisoner. "I will never make it through these mountains."

"You must try," said Ingrid. "You mustn't give up hope now that you are free."

"I will try," he said. "But I don't want to hold you up. I have accepted that death is coming soon."

"Do you have any food?" asked the first prisoner. "We haven't eaten in days. If he eats something or just drinks water, he may have enough strength."

They had stuffed their pockets and knapsacks with bread, dried beef, and cheese that Max had given them. They shared it with the two prisoners, who savored every bite as though it was a royal feast.

"What are your names?" asked Wilhelm.

"My name is Otto. I don't know his name," said the healthiest of the two as he pointed to the other.

"My name is Chayim."

"There will be *SS* and *Wehrmacht* waiting for us at the top," said Wilhelm. "We may need to alter our plans, Domingo. You know this mountain. Where do you think we should jump?"

"At Urdos. The track makes a sharp curve there. The engineer will need to slow the train to avoid derailment. That will give us the best opportunity to jump safely. Unfortunately, it will add another two hours to our journey. If we don't show up in a reasonable time, our escort may leave without us."

"How much longer before we jump?" asked Uri.

"An hour," replied Domingo.

"How long is the entire journey?" asked Joseph.

"With this many people and traveling from Urdos, it will take over six hours."

"Six hours in the snow?" asked Miriam.

The group looked toward the two prisoners. There was the unspoken consensus. They would never make it.

Urdos, France

Domingo slid the door open. The freezing air stung their faces as it blew into the freight car.

Wilhelm placed his shoulder through the leather strap of the Mauser before inching his to the edge.

"The train will begin to slow," shouted Domingo.

Right on cue, they felt a jerking sensation, making it difficult to keep their balance. It continued to decelerate as the engineer applied the squealing brakes.

Domingo shouted, "Go!"

Without hesitation they went—First Wilhelm and then Uri, followed by the children and their mothers. Behind them were the two prisoners, Otto and Chayim. Joseph leaped ahead of Domingo, who jumped last.

The deep snow welcomed them as it softened their landing.

After rolling and rising to his feet, Wilhelm glanced back at the train and said to Domingo, "What if they saw us?"

"We don't have time to worry about it. Let's get moving."

Pau, France

Salvador was in the lobby sweeping, and Max was in the café serving cognac to a table of *Wehrmacht* officers.

"Would you like another glass, *monsieur*?" asked Max.

"*Oui*."

As he turned for the bar, an *SS* staff car and lorry stopped in front of the café. An *SS Hauptsturmführer* climbed out of the staff car, and six soldiers leaped from the lorry. Three went to Max in the café, and the others cut though the passageway to Salvador in the hotel lobby.

They were both arrested.

Shoving Salvador against the wall, the *Hauptsturmführer* said, "Where is Major Zeigler's room?"

"No! Leave him alone," shouted Max. "I'll show you."

Once in the room, Max watched as the officer ordered two *SS* soldiers to tear the room apart. They first opened drawers and then the closet, throwing the major's belongings everywhere. After they had flipped the mattress, they went to each room of the hotel and repeated the process.

The *Hauptsturmführer* then found the attic door and climbed the stairs.

Max and Salvador stood motionless on the third floor. They watched and listened as their lives were demolished in a matter of moments.

Returning from the attic were the heavy boots of the *Hauptsturmführer* coming down the stairs.

When the attic door opened, he addressed Max. "I find it odd you would rent space in your attic when your hotel has available rooms. Why don't you tell me about your guests and what Major Zeigler knows about them?"

Pyrénées Mountains
Northern Face

"Step where I step," shouted Domingo as he forced his feet into the knee-deep snow. "My footprints will keep you from losing your balance and falling down the mountain."

It had been five hours since they'd jumped from the train. The mountain wind was cutting, and their lungs burned from breathing the frigid air. The late afternoon sun and their physical exertion offered protection from hypothermia.

"Can we rest again, Domingo?" asked Miriam.

"Once we get to the tree line we can rest. Until then, we must keep moving. It isn't good to be in the open. The wind will cause frostbite, and the *Luftwaffe* search these mountains. If they spot us, a patrol will be sent after us."

Eight-year-old Dreyfus was struggling to keep up. Joseph stayed with him as the others advanced.

"You are doing great, son. I'm proud of you."

"I'm tired, Papa. And I'm hungry. When can we stop?"

"We are just about there, Dreyfus. Do you see those big trees at the top? Once we reach them, we will rest."

When they arrived, the canopy of the thick forest offered shelter. Moans were heard as their exhausted bodies sat down in the soft undergrowth. They ate bread and cheese and fed themselves handfuls of snow to quench their thirst.

Alfred and Esther cuddled together next to a large tree. After watching Otto and Chayim lay down in the underbrush, they gathered leaves and twigs and covered the two men to help them stay warm.

The air turned so cold that even those who had gloves

had numb fingers. The condition of their feet was worse. Domingo and Wilhelm were the only two with boots. The rest of the group had leather shoes that were soaking wet and frozen.

Wilhelm and Domingo had walked away for several minutes, then returned with branches of various sizes.

Domingo said, "When we continue, use these as walking sticks. The mountain will soon get steeper and they will help you pull yourself up."

"Can we rest a little longer?" asked Ingrid.

"No, I'm sorry. We must get going. Your guide to Spain is waiting on us. We have only a few more hours of daylight. As cold as it is now, it will be twenty degrees colder when the sun sets. The rest of the journey will be through the forest. We won't have the warm sun shining on us, but the snow won't be as deep."

Even though it was bitter cold, everyone wanted to stay and sleep.

"We will freeze to death if we spend the night here," said Wilhelm.

Everyone stood except Otto and Chayim.

Domingo walked over to where they were laying, knelt and shook them. Standing and turning to the group, he said, "They're dead—both of them."

Pau, France

It was a beautiful day. The sun was bright, and the buildings around the courtyard blocked the cool winter wind.

Though the shortages of life's necessities were worsening, the people of Pau still liked to window-shop for what little was available. It gave them a sense of normalcy.

The peace they enjoyed was abruptly interrupted by the roaring engine of a lorry racing around the corner.

The squealing brakes brought it to stop in the center of the roundabout, and four *Wehrmacht* soldiers leaped from the back.

They grabbed two prisoners, each with their hands tied in front of them.

After shoving them against the only wall without a storefront window, the four soldiers positioned themselves twenty meters away.

"Prepare to fire," shouted the *SS Hauptsturmführer*.

"We did the right thing, Max."

"I know we did, Papa. I love you."

"I love you too, Max."

"Fire!"

Astun, Spain

The final and the most dangerous part of the journey was ahead. Dusk settled and the evening air was colder than any of them had ever experienced.

Domingo had led more groups than he could remember through this passage. But those were in the spring or summer. Even the summers were cold at these altitudes, but the Pyrénées in the winter were dangerously cold.

"Mama, I can't feel my feet," said Dreyfus.

"I know, honey," said Ingrid. "We are almost there. Isn't that right, Domingo?"

"We are at the final part of the journey," Domingo said

as he held his hand up, instructing the group to stop. "I need everyone to listen carefully."

Pointing up a steep incline, he said, "The outpost is on the other side of that slope. As you can see, the rock facing goes straight up, so we can't travel that way. Our path will be a ledge that bends around the top. It is narrow in two spots, but most of it is wide enough for two people to pass at the same time.

"We can only rest briefly. We need what little daylight we have left to see where we are stepping."

"I'm afraid of heights," said Miriam.

"Don't look down, and remember that on the other side of the ledge is a warm cabin," said Domingo.

"Will there be a fire?" asked Uri

Domingo said, "Once the sun goes down, but not while we have daylight. A fire generates smoke, and smoke informs bad people that we are up here."

"Do you mean Germans?" asked Joseph.

"The cabin is in Spain, so although the *Wehrmacht* and the *Waffen-SS* are not likely to cross over from France, *Gestapo* agents are a possibility. But I'm more concerned with the *bandidos* who kill for fun and rob their victims."

"Will your Spanish contact be at the cabin?" asked Joseph.

"I hope so," said Domingo. "But sometimes they have been two days late, and other times they didn't show up at all. There is political unrest in Spain, and helping refugees is not always a priority. If he isn't there, I will escort you down the other side myself."

After resting, they continued the journey, keeping the same single file formation they had been in since leaving the train. After twenty minutes, the frigid wind increased. The trees thinned, and before them was a drop-off that took

The Heroes of Sainte-Mère Église

their breath away. The valley below was deep, and the rocks were jagged. To the right, their path continued around the cliff. The narrow ledge above the massive drop came into view.

"Oh God, no—I can't cross here," cried Miriam. "Isn't there another way?"

"If there was a better way, we would take it," said Domingo.

"You have no choice, Miriam," said Uri. "Just remember, the outpost is not far from the other side of the ledge. Once there, we can rest for the night, then down into Spain we go."

The setting sun created an orange sky over the valley.

"Under different circumstances, this view would be something to celebrate," said Wilhelm.

With Domingo leading the way, they continued in the single file formation. Uri was behind Domingo, followed by Miriam, who kept reminding herself not to look down.

The farther they went out on the ledge, the harder the wind blew. The ledge was still wide enough for two people. Domingo took small, choppy steps so everyone could keep up. Alfred followed Esther, then Ingrid, Dreyfus, and Joseph, with Wilhelm in the back. Joseph carried his suitcase, Wilhelm the Mauser.

Below them was a six hundred-meter drop.

"It will soon narrow," shouted Domingo through the whistling wind.

Fourteen steps later, the ledge tapered inward, and their shoulders were forced against the mountain facing.

Miriam stopped. "I can't do this," she shouted, her voice barely loud enough to be heard through the wind.

"Yes, you can, Miriam," said Uri. "I am right here with you. Esther is behind you. We are both counting on you to continue. You must be strong. We are almost there."

"You can do it, Mama," shouted Esther.

Miriam was proud to hear how brave her fifteen-year-old daughter was and suddenly felt ashamed of her own fear.

"I will make it," Miriam shouted.

At its most narrow point, they pressed their backs against the mountain face.

Domingo continued his small steps. "Just a few more meters. Once we are around this bend it will widen, then up a short slope, and we will be back in the trees."

Step after step, not looking down and feeling the strong, cold wind across their faces, they turned the last bend of the narrow trail. One by one, they pulled each other up into the forest with Wilhelm being the last.

Once there, they embraced in celebration. The forest was dark, but they were once again on a solid footing.

"How much farther, Domingo?" asked Joseph.

"Just look through those trees."

The sparse daylight that remained showed a silhouette of a little cabin through the pathway.

"It will be so nice to sleep," said Ingrid

They made their way down the curvy path. As they glanced through the last patch of trees, they could see the cabin was pitch dark inside, but there was a car parked in front. It was a black Mercedes.

"Is that our ride to Spain?" asked Ingrid. "Will we all fit in that car? Did the guide not know how many of us there were?"

Domingo held his hand up, "Stop, and be silent."

Wilhelm made his way to the front and stood alongside Domingo. "Where the hell did that come from?"

The Heroes of Sainte-Mère Église

"What is it?" asked Joseph.

"It is a German staff car," replied Wilhelm.

Joseph said, "I thought you said the German military wouldn't be up here, Domingo. You said the Spanish government didn't want them here."

Domingo replied, "Sometimes they get arrogant and do what they want. Other times, they just get lost."

"Could they be *Gestapo*?" asked Joseph.

"I don't think so," said Domingo. "That car has Nazi written all over it. The *Gestapo* keeps a low profile in Spain."

"What are we going to do?" asked Miriam "We need that cabin tonight. It has been a long day trekking up this mountain. We are all exhausted. There are three children with us. If we sleep out here, we will freeze to death like Otto and Chayim."

Uri raised his voice and pointed his finger at Domingo. "Where is the escort you said would be here? I didn't seal my family up in crates, ask them to leap from a moving train, march through deep snow, and balance on a four-meter-wide ledge so they could freeze to death in this forest."

"Don't overreact, Uri," said Joseph. "We need to stay calm and think."

"Think about what, Joseph? Turning blue? At least the mountain lions can feast on our bodies when we thaw in the spring."

"You are frightening the children, Uri," said Ingrid.

"Stop this talk of defeat," demanded Wilhelm. "You forget I wear the uniform of a major in the German army. I'll approach them and find out who they are and how long they will be here."

After handing the Mauser to Domingo, Wilhelm walked toward the cabin. His steps were cautious as he tried not to make any more noise than necessary. Watching his surroundings for clues of danger, he noticed multiple tire tracks in the snow.

He pressed his ear against the side of the cabin but heard nothing. Stepping around to the front door, he looked toward his companions standing in the woods, took a deep breath, and knocked. There was no answer, so he knocked louder. Still no answer.

Wilhelm pulled his Luger from the holster, grabbed the doorknob, and entered the cabin.

"What could be happening in there?" asked Uri.

"He is probably talking to them," replied Domingo.

"What could he possibly do?" asked Ingrid. "If there are two or three Germans in there, he can't just throw them out."

"What if they arrested him? They will be out here for all of us soon," said Miriam.

Wilhelm appeared from the front door of the cabin and ran over to the group and said, "I don't know what happened before we arrived, but there are two dead bodies in there. A *Wehrmacht Oberst* and what I guess to be his mistress. They are both tied to chairs, have been savagely beaten, and have bullet holes in their heads."

Miriam gasped.

"Who would have done that?" asked Joseph.

"There are three possibilities," replied Domingo. "It could have been *bandidos*, Spanish soldiers, or antifascist rebels. Maybe even the same rebels who are supposed to escort us down the mountain."

"You mean your uncle's men?" asked Joseph.

The Heroes of Sainte-Mère Église

"Yes, my uncle's men. These mountains are dangerous. Not just because of the weather, but also because it is lawless. The people here make their own laws and trust nobody."

"Does this mean we can't go in and get warm?" asked Esther.

"No, Esther," Wilhelm replied. "You will be in there sleeping peacefully soon, I promise. Just wait a little longer."

Looking at Ingrid he said, "Go, take the children and sit between those two boulders. They will protect you from the cold wind. Once we have finished cleaning the cabin, we'll come get you."

"Come on, children. Those large rocks will keep us warm," said Ingrid.

The men walked to the cabin, with Wilhelm leading the way. Once in, the others were disgusted at the sight of the blood and bodies.

The dead *Oberst* was in his fifties. His coat and boots were missing, and Wilhelm searched his shirt and pants pockets and found nothing. No papers or money, and both bodies were void of any jewelry. They also couldn't find the keys to the Mercedes. The female was in her thirties. She wore a red wool dress, and unlike the *Obrest's* boots, her leather shoes were still on.

Three storage crates had been pulled out from under the beds. The lids were open, and they were empty.

"Those contained food and blankets," said Domingo. "I was counting on those to get us through the remainder of the journey."

Wilhelm pointed to the corner. "I know they are covered in dried blood, but at least we have those blankets over there," he said.

"Why didn't they take the car?" asked Joseph.

"Because the Spanish army has patrols everywhere," Domingo said. "The car is a target."

The four men took the two corpses to the rear of the cabin and dragged them into the woods.

Uri said, "It is pitch black out here. This is creepy walking through these woods carrying these two bodies. I can't even see where we are stepping."

Once they were out of sight of the cabin, they laid the bodies down and covered them in leaves and other debris.

As the others turned to walk back to the cabin, Domingo said, "I'll be right there. I need to piss."

Out of respect for the dead, he strolled several meters away from the bodies. He found a patch of tall bushes and relieved himself. On his return trip to the cabin, he stumbled over what he thought was a log. Before standing, he found a bare foot.

We didn't stash the bodies here.

Removing the leaves covering the body, even in the darkness, he recognized the victim as someone he had met here before.

Time for a change of plans.

Astune, Spain

Entering the cabin, the women and children noticed it had a foul odor, but nobody complained, not even Miriam Edelman. Without cleaning supplies, there was little the men could do to remove the bloodstains. Much of it had been absorbed into the wood floors and walls.

"We are sorry for the blood. But at least the bodies are gone," said Wilhelm.

The Heroes of Sainte-Mère Église

There was a fireplace and plenty of dry wood in the corner, and although the mental image of a roaring blaze was on everyone's mind, they remembered Domingo's warning about the smoke giving away their position.

There were just two beds on either side of the small cabin. They were built with wooden planks, and slightly larger than a cot. Each had a mattress stuffed with straw.

"Fortunately, in these temperatures, bed bugs would never survive," joked Uri.

The families climbed into their separate beds and cuddled closely with each father wrapping his arm around them to keep them warm. They were asleep in moments. Wilhelm and Domingo covered them with several of the blood-stained blankets and then laid the remaining blankets on the floor for themselves.

"Is it dark enough to start a fire, Domingo?" asked Wilhelm.

"We should be safe to build one now, but we need to have it extinguished long before sunrise."

Wilhelm said, "I'll get one started and take the first watch. You deserve a rest, Domingo." He then asked, "Do you think our escort will ever arrive?"

Sitting on a blanket with his back to the wall, Domingo pulled some dried beef, cheese, and a pack of cigarettes from his knapsack. "I'm afraid we are on our own, my friend. Our guide is lying in the woods next to the Nazi and his girlfriend."

Chapter Forty-Nine

JANUARY 10, 1943

Astun, Spain

Alfred was the first to awaken. He rolled out from under his father's warm coat and walked across the room to check on Esther and her family.

He stood for a moment and stared at Esther's face. It was exposed above her father's shoulder as he lay on top of her to keep her warm. She looked beautiful.

There was nothing he wanted more than to take Esther away from all of this and put her someplace safe. He would even come back and endure all this by himself, if he had to, as long as she was protected.

Now I know how Jean-Pierre felt about Angélique Lapierre.

His mind wandered to his old friend from Sainte-Mère-Église. To their fun times together, and to the day they first met at the schoolyard, when Jean-Pierre saved him from Maurice Fuquay.

I hope you are well, my friend. One day, I will return to Sainte-Mère-Église.

A sound in front of the cabin shook him from his daydream. He stepped out of the front door to see Domingo and Wilhelm trying to start the car.

"Good morning, Alfred," said Wilhelm, who was behind the wheel with the door open. Domingo was laying under the engine with his legs exposed.

"Are we going to be riding in this car?" asked Alfred.

"If we can get it started," said Wilhelm. "We can't find the keys, but there are ways around such things if you have a brilliant mechanic like Domingo working on a solution."

"Don't get the boy's hopes up," shouted Domingo from underneath the car. "If I were so brilliant I would be living on a tropical island right now, away from Nazis and cold weather."

After banging his fingers and spewing a series of profanities, he added, "If I only had tools. Trying to jump the ignition wires with my bare hands and a knife is not working."

"Maybe there are tools in the trunk," said Alfred. "I once saw my friend Jean-Pierre's papa get into a car trunk by removing the back seat."

As he shifted from the front seat to the back, Wilhelm said, "Alfred, you are officially the brains of the outfit. Let's see what is back here."

Wilhelm and Domingo each put the blades of their knife between the back of the seat and the window panel. After two tugs, the seat came loose and they exposed the trunk.

Inside was a treasure they didn't expect.

Wilhelm climbed in and shouted, "We have an early Christmas. There is wine, bread, cheese, a little dried beef, and what appears to be a fully cooked ham."

"What about tools?" asked Domingo.

After feeling around and finding a large canvas bag, Wilhelm handed it to Domingo.

"Everything we could possibly need is in here," said Domingo.

Wilhelm entered the cabin to find both families waking up. He shared the good news with them as he laid the food out on a blanket.

Joseph asked, "Where did that come from?"

"The trunk of the car," said Wilhelm. "Whoever was here never bothered to check it."

As Wilhelm used his bayonet to slice the nearly frozen ham, Joseph said, "You know we can't eat that, don't you, Wilhelm? We are Jews."

"I'm sorry, Joseph. I didn't think. We have plenty of bread, cheese, and a little dried beef. You can eat that, can't you?" asked Wilhelm.

"Yes, of course," he replied

"Children, you eat first. Then Miriam and Ingrid," said Joseph. "If there is any left, Uri and I will eat. Wilhelm, you and Domingo get that whole ham to yourselves."

"I want ham, too," said Ingrid.

"No, Mama," said Alfred.

Angrily raising her voice, she said, "We left Sainte-Mère-Église over two years ago. We have been hungry the entire time. We have lost so much weight our clothes no longer fit. What does God expect of us?" Waving her finger at Joseph, Uri, and Miriam, she asked, "Does God expect our children to starve because of a two thousand-year-old passage in the Torah? I say he does not. If he does, he is not a god I want to worship."

After Ingrid's outburst, the room remained silent. Then Joseph broke the silence. "My family will take part in your feast of ham, Wilhelm."

"As will mine," said Uri. "Esther, you go first. It is okay."

The sun had been up for two hours. Behind the steering wheel, Wilhelm drove them away from the cabin. Domingo was in the passenger seat, the Mauser propped between his legs. In the middle, Alfred's legs hung over the bench seat, his feet just above the floorboard. The parents of the two families were in the back, with Dreyfus and Esther sitting on their parents' lap.

"Are we safe traveling in this car, Domingo?" asked Joseph. "I thought you said whoever murdered the *Oberst* and his mistress left it because it is a target."

"It is a target," replied Domingo. "But the alternative is to walk down the mountain. That would take days in the same frigid temperatures we experienced on the way up here."

"I see your point," said Joseph.

"How much petrol do we have, Wilhelm?" asked Domingo.

"Half a tank," said Wilhelm.

"That should get us to Jaca," said Domingo. "The remainder of the journey, our threat will be from *Gestapo* agents, Spanish soldiers, *bandidos* and the *Falange Españolas*."

"Who the hell are they?" asked Wilhelm.

"They are a rebel wing of Franco's Fascist movement who roam this side of the mountain pass. They are nothing but a pack of thieves who rob and extort money from refugees."

Miriam asked, "Is there anyone left in this world we don't have to worry about? Everyone either wants to rob us, kill us, or both."

The passengers remained quiet for the next hour. The children and Miriam had fallen asleep. The warm car offered comfort they were not accustomed to.

"We are about to clear the forest canopy," said Domingo. "Then we will be out in the open for all the world to see."

There was a thick, low cloud cover. The type they knew was waiting to unload snow.

Wilhelm drove slowly. The roads were steep, narrow and unpaved. A string of hairpin turns overlooking the valleys below made a potential mistake deadly.

They had traveled for an hour when Dreyfus said, "I need to pee."

"I could stand a little relief myself," said Wilhelm, who then found a safe place to pull over.

Ingrid, Miriam, and Esther walked into the woods at the side of the road. The men, along with Dreyfus and Alfred, urinated at the edge of the road, enjoying the view of the valley below.

After they returned to the car, Domingo lit a cigarette. "What are your plans, Wilhelm? You can't go back to Germany anytime soon."

"I have been thinking about that. My biggest concern is for my mother, father, and sister. My family owns a leather goods shop in Berlin. It won't be long, and word will spread that I am a deserter. My family will be disgraced, and nobody will do business with them. It will ruin them. They won't understand, and I can't contact them to explain."

Ingrid approached Wilhelm. "Your parents are well respected in Berlin. They have many friends who won't abandon them."

"It has been a long time since you left Berlin, Mrs. Shapiro. It isn't the same. The Nazis terrify everyone.

Nobody goes against them or wants to be associated with anyone who does. My family will be guilty because I am guilty, and anyone who is friends with my family will be guilty for the same reason."

"One day they will know what you did. They will be proud of you for risking your life to save ours."

Before Wilhelm could respond, Domingo shouted, "We have company."

Climbing the hairpin road, a canvas-covered troop carrier trudged its way up the hill.

Joseph shouted, "Alfred, take the ladies and Dreyfus into the woods and hide there. We will deal with whoever this is. Here, take my suitcase with you."

"Yes, Papa."

Alfred grabbed Esther's hand and led her, his mother, Miriam, and Dreyfus into the woods.

As the lorry made its way up the steep, winding incline, Wilhelm handed Domingo his Luger. He then stepped behind the Mercedes with the Mauser and crouched down so he could conceal the uniform.

With Domingo in the front, the four men watched the truck approach them and stop.

Six men leaped from the rear. The driver and the passenger climbed down from the cab. The massive passenger struggled on his way to the ground. He was a towering figure, and his thick waist was unusual during these times of limited food. He appeared to be in his fifties and had a bushy black beard to match the hair on his head.

The men with him were well armed. Those from the back carried bolt-action rifles. The two from the cab were holstering handguns. The driver carried an Eibar and the passenger a semiautomatic Spanish Astra.

"Uncle Marcos!" shouted Domingo.

"Domingo?" said the big man, speaking in broken French. "What are you doing this far into Spain? You should be well back down the north face by now."

"No, Uncle. The man you sent to meet us at the cabin is dead. Along with a *Wehrmacht Oberst* and his mistress."

"Dead? How did that happen?"

"Someone murdered them. Whoever did it was brutal."

"It was Franco's *Falanges*," said Marcos. "They have grown weary of us. We are an irritant, and they look for our hideouts. When they find one, they don't care who is there—they just want to send a message. I'm sure they viewed the fact that one of their victims was a Nazi as an added bonus."

Joseph motioned for Alfred to bring the others out of the woods.

Marcos focused on Wilhelm. "Where did you get this car, and why is there a *Wehrmacht* officer with you? Shouldn't he be standing in front of you with a gun in his back?"

"This is Major Wilhelm Ziegler, Uncle. He is one of us. He helped me get these good people out of France," said Domingo as he pointed to the others who were approaching from their hiding place. "Now he is on the run with them."

"Are you sure we can trust him, Domingo?"

"He hid these two Jewish families in a hotel for over two years. They would have been arrested at the train station had he not intervened. I trust him like a brother."

Walking around the Mercedes, Marcos looked Wilhelm up and down and then spit on the ground. "A major, are you?"

"Yes, sir."

"You are lucky. I have sharpshooters positioned all throughout this part of the mountain. If they would have seen you dressed in that fascist costume, they would have put a bullet in your head."

Turning to Domingo, he said, "We need to hide this Nazi car. Although I am glad you are alive, I am disappointed in my men for letting you get this close to our safehouse."

Joseph looked up at the thick clouds as the snow fell. "Can you get us someplace safe?"

With a deep chuckle, Marcos said, "You are with me, *señor*. In these mountains, there is no safer place."

Turning to Domingo, he said, "Follow us. My snipers won't shoot you if you stay close behind me. But if you fall back too far, I can't make you any promises. We better get going—those clouds are about to bury us in snow."

Southern Face
Pyrénées Mountains

Wilhelm followed Uncle Marcos's lorry back up the spiraling road. After several kilometers, they turned onto a narrow path that was barely visible from the main road. The forest was thick, and the tree branches scraped the side of the truck as it bounced along the bumpy trail.

"Do you know where they are taking us, Domingo?" asked Wilhelm.

"No. I have never been on this road. I haven't been on this side of the mountain since I was a small boy. My job has been to take people to the top and leave them at the outpost."

They traveled over the snow-covered passage for what seemed like an eternity. The path was rough, and at times it appeared to go straight up before leveling off and then sloping down at an equally sharp angle.

The snowfall increased, and when they were away from the trees, there was a screen of white.

"I hope we get there soon," said Miriam. "We can barely see Uncle Marcos."

After a few more turns, a large cabin appeared in the distance. It stood two stories tall, situated under a canopy of massive trees which made it impossible to see from an airplane. The dirt road approaching the house had sandbags stacked high on each side, with armed guards positioned behind them.

Once past the sentries, a better view emerged of the cabin. Its enormity made it appear out of place in the rugged environment. It was positioned in the center of several single-story structures that could best be described as barracks. In the back was a barn and a series of chicken coops.

Around the perimeter of the entire facility were dozens of armed guards with submachine guns.

Joseph said to Domingo, "I see what your Uncle Marcos said about being safe with him. This isn't an outpost—it is a military compound."

As the vehicles came to a stop, the armed men in the lorry leaped out as they had before, with Marcos walking back to the Mercedes. He made it a point to approach Wilhelm's side first so that his men could see that the German uniform was no threat.

"Follow me into the main cabin. You will be fed and shown your living quarters," said Marcos.

As they exited the Mercedes, they noticed the temperature had dropped considerably.

Inside the main cabin was a flurry of activity. The first

floor was a large open area. In the center was a long, wooden dining table with bench seats running the length of both sides, and a chair at each end.

Eating at the table were a group of people of different ages and in various forms of dress. They were old, young, and in between. There was even an infant. Some were dressed in regular street clothes. Those who had coats were wearing them. It was still too light outside to burn the immense fireplace in the corner.

There were also people dressed in the gray uniforms, like Otto and Chayim.

"They escaped from the Germans and made their way here," said Marcos.

"They were brought here by guides," said Domingo. "Guides like me. There are four of us. There were more, but some have been caught and executed."

"You are sharing too much information, Domingo," said Marcos. "Always remember, nobody should know more than they need."

"I'm sorry, Uncle Marcos. Sometimes I forget."

While playfully putting Domingo in a headlock to let him know he was forgiven, Marcos said to the others, "After dinner, you will be shown to your cabins. We have several outbuildings around the perimeter of our compound that are empty. There are three available for you."

"This is a small city," said Wilhelm.

"No, Major, this is a small country," replied Marcos. "We answer to nobody, have no government, pay no taxes, and are completely self-sustaining. We believe in the Marxist principle of 'From each according to his ability, to each according to his need.'"

"I guess that works for a group this size," said Joseph.

"It will work for any size. It is working in Russia, isn't it?" said Marcos.

"People are starving in Russia," said Joseph.

"That is coming from a man who is about to eat our food because he has none for himself."

Ingrid said to Marcos, "Sir, we appreciate your generosity. Forgive my husband for his desire to challenge your political views while we are your guests."

Without responding to Ingrid, Marcos climbed the stairs until he reached the top. He then turned and yelled to the women serving those at the table, "Be certain that our guests eat. Provide them with a feast."

Chapter Fifty

JANUARY 11, 1943

**Uncle Marcos's Compound
Southern Face
Pyrénées Mountains**

The Shapiros and Edelmans each had their own cabin. Wilhelm, who shared his with Domingo, woke before the others. The wood-burning stove in the center of their room had lost its flame during the night, leaving a crisp chill in the air.

Wilhelm made his way to the main cabin, hoping to find breakfast. As he entered the door, he paused. Sitting around the table were two RAF airmen. The first whispered something to the second, and they stood to face Wilhelm.

They don't appear to be fans of my Wehrmacht uniform.

After a brief stare-down, they stepped toward him, fists clenched.

Should I stand my ground or return to the cabin and hope they don't follow me?

"Let's get that bloody Jerry bastard," shouted the first one.

With momentum on their side, they tackled Wilhelm with enough force to drive him out of the door he just entered.

The three scrambled in the dirt, punches thrown from all directions, with Wilhelm getting the worst of it.

"Get off of him!" shouted Domingo.

Both men flew off of Wilhelm as Domingo sent them sailing with a running body slam.

The pilots stood up to go after Domingo, but abruptly stopped when Marcos stepped out of the main cabin.

In a booming voice, he shouted in French, "That is a fine way to treat your future traveling companions."

Squadron Leader Virgil Pierpoint, and Flight Lieutenant Kingsley Dalton, who only spoke English, didn't understand Marcos, but they sensed it was best to end the skirmish.

Chapter Fifty-One

MAY 19, 1943

Above the English Channel

"Approaching enemy territory," was the alert from the pilot in the lead B-24 bomber.

This was a radio call that U.S. Army Air Corps Captain Jim Ewens had heard more times than he could remember. Today was his twenty-fifth birthday, and the young redhead from Hartford Connecticut was spending it flying his eighteenth escort mission. A skilled P-51 pilot, who already had seven reported kills, Ewens never feared a fight in the air or on the ground, even though he stood slightly shorter than the average man.

He liked to lie behind the formation of B-24s, knowing the ME-109s would swoop down from above and take out the bombers highest in the formation. As they focused on their target, he would pounce.

The sun was high, and the cloud cover was moderate. This was both a blessing and a curse. Clouds were a blessing for the fighter planes because they provided cover from the enemy, but a curse for the bombers because their view of their targets was obstructed.

Glancing down, Captain Ewens could see the coast of France.

Their target was an airfield in Nantes which was further into the country than he had ever flown.

Over the radio, a crew member of one of the B-24's shouted, "Enemy—six o'clock high!"

"I see him," shouted his tail gunner.

Ewens looked up to see two ME-109s diving on the bombers. He opened his throttle and took off for the one in the rear.

You will be my eighth kill, and a birthday present to myself, you unlucky Kraut bastard.

He first went high and then dove hard left, putting himself directly behind both planes as they zeroed in on the group of B-24s.

Ewens positioned himself behind the second plane. He opened fire, missing with the first barrage, then repositioned himself and fired again, hitting the fuel cell in the right wing, causing it to explode and separate from the fuselage. Ewens watched as the remainder of the plane burst into flames and drop from the sky and into the English Channel. He never saw the pilot's chute.

One down, one to go.

The other ME-109 was not in sight. Ewens was a student of his craft. When he'd arrived in England, he had queried the best British pilots he could find. He found those who had racked up the most kills and flight hours against the *Luftwaffe*.

He remembered them saying, *They work in teams of two. When you are focusing on one, the other trails behind you to take you out.*

Those discussions allowed his instincts to kick in, and he sensed that the other ME-109 was behind him.

He rolled his plane hard left then pulled back on the control stick, forcing his P-51 to loop under the ME-109. Once he was behind the enemy aircraft, he rolled again and leveled off, positioning himself directly behind his target.

Damn! I'm right on his tail. I'm too close. If I score a hit, he will blow up in my face.

The ME-109 pilot cut back on his throttle, hoping Ewens would fly right past him.

Oh, no you don't. I'll take my chances.

Ewens opened fire, ripping the tail rudder to shreds and causing the plane to explode in a massive fireball.

Metal and debris flew in every direction.

A large piece of the ME-109 hit Ewens' canopy. It shattered and broke away from his plane. The sound was deafening.

As his P-51 began to roll, Ewens unbuckled his seat belt, and the force of the spinning plane separated him from the cockpit. Within seconds, he was floating.

He looked up to confirm that his primary parachute had opened.

No need for the secondary chute.

He surveyed his location below.

Shit, I'm over the Channel. I knew I should have taken those swimming lessons.

The wind was blowing hard, and he was drifting south over the Cotentin Peninsula.

That's right, baby, keep blowing me to land.

With the Channel to his back, he no longer feared the water.

The Krauts are probably watching me. I hope they wait for my boots to hit before they shoot me.

During the descent, he studied his surroundings, looking for approaching vehicles and a safe place to hide once on the ground.

Directly below him was a cow pasture.

Several kilometers to the south, a convoy of trucks was moving toward him.

Krauts! This birthday is turning out to be a bust.

To the east, a pickup truck was speeding his way.

That thing is hauling ass.

They zigzagged their way down dirt roads, through hedgerow openings, and over open fields. They initially lost track of the descending parachute before locating it again.

"There it is, Jean-Pierre," said Angélique. "It is coming down in that field."

Jean-Pierre drove down the narrow road until they approached a break in the hedgerow.

"Turn in there," said Angélique.

As he turned into the pasture, the pilot suspended from the chute landed on the ground and rolled to his side, then swiftly got to his feet.

Jean-Pierre accelerated through the field, with mud flying under his tires. They arrived as Ewens collapsed the chute and unbuckled his harness.

"He isn't a Brit, Angélique. He's an American."

Speaking in French, Jean-Pierre said to Ewens, "We are with the Resistance."

Uncertain if he understood correctly, Ewens asked, "Resistance? You said you are with the Resistance?"

"*Oui!* We are members of the Resistance."

Pointing south, Ewens said, "Germans! They are coming."

Searching his memory for one of the eight French phrases he taught himself, *"Je suis un Américain. Pouvez-vous m'aider?"* I am an American. Can you help me?

The three worked together to gather his parachute and place it in the truck bed under a pile of hay.

Jean-Pierre put the truck in gear and stepped on the accelerator. The tires spun, shooting mud from the rear. They were stuck.

"Take the wheel, Angélique."

Jean-Pierre and Captain Ewens leaped from the cab and pushed. The rear wheels gaining traction as their shoulders pressed against the tailgate.

After the truck was freed from the mud, Jean-Pierre turned the truck around and retraced the tracks he had created when he entered the field.

Exiting—first a sharp left, then a right, then into an isolated path deep in the woods that was difficult to see from the road.

Once hidden, Jean-Pierre parked the truck and shut off the engine.

"We need to bury his chute, Angélique. Then find a place to hide him."

"He can stay at my house, Jean-Pierre. I think Mrs. Abraham speaks English. She can translate for him."

"I was hoping you would suggest that. Are you sure your mama won't mind?"

"What is one more guest? It has been nice having a houseful of people."

Captain Ewens listened to the conversation, assuming they were discussing what to do with him.

These two are just kids. Their mothers are probably still wiping their butts.

They heard vehicles coming. It sounded like several trucks, but they couldn't see through the thick tree line.

Ewens reached to his holster and pulled out his Colt M1911 handgun.

Jean-Pierre reached under the seat and grabbed two M1A1 submachine guns, handing one to Angélique.

Jesus Christ, I've been rescued by Bonnie and Clyde.

The three positioned themselves behind the truck, ready to unload on anything that came down the narrow path.

The rabbling trucks passed them one after the other. It sounded as though there were no less than four.

After the last vehicle had passed, Jean-Pierre said to Angélique, "When they don't find him, they will have troops scattered all over these fields. We need to get him to your house."

When they turned around, Ewens was digging a hole with his knife to bury his chute.

Jean-Pierre reached under the seat and exchanged the machine guns for a shovel.

Sainte-Marie-du-Mont, France

"He can stay in my room, Mama, and I'll sleep with you."

"That will work fine, Angélique. I'm more concerned about the hidden room. I don't know if we can squeeze a fourth person in if the Germans pull up to the house. If not, we will need an additional hiding place."

"What about the attic?" asked Jean-Pierre.

"That is too obvious. That will be the first place they check."

Mr. Rubin said, "We can fit him in the hidden room with us, Brigitte. The last time you had us make a practice run, I noticed there was room for at least one more. But it will be tight. He is much larger than the rest of us."

"Let's try it," said Brigitte.

After Mrs. Abraham translated the conversation to Ewens, they made their way to the second-floor guestroom. It was in the rear of the house. There was a space between the wall and the stairwell.

Pascal and René had created a door for easy access. They hid it behind an oak bookcase.

Brigitte and Angélique practiced pulling the bookcase away from the wall and quickly replacing it after the Rubins and Mrs. Abraham had climbed in.

"Let's try this again," said Brigitte. "This time, Captain Ewens will climb in with you."

"Should we start downstairs and time it like we did last time, Brigitte?" asked Mr. Rubin.

"Not this time. Let's just see if everyone fits."

Ewens tried to help with the bookcase, but Brigitte would have none of it.

"Mrs. Abraham, please tell Captain Ewens that although we appreciate his chivalry, Angélique and I need to master this process by ourselves."

Once the bookcase was away from the wall, they climbed in, with Ewens entering last.

He got most of his body in, but his right leg and arm were still out, with his flight boot still flat on the floor.

The other three moved further inside as Angélique and Brigitte attempted to push him in.

Jean-Pierre chuckled, "This is the most entertaining

thing I've seen since I went to the movies to see Laurel and Hardy."

"We are glad you find us amusing," said Angélique.

"This will never work," said Brigitte.

"What else can we do, Mama?"

Jean-Pierre said, "Maybe my papa and Pascal can come back and create another hiding place in the wall."

"Your papa needs to stay hidden, Jean-Pierre. You need to be careful yourself. Every German on the Cotentin Peninsula is on the lookout for your father. If you get stopped and they see your last name on your papers, things might not turn out well."

Mrs. Abraham translated the conversation to Ewens, who wandered around the corner. He first glanced up the attic stairs, then opened a closet in the hallway.

After closing the door, he heard a vehicle.

He made his way to the front window, where he watched a German troop carrier approach the house.

"May I help you?" asked Brigitte as she stood on her front porch watching a dozen soldiers run into the woods.

Using his left arm, the *Oberstleutnant* moved Brigitte aside. "We will search your home."

Entering the door behind him were six *Wehrmacht* soldiers. Three went upstairs while two more remained on the first floor.

"Who lives here with you?"

"My mother, my daughter, and my son."

"Where are they?"

"They are all upstairs. My daughter is tending to my mother and my son. They are terribly ill."

The Heroes of Sainte-Mère Église

"Show me."

As they entered Brigitte's bedroom, Mrs. Abraham and Jean-Pierre were in the bed under the covers. They were both coughing frequently and uncontrollably. Angélique was applying a damp cloth on Mrs. Abraham's forehead.

"What is wrong with them?"

"We aren't certain. Dr. Pelletier is treating them for measles."

The *Oberstleutnant* said, "Measles are highly contagious. We need to step out of the room."

After they exited and closed the door behind them, he said, "Let me see all of your papers."

Brigitte said, "They are in there with them. Wait here and I will get them."

From her dresser, Brigitte retrieved four documents and stepped back out into the hall with the *Oberstleutnant*, closing the door behind her.

He glanced through Brigitte's and Angélique's papers without questioning them.

He read the third name out loud, "Agathe Jacques. That woman in bed in there is supposed be your mother?"

"She is my mother, yes."

"These papers indicate she is sixty-eight years old. That woman lying in there appears to be in her eighties."

"She has been ill for several weeks. Her health has declined rapidly."

Looking into Brigitte's eyes, he held the stare, refusing to look away, anticipating a sign of deception.

Checking the next document, "Armand Lapierre. Your son is of military age. Is he not in the French army?"

"He was exempt. My husband died in an accident a few years ago. I need my son to help me on our farm."

The *Oberstleutnant* returned the papers to Brigitte while maintaining a look of curiosity.

"We are sorry we bothered you, madame. *Au revoir*."

Addressing two soldiers who had finished checking the other rooms, he said, "Get everyone back in the lorry."

Once the soldiers were gone, they let Captain Ewens and the Rubins out of the hidden compartment.

Mrs. Abraham asked Brigitte, "Who is Agathe Jacques?"

"My late mother."

Chapter Fifty-Two

JULY 15, 1943

Le Vrétot, France

Captain Ewens stood in the tree line. He watched the silhouette of the three teenagers taking their positions in the open field.

He had been holed up at the Lapierre farmhouse for two months. Other than when he was forced to hide in the wall compartment during the *Wehrmacht* raid, his stay had been uneventful.

He thought about Brigitte and Angélique and how kind they were, not just to him but to Mrs. Abraham and the Rubins. They had so little, but what they had was shared with others first. They were putting their lives at risk to save other people.

"Are you ready to return to the fight?" asked Martin Laurent.

"You're damn right. I'll be back in the air in a few days, and I plan on racking up kills like never before. We need to help you get your country back."

"We are glad you Americans finally joined the fight."

"You can thank the Japanese for that. If it hadn't been for Pearl Harbor, we would be sitting comfortably eating apple pie and watching baseball while Hitler conquered the world."

Laurent looked to the sky. "There it is."

It was too dark to see, but they heard the buzz of a single-engine plane. Then the three torches ignited, lighting up the field in a single file line.

Ewens saw Angélique in the center of the field. He watched as the reflection of the dancing torch bounced off her dress. A dress her mother had made her from the fabric of her father's work clothes.

What a brave girl she is.

Ewens watched as the plane landed. Laurent grabbed his arm, and they ran. Moments later, they were back in the air and on their way to England.

Chapter Fifty-Three

AUGUST 7, 1943

Sainte-Mère-Église, France

Jean-Pierre parked his father's 1934 Ariel 600cc motorcycle in front of Mayor Renaud's pharmacy. Angélique climbed off the back before Jean-Pierre swung his leg over the seat.

They surveyed the German soldiers and French police, whose numbers had increased. There was another group that had joined them who wore a different uniform. They wore all black and wielded billy clubs.

"Who are they, Jean-Pierre?" asked Angélique.

"I have no idea, but they aren't German. They are French. Look at their vehicles. Let's see if the mayor knows who they are."

There were no customers in the pharmacy, and the mayor was in the back of the store. The shelves behind the counter were nearly bare.

Jean-Pierre rang the bell on the counter.

Coming from the rear of the store, the mayor said, "*Bonjour*, Jean-Pierre, Angélique. What can I get for you today? Not that I have much of anything. The Germans have cleaned me out, and much of what I order gets confiscated."

"We aren't here to purchase anything, Mayor. We were questioning who those Frenchmen in the black uniforms are. Do you know?"

"Gabrielle Hall overheard a conversation last evening. They are referred to as *Milice*. They are here to manage the Jews departing from the train station."

"Where did they come from?"

"Look closer, Jean-Pierre. They didn't come from anywhere. They are locals. Don't you recognize them? There is Didier Lécuyer and Constantin Boucher and—"

Before the mayor could finish his statement, Jean-Pierre watched the last man leap from the back of the lorry. "Maurice Fuquay."

"You know Maurice, do you, Jean-Pierre?"

"Yes. I went to school with him. He is a big fat Jew-hating bastard."

Chapter Fifty-Four

FALL 1943

Martin Laurent had spent the past two years traveling back and forth between France and Britain. Each time he arrived in France he provided the Resistance with supplies. But most of all, he provided them with hope. Seeing Margot regularly helped his spirits and hers.

When he returned to Britain, he supplied valuable intelligence that became more precise and more respected by the SOE.

Gabrielle continued to get information from the officers at the café.

Angélique, seventeen and prettier than ever, was at an age where she could chat with the younger German soldiers, proud to boast of the work they did for the war effort. Frequently, they shared information with her that was considered classified.

Jean-Pierre and Luke had become masters at traveling the roads of Normandy, looking for specific details. Martin trained them how to look for clues of troop movements, force strength and weapons positioning, and most of all, the status of the Atlantic Wall.

Martin's recent return to Britain had been after his longest stay in France since he first connected with the Resistance.

Back in England, Martin noticed how things had transformed since the Americans arrived. GIs everywhere. American ships were tied to docks throughout coastal Britain.

To and from the port cities were convoys of trucks. Painted on the doors were the unmistakable images of a white star. The symbol of the U.S. Army.

He was seeing what the people of Europe were longing for. Britain, France, and the other Allied nations were no longer in the war by themselves. He believed he was witnessing the beginning of the end of Nazi Germany.

Chapter Fifty-Five

FEBRUARY 5, 1944

Quorn, England

"What is this place?" asked a voice from the rear of the bus. "Is it some kind of castle or something?"

"They consider it an estate," said Captain Jack Wakefield, who had recently been promoted after leading a group of men through fierce fighting in Italy. "It's owned by a family named Farnham. Apparently, the British government has requisitioned this property for the war effort. Don't get too excited. We won't be staying in the main house. There is a group of temporary barracks that have been built somewhere in those woods. That is where we will stay with much of the rest of the 82nd."

After driving around to the back and through a short canopy of trees, the bus stopped in front of a row of huts. The roofs were made of metal and curved to form a half moon.

"Here we are, boys. Hut thirteen is your new home. Get out, and find a bunk."

"Hut thirteen?" said a soldier in the back. "We are doomed."

"Just be glad there aren't 666 huts, soldier, or I would put you in that one," said Wakefield.

They climbed out of the bus and into the cold February air. After entering the building, Wakefield headed for the bottom bunk closest to the door.

"Excuse me, Captain," said a voice from the other side of the barracks. It was Staff Sergeant Hicks. "Will you be bunking with the men, sir?"

The husky, battle hardened, Staff Sergeant Hicks was tough as nails and had earned Captain Wakefield's trust, quickly becoming his right-hand man.

Wakefield responded to Hick's question, "That's right, Staff Sergeant. They offered to put me up in the house with the other officers, but I've been through hell and back with these men. We have some intense training ahead of us. I might as well stick close by to make certain everyone stays out of trouble."

The 505th Parachute Regiment of the 82nd Airborne Division had just arrived in England after months of fierce fighting. It started in North Africa, then into Sicily and up the coast of the Italian boot.

They were grateful to be in England, where they were promised time off before training began. The next mission was rumored to be an invasion of Western Europe. When and where was still top-secret information.

"What do you plan on doing this evening, Captain?" asked Hicks.

"I saw a few bars in town when the bus drove through. How about we go visit one, and I'll buy you a drink?"

Military regulations limited fraternizing between officers and enlisted personnel. However, Staff Sergeant Hicks and

Captain Wakefield had fought side by side since North Africa. At the time, Captain Wakefield was still Second Lieutenant Wakefield and Staff Sergeant Hicks was still Private Hicks.

They had eaten together, stood watch in foxholes together, and, most of all, dug the temporary graves of their men together. They trusted each other, and in the eyes of Captain Jack Wakefield, they were equals. The only difference was he had graduated from college at the University of Virginia.

After taking the bus into town, Wakefield and Hicks walked the streets of Quorn.

Although the restaurants and shops enjoyed having the influx of business from the American GIs, many of the locals were not pleased. The tension was particularly noticeable among the young British men. They didn't like the increased competition for their girls, many of whom had grown up watching American films and hoped that all American men would look like Clark Gable. Although disappointed they didn't, there was an intrigue difficult to resist.

"Let's try that place over there—The Blacksmith's Arms," said Jack.

"Looks as good as any," said Hicks.

Captain Jack Wakefield wasn't tall but had broad shoulders and what his mother referred to as a "kind face." This combination seemed to attract the attention of some good girls, but not those who were considered the most beautiful, although that was always where his eyes would roam. Once he spoke to them, he was able to win them over with his sense of humor and quiet confidence. Traits that also earned him the respect and admiration of the men he led.

Sitting down at the bar, Wakefield said to the barmaid, "We'll have two beers."

In a barely understandable British accent, she asked, "And what will it be, mates, dark or light? Do you want full pints or a half?"

"Two fulls and make them dark," said Wakefield.

Pouring the brews while trying to limit the foam, the barmaid said, "Welcome to Quorn." She appeared to be in her early sixties, about five-foot-three, thin with short brown hair. "My name is Gassoway. Elizabeth Gassoway. My husband Terrence and I own this establishment. Been in the family for four generations. He isn't here right now. He had to go to the machine shop to get a part made for the brew kettle. The darn thing is always breakin' down."

"We are pleased to meet you. I am Captain Wakefield with the U.S. 82nd Airborne, and this is Staff Sergeant Hicks."

"Some will tell ya they don't want ya here, but let me tell ya, I for one am glad ya here. We have been fighting the Jerrys since May of '40. They have nearly whooped us a handful of times. First at Dunkirk, then in the air during the Battle of Britain. One would have to be a fool to think we could win this war without ya Yanks."

"We hope to do what we can, as quick as we can, and then return home in one piece," said Wakefield.

"I pray that's the case, young man."

As the conversation continued, they heard a commotion as Gassoway looked behind them toward the front door. She then shouted, "See here, mates, we will have none of that in this establishment."

The Heroes of Sainte-Mère Église

Wakefield and Hicks turned around to see a private in their unit rolling on the floor with a local Brit.

Sergeant Hicks said to Wakefield, "I'll take care of this, Captain."

He went over, grabbed the private by the collar, and pushed him out the front door.

Wakefield watched as an Army MP approached Sergeant Hicks.

After a brief discussion, the MP grabbed the young soldier and escorted him away.

Returning to the bar, Hicks spoke briefly with the local man, who was still dusting himself off. He then shook his hand and shouted to Gassoway, "This man's next round is on me."

Wakefield followed with, "I'm sorry that happened, ma'am. We have told our boys they are guests here and they are to be on their best behavior. But some just don't listen."

"I'm just glad you were here. The next time, someone might get hurt. Worse still, somethin' might get broken."

Chapter Fifty-Six

MAY 13, 1944

**Uncle Marcos's Compound
Southern Face
Pyrénées Mountains**

Domingo and Wilhelm had been summoned by Uncle Marcos before the sun came up. He asked them to be in his office before breakfast.

Uncle Marcos's office was modest. It was large enough for his wooden desk and chair, and two more chairs for meetings, but there was little room to move around if there was more than one person. The dark wooden walls and low ceiling were reminiscent of a cave.

On the wall behind Marcos was a picture of himself with Manuel Azaña, the previous president of Spain. Azaña lost power after being overthrown by Francisco Franco. Next to the picture was a series of military medals enclosed in a picture frame.

"Would you care for a cigarette, gentlemen?" asked Uncle Marcos.

The Heroes of Sainte-Mère Église

Wilhelm waved the offer off as Domingo reached for one along with a match.

"Domingo, you and your group have been here more than a year. I'm glad I have been able to provide you refuge from the evils of the world; however, we have accumulated more Jews and pilots than we can feed. We even have Americans now, and those boys can eat. I am getting desperate. We need to start sending refugees down the mountain and we are going to start with yours."

Tilting his head back and blowing smoke into the air, Domingo said, "We have known this time would come, Uncle. We have been growing restless ourselves. We are ready to go."

Uncle Marcos said, "In addition to the nine in your group, you will be escorting two British airmen. They are the same two you got into a skirmish with when you first arrived. You will take the airmen to a safehouse in San Sebastian. The Shapiros and the Edelmans will need to cross through Spain into Portugal."

Domingo asked, "Portugal? Why Portugal? The plan has always been to take them down the mountain and into Spain."

"There are few safe places in Spain. Something has happened. Although Franco has troops up here as a deterrent to keep the German army out of Spain, Franco and Hitler have made some type of arrangement."

"What do you mean by 'arrangement?'" asked Wilhelm.

"My informants have found evidence of transfers through the Canfranc rail line traveling in both directions. Gold from France to Spain, and tungsten from Spain to France."

"The tungsten is used to build German weapons I'm assuming?" said Wilhelm.

"Precisely," said Marcos. "Then there are the *Gestapo* agents drifting throughout the country. If Franco really wanted them out, he could crack down and force them out. Personally, I believe Franco doesn't want an influx of Jews pouring into Spain, so he tolerates Hitler's agents since they wander the country rounding them up."

Domingo asked, "So how do we get down the mountain, Uncle? We can't drive the Nazi staff car. For one, there isn't enough room for ten people, and we would never make it through the checkpoints."

"Yes, checkpoints are certainly a problem. The Spanish army has them everywhere. To make matters worse, they move them almost daily," said Marcos. "Then of course, there is always the possibility of crossing paths with *bandidos* who are roaming the southern face of the mountain looking for refugees to steal from."

Opening his desk drawer and pulling out three glasses and a bottle of brandy, Marcos said, "I know it is early in the morning and you haven't had breakfast yet, but I need this, and I hate to drink alone."

Without asking if they wanted any, he filled their glasses and slid them across the desk, then tipped his glass back and downed the contents in one swill.

Marcos then said, "You will be traveling down the mountain in a lorry. My men have mapped out a route for you through the most remote, desolate roads. The roads will be terrible. You will need to travel slowly, but it will be far less likely that you encounter trouble."

"When will we be leaving, Uncle?" asked Domingo.

"Just as soon as my men can commandeer another lorry. I don't have one to spare."

"What do you mean by commandeer?" asked Wilhelm.

"Just let me and my men worry about that. In the meantime, I want you to go find one of my lieutenants. His name is Poncho. He is going to supply you with weapons and ammunition. You may need them."

Chapter Fifty-Seven

MAY 14, 1944

**Two Thousand Meters
Quorn, England**

Captain Wakefield found night jumps to be exhilarating. He stood at the edge of the open door of the C-47 staring down into complete darkness.

England, as with much of Europe, had been under a blackout state for the past four years.

When the go order was given, the men leapt into a sea of black nothingness. They hoped they landed in an open field covered in soft grass.

During earlier training jumps, most of the men had landed in trees, lakes, or on the top of houses. The lakes were the most dangerous. The 101st had already had two drowning victims. The second most feared were the houses.

Jack grabbed Hicks by the sleeve and put his mouth to his ear. Over the roar of the engines he shouted, "Try not to land on an old lady's house this time. I don't want to have to go knock on the doors of any more Brits to apologize for your poor luck."

"I'll keep that in mind, Captain. I'll aim for a tall tree so you must climb up and cut me down."

"I'll send a corporal up after you. Or maybe leave you up there."

As the plane made a sharp bank to the right, Hicks asked, "How many more training jumps before the real thing?"

"I have no way of knowing. Let's just keep jumping, running, marching, and chasing British women until Ike unleashes us like a pack of wild dogs."

"Prepare to jump," shouted the copilot as he turned on the red light.

Hicks turned to the men and shouted, "Up!"

They stood and connected their snap hooks to the static lines above their heads.

"Check the man in front of you and behind you. Be certain they are hooked," shouted Hicks.

"I'll go first this time, Sergeant. You check the last man then follow him out. I'll see you on the ground."

"Yes, sir, Captain. Keep your feet dry."

"Green light—go!"

Chapter Fifty-Eight

MAY 15, 1944

Uncle Marcos's Compound
Southern Face
Pyrénées Mountains

Uncle Marcos greeted his men as they returned to the compound with the lorry, "Where did you get this from, Poncho?"

"From the same *bandidos* who murdered the priest last month. They have a camp outside of Candanchú."

"I see by the blood on the side, they didn't just hand it over," said Marcos.

"No, General, there was a bit of a firefight. Let's just say, they won't be murdering anymore priests."

"What did you do with the bodies?"

"We threw them down a shaft in one of the caves. They will never be found."

"How did your men make out?"

"Not a scratch. We caught them completely off guard."

"Well done, Poncho."

"Thank you, General."

"What about weapons?" asked Marcos. "Will Domingo's group be well armed as they travel down the mountain?"

"Yes, General. In addition to the Mauser and Luger Major Ziegler arrived here with, we also gave them three more Mausers. One for Domingo and one for each British airman."

Addressing the small group standing with Poncho, "Thank you, gentlemen. Wash the blood from the side of the truck. Then eat, and get some rest. I will tell Domingo and the other guests we are just about ready to send them to Jaca."

Chapter Fifty-Nine

MAY 17, 1944

Uncle Marcos's Compound
Southern Face
Pyrénées Mountains

Alfred knocked on the door of Domingo and Wilhelm's cabin. After it opened, he said, "You wanted to see me?"

"Come on in, Alfred," said Wilhelm.

Although Alfred was now seventeen, he was still small in stature. With a look of apprehension, he stepped into the room and sat in a wooden chair next to Wilhelm's bunk. Domingo stood with his shoulder leaning against the wall as he lit a cigarette. Wilhelm took a seat on the edge of his bunk within reach of Alfred.

"Alfred, we need to ask something of you," said Wilhelm.

"What is that?"

"We need you to help us escort the others down the mountain. The others we are referring to are your parents, Esther, Esther's parents, and two British pilots."

The Heroes of Sainte-Mère Église

"What do you mean by escort?"

Wilhelm said, "Until now, you have been along for the ride. That needs to change. We need you to help us help the others."

"What do you want me to do?"

"Have you ever fired a weapon before?" asked Domingo.

Looking up at the standing Domingo, he said, "No. My father carries a gun in his suitcase, but I have never fired it."

"Well as of today, that is going to change," said Wilhelm, as he removed the leather holster from his belt. Handing it to Alfred he said, "I am going to teach you how to fire my Luger."

Alfred took it with hesitation, surprised at how heavy it was.

"Why do I need to know how to fire this?" asked Alfred.

Domingo said, "The likelihood of you ever needing to use it outside of target practice is small. However, while we are making the journey down the mountain we might run across some bad people. If that happens, we hope that when they see we are well armed, they will leave us alone. But just in case they don't, we want as much fire power as possible. So, you will need to know how to use it. There will be two British airmen with us. They will also be armed with Mausers."

"I need to ask my parents first."

Wilhelm—still sitting on the edge of his bunk—leaned forward to get closer to Alfred. He then asked, "How old are you, Alfred?"

"My seventeenth birthday was last week."

Wilhelm shook his head in frustration. "There are soldiers dying on the battlefield who are younger than you, Alfred. Why do you need to ask your parents?"

"I just always have."

Wilhelm said, "That needs to stop. It is time for you to grow up. Your parents, Dreyfus and the Edelmans are counting on you. You want to protect Esther, don't you?"

"Yes, of course I do. I would do anything for her."

"Well, okay then," said Wilhelm. "Her safety may depend on you learning everything we need to teach you. Do you understand, Alfred?"

"Yes. I understand. I'll do it."

Chapter Sixty

MAY 25, 1944

**Spain
Southern Face
Pyrénées Mountains**

The lorry sat empty with the engine idling. The front end pointed toward the same entrance of Uncle Marcos's compound they'd arrived through seventeen months earlier.

Domingo said, "I'll drive. If we encounter a Spanish checkpoint, I'll have the best chance of talking us through it."

Looking toward Wilhelm, Domingo said, "You will be in the front cab with me."

"Miriam and Esther, I'll need one of you to stick close to the Brits in the back at all times, since you are the only two who speak English. I may need you to translate for me."

The Brits climbed in the back first. Once they were in, they each turned and reached out a hand to pull Miriam, Esther, and Ingrid up into the canvas covered truck bed. They were followed by Dreyfus. Uri climbed in next.

Standing outside of the lorry were Uncle Marcos, Domingo, Wilhelm, Joseph, and Alfred.

"Are you ready, Domingo?" asked Uncle Marcos.

"Yes, we are ready. Thank you for everything, Uncle."

"Why are you thanking me? You are the ones putting your lives at risk. You could have just stayed in Pau and lived a relatively peaceful life, Domingo."

Turning to Wilhelm, now dressed as a civilian in blue pants and a gray sweater, "And you Wilhelm, you could have just stayed in the German army and obeyed orders."

Wilhelm said, "I couldn't do that. I had already seen enough evil to know I could no longer just sit back and do nothing."

"I understand, my friend. If only Germany had more men of your character."

"They exist, General. Unfortunately, they are either in forced labor camps or dead because they stood up for what is right. Others are just too terrified to speak up."

Uncle Marcos then approached Alfred and pointed at Wilhelm's Luger which was holstered to his belt, "Do you know how to use that thing if you need to, Alfred?"

"Yes, sir. Wilhelm spent a lot of time teaching me. I shot two of the rabbits we had for dinner last night."

"He's ready," said Wilhelm. "He is already a better shot with that thing than I ever was."

Uncle Marcos turned to Domingo, "I am going to have one of my men lead you out of this tangled maze. He will get you as far as the east road I told you to take. Once on it, you are on your own."

Joseph Shapiro had been standing off to the side. When he sensed the goodbyes were coming to an end, he laid his suitcase on the ground, opened it, and removed a purse of gold coins that were buried under a stack of French francs.

The others watched as he approached Uncle Marcos who towered over him. "General, please take these gold coins. You have provided my family with a safe haven from the evils of the world for many months. I will always be grateful."

Uncle Marcos towered over Joseph. He initially stared at him without responding. He then said, "Shapiro, that suitcase of yours has been a mystery to me since I first saw you with it. You cradle it as though it is the Messiah himself. But then I realized that it is made of Italian leather and has your initials embossed on the side. My advice to you is, if you really want to hide your wealth, don't carry it around in a case that cost more than the average man's annual wages.

"Normally, I would not accept your capitalist greed, Shapiro. But I have a compound full of desperate people. They have come from all over Europe to escape a Nazi wave that is even more evil than the wealth that funds it. They need to be fed. So, I will accept your gold."

Joseph replied, "Whatever your motivation, General. Please know it is offered with my sincere gratitude."

Uncle Marcos hesitated before shaking Joseph's hand with a firm grip that nearly brought him to his knees.

Once everyone was loaded in the lorry, Uncle Marcos looked up at Domingo who was behind the wheel, tapped on his door and said, "Drive safely, nephew. At least the spring weather is breaking. It only drops below freezing when the sun goes down."

After a few minutes on the road, Miriam took the opportunity to speak to the two British airmen in English.

"Gentlemen, my name is Miriam Edelman, this is my

daughter Esther. We both speak English so if you need something translated, just let one of us know. We would be happy to help you."

"That is truly kind of you, Madame. I'm Squadron Leader Virgil Pierpont, Royal Air Force," said the first Brit who appeared to be about thirty.

"And I am Flight Lieutenant Kingsley Dalton. We are pleased to make your acquaintance," said the twenty-one-year-old as he tipped the flat cap he wore on his head.

The two British airmen, like the others, were wearing civilian clothes. Uncle Marcos knew they would be targets for opportunists looking to cash in with the *Gestapo* agents roaming throughout Spain if they were in uniform.

Miriam pointed out the other members of their group who were sitting in the back of the lorry, and one by one explained their relationship and how they had met. She also explained their history with Wilhelm and Domingo, who were in the cab.

Upon hearing of Wilhelm's heroics, Virgil Pierpont said, "We hope that Wilhelm chap doesn't hold any hard feelings over the scuffle we got into with him. When you get a chance, let him know it is all forgotten with us, will ya ma'am?"

Miriam said, "It was a long time ago, Virgil. I'm sure it is long forgotten. But I will pass on the message."

Kingsley Dalton addressed Esther, "Where did you learn to speak English, young lass?"

"My mother was a professor of language at the University of Warsaw before the war started. She has taught me English, Spanish, French, and German."

"So, you are smart as well as pretty," said Dalton.

Alfred, not understanding what was said, became

The Heroes of Sainte-Mère Église

jealous as he sensed what might be a flirtatious laugh from Esther.

Esther, like Alfred, had just celebrated her seventeenth birthday before leaving Uncle Marcos's compound. Although still small, she was not the petite little girl Alfred had met at Mont-Saint-Michel. She was developing into a beautiful young woman, and he didn't want other men to notice.

It had been several hours since they left the safety of Uncle Marcos's compound.

The road he instructed them to take was in poor condition. It had many twists and turns and was riddled with holes, but would be less likely to have checkpoints.

Domingo said, "With all of these bumps and the hairpin turns; it will take us into the early morning to get to Jaca."

After another kilometer, the road leveled off and the holes were fewer.

They drove through an area with thick trees and overgrowth to their right that rested on a steep hill. To their left were fewer trees and a drop-off that sloped sharply and would cause the lorry to roll for a hundred meters if they went over the edge.

"Domingo, I think we should stop, and let everyone stretch their legs," said Wilhelm.

"I'm ready for a break myself," said Domingo, as he stopped in the middle of the narrow road.

After everyone climbed out, they wandered around the lorry. The women went down the hill to relieve themselves. The men urinated on the side of the road where they stood.

Nine-year-old Dreyfus said, "I have to poop, Papa."

"Go up the hill, Dreyfus. You will have more privacy in the thick woods up there," said Joseph.

"I'll go with him," said Alfred.

"Don't be gone long," said Domingo.

"We won't," said Alfred as he followed his little brother up the hill and into the thick tree line.

After the ladies returned, Ingrid said, "It feels like it is getting cooler."

Wilhelm said, "Jaca is near the base of the mountain. It will be warmer at lower altitudes."

They were enjoying being on their feet after the long ride. The view overlooking the valley below was peaceful. In the trees, they heard snow finches singing.

Standing near the front of the lorry, Virgil Pierpont and Kingsley Dalton were telling Esther and Miriam of their adventures as British airmen. Miriam would translate the conversation to Ingrid. Joseph and Uri were standing a few meters away, engrossed in their own conversation. Domingo and Wilhelm were also in front of the lorry but had walked several meters away from the others.

Before Domingo and Wilhelm could react, they heard a vehicle approaching from the direction they were walking. When they looked, they saw road dirt stirring under the wheels of a pickup truck speeding in their direction. There were two men in the front cab, and two standing in the bed holding onto the roof.

"Who could that be?" asked Uri.

"Probably *bandidos*," said Domingo. "Back to the lorry, and grab your Mauser."

Before they made it, machine gun fire sprayed the ground around them, causing them to stop in their tracks.

The pickup skidded to a stop. The four men leaped out. Three of the men had Mausers, a third had a MG 40 machine gun. Two of the men stayed with Domingo and Wilhelm. Two others ran to Ingrid, Miriam, and Esther as they instructed Joseph and Uri to join them. Everyone was then corralled into one group where they were surrounded.

The absence of the two Brits was obvious to everyone but the *bandidos*, who didn't notice them before they disappeared.

The two *bandidos* with their Mausers pointing at Domingo and Wilhelm were the oldest of the group. One in his late thirties, and the other in his fifties. The older man had a German Luger holstered to the belt wrapped around his thick waist. He was missing teeth. The other two *bandidos* were much younger, appearing to be in their early twenties. All four men had thick dark hair, facial stubble, and were filthy. Their body odor was noticeable from several meters away. They apparently only bathed when it rained, and there had been a dry spell.

In Spanish, Domingo spoke first, "What do you want with us?"

The oldest among them said, "You have our lorry. You murdered our comrades. Now, we will murder you."

Domingo replied, "We purchased this lorry. We were walking down the mountain, and six men we didn't know pulled up and offered to sell it to us for just a few pesetas. We paid them, and they drove off in another lorry. You must believe us. Do we look like a pack of murdering thieves?"

The man replied, "No, you don't. We know what murdering thieves look like. They look like the four of us, which is unfortunate for you. It doesn't matter. Our comrades are dead, and someone must pay. That someone is all of you."

Miriam and Esther understood the words of the Spaniard. Esther started to cry. Miriam held her tight.

The oldest man said to the other *bandidos*, "Search the lorry."

One of the young ones went to the back and the other climbed into the cab.

They each returned with Mausers they had found. The young man from the back also had Joseph's suitcase. Everything they found was laid on the ground at the feet of the oldest man in charge.

Domingo and Wilhelm immediately noticed the same thing, *Two Mausers are missing.*

The oldest man knelt next to Joseph's suitcase. "Where is the key?" asked the man in Spanish.

"He wants your key, Joseph," said Domingo.

Joseph hesitated.

"Tell him I won't ask again," said the *bandido*.

After Domingo relayed the information, Joseph reached into the breast pocket of his jacket and removed the key, then tossed it on the ground—far enough away that the man had to stand to retrieve it. As he did, he glanced at Joseph in disgust.

As he knelt back down at the case, he pointed to Joseph and said to his three comrades, "I want to kill that one myself."

After inserting the key and opening the case, the man was elated. He shouted, "I am rich!" as he rummaged through the piles of francs, jewels, and gold coins.

Disgusted at watching his family's financial security get pillaged, Joseph pulled his own Luger from the rear waistband of his trousers. He aimed and fired, hitting the man in the head, causing a spray of blood, and killing him instantly.

The Heroes of Sainte-Mère Église

He then turned and fired at a second *bandido*, missing the mark but catching a bullet himself as the man fired back. Joseph fell to the ground, grabbing his chest and grasping for air.

Alfred leaped from behind the lorry and fired Wilhelm's Luger twice, killing the man who just shot his father.

As a third *bandido* turned and aimed his machine gun at Alfred, a rifle crack was heard from the woods, killing the third *bandido* and dropping him to the ground. Virgil Pierpont and Kingsley Dalton ran from the woods. Dalton's Mauser had one less bullet in it.

The fourth and final *bandido* dropped his weapon and raised his hands over his head.

Ingrid fell to her knees next to her husband. "We will get you to a doctor, Joseph."

"I will never make it," whispered Joseph as he painfully coughed up blood.

Wilhelm grabbed the rifle that the last remaining *bandido* had dropped to the ground and held it on him.

Virgil Pierpont pushed Ingrid out of the way and knelt next to Joseph before applying pressure to the wound with his bare hands.

Still holding Wilhelm's Luger, Alfred dropped to the ground next to his father. They stared into each other's eyes.

"I'm sorry, Papa. I should have shot sooner. I could have saved you."

"You saved our family, Alfred. I am proud of you," said Joseph Shapiro, before taking his final breath.

Twenty minutes had passed. Ingrid was still kneeling at Joseph's side wiping dried tears from her eyes. Dreyfus sat on the ground next to her, still weeping uncontrollably. Alfred stood and looked down at the lifeless body of his father. Like his mother, his tears had stopped flowing but the disbelief of losing the patriarch of the family in a violent burst of gunfire was still stinging.

"We need to get moving, Ingrid," said Domingo. "I hate to inform you of this, but we must leave Joseph behind."

"He is my husband," said Ingrid. "I won't just leave him to rot on the side of this mountain."

"We have no choice, Ingrid," said Uri. "We still have a long journey, and there are still many dangers. We will bury him respectfully."

"Uri is right," said Wilhelm. "Joseph was a brave man who loved you and the boys. He did everything to protect you. He would want what is best for you. And what is best for his family is to move down this mountain as quickly as possible. It will be dark soon. We must keep moving."

"They are right, Mama," said Alfred. "Let's bury Papa, and get moving."

Once they buried Joseph, Domingo instructed the others to climb into the rear of lorry. Then he, along with Wilhelm and Alfred, escorted the fourth *bandido* down the steep hill.

"Keep your hands on top of your head so we can see them," said Domingo.

Several meters down the hill they stopped.

Speaking in French so the *bandido* wouldn't understand, Domingo asked Alfred, "What do you want to do with him? He was part of the gang that killed your father. If you want to shoot him yourself, we will not judge you. If you want me to do it, I have no problem doing so. His type is nothing but thieves, rapists, and murderers. The world is better off with none of them."

Alfred looked at the *bandido*. For the first time, he got a good look at him. He was filthy, dressed in rags, and wasn't much older than himself. He was just another victim of the evil the world had become.

"What if we leave him here, Domingo? What will happen to him?" asked Alfred.

"He will make his way to another set of thugs just like the ones laying in the road at the top of the hill. Within days, he will be robbing and murdering someone else.

"If it is okay with you, I would like to just let him go. If he has no weapons, he is no threat to us."

Domingo turned to the young *bandido*. "Today is your lucky day. You will go free. But if we run across you again, you won't be so lucky. Keep marching down the hill and don't turn around."

The boy looked at Alfred—their eyes locked momentarily. Alfred saw the pain in the boy's face from what life had dealt him. Alfred realized they had that in common as the young man turned and made his way down the steep hill.

Chapter Sixty-One

MAY 26, 1944

The Banks of the Aragon River
Jaca, Spain

"We can't obtain fuel until the morning," said Domingo. "I will park next to the river under those trees."

Once they parked, everyone got out and sat under the trees and waited for the sun to rise. The sound of the flowing river offered a hint of peace.

Ingrid sat Joseph's suitcase on the ground and stared at it.

"This case cost Joseph his life," said Ingrid.

"No, it didn't," said Domingo. "The thieves who roam the Pyrénées never leave witnesses. Joseph, Alfred and Kingsley Dalton saved our lives. Had they not acted; we would have all been murdered. As for that suitcase, I don't believe your husband was a greedy man. It wasn't the wealth in the suitcase that was important to him. It was the security it provided to you and your boys that was important to him."

"Thank you, Domingo. Your words are comforting."

Ingrid walked to the riverbank and stared at the flowing water. She thought of Joseph—the man she had married over twenty years ago. He was still on the mountain, buried in a hole on the side of a winding road. A road she knew she could never find again. The thought made her weep.

Alfred and Dreyfus went to their mother and hugged her. Their emotions overcame them. The stress of being on the run for years poured out, and they all wept uncontrollably.

Even though they had made it to Jaca, it was a hollow victory. The head of their family, the man who had brought them out of Berlin, Sainte-Mère-Église, and Mont-Saint-Michel and through the Pyrénées Mountains was gone.

The others watched, wishing they knew what to say. Esther walked up to Alfred and embraced him. Then Uri and Miriam joined them. They took turns comforting each other.

The group sat in a circle under the trees.

The conversations went in many directions. Less concerned with scarcity, they shared the little bit of dried beef, cheese, and bread that still remained.

Through Miriam's translation, Virgil Pierpont asked Domingo, "When do we leave for San Sebastian?"

Domingo replied, "Miriam, tell him that in the morning, we will get fuel and stock up on food, then we will head out. When we get to San Sebastian, it may take time to find the British safehouse. I doubt that it will have a big sign and a flashing light."

After translating the comments, Miriam asked Domingo, "What about the rest of us. Will you be making the journey to Portugal with us, Domingo?"

"I don't believe so, Miriam. There are many others in France who are desperate to get out. I have much work to do."

"Have you ever been to Portugal, Domingo?" asked Wilhelm.

"No, never. I hear it's beautiful," said Domingo.

After lighting a cigarette, Domingo asked, "Have you decided what you are you going to do, Wilhelm?"

"I have been thinking about something, Domingo. The best thing for Germany is for Hitler to get removed from office and for the war to end. Maybe I can accelerate that process. What if I were to surrender to the British? They could use me for intelligence gathering."

Domingo said, "Although admirable, do you really believe that is where your heart lies? You would provide the British with information they would use to kill your fellow Germans."

Wilhelm replied, "As a *Wehrmacht* officer, I saw German Nazis send German Jews to death camps. I personally loaded them up in cattle cars, slammed the doors, and locked them in. The faces of the children staring back at me as I closed the doors wakes me up in the middle of the night. I already have German blood on my hands. I know things. I could provide the British with information that could save many lives, even though it would destroy others. I wouldn't view it as betraying Germany. I would view it as saving Germany from a Nazi political party that is destroying my country. I'm willing to do anything to stop that destruction, Domingo."

Chapter Sixty-Two

MAY 27, 1944

San Sebastian, Spain

"Uncle Marcos said to drive to the waterfront on the eastern side of the San Sebastian, and look for a small community called Lezo. He said the British safehouse will be found on a narrow street near the docks. The address is 4 Gurutze Santuaren Plaza."

Once they arrived, Wilhelm asked, "Are you sure this is the correct place? It looks like an abandoned warehouse. Most of the windows are broken."

"I'm sure. I memorized the address," said Domingo. "I'll go in first. I'll take Pierpont and Dalton with me."

"Won't you need Miriam to translate?" said Wilhelm.

"We'll figure it out without her. I don't know what we will find in there. I won't needlessly put her at risk."

Wilhelm remained in the passenger side of the lorry. He noticed a group of boys kicking a football in an alley between the buildings across the street. They stopped and watched as Domingo and the Brits entered the warehouse. Then one of them ran off.

Wilhelm thought to himself, *That's strange. Why are they playing football in the warehouse district?*

When they entered the building, Domingo and the Brits found it to be vast and open, with a row of I-beam in the middle.

There were crates on one end, and at the other were two boats. Each were closed bow, twenty-four meters in length.

The trio walked the warehouse, not wanting to yell, but hoped to get someone's attention.

A door in the back opened, and a large man with a bald head and a British accent said in Spanish, "May I help you?"

Excited to hear the accent, Virgil Pierpont said, "You wouldn't happen to have some fish and chips stashed away, do ya, mate?"

"And who might you be?" asked the man in English.

"I am Squadron Leader Virgil Pierpont, Royal Air Force."

"And I am Flight Lieutenant Kingsley Dalton. We hear this is the place to come if we want to get home."

"Ya heard right, mate. Good to see ya made it safe. I heard rumors you were on your way."

Returning to Spanish, the man approached Domingo and shook his hand. "Thank you for bringing them here, *señor*. I don't believe I have met you before. Are you new?"

"I stay on the other side of the mountain. Unusual circumstances brought me here."

"My name is Finley," said the large Brit. "Come on back. You must be starving. Please join me for lunch."

"Finley?" asked Domingo. "Is that your first or last name?"

"It is neither. You need not know my real name—first or last."

"I have more outside—Jews." Clearing his throat, "And a *Wehrmacht officer.*"

"A what?"

"You heard me correctly. I have a German officer with me. He deserted to help us. We would have never made it without him."

"You shouldn't have brought him here," said Finley.

"You can trust him," said Domingo. Nodding toward Pierpont and Dalton, he said, "Just ask these two."

Once off the truck, the group sat in the back room of the warehouse. It was clean compared to the rest of the building. It had a full kitchen, a bath, and sleeping quarters for up to eight people.

"What's next?" asked Uri.

Domingo had to interpret Uri's comments for Finley.

Finley replied, "First, I must get false papers made for the lot of you. That will take time. There are nine of you. Some of you will be here a week or more."

Domingo asked, "Can you get papers for me, too? I never returned to work after I got these people out by rail. The Nazis aren't stupid. They will know I was involved."

"Yes, I can do that. You will be a Spanish businessman. That will get you over the Confranc railroad and back into France."

Pointing toward Pierpont and Dalton, Finley said, "These two here—they will go first. Once they have their papers, someone will drive them to the British Embassy in Madrid. Then they will be escorted to Gibraltar, where they will be returned to Great Britain by boat or plane. Within a few weeks they will once again be dropping bombs on Germany."

"Gibraltar? I thought you sent them directly across the Channel from here," said Domingo.

"Not in a year. The Germans now patrol these waters. They have captured some of our transport boats. Others they blew out of the water. Their *Gestapo* agents hidden in Spain haven't figured out our path to Gibraltar yet."

"What about the Jews?" asked Domingo.

"The best place for them is Portugal. If they stay here in Spain, they will eventually get arrested and imprisoned, or turned over to the *Gestapo* for bounty money. It won't be long before Portugal cracks down on them, too. Apparently, nobody wants Jews."

Miriam and Esther sat quietly and listened, never letting on to Finley that they both understood Spanish. It was painful to listen to him discuss their plight as if they were stray dogs everyone refuses to feed in hopes they will go away.

"What about, Wilhelm?" asked Domingo.

"Your friend the Jerry over there? I should arrest him and send him back to Great Britain for interrogation. He might be of value. He probably has information we could benefit from. But he is your friend, and you say he helped you. So, off with him wherever he wants is my attitude."

Chapter Sixty-Three

MAY 30, 1944

San Sebastian, Spain

They had been at the safehouse for three days. Finley woke early and went into town to meet with the forger. He returned with the false documents for Pierpont and Dalton. He arranged for a car from the British Embassy to pick them up. He also had a set of documents for Domingo.

That afternoon, they stood outside and said their goodbyes.

Pierpont and Dalton embraced Miriam and Esther, who they had bonded with due to their ability to speak English.

Alfred was glad to see them drive off. Especially Kingsley Dalton, who was clearly smitten with Esther.

Moments after the Brits drove off, Domingo stepped out of the warehouse, where he found Wilhelm, the Edelmans, and what remained of Joseph Shapiro's family—Ingrid, Alfred, and Dreyfus, who kept getting scolded for wandering off. Alfred and Esther were holding hands.

Approaching the group, Domingo said, "It is time for

me to go. I have a bus back to Jaca to catch. Then over the Pyrénées and back to Pau. Finley has given me new papers. No more Domingo. But for my safety, Finley instructed me to not share my new identity. So, to you, I will always be Domingo."

Wilhelm spoke first, shaking Domingo's hand. "I knew this day would come, my friend. I guess it is time for all of us to move on."

"And you, Wilhelm? Where will you go?"

"You said Finley is considering arresting me. I'm hoping he does. I haven't been to England since I was a boy. I'm sure it is beautiful this time of year."

With a grin on his face, Domingo said, "Maybe if you beg him. At any rate, take care of yourself, Wilhelm."

Moving to the others, he embraced them all. One by one, they thanked him for his courage and getting them through the Pyrénées.

"When you get back, give our regards to Max and Salvador, will you?" said Uri.

"Of course. I know they will be pleased you are safe." He added, "I know this is a crazy thing I do—smuggling people through the mountains. But I must admit, it makes me feel alive in a world blanketed in death."

He then turned and walked away with his new identity.

Chapter Sixty-Four

JUNE 3, 1944

San Sebastian, Spain

Wilhelm, the Shapiros, and the Edelmans were waiting to obtain their false papers. It had taken longer for Finley's source to create them since there were so many.

Finley said, "I need to go into town. We are running low on supplies. I will check on the status of your documents. I hope to have them with me when I return."

After Finley left, there was an eerie stillness in the building. They all sensed it.

"It's strange being here by ourselves," said Ingrid. "It feels as though something isn't right."

Wilhelm said, "You feel like that, Ingrid, because we traveled through those mountains with our small group. Now it is even smaller."

"I'm glad you have decided to go to Portugal with us, Wilhelm," said Ingrid. "We will stay there until the war is over. Maybe one day we can all return to Berlin together. I would love to see your mother again."

"As would I," said Wilhelm.

Suddenly, sirens could be heard a few blocks away. It was a sound they had grown used to in the warehouse district of the docks. The blaring sound got closer, then closer still, before stopping outside their warehouse. There were several vehicles. Brakes squealing, doors slamming. Then two of the side doors of the warehouse opened and in ran several Spanish police officers with submachine guns. There were at least a dozen.

"I'm scared, Mama," said the usually silent Dreyfus, as he nuzzled close to Ingrid, wrapping his arms around her waist.

The small group who had been through so much together stood in silence as the armed squad of police officers surrounded them.

Miriam said in Spanish, "What is this about?"

"You are under arrest, *señora*," said a police officer.

"Under arrest for what?" asked Miriam.

Without answering the question, the policeman then asked, "Where is the one who calls himself Finley?"

"We don't know who that is."

"You are lying," said the policeman.

Miriam stood quietly, realizing talking would bring more questioning.

Several of the policemen scattered in different directions, searching the warehouse.

Outside, another vehicle approached, but with no siren. They heard two car doors slam. Moments later a man in civilian clothes entered the warehouse. He was sharply dressed in a wide brimmed felt hat and a long leather coat. Wilhelm sensed who they were dealing with—the *Gestapo*.

The warehouse was silent other than the *Gestapo* agent's well-polished leather shoes as he approached the group.

The Heroes of Sainte-Mère Église

Addressing the policeman, he said in Spanish, "Fine work, *Comisario*."

Switching to German he said to the group, "You almost made it, didn't you? Fortunately, corruption in Spain these days is rampant. If you slip enough gold into the right pockets, you can get anyone to help you."

Wilhelm remembered the boys playing outside of the warehouse the day they arrived. *One of them ran off.*

The *Gestapo* agent then reached in his pocket and pulled out a wanted poster, glanced at it, and approached Wilhelm.

After getting close enough that Wilhelm could smell his disgusting breath, the agent said, "You are a treasonous pig. You betrayed your country, your family, and your honor. Why? To help a group of Jewish swine. If I had my way, they would slaughter you in the same trough as them. But unlike you, I am disciplined. My orders are to take you to Cherbourg for court-martial. Where is your uniform?"

"At the top of the Pyrénées mountains. Would you like me to take you to it?"

The agent snickered, "Soon you won't find life so humorous, Major."

Ingrid knelt and hugged Dreyfus. Alfred held Esther close.

The police surrounded them, and they were led toward the lorries outside. Both Ingrid and Alfred realized that Papa's suitcase was hidden under a bed in the warehouse.

Ingrid thought to herself, *Hidden? Sliding a suitcase filled with cash, jewels and gold under a bed is not hiding it. Joseph would be furious.*

As they were escorted out of the building, Ingrid realized it made no difference anymore.

What good is the case now?

The group sat in the back of the lorry, watching through

the opening of the canvas. They watched as a police officer exited the warehouse and presented the *Gestapo* agent with Joseph's case. Unlike the thief on the mountain, he didn't ask for the key. He simply pulled a knife from his breast pocket and cut into the side. Miriam looked on as she watched the knife rip through Joseph's initials embossed in the leather.

Alfred, also watching, remembered searching the field in the pouring rain after their truck rolled over.

Papa's case. It couldn't save us after all.

The driver of the truck released the brake, and they rolled forward.

"Where are they taking us, Wilhelm? Do you have any idea?" asked Uri.

"The *Gestapo* agent said something about taking me to Cherbourg for court-martial. The only logical way to get there from here is by plane or boat. They surely won't escort us back through the Pyrénées."

The truck didn't travel far. It seemed like less than a kilometer before it stopped at the end of the docks.

A different set of men in Spanish police uniforms were there.

"*Raus jetzt. Schnell!*" Get out now. Quickly!

They are speaking German, Wilhelm thought to himself.

After climbing down from the back of the lorry, they saw a series of piers with various types of boats tied to them. Most were fishing boats.

Moored to the pier they were on was an inconspicuous motor cruiser.

It appeared to be about forty meters. It flew a Spanish flag.

Using their rifles, the policemen shoved them down the

pier until they were next to the cruiser. Once there, they were herded aboard and forced below decks.

Chapter Sixty-Five

JUNE 4, 1944

United Kingdom

The streets in England had been different for the past week. There were no longer U.S. soldiers and sailors in every bar and restaurant. The British girls were missing their Yank boyfriends, who were now restricted to their bases.

The assembly had started. The day all of Europe had been waiting for was looming.

From Wales to East Anglia to the White Cliffs of Dover, the United Kingdom had been a beehive of activity. Even the smallest hamlets provided support to the nearly three million Allied troops preparing for the invasion.

In addition to the soldiers, sailors, and airmen, the island was a staging area for two and a half million tons of supplies, eleven thousand airplanes and seven thousand combat and support ships. Soon, one-hundred-fifty-six-thousand men will penetrate Adolf Hitler's Atlantic wall.

"When do you think we are going, Captain?" asked Staff Sergeant Hicks.

The Heroes of Sainte-Mère Église

"Soon," said Captain Wakefield. "Did you write your suicide letters?"

"Nineteen of them," replied Hicks.

"Oh, that's right, you have that big ass family."

"The hardest one was to my son. He is only twenty months old, and I have never met him. Here's his picture."

"He's beautiful. Are you sure he's yours?"

"He gets his looks from his mother."

"Obviously. What's his name?"

"Baldwin Jr."

Laughing, "Your first name is Baldwin?"

"Yes, Captain it is. What of it? You should be glad. Its origin is Norman and means 'loyal friend.' So, when we parachute into Normandy, there is no better man to have by your side than me."

"Hicks, I knew that before you told me your first name."

"How many did you write, Captain?"

"I wrote six," replied Wakefield. "When we get back, you, me, and every member of the 82nd Airborne will start a bonfire and burn the damn things."

"Attention!" shouted a corporal near the door of the assembly room.

"At ease, men," said General James Gavin.

With the rumble of wooden chairs and boots sliding across the floor, the platoon sat down to listen for their orders.

General "Jumpin' Jim" Gavin was highly respected among his men. Other than the stars on his helmet, he led as though he was one of them. Many in the room fought side by side with him in North Africa and Sicily. He not only carried an M1 Carbine rifle, they saw him use it.

In front of the room was a map of the Cotentin Peninsula. Grabbing the wooden pointer from the desk, he touched it to the map,

"Our job, gentlemen, is to cut off German access to Cherbourg from Carentan. The main road between the two is N-13. Our mission is to take control of it. To carry out this order, our objective will be to capture this little village here—Sainte-Mère-Église."

Cherbourg, France

The seas were calm during the twenty-six-hour trip from San Sebastián to Cherbourg. It was early evening when they arrived. They had not received food or water since breakfast the previous day.

As they waited to exit the boat, Wilhelm said to Ingrid, "I'm sorry I couldn't get you to Portugal."

"You gave us four extra years of life, Wilhelm. Had it not been for you, they would have shipped us to a work camp from Pau."

"If you ever see my mother again, please tell her I love her. My father and sister, too."

"I will, Wilhelm."

They both sensed it was a pointless request. He said it in part to give her one last glimmer of hope.

They opened the hatch, and a *Wehrmacht* soldier yelled down, "Komm *jetzt hier hoch. Schnell!*" Get up here now. Quickly!

After being taken down the pier, Wilhelm had his hands cuffed behind his back. He was escorted into a building at the end of the pier that was once Daniel Girard's pilothouse.

They placed the others in the back of a lorry where they sat for more than an hour.

Through the back canvas, they stared at the building Wilhelm had been taken into.

"There he is. There is Wilhelm," said Alfred. "They are bringing him out."

They watched as he was escorted from the pilothouse with his hands still cuffed behind his back, still dressed in civilian clothes. His head was held high, his face stoic. They marched him across the dock and pushed his back against the corner of the maintenance shop. The same maintenance shop where René had first met DuBois.

They shackled his feet and blindfolded him. Five *Wehrmacht* soldiers lined up fifteen meters in front of him and aimed their Mausers at his chest.

In the lorry, Ingrid turned away and covered Dreyfus's eyes. The others looked away, too, except for Alfred who held Esther close, her face buried in his chest so she wouldn't see.

A *Wehrmacht* officer stood next to the soldiers. He raised his hand then abruptly lowered it, and with the crack of five Mauser rifles, the life of a hero was over.

Bushy Park, London England

General Dwight D. Eisenhower, Supreme Commander of the European Theater, entered his office. He strode past the microphones and recording devices and sat at his oak desk.

Opening the top right drawer, he pulled out two speeches he had been drafting for four months. The first accepted full responsibility for the D-Day invasion in the event it should fail. After glancing at it briefly, he placed it back in the drawer, praying he would never need to read it publicly.

He then read the second speech. Although he had edited it dozens of times, and shared it with others for their input, he still marked through several sentences, added notes, and made additional changes.

Handing it to his aide to type the final draft, he sat back in his chair and stared at the posh office the British government had provided for him. The paintings on the walls were stunning. Some were of the English countryside; others were of British royalty from generations past.

Less than twenty-four hours earlier, he had given the order to go.

He thought about the mothers, fathers, wives, sisters, brothers, and children who would be notified of the loss of their loved ones. These notifications would be received in the U.S.A., but also in Britain, Canada, Australia, France, Poland, New Zealand, Greece, and a dozen other countries who would sacrifice their sons to liberate the continent of Europe.

His aide handed the final draft back to him, and he read it one last time. Looking up, he nodded toward the sound engineer who started the recording device. The recording would be heard by the nearly three million Allied soldiers, sailors, and airmen about to take part in Operation Overlord.

When the sound engineer pointed for him to begin, General Eisenhower read the following words:

Soldiers, Sailors, and Airmen of the Allied Expeditionary Force!

The Heroes of Sainte-Mère Église

You are about to embark upon the Great Crusade, toward which we have striven these many months. The eyes of the world are upon you. The hopes and prayers of liberty-loving people everywhere march with you. In company with our brave Allies and brothers-in-arms on other Fronts you will bring about the destruction of the German war machine, the elimination of Nazi tyranny over oppressed peoples of Europe, and security for ourselves in a free world.

Your task will not be an easy one. Your enemy is well trained, well equipped, and battle-hardened. He will fight savagely.

But this is the year 1944! Much has happened since the Nazi triumphs of 1940-41. The United Nations have inflicted upon the Germans great defeats, in open battle, man-to-man. Our air offensive has seriously reduced their strength in the air and their capacity to wage war on the ground. Our Home Fronts have given us an overwhelming superiority in weapons and munitions of war and placed at our disposal great reserves of trained fighting men. The tide has turned! The free men of the world are marching together to Victory!

I have full confidence in your courage, devotion to duty, and skill in battle. We will accept nothing less than full Victory!

Good Luck! And let us all beseech the blessing of Almighty God upon this great and noble undertaking.

Sainte-Mère-Église, France

As the lorry moved east down N-13, Alfred looked past the soldier sitting on the bench at the rear. He recognized the countryside.

"We are approaching Sainte-Mère-Église, Mama."

"Nicht sprechen," shouted the guard. No talking.

Alfred thought about when they'd left. It was May 10, 1940. The day before his thirteenth birthday. He recalled walking home from school with Jean-Pierre. His papa stopping the old truck, and mama telling him to get in.

We are leaving for Spain, she'd said.

It was so long ago. So much had happened since.

After an hour drive, the truck came to a stop at *Gare Chef du Pont*.

"Aus-Out!" shouted the guard.

The train station was a flurry of activity. Prisoners in the same gray uniforms they saw in Pau were loading the train with supplies. Primarily crates of food. But also horses and people—people who were dressed in the gray uniforms and crammed onto cattle cars.

Alfred noticed an open field with a large holding area in the center. They had fenced it in with tall wooden posts and chicken wire.

Inside were dozens of people, some dressed in gray prison uniforms and many others in civilian clothes. They had yellow stars sewn into their clothes, something he had not seen before. There were women and children along with the elderly.

Their scrawny frames made their clothes baggy. Their eyes were sunken, and they were frail.

How long has it been since they have fed these people?

The Heroes of Sainte-Mère Église

Esther looked up at Alfred. "These people remind me of Otto and Chayim before they died," she said.

"Be quiet. No talking," shouted the guard as he shoved them into the pen.

The push forced Ingrid to the ground.

"I'll help you up, Mama," said Alfred.

A voice murmured. "If you want to speak, move to the center of the pen. The guards can't see you in the middle of all these people."

Taking the stranger's advice, the Shapiros and Edelmans made their way to the center.

"Where are you from?" someone asked.

"I am from here," said Ingrid. "Sainte-Mère-Église."

"Ingrid?" said a voice behind her.

Ingrid turned to see one of Joseph's colleagues from the bank.

"Yvette? Yvette Babin? Is that you?"

"Yes, it is me, Ingrid."

"What is happening here?" asked Ingrid.

"We are being deported to labor camps in Germany. It is dreadful, Ingrid. Where have you been? Where is Joseph?" asked Yvette.

Ingrid explained their entire journey over the past four years, including Joseph's death at the hands of the *bandidos* in the mountains.

"What about you, Yvette? Why are you here? You aren't Jewish."

"Do you recall the Schwartz family?"

"Yes, of course."

"I was hiding them in my attic. Someone found out and turned me in. The Schwartz family was deported last month. They have kept me in a separate prison until they decided what to do with me."

Ingrid and Yvette shared the hardships they had experienced and reminisced about Joseph and how nice of a man he was.

Alfred and Esther stood together staring out toward the train. Its steam engine hissed and spat as it remained idle, waiting for everything to load. They noticed the cattle cars.

Esther said, "Do you remember what Wilhelm said? People are closed in those cattle cars for days with no food or water. There is no place to use the toilet, he said." Her tears flowed as she held Alfred close and said, "I'm scared."

"I don't want you to suffer in there, Esther. I am seventeen now. I am a man. I will protect you."

"It is no use, Alfred. How are we going to escape?"

"I'll find a way."

As Alfred looked around, he became furious.

How could this happen? Why didn't we fight back? None of this nightmare makes sense.

Still looking toward the train, he saw a familiar face on the platform directing the prisoners. It was Maurice Fuquay. The boy who bullied him when they were young. The one Jean-Pierre beat up.

It would only make sense that he would take a job that would allow him to push Jews around. It is the perfect job for him.

Alfred continued to stare at Maurice with contempt.

As dusk came, the guards rotated their positions, and Alfred saw Maurice and another guard walking his way. They would watch the pen now.

Maurice and the other guard walked past the side of the enclosure, looking in at the prisoners. He looked the same, just a much larger version of the same pudgy oppressor he once knew.

As they approached, Alfred knew he should be quiet,

not wishing to give him the satisfaction of seeing him trapped. But he couldn't help himself.

"Maurice!" shouted Alfred. "I see you are still an asshole."

"Shapiro? I see you are still a Jew boy. Where have you been? I thought you went to Spain."

"Go to hell."

Looking at Esther, Maurice asked, "Is that your wife, girlfriend, or just a whore you met?"

Alfred refused to answer. He didn't want to get Esther involved in the discussion.

Speaking to the other guard, Maurice said, "This Jew was in my class in school many years ago. I used to kick the shit out of him. Now look at him."

The two laughed and continued on their way. Alfred was simmering.

"Calm down, Alfred," said Esther. "Getting angry will not help us."

After some time passed, Maurice returned to the side of the holding pen. He was alone this time. He got Alfred's attention and called him over.

Whispering to him, he said. "Tonight, when the sun goes down, meet me at the back of the pen. Over there in that corner. Be there around midnight."

The Germans had confiscated everyone's possessions, without a watch there was no way to know when midnight arrived. So, Alfred waited until most of the prisoners were asleep in the grass, then made his way to the fence.

Crawling on his belly, he made it to the corner of the pen and waited. It was pitch black. Everything was in a blackout condition.

Maurice appeared from the tall grass nearby. He, too, had crawled on his belly so he wouldn't be seen. He had a canvas bag with him.

"Shapiro?" he whispered.

"I'm here."

Still on their bellies, they crawled to the same section of the fence. Their faces nearly touched with only the chicken wire between them.

Maurice reached in the bag and pulled out bread, cheese, dried beef, and four apples.

There was a hole under the fence, camouflaged with tall grass.

Sliding the food to Alfred, Maurice said, "Here. Take this."

"What is it?" said Alfred.

"What does it look like, Shapiro? It's food. Look, I'm sorry I was so rough on you earlier. I had to be like that because of the other guard. I couldn't tip him off. I'm not like that kid who used to bully you. I took this job to try to help the prisoners before they get shipped off. I smuggle as much food to them as I can. It isn't much, but I must do something. I can't just sit and watch so many suffer and simply turn my head."

"I appreciate the food, but you can do more. You can get us out of here."

"How? You see what it is like around here? There are *Waffen-SS* everywhere. As we speak, there are guards within fifty meters in every direction. Do you know the risk I am taking just by being here?"

"Maurice, I am begging for your help. You are the only thing between my family and a Nazi slave camp."

Maurice Fuquay looked at the face of Alfred. He saw the little boy he used to treat so horribly. The boy he had once shoved to the ground and kicked and spit on unmercifully. Now, he also saw a man. A man that was just asking for mercy for his family.

"How many are with you, Shapiro?"

"There are six of us."

"Can everyone run?"

"I have my mother who is nearly fifty, and Esther's parents. They are the same age as my mother. I also have my little brother Dreyfus, who is nine, and Esther, who you met. We are all weak. We have been through hell. But we will do whatever we have to."

"Tomorrow, bring them to this same spot at the same time. Discuss this with no other prisoners. If I get here tomorrow and there are fifty people here with you, I will just keep crawling through the tall grass and you will never see me again. Got it, Shapiro?"

"Got it, Maurice."

PART III
Liberation

They fight not for the lust of conquest.
 They fight to end conquest.
 They fight to liberate.

> President Franklin Delano Roosevelt

Chapter Sixty-Six

JUNE 5, 1944

**1858 hours
Greenham Common Airfield, RAF
Greenham, England**

They assembled between their tents, waiting to board the C-47 airplanes that would take them over the Cotentin Peninsula of Normandy, France. The men of Company E, 502nd Parachute Infantry Regiment, 101st Airborne Division, had blackened their faces with burned cork, cocoa, and cooking oil to blend into the darkness.

"Are you nervous, Sergeant?" asked a nineteen-year-old baby-faced corporal from Brooklyn, NY.

The tall, battle-hardened Sergeant said, "We are all uneasy, Corporal. Some of us are terrified. Just remember your training. Do what we have taught you, and you'll be fine."

"That is bullshit, Sergeant. Many of these men standing next to us will be dead in a few hours."

"If you think like that, Corporal, you will be one of

them. Again, I'm telling you: remember your instructions, pay attention to your surroundings, and draw comfort in knowing they are unaware we are coming. By the way, keep your bad attitude to yourself."

"I hear ya, Sergeant."

Moments later, there was chatter among the troops. Traveling toward them was a U.S. Army, 1942 four-door Studebaker. Attached to each front fender was a bright red flag, each containing five white stars.

"Is that General Eisenhower?" shouted a voice from the back.

"Well, I'll be damned," said another.

The car approached the waiting paratroopers as they looked on.

"What is he doing here?" asked another voice.

"He wants to give us a good word before we jump to our death."

The last comment broke the tension, and the group erupted into nervous laughter. The humor in the statement stemmed from its truthfulness.

General Eisenhower's driver, Mrs. Kathleen Summersby of the British Mechanized Transport Corps, stopped the vehicle several meters from the paratroopers. Ike's personal aide exited the front passenger seat and opened the rear door, where the general was sitting.

Wearing his trademark short waistcoat and cap, the general approached the members of the 101st Airborne.

"Good evening, General," the men shouted in unison.

"Good evening, gentlemen. How is everyone feeling tonight? Are you ready to give 'em hell?"

"Yes, sir!" they shouted.

Stepping over parachute packs and weapons that laid at the feet of the men, he approached a few soldiers and

The Heroes of Sainte-Mère Église

reached out to shake their hands. Individually, he asked them, "What is your name, soldier?"

"First Lieutenant Wallace Strobel from Michigan, sir."

"Oh, yes, Michigan. Great fishing there. I've been many times. Do you feel you are ready for the operation, First Lieutenant? Have you been well briefed?"

"I believe we are ready, sir," replied Strobel.

"It is no wonder you volunteered for the Airborne. You must be tough to make it through those Michigan winters," replied Ike.

A corporal from the back shouted, "I'm sure you grew up with some harsh winters in Kansas, sir."

"That's why I moved away. Too cold for me," replied Ike.

"How about you, Corporal? Where are you from?"

"I'm Corporal Joe Alvarez from Arkansas, sir."

"I've been to Arkansas, too. I have a cousin who lives in Hopewell. We once went hunting for wild hogs. I believe you call them razorbacks. They are mean rascals. You better get them with the first shot, or they will come after you."

"Yes, sir. You are right," replied the corporal. "I once lost a dog who jumped out of my truck and ran into the woods after several of them. All I heard was my dog yelping. By the time I got there with my shotgun, the razors were gone, and my dog laid there bleeding to death. It was an awful sight to see."

"Well unlike those hogs, you'll whip those Germans. They won't know what hit 'em. You will leave them bloody, I'm sure of it, soldier."

"Yes, sir, I will."

Another voice from the back shouted, "Sir, I am from Texas. My family owns a ranch. If you need a job after the war, just let me know. I'll teach you how to rope. The great thing about working on a Texas ranch is there is always plenty of fresh beef to eat."

"I appreciate the offer, soldier. I'll make you a deal. You get over the Channel and end this war, and I'll come work for you. How does that sound?"

"I'm holding you to it, sir."

"You know how to get a hold of me, soldier," said Ike.

That evening, General Eisenhower spent over an hour mingling among the members of the 101st Airborne. Those who survived the invasion later said his words were encouraging and calming and put the men at ease in preparation of the daunting task ahead of them.

With the massive engines of the C-47s roaring in the background, General Eisenhower raised his voice. "I have complete faith in all of you. The world is counting on you. Your families back home are counting on you."

"We won't let them down, sir," shouted an enthusiastic voice from the back.

"I know you won't," Ike shouted back. "May God be with all of you."

Kathleen Summersby later reported that when General Eisenhower left the encounter with the 101st Airborne and returned to his car, he wiped tears from his eyes.

He returned to his headquarters at Bushy Park, around 1:15 a.m., where he waited throughout the morning for reports of the D-Day landings.

Chapter Sixty-Seven

JUNE 5, 1944

2218 hours
Liberté
Saint-Cyr, France

"Do you think it will be tonight, Martin?" asked Pascal as the group listened to the BBC over the shortwave.

"It won't be much longer. When I was in England last week, the massive numbers of men and equipment moving toward the coast was staggering. Something will happen; the invasion is imminent."

In English, the BBC was reporting on the latest air raids, weather, and movies from the American films playing in the theaters.

"Let's review our assignments," said René. "Jean-Pierre and Angélique, what are you to do?"

"We blow up the German communication lines between Carentan and Sainte-Mère-Église."

"Good. Arthur and Luke?"

"We have the communication lines near the main garrison at La Madeleine."

Resting his hand on Luke's shoulder, Pascal said, "Are you ready, son?"

"I won't let you down, Papa."

Looking at Arthur, he said, "Take care of him."

Arthur said, "I couldn't ask for a better partner. He'll do great."

René said, "Laurent, Pascal and I will cut off the head of the snake."

Looking back at Arthur, he said, "By the way, Arthur. How do I say in German, 'Do you remember me, Dettmer? You gave the order to burn my house to the ground'?"

"Let me make it easy for you, René. Just tell him, *'Zeit fur dich, das Arschloch zu sterben.'* That means 'Time for you to die, asshole.'"

"That's even better, Arthur. I never knew you had such a way with words."

Arthur said, "It's getting late. It doesn't look like we will receive the signal tonight. Maybe we should go home and come back tomorrow."

"Let's give it thirty more minutes. If we don't hear by then, we leave," said Martin.

While they waited, they cleaned their firearms and sharpened their knives. With five minutes to spare, the BBC broadcast abruptly turned to French.

It first repeated what they had just reported in English. Then Laurent heard what he was waiting for, the first four notes of Beethoven's Fifth Symphony. Upon its conclusion, the announcer quoted the following line from the French poem *"Chanson d'automne:"*

"Bercent mon coeur d'une langueur monotone." Lull my heart with a monotonous languor.

Martin rose from his chair. "That's our signal. Grab your weapons—the invasion is tonight. It's time to take our country back."

2353 hours
Fauville, France

With the night air blowing her long dark hair, Angélique wrapped her arms securely around Jean-Pierre as he drove his father's motorcycle.

Traveling down narrow roads few people knew about, they passed through pastures and fields, with the headlight off so they wouldn't be noticed.

Overhead, they heard the rumble of Allied aircraft engines. From the direction of Sainte-Mère-Église, air raid sirens could be heard intermixed with the sound of bomber payloads exploding as they hit the ground.

Jean-Pierre and Angélique had already scoped out a suitable place to blow the communication lines coming in from Carentan.

Wehrmacht engineers had run the lines under the base of a steel bridge that crossed over a shallow stream. They then went through a row of bushes before being mounted on a series of utility poles.

When they arrived at the location, Jean-Pierre laid the motorcycle down beneath a row of bushes along the side of the road.

"Angélique, we need to blow at least six of these poles to be certain they can't be repaired before the invasion. I'll set the charges for three, and you get the other three. Do you remember how my papa showed us?"

"Yes, I remember, Jean-Pierre. I can do it."

After setting the charges, they heard the rumble of engines. A column of lorries was driving toward them.

"Behind the bushes, Angélique," shouted Jean-Pierre as he dove to the ground.

After the trucks passed, Jean-Pierre said, "They must know something is happening."

As he reached for the detonator to connect the wires, he paused.

"I just thought of something. Gabrielle Hall said there is a garrison of *Panzer* tanks stationed near Carquebut. If they come here, they will need to cross this bridge. I have extra explosives in my saddlebag. We will take out the bridge, too."

Angélique watched as Jean-Pierre waded into the water. He then climbed up into the underside of the bridge, where he laid the additional charges.

After returning to the bank of the stream, Angélique handed him the detonator, and he attached the wires to the contact points.

"You will have the pleasure, Angélique," he said as he handed the detonator back to her. "When I give you the word, twist the lever and then hop on the back of the bike, and we will ride like hell. We need to get back to Sainte-Mère-Église in case my papa needs me."

Jean-Pierre lifted the motorcycle from the ground and pumped his foot, causing it to roar to life. He revved the throttle one last time, before nodding to Angélique.

With a single twist of her hand, the German army lost their communication lines—and access to a garrison of *Panzer* tanks.

2358 hours
Sainte-Mère-Église, France

The sirens were deafening. The sound woke the prisoners from their sleep on the wet grass as a light rain fell through the night sky.

"What is happening?" asked Miriam Edelman.

"Stay down on the ground—it's an air raid," said a woman next to her.

As every prisoner in the holding pen hugged the ground, the woman next to Miriam said, "Brace yourself. The bombs are about to fall."

"Bombs from where?"

"The Americans. They used to fly over twice per week. They recently increased to every day."

"Why are they dropping bombs on innocent civilians?"

"They are dropping bombs on Germans. We happen to be in the way. There is a rumor they are about to invade. We hope they come soon before we get put on the trains."

"Airplane engines—B-24 Liberators," shouted a voice in the pen.

"Cover your heads," someone else shouted.

Moments later, massive explosions could be heard a kilometer away. Some landed closer. The ground shook and the smell of burned metal and dirt permeated the air.

The ground kept rumbling, and the explosions got louder.

They felt blast after blast as the sixty-plus planes carpet-bombed the vicinity of Sainte-Mère-Église.

Alfred crawled on his belly. First to Esther, then to his mama and Dreyfus. Then to Esther's parents.

"Follow me. I'm getting us out of here."

"You are doing what?" said Uri.

"Don't ask any questions—just follow me."

As the blasts got nearer and increased in frequency, Alfred noticed there were no guards in sight. They were all in holes they had dug for themselves after previous air raids.

"Get to your feet and run. Stay close behind me."

When they arrived at the rear fence, Maurice was already there. When he spotted them coming, he pulled wire cutters from a bag and began to cut a hole in the wire fencing.

Alfred said, "Hurry, Maurice. Once the bombing stops, the guards will return."

"Almost there, Shapiro. Just a few more cuts."

Snip-snip!

Maurice ripped the last piece of wire away, creating a hole for them to escape through.

Alfred waited for the others to climb through before exiting himself.

Once they were through, Maurice said, "Follow me. I will hide you in my father's factory."

Chapter Sixty-Eight

JUNE 6, 1944

**0112 hours
The Skies Above
Cotentin Peninsula**

The C-47 bounced in the darkness. Around them was the thunder of the two engines and endless exploding *yak-yak* from the antiaircraft fire below. The shrapnel pounded on the wings and fuselage of the airplane.

"I don't know what the Krauts have planned for us on the ground, but it must be better than being in this flying casket," shouted a voice from the back.

"Red light! Everybody up," yelled Staff Sergeant Hicks.

As the men stood, they hooked to the static line as they had done dozens of times over the past year.

Captain Wakefield was standing at the open door, hanging on tightly, preparing to be the first man to jump.

"This is it, gentlemen," shouted Wakefield.

"Remember, if you get separated, don't give your position away by talking. Use your clickers to find us. One click followed by two clicks, followed by the words 'flash, thunder, welcome.' Does everyone have it?"

"Yes, sir!" shouted the small squad in unison.

Wakefield looked out of the open door. Below him, C-47 airplanes could be seen in a every direction. In his briefing, he learned there were over eight hundred planes participating in the invasion, each carrying sixteen to twenty-eight paratroopers.

As the aircraft bounced and tilted below his feet, he held on tight and watched as a plane above was hit with flack, causing it to explode into a fireball.

"Shit! How much longer?" he shouted to the pilot.

"Three minutes."

Wakefield shouted, "Get ready, men. I'll see you in Sainte-Mère-Église."

0123 hours
Pleinmont
Guernsey Island

"No, Philippe, stay here," Claire pleaded as she held the crying baby Oliver.

"I can't. That antiaircraft fire has been nonstop for two days, and they are shooting at Allied aircraft. Something is happening in France. I have to do my part, no matter how small."

"But what are you going to do? What if they kill you? I just lost my father. Don't let me lose you, too."

"I love you, Claire," Philippe said as he kissed his wife and baby Oliver before leaving the house.

0136 hours
Neuville-au-Plain, France

After jumping from the C-47 at less than one thousand meters, Captain Wakefield hit hard, landing in a pond of waist-deep water. His boots sunk into the mud as his parachute softly collapsed around him.

As he unhooked the chute, the smell of the stagnate swamp he stood in was revolting.

In the sky above, tracers from antiaircraft fire lit up the night, sometimes followed by a massive explosion as a C-47 blew apart after absorbing the shrapnel.

From every direction, he heard machine gun fire. He recognized the distinctive ripping sound of the German MG 42, intermixed with American M1A1s like the one he carried himself.

Jesus, God, get me out of here. All hell is breaking loose.

Once out of the water, Wakefield ran through an open field and dove into a thicket of bushes in the woods.

Seeing no movement around him, he tried to find a familiar landmark from the aerial photos he had studied during his briefing.

There was a house to his west. Light was shining from behind a curtain. After cautiously approaching, he knocked on the door, then stepped to the side with one hand on his .45, ready to draw.

An elderly man opened, his wife standing behind him.

Wakefield pointed to the American flag on his shoulder and in French said, *"Bonjour,* I am an American. I need your help."

The couple grinned, grabbed him, and pulled him into their kitchen.

At the table eating apples were Staff Sergeant Hicks and two corporals from their unit.

"I see you guys are giving the Germans hell," said Wakefield.

"Boss, we were trying to interpret their directions to Sainte-Mère-Église. They don't speak English and we don't speak French."

Wakefield pulled a map from his jacket pocket and laid it in on the table. In French he said, *"Monsieur,* could you please tell me the best way to get to Sainte-Mère-Église?"

The old man first pointed to the location of his house, then used his finger to trace a route through a series of backroads and pastures.

Wakefield nodded. *"Merci beaucoup, Monsieur. Madame,* we are so sorry we disturbed you."

She replied, *"Non, Monsieur.* You are not disturbing us. We have been waiting for you. You are our liberators—our heroes."

Addressing his small squad, Wakefield said, "Let's go see if we can find more of our boys."

0138 hours
Guernsey Island

The petrol rations had been cut off for weeks. Those who still had fuel had managed to hide it from the *Wehrmacht* searches.

Philippe poured the last can into the pickup truck and sped down the long driveway.

The wind was blowing in from the Atlantic Ocean, and

the light rain drenched his face as he rode with the window down.

Keeping his headlights off, he traveled to the source of the tracer rounds lighting up the sky.

When he got closer to the hilltop bunker, a single sentry stopped him.

"Halt!" the young soldier said as he pointed his rifle at Philippe. "*Warum bist du aus der Ausgangssperre?*" Why are you out past curfew?

As Philippe looked into the soldier's eyes pretending to answer, he raised a revolver from his lap and pulled the trigger, hitting the sentry squarely in the face.

Grabbing Oliver's rifle from the seat next to him, he climbed to the top of the hill and glanced over the edge. The sound of the continuous antiaircraft fire was thunderous, but it was also perfect cover. He could snipe the crew one by one as they were distracted by their mission of loading, firing, and reloading. There were three members of the team, and they performed with rapid efficiency.

Philippe aimed the Mauser, then squeezed the trigger, dropping the first soldier. Pulling the bolt of the rifle back and firing two more times in rapid succession, he eliminated the threat of the first of four antiaircraft guns during the early morning hours of the liberation.

0213 hours
Neuville-au-Plain, France

The sound of the metal clickers they were issued was distinct. *Click ... click-click* was the exchange between Wakefield and a small group of paratroopers on the other side of the hedgerow.

"Flash."

"Thunder."

"Welcome."

The two small squads peeked over the mound of rock and mud for a final confirmation that the other side was friendly.

"I'm Captain Wakefield, with the 505, 82nd."

A tall gangly officer responded from the other side, "Lieutenant Douglas, 502, 101st. Where the hell are we?"

Wakefield said, "Near as I can tell, we are in Neuville. Mésieres is north of here, and Sainte-Mère-Église is in that direction to the southeast."

"Judging by the way the night sky is lit up, it looks like the entire town of Sainte-Mère-Église is ablaze," said Douglas.

"That will make it easier to find," said Wakefield.

"Do you want us to stick with you, Captain?"

"What is your objective?"

"We are supposed to capture a bridge in Neuville."

"Stick with your plan, Lieutenant. Go find your bridge. Good luck."

"Good luck to you, Captain."

After separating from Lieutenant Douglas, Wakefield's small squad of four continued to Sainte-Mère-Église. They stayed close to hedgerows and wooded areas as they traveled the countryside.

In between the occasional moments of quiet, machine gun fire could be heard, and mortar rounds became closer and more frequent, causing the ground to shake with each blast.

In the distance, they could hear a church bell ringing.

The Heroes of Sainte-Mère Église

"Where is that coming from?" asked Hicks.

"It sounds like it is coming from Sainte-Mère-Église," said Wakefield.

Hicks said, "They picked a hell of a time to announce a church service."

The rumble of approaching engines caused them to dive behind a hedgerow as they watched two German lorries zip past.

"Don't move," said one corporal. "I see Krauts in the corner of the field."

After spotting an MG 42 sitting on a tripod aimed in their direction, Wakefield said, "So far they haven't seen us. If they had, we would be dead by now."

"What are we going to do, Captain?" asked the corporal.

Hicks said, "We will lay our asses nice and quiet until they look the other way."

"What if they don't? The sun will be up soon. Then we won't have the darkness on our side," said Wakefield.

"What do you suggest, Captain?" asked Hicks.

"Well, we are here to win the war, which means the enemy must die. Besides, there will be more Airborne units cutting through here soon. If we leave that MG 42 buzz saw to mow them down, what does that make us?"

Hicks said, "I'm all in boss. What do you have in mind?"

"These two green corporals who have never been in battle are going to stay right here and not move a muscle. Can you do that, boys?"

"Yes, sir. We can do that."

"Good. Because if you fail at that simple task, you will get us all killed."

"What about us, boss?" asked Hicks.

"You and I will crawl through that opening in the hedgerow. Once through, we will stay low, loop around the back of those bastards, and open fire with everything we have."

"I'm right behind you, Captain."

The forty-meter crawl took them fifteen minutes. They were careful not to make any sudden movements.

Once through the gap, they got to their feet and made certain their heads were always below the top of the hedgerow.

At the corner, they turned right and made their way toward the gun emplacement, slowing as they got closer.

Wakefield raised his hand for Hicks to stop. He then held up three fingers, indicating the number of *Wehrmacht*.

They had been in enough battles together that they knew the routine. Wakefield fires first, then Hicks as they take out the enemy together.

Moments before Wakefield made his move, the MG 42 opened fire with a ripping sound, as tracers sailed across the open field to where they had just come from.

Wakefield and Hicks returned fire, each hitting a man, before the third man ran into the woods.

Hicks shouted, "I'm after him, boss!"

He followed him into the woods.

"No, Hicks!" shouted Wakefield, but it was too late. Hicks was soon out of sight.

Wakefield approached the two dead *Wehrmacht* soldiers on the ground, the barrel of the MG 42 still smoking.

He then looked across the field toward the two dead corporals. Their bodies lay motionless—one sprawled out across the top of the hedgerow where he attempted to escape the machine gun fire. The other on the ground just meters from where he had left them.

The Heroes of Sainte-Mère Église

From the forest, a shot—*crack*. A single rifle blast.

That's not Hicks. He has a machine gun.

Wakefield ran into the woods, keeping low, as he ducked behind tree after tree, slowing to a walk, unable to see much in the dark forest.

He heard a faint gasp. "I'm over here, boss."

Wakefield made his way to Hicks while staying on the alert for the German who'd shot him.

Kneeling down, he asked, "Where'd he get you, Hicks?"

Hicks tried to speak but only coughed up blood. He had a chest wound that entered from the back.

With blood flowing from the side of his mouth, he said, "Boss, tell little Baldwin Jr. about me. Tell him I was a brave soldier. Tell him I loved him. Tell his mother the same. Will you do that for me, boss?"

"You will tell them yourself, Hicks. Because I will carry your ass out of here and get you to a medic. Do you understand me, Hicks? Do you understand me?"

His words fell silent as he stared down at the lifeless body of Staff Sergeant Baldwin Hicks.

Trying not to weep, Wakefield laid his hand on Hicks's chest. *Loyal friend.*

0257 hours
Sainte-Mère-Église, France

Wakefield advanced on the perimeter of Sainte-Mère-Église. He positioned himself in an alley overlooking the courtyard. Dead paratroopers lay everywhere.

The blaze they had seen from a kilometer away was a barn on the edge of the courtyard. The flames reached as high as the church steeple and were intense enough to make the courtyard look like it was daytime.

German soldiers abruptly looked up and fired.

Wakefield watched as another stick of paratroopers dropped from above.

Jesus Christ, those guys don't stand a chance.

The first few landed in the center of the courtyard. Before they could get untangled from their chutes, they were mowed down by MP 40 machine guns by a dozen *Wehrmacht* and *Waffen-SS*. Others landed in trees and were killed before their boots ever touched French soil.

Bullets ricocheted off the shoulder-high wall in front of him and the building behind him.

Pinned down, Wakefield kept his head low.

Shit! I'm useless here.

Six more parachutes descended on the courtyard. The first was directly over the church.

He's landing on the roof.

Wakefield watched as the parachute draped the corner spire. The soldier continued to fall until the suspension lines jerked him tight like a dog running out of leash.

More came down. Some pulled their weapons free and were shooting down at the Germans below.

Wakefield watched as another paratrooper hovered over the burning barn.

Oh, God help him.

He could hear the cries of the man as the heat drew him into the bright orange flames.

The massacre that Wakefield was witnessing repeated itself with two more sticks. It went on for what seemed like an eternity.

After the chaos ended, he kept his head low behind the stone wall, peeking over occasionally to see what was

The Heroes of Sainte-Mère Église

happening. There was an opening at one end of the alley and a house at the other.

I need to find more Americans. I can't capture this town by myself.

Searching for an escape route, he glanced over the wall.

He watched as three Frenchmen, with their hands tied behind their backs, were escorted across the courtyard by *Wehrmacht* soldiers. As they approached the officer, one of the *Wehrmacht* shouted something in German. The only thing Wakefield could make out was the officer's rank and name, "*Sturmbannführer* Dettmer."

After Dettmer replied, they followed him into the house.

Wakefield waited for the activity in the courtyard to settle before he moved toward the house.

As he did, he kept his head below the wall. German voices were on the other side.

He made his way to the backyard and pressed himself between a row of bushes and the house. With the church courtyard now quiet, he realized the machine gun and mortar fire were getting closer. Other airborne units were closing in on the village. Help was on the way.

Come on, boys, you are almost here. Keep coming. I need you.

He positioned himself under a window, raised his head, and peeked in.

The three Frenchmen were in wooden chairs in the middle of the kitchen, their hands still tied behind their backs.

Two of them were seated as they watched the *SS* officer continually beat the third one with a wooden baton. Blood flowed from his mouth and nose, his hair awash in red.

The officer shouted in remedial French, "I have had enough of you and your little group, Legrand. You have wreaked havoc on my entire operation. You have made my life miserable. Did you cut my communication lines?"

Lifting his chin from his bloody shirt and spitting blood as he spoke, he replied, "No, I did not cut your communication lines. That was my son. And he didn't cut them, he used explosives."

Enraged by the comment, Dettmer raised the baton high in the air and brought it down on René's skull, knocking him unconscious. They then dragged the three Frenchmen back out of the front door and into the courtyard.

Wakefield made his way around to the alley wall. When he arrived, there were two teenagers standing several meters from where he was before. A male and a girl with long, dark hair. The young man was holding a bolt-action rifle. They glanced at Wakefield, who pointed to the American flag on his shoulder.

In the courtyard, the SS officer laid the unconscious René on the ground. He made Pascal and Martin Laurent kneel beside him, then pulled his Luger from its holster.

Pointing it at the bloody body on the ground, the officer said, "Legrand, I wish you and your entire family were in your house when I burned it down."

With the crack of a single rifle blast, the head of the SS officer jerked back as blood from his face sprayed into the air.

To Wakefield's left, the young Frenchman pulled the rifle down and ducked behind the wall. German soldiers dove to the ground, not knowing the location of the sniper.

Moments later, the earth shook from a mortar round that landed on the other side of the house. The blast knocked Wakefield and the two teens off their feet. They all lay staring at each other next to the base of the wall.

Before they stood, on the other side of the wall, a barrage of machine gun fire erupted. It was nonstop and enormous in numbers. The house became sprayed with bullets, ricocheting in every direction. Without standing to look, Wakefield recognized the sound.

M1A1s—American.

As the gunfire subsided, he heard shouts of, *"SchieBen Sie nicht, SchieBen Sie nicht!"* Don't shoot, don't shoot!

Rising to his feet, he saw masses of American paratroopers everywhere. They were in the courtyard, the sidewalks, the streets. The few German soldiers who remained alive held their hands over their heads with their weapons at their feet.

Wakefield watched as the young Frenchman who fired the shot leaped over the wall and ran to the man on the ground who had been beaten. The other two who were kneeling checked for signs of life.

From the pharmacy, two men ran across the courtyard. One carried a medical bag.

Chapter Sixty-Nine

JUNE 6, 1944

**0814 hours
Sainte-Mère-Église, France**

The smell of smoldering hay and wood from what was left of the barn permeated the air. With sunrise came the reality of war. The bodies of both American and German soldiers lay everywhere throughout Sainte-Mère-Église.

Climbing the trees in the church courtyard, a group of paratroopers cut down the bullet-riddled remains of their buddies. Their bodies hung suspended over the ground as their parachutes lay tangled in the branches of the trees.

Captain Wakefield noticed a small group of citizens gathered around the pharmacy. Inside, the doctor treated the Frenchman who had been beaten. The young man who'd shot the *SS* officer sat on the curb with the girl.

Across the courtyard, GIs were smoking cigarettes in front of Le Café du Quartier. They sat in chairs that moments earlier laid on their sides, scattered across the sidewalk.

The Heroes of Sainte-Mère Église

Wakefield joined them, and they offered him a smoke, which he refused.

"What units are you boys from?" asked Wakefield.

A corporal said, "I'm with the 101st."

"I'm with the 82nd," said another as he adjusted the bandage of his bloody foot.

"What happened to you?" asked Wakefield.

Pointing to a parachute hanging from the church spire, he said, "You see that up there?"

"Was that you? I watched you come down last night."

"Yes, that was me. I hung up there for what seemed like hours. A Kraut took a shot at me and hit my foot. There was a wounded GI on his back who saw what was happening. Even though he had a belly wound, he took his .45 and shot the German before he could get another crack at me. That GI saved my life. I'll never forget it. After that, I played dead."

"How did you get down?"

"Two Krauts in the tower dragged me in. They took me to a holding area where there were other Paratroopers. It was the darnedest thing. Once the guards realized they were surrounded by Americans, they hauled ass and we just walked away."

"Or in your case, hopped."

"I used a branch as a crutch."

"What is your name, soldier?"

"I'm Corporal John Steele, sir, from Illinois."

During their conversation, they noticed a group of American GIs who walked into town. They looked exhausted and the enlisted men sat down in a clump of grass next to the courtyard.

A first lieutenant from the group walked over and propped up a chair next to them.

Wakefield looked at his shoulder patch. "Fourth Infantry? Where did you come from, First Lieutenant?"

"The beach. We hit Utah about 0630 hours yesterday morning."

"What was it like? Was there heavy resistance?"

"The good thing was, the current carried our boats off course. Where we landed wasn't too bad. They slaughtered our boys who ended up where they were supposed to be. We didn't see heavy combat until we moved inward. Then all hell broke loose. We ran into everything from land mines to 88s. Much of the time we were in open dunes, which made us easy targets. That's why I'm here. I rode an ambulance with some of my men to a field hospital down the road."

Reaching his hand out to shake Wakefield's, he said, "By the way, I'm First Lieutenant William Surratt from Montgomery County, North Carolina."

"We are practically neighbors, my friend. I'm Captain Jack Wakefield, Bedford, Virginia."

Chapter Seventy

AUGUST 25, 1944

**1200 hours
Sainte-Mère-Église, France**

On the very day the first American tanks rolled into a liberated Paris, Jean-Pierre stood at the altar of the eight-hundred-year-old Notre-dame-de-l'Assomption, the centerpiece of Sainte-Mère-Église. The church stood tall and proud like the people it served.

Outside, meters away from the ancient Roman distance marker, his father's dried bloodstains remained visible from the beating he took at the hands of *SS-Sturmbannführer* Gunther Dettmer. The buildings surrounding the courtyard were still damaged from mortar fire from the night of the liberation.

Across the street from the courtyard, American soldiers sat at tables and ordered drinks in front of Le Café du Quartier. They would never know the pleasure of being waited on by Gabrielle Hall, who had resigned her position the day after the village was set free.

Doctor Pelletier moved back home and was seeing patients in his first-floor office again.

Jean-Pierre looked on with pride as much of the town sat in the church pews in front of him. Scanning the crowd, he saw the mayor and his family seated in the back. Pascal and Luke were seated with Arthur and Gabrielle Hall. Next to them, Margot and Martin Laurent. Standing in the back was Maurice Fuquay, who signaled to Jean-Pierre with a thumbs-up.

In the front row, his mama sat next to his papa, who tended to forget things due to his head injuries. Next to them, his brother Philippe with his new bride Claire. In her lap, baby Oliver slept quietly.

Standing at the altar with Jean-Pierre, stood Brigitte Lapierre and Father Rousseau. To his left, his best man, Alfred Shapiro, who couldn't stop telling him how much he loved Esther, also in the crowd with her parents and Mrs. Shapiro.

As the noonday church bell rang, as it had done for centuries, the congregation turned to the back of the sanctuary as two young boys dressed in black opened the large oak doors of Notre-dame-de-l'Assomption.

Jean-Pierre stood mesmerized. Before him, stepping into the church and walking down the aisle was the most beautiful sight he had ever seen. Wearing her mother's long, white wedding dress, Angélique approached the altar. Her eyes stared back at Jean-Pierre. The smile on her face illuminated the church.

Acknowledgments

When I first made the decision to publish a novel, I envisioned doing everything myself. However, after informing others of my plan, the number of people who voluntarily offered to assist in the endeavor was humbling. In the end, I realize I couldn't have finished without them. There are numerous people to whom I owe my gratitude.

First, I would like to thank the citizens of Sainte-Mère-Église. I found their welcoming spirit and gracious embrace of visitors to their charming village to be inspiring. More times than I can count, they spoke the words, "We will never forget."

I would also like to thank, Dawn Gardner, Elizabeth Gassoway, Katie Keene, Mike Buser, Sarah Smith and Terry Gassoway for traveling with me on my research journey to France. Because of you, the trip exceeded my wildest expectations, which were enormously high before we departed.

Also, the following individuals contributed significantly in the form of, editing, researching, advanced reading or a combination of all three: Andy Keene, Colin Fradd, Elizabeth Gassoway, Evan Keene, Genevieve Montcombroux, Joe Alvarez, John Kruger, Katie Keene, Kim Morrison, Mark Keene, Phyllis Sawyer and Terry Gassoway.

Finally, I can say with certainty that this project would have never been completed without the support of two people in particular. My sister, Elizabeth Gassoway, read the manuscript nearly as many times as I have. Her knowledge of the English language and patience in correcting my mistakes were invaluable. Also, my wife, Katie Keene, tolerated my twenty-hour writing weekends and four-hour writing evenings as I trudged along, word after word, paragraph after paragraph. Her constant words of encouragement kept me going.

Also by J.D. Keene

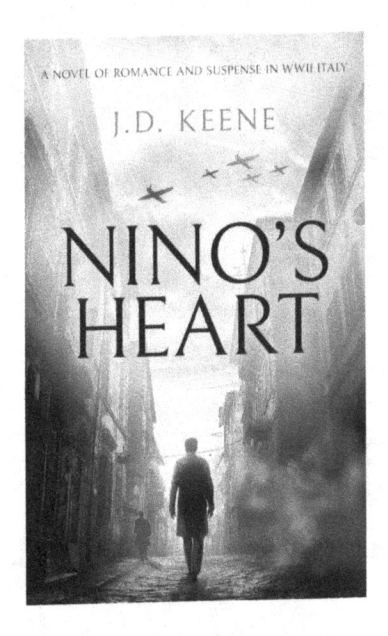

www.vinci-books.com/ninos-heart

In 1938 Italy, a Catholic priest in training and a Jewish widow must choose between faith and forbidden love.

Turn the page for a free preview…

Nino's Heart: Chapter One

BRONX, NY 1934

He sat in the back of the classroom because that's what his father had instructed him to do. His older brother, Angelo, who attended a different school, did the same.

"Watch your back, and never let anyone behind you," their father would say.

They obeyed because the consequences of doing otherwise were severe.

Even though he was in his second year at Saint Francis Preparatory School for boys, he barely knew any of the other students. They kept their distance from him, and he knew why.

"We're sorry, Nino, but our parents told us to stay away from you," they would say.

This led to a lonely existence for the fourteen-year-old Nino DiVincenzo, who was also self-conscious of his small size.

The details of his father's companies were unknown to Nino—that was intentional. There were many men who

Nino's Heart: Chapter One

worked for him. Some of them came by the apartment once per week and dropped off large sums of cash.

Frequently out all night, Nino's father would come home and sleep for a few hours, then leave again for several days. During his long absences, Nino's mother would sometimes sit and stare out the window. On rare occasions, she would get angry and swear in Italian.

"Salvador DiVincenzo, *sei un maiale e anche le tue puttane sono maiali*," she would say. *You are a pig and your whores are pigs, too.*

Why she switched to Italian when swearing, Nino never knew. By order of their father, she had taught her sons to speak Italian as well as any Sicilian. After her outbursts, she would pray the Rosary and apologize to Nino and Angelo for her coarse language.

After being dismissed from his final class of the day, Nino grabbed his books, pulled his flat cap over his thick, black hair, and sprinted down the stairs. Once free of the building, he slowed his pace to a walk. The early September air had an unusual chill, but Nino's blue blazer, which displayed his school's red emblem, kept him warm.

His family lived in Hoffman Towers, one of the most prestigious apartment buildings in the Bronx. Although it was out of the way, Nino would take East 188th Street home. He liked to stop at Giovanni's Drugstore. Mr. Giovanni was kind to Nino. He was kind to everyone, always addressing each of his customers by name. He was popular with the local children because he handed out free candy and had been doing so for two generations of neighborhood kids.

"Good afternoon, Nino. How was school today?" Mr. Giovanni said as a bell over the door rang when Nino entered.

Nino's Heart: Chapter One

Mr. Giovanni had a thick Italian accent he'd never been able to shake, even after three decades in America.

"It was fine, Mr. Giovanni."

Wearing his white pharmacist coat, Mr. Giovanni turned to the icebox behind the counter.

"Do you want the vanilla or do I mix the strawberries in your ice cream today?"

"I'll stick with vanilla," Nino said as he set his books and cap on the soda fountain counter and climbed up on the stool.

Mr. Giovanni said, "I have seen no Angelo, how is your brother?"

"His school suspended him two weeks ago for fighting. They won't let him return until next year. Papa isn't happy and is making him work loading trucks at the docks."

"Work is good for a young man. It will help him grow up."

"That's what Papa says, too."

As Mr. Giovanni turned to set the porcelain bowl on the counter, it slipped from his hand. When it hit the wooden floor, it shattered, splattering ice cream in all directions.

"*Sarò dannato, Mamma mia*," Mr. Giovanni said. "I'm so sorry, Nino. After I clean this up, I will make you more."

"I'll help you, Mr. Giovanni. I'll go get a bucket and a mop from the storage room. I know where they are. You keep them next to the big sink near the toilet."

"Thank you, Nino. While you do that, I'll make you another ice cream."

Nino jumped down from the stool and stepped behind the curtain separating the front of the store and the storage room. He made his way to the rear and placed the bucket in the deep sink. While he was filling it, he heard the bell at the front door.

Nino's Heart: Chapter One

Another customer, Nino thought.

He shut off the water and heard what sounded like pleading from Mr. Giovanni. He was begging for something.

"Please, please, I will pay you I promise," Mr. Giovanni said from the other side of the curtain. "Business has been slow. I don't have the money right now. Please, give me more time."

"I don't want excuses," said the other man in a deep, gruff tone. "I have given you plenty of time. Too many in this neighborhood have fallen behind on their payments. I need to make an example of someone and today is your unlucky day."

"No, no please, I beg you," shouted Mr. Giovanni before his words turned into a series of gurgles and gasps.

Nino left the bucket in the sink and ducked behind a row of shelves, caution in each step. Crashing and banging echoed throughout the building. It sounded as though everything was being knocked over and thrown about the store.

When the clanging stopped, Nino crawled toward the front on his hands and knees. The store was quiet now. He pulled the curtain back just enough to see past it. He saw Mr. Giovanni lying on the floor behind the counter. His blood flowed like a small river before mixing with the melting ice cream.

Bent at the waist and standing over Mr. Giovanni's body, a large man wiped a bloody knife on the white coat of the corpse. Nino couldn't see his face. He wore a wide-brimmed hat and a trench coat. Nino let loose of the curtain and ran to the back door. The swaying cloth drew the man's attention toward the storage room entrance. When Nino arrived

Nino's Heart: Chapter One

at the door, his hope of escape vanished when he found the rear exit locked.

I'm trapped.

Moving swiftly for a man his size, the pursuer was at Nino in an instant.

Nino turned and saw the massive killer glaring at him. Evil reflected in his eyes. He held the knife in his right hand. The remnants of Mr. Giovanni's blood clung to the blade that was as long as Nino's forearm.

I've seen him. He works for Papa. He has been to our apartment.

Nino stood with his back pressed against the door. His stomach tightened. His mind raced as he fought the urge to vomit.

The man paused and tilted his head to the side, squinted his eyes, and stared at Nino as though he was studying him.

He recognizes me. He knows who I am. He knows where I live. He will kill me.

Without saying a word, the man slipped the knife in a pouch sewn into the inside of his trench coat. He then turned and casually walked to the front of the store. The hard leather soles of his shoes scraped over the floor. Nino heard the bell at the entrance ring as the man exited Mr. Giovanni's drugstore.

The apartment occupied the entire seventh floor of Hoffman Towers. The doors of the elevator opened in front of two large oak doors that led into a foyer of marble floors, walls accented with cherry wood, and a gold chandelier imported from South America.

With the live-in maid out of town visiting family, Maria

Nino's Heart: Chapter One

DiVincenzo was in the apartment by herself. She stood at a cast-iron stove preparing dinner.

One of the large double doors of their apartment swung open, then slammed.

"Mama! Mama! Where are you?"

"I'm here, Nino. I'm in the kitchen. What's wrong?"

As he approached her, he wiped the tears from his cheeks.

"Mr. Giovanni has been killed. I was there. I saw it. Mr. Giovanni is lying on the floor of his drugstore. He is behind the counter. I saw the man who killed him, and he saw me. He is one of the men who works for Papa. We need to tell him. Papa needs to tell the police."

Maria knelt next to her son. "Are you sure, Nino? Are you sure this is what you saw?"

"Yes, Mama." The words spewed out of him like a firehose. "I was in the back room of the drugstore filling a bucket with water. First, I heard Mr. Giovanni talking to the man. Then, I heard Mr. Giovanni begging for his life. After that, I looked through the curtain and saw Mr. Giovanni on the floor. Blood was flowing out of him. That big man who works for Papa was standing over him. I tried to get away, but the back door was locked. He had me trapped in the storage room. I thought he would kill me, too, but then when he looked at my face, he just stood there. Then he turned and left the store. He has been here before. He knows where I live. He will come after me."

She embraced him. "No, Nino. He will never come here again, I promise. I will speak to your father, he'll make certain of that."

He pushed her away. "I don't understand. How can Papa do that? I walk to school by myself. If the man wants

Nino's Heart: Chapter One

to kill me, how can Papa stop him? We need to call the police."

She grabbed his hands and looked into his eyes. "Listen to me, Nino. Everything will be fine. Your father will take care of this. Now, let me ask you something, and this is important: Was there anyone else there? Did anyone see you leave Mr. Giovanni's drugstore?"

"Nobody else was in the store. When I ran out, I passed a few people on the sidewalk. Some of them looked at me, but I just kept running until I got home."

"Did you know any of those people? Would they know you if they saw you again?"

Nino paused and said nothing while he stared into his mother's eyes.

Why was she not concerned about Mr. Giovanni?

Pulling away from her grip a second time, his voice crackled with emotion. "I don't understand, Mama. Why are you asking me these questions? Why aren't we going to the police station to tell them what happened?"

Maria noticed the look of confusion in her son's eyes. "Nino, we need to wait for your father to come home before we do anything. He will know what to do. But in the meantime, you mustn't tell anyone what you saw. Not your teachers. Not your classmates at school. No one. Do you understand, Nino? Will you promise me you will tell only me?"

Nino stood speechless as he weighed his mother's response to the bloodshed he had witnessed. Confused, he turned, ran into his bedroom, and slammed the door.

Nino's Heart: Chapter One

The Roseman Cameo Shop
Chicago, IL

As Hannah Roseman stepped onto the bus, the eyes of other passengers locked on to her as if she were an actress stepping on stage. They studied her every movement, watching as she paid the fare. While they gazed at her, she brushed her long sandy-blond hair from her face, her brown eyes searching the rows for an open seat. The experience of being gawked at was neither unusual nor significant for Hannah. It's simply how it was. It had always been that way. Several men stood, offering their seats to her. She refused their generosity, yet thanked them, as she made her way to the rear. Halfway down, a little girl in an aisle seat dropped her doll. Hannah bent down and retrieved it. "Here you are, sweetheart."

"Thank you, ma'am."

"You're welcome. Your doll is very pretty, just like you."

The little girl looked up at her and smiled.

Upon finding an open seat, Hannah removed one of her white gloves and brushed dirt from the wooden surface. She didn't want to soil her new blue skirt and matching waistcoat. After sitting, she took several deep breaths. Motion sickness overcame her even though the bus had barely left the curb. She was in the twelfth week of her second pregnancy, having lost her first child shortly after conceiving.

Following her exit from the bus at the corner of Michigan Avenue and Lakeshore Drive, she walked half a block to the Roseman Cameo Shop.

"Good morning, Clara," Hannah said, entering the showroom.

Nino's Heart: Chapter One

"Good morning, Mrs. Roseman. I trust your doctor's visit went well."

"Dr. Jacobs said the baby appears to be healthy."

"I say my prayers for you, Camillo, and the baby. I know you will make wonderful parents."

"You are very kind."

"When is Camillo due back from Italy?"

"Not for two more weeks. I wish it were sooner. I miss him terribly."

"I was wondering if you could help me with something, Mrs. Roseman?"

"What's that?"

"At Camillo's request, I sent several cameos to a customer in Kansas City. Yesterday, we received a telegram from the man, and he said he never received them. He demands an immediate refund. What should I do?"

"I'm awfully sorry, but I can't help you. The customer will need to remain patient until Camillo returns. I don't get involved in his business affairs."

The door opened and two elderly women walked in. As Clara waited on them, Hannah made her way to the door. "I'm going home to rest, Clara. I'll bring you lunch today since you're here by yourself. Do you like navy bean soup? I just prepared it yesterday."

"That sounds delightful, Mrs. Roseman. You're always so very thoughtful. Thank you."

"I'm happy to do it."

After Hannah left, one of the customers said, "That young woman was strikingly beautiful. Is she the owner of the store?"

"Her husband is. He comes from a wealthy Italian family. They own other stores in Italy. He is there now on business."

Nino's Heart: Chapter One

The Meatpacking District
Manhattan, NY

Fourteen men wearing fedoras and three-piece suits in varying shades of dark paced the floor of the warehouse. They smoked cigarettes and discussed the murder of Giovanni the druggist.

Fredo Romano stared at his watch in thirty second intervals as he stood in the back waiting for Salvador DiVincenzo to arrive. It was early Friday evening, and he was late. He was always late. Although never verbalized, each of the men standing in the dank, dusty building knew the purpose of his delay. It was a statement of power. A tactic Salvador had learned from his father—Alfonso DiVincenzo, the *Capo di tutti capi* of Sicily. Salvador's lieutenants were to be there at 6:00 p.m., but Salvador arrived when he arrived. Usually around 6:20 p.m., but often later—much later when he was pissed off, and Fredo Romano's last glance at his wrist read 7:06 p.m.

The purpose of their meetings was to review their individual business dealings. Salvador's lieutenants ran brothels, drug distribution rings, and illegal distilleries. Others, like Fredo Romano, controlled various forms of racketeering. Most commonly, extorting money from local businesses for protection against vandals and other ruffians.

"He's here," shouted one of the men peeking through a scratch in the painted glass.

Two men ran over and grabbed the handles of the bulky carriage doors and pulled. With headlights shining in their eyes, the assembly of thugs watched the Cadillac V-16 452 Fleetwood roll in. Dim, overhead lights in the warehouse reflected on the polished black paint. The rumble of the engine reverberated off the brick walls as the men

Nino's Heart: Chapter One

stepped to either side, the vehicle dividing them like Moses parting the Red Sea.

After bringing the vehicle to a stop, the driver exited before opening the door for his boss.

"Good evening, Mr. DiVincenzo," the group shouted in unison as the Don stepped out of the limousine.

Without responding, he strutted to the back office with a forty-dollar cigar hanging from his mouth. He was pudgy, yet sharp. He dressed to the nines in dark, pinstriped suits that cost most men a four-month wage. He exuded confidence.

"Fredo Romano, in the office. Now!" Salvador DiVincenzo shouted. "DeFazio and Moretti, I want you in there, too."

With their eyes locked on Fredo, the other men made a path for him so he could trail behind Salvador. DeFazio and Moretti, both as large as Fredo, brought up the rear as they entered the office.

"Close the door, Moretti, and have a seat, Romano," Salvador said.

Fredo sat down behind a desk covered with old newspapers and coffee cups that held more mold than a high school science project.

Standing in the middle of the office, Salvador said, "What the hell happened, Romano? I never told you to cut nobody."

"I'm sorry, Mr. DiVincenzo. I lost my head. The druggist was the fourth person of the day I went to collect from who said they didn't have no money. I had to make an example of someone."

Salvador removed the cigar from his mouth and walked toward Fredo, "You make an example of someone by busting up their place or breaking their fingers. You don't

Nino's Heart: Chapter One

slice nobody unless I tell you to slice them. You are one dumb shit, Romano. This will stack heat on me like I was rolling in a coal furnace."

Salvador paced back and forth in the office, taking a quick puff of his cigar. He then walked back toward Romano. "I hope you were at least smart enough to make certain nobody saw you. Were there any witnesses, Romano? Did anyone see you leave that store?"

Fredo leaned forward thinking he might be ill. He twisted the wedding ring on his finger, wondering if he would ever see his wife and children again. Beads of sweat rolled down his forehead. Lying would only make it worse. He sat in the chair speechless.

Breaking the silence, Salvador said, "The fact that you ain't sayin' nothin' tells me you don't have good news. How many saw you, Romano? Did you recognize any of them? If you know them, tell me now so I can send DeFazio and Moretti to shut them up."

Knowing he could no longer stay silent, Fredo blurted out, "It was Nino, Mr. DiVincenzo. Your son, Nino."

Salvador paused and said nothing. Holding the cigar in his hand, he tilted his head to the side, stared at Romano, then at the other two men in the room. He flicked his cigar on the floor and slammed his forearm on the desk before swinging it across the top, sending the newspapers and coffee cups against the wall.

Moving his face inches from Fredo's, Salvador said, "My son Nino was there? You killed a man while my son watched you do it?"

"No, no, no, Mr. DiVincenzo. Let me explain. It wasn't like that. It wasn't like that at all. Nino was in the back room. I didn't know he was there. He must have heard the noise and peeked around the curtain and saw me standing

Nino's Heart: Chapter One

over the dead guy. At first, I didn't know it was him. He ran to the back of the storage room, and I went after him. I was going to take him out, but when I got there, I saw it was Nino. So, I turned and left the store."

Salvador stood up straight and stared down at Romano. "When did all of this happen?"

"This afternoon, about three thirty."

Salvador turned and opened the office door then said to DeFazio and Moretti, "Don't let this fat shit out of your sight. I would tell you to take him out back and shoot him, but somebody is going to the electric chair for this, and it sure as hell ain't going to be me."

Hoffman Towers
Bronx, NY

"I'm home, Mama," Angelo shouted while crossing the foyer of their apartment. His work boots left a trail of dirt across the marble floor.

"Take your shoes off at the door," Maria yelled from the master bedroom. "And leave your brother alone. Say nothing to him until your father comes home."

Angelo and Nino shared one of the three bedrooms in the apartment. The live-in maid, Elsa, stayed in another, and Salvador and Maria occupied the master suite.

Angelo grabbed the doorknob of the bedroom, but it wouldn't turn.

"Unlock the door, Nino. What are you doing in there, playing with yourself again? Come on, open up. I need to change my clothes and wash up before dinner."

"Go away, Angelo," Nino shouted.

Angelo beat on the door. "I don't have time for this. Open up."

Nino's Heart: Chapter One

Nino unlocked the door and let his brother enter their bedroom.

"What the hell is wrong with you, Nino?"

Saying nothing to Angelo, Nino crossed the room and sat in a wooden chair in the corner. His face was red, and he stared at the floor. He was trembling.

Angelo said, "Talk to me, little brother. I have never seen you like this. I know something is wrong because Mama told me not to talk to you until Papa gets home."

Nino remained silent. Angelo crossed the room and sat on Nino's bed.

"Nino, it's me, Angelo. I know I treat you like crap, but you know I have always been there for you when you needed me. And you look like you need me now. What's going on?"

"I saw Mr. Giovanni get murdered today."

"Oh, shit. Is that what happened? I heard the cops were hanging out at his store, but nobody knew why. So, you are telling me somebody whacked Mr. Giovanni and you saw them do it? Did the guy see you?"

"Yes."

"What did he do?"

"He did nothing. He just stared at me. I thought he was going to kill me, then he turned and walked away."

"Have you ever seen him before?"

"It was that really big guy who works for Papa. The one who comes here sometimes and gives him money."

"Fredo Romano, Nino? Was it Fredo Romano?"

"I don't know his name."

"What happened? What did you see?"

Nino explained every detail to Angelo, including their mother's indifference toward Mr. Giovanni's fate.

Nino's Heart: Chapter One

"Just like Mama told you, you can't tell nobody what you saw. Do you understand that?"

"No, I don't understand. Mr. Giovanni was a nice man. He was my friend, and I'll tell the police."

Angelo said, "For someone who is so smart, you sure can be a moron sometimes."

"Don't talk to me like that."

"It's time someone opens your eyes to what goes on around here and it will be me right here, right now. If I don't, you will screw everything up for all of us—our whole family."

"What are you talking about?"

"Wake up, Nino. Have you ever wondered why we live in a big ass apartment on the seventh floor of this building? You go to a private school with the wealthiest kids in New York City, but everyone else around you is standing in soup lines or begging for food. Have you ever asked yourself those questions?"

"I just figured it's because Papa owns all of his companies. That's what Mama says."

"And what the hell do you think those companies do?"

"I don't know, Angelo. You work for Papa, you tell me."

"Okay, brace yourself, little brother. I'll start with the best part. My favorite. Do you know what a whore is?"

"I think it is a woman who has sex for money."

"That's right. And when the whores here in the Bronx have sex for money, who do you think keeps the money?"

"I don't know. I guess they do."

"No, Nino, they don't. All the whore gets is a chance to not get the crap beat out of her by one of Papa's men. The person who gets the money is Papa. Papa owns all the whores in the Bronx."

"That's a lie. I don't believe it."

Nino's Heart: Chapter One

"Believe it, Nino. I have seen it myself. And that's just the beginning.

Nino stood up to leave the room, but Angelo grabbed his arm.

"Sit down. There's a lot more for you to know, and you need to know all of it. I'm telling you because if you go to the police and tell them about what you saw, Papa may go to the electric chair."

"You're wrong. Papa didn't kill Mr. Giovanni, that man did. I saw him."

"But don't you see, Nino? That man works for Papa. Papa ordered that man to go see Mr. Giovanni. That man's job is to collect money from the businesses in the Bronx."

"Collect money for what?"

"Collect money to keep Papa from busting up their stores and beating them up."

Nino bowed his head and wept.

"Get control of yourself, little brother. You'll learn to accept the family business. Just like Mama and I have. Papa has big plans for both of us, especially you. I've heard Papa tell Mama many times that since you are the smart one, he is sending you to law school when you get older. That's why you are going to that expensive prep school. Papa has many lawyers who work for him. You will be in charge of all of them. He says, 'I need someone I can trust, and there's nobody you can trust like family.'"

Nino stood and stepped toward the door.

"I don't believe any of this, Angelo. You are making it all up. But if what you say is true, I'll never work for Papa."

Nino's Heart: Chapter One

The Cadillac Fleetwood came to a stop in front of Hoffman Towers. The sun had set, and there was a chill in the air. Salvador DiVincenzo didn't wait for the driver to open his door before sprinting through the light drizzle and up the six steps to the entrance. Ignoring the doorman's nod, he opened the door of the lobby to see Deputy Inspector Murphy of the 43rd Precinct.

"What the hell are you doing here, Murphy?"

"Good evening, Mr. DiVincenzo. I am here because I have a message for you. It's important. Is there someplace we can speak in private?"

Salvador looked at the doorman. "If anyone comes by to see me or my family—I don't care who it is—we ain't home, you got it?"

"Yes sir, Mr. DiVincenzo."

Salvador reached for the elevator button and said to Inspector Murphy, "Come up to the apartment."

On the elevator, Salvador said, "Are you stupid? You and me together don't look good."

"I'm sorry, Mr. DiVincenzo, but what I have to say to you is urgent."

Exiting the elevator, the two men entered the foyer of the apartment. Salvador shouted, "Maria, I'm home. I have a guest. We will be in my den. Don't disturb us."

They entered the office and Salvador closed the French doors behind them before walking around the oak desk.

Salvador sat in his leather chair. "Would you like a cigar? They are Cubans."

"No, Mr. DiVincenzo. I'm fine. Thank you."

"Have a seat, Murphy, and tell me, is this about that druggist?"

"Yes, Mr. DiVincenzo."

Nino's Heart: Chapter One

"What the hell am I up against? What does the brass down at the station know?"

"It ain't good, sir. Everyone suspects you were behind the murder of the druggist."

"Of course they do. Every time someone gets whacked, I am the number one suspect. But I tell you, Murphy, I ain't got nothin' to do with it. My lawyers will clear me. They always do."

"That may be the case, Mr. DiVincenzo, but there's a twist to this story."

Placing his cigar in an ash tray, Salvador leaned forward and put both elbows on the desk. "What the hell are you talking about? What is this twist that has you all worked up?"

"When our boys at the scene showed up, there was a cap and schoolbooks on the counter of the drugstore."

Salvador picked up the cigar and puffed while leaning back in his chair. "Why is this of interest to me?"

Leaning forward toward Salvador, Murphy said, "There was a name in the hat. The name was Nino DiVincenzo."

Salvador stared back at Murphy, "How can you fix this for me?"

"I'm sorry Mr. DiVincenzo. Had I been the first on the scene, I would have walked out of there with Nino's stuff. But by the time I arrived, it was too late. All the other cops who were there are clean. I was the only one on your payroll."

"What happens now?"

"The good thing is I'm here is to bring Nino down to the station for questioning. Two other guys were supposed to come with me, but they were called away to a mugging. Since it's just you and me, we can talk to Nino and come up with a story."

Nino's Heart: Chapter One

Salvador paused and looked up at the ceiling. "I know nobody else was there when it happened. Nino was the only witness."

Murphy said, "I won't ask you how you know that."

"Don't."

Salvador rose from the chair. "Stay here, I'll get Nino."

Opening one of the double doors, Salvador yelled through the apartment, "Nino, come here now!"

Maria crossed the foyer from the kitchen. "What is it Salvador? What is so urgent?"

"Go find Nino, Maria, and bring him here to my den, now!"

Maria turned and made her way down the hallway before knocking on the boy's bedroom.

"Come in," Angelo said.

"Where is Nino? Your father wants to speak to him."

"I don't know, Mama. I thought he was with you. He left here about an hour ago, and he was really upset."

Maria turned and walked through the apartment, checking each room and shouting, "Nino, your father needs to see you."

Salvador approached Maria. "Well, where the hell is he?"

"He's not here. He must have snuck out of the apartment. I told him to stay in his room until you got home."

"Where the hell could he have gone?"

Angelo stepped out of his bedroom. "He said he was going to go to the police, but I thought I'd talked him out of it."

Grab your copy…
www.vinci-books.com/ninos-heart

About the Author

J.D. (Jim) Keene was born in Crown Point, IN., where he lived until he enlisted in the United States Navy at the age of seventeen.

While in the navy, he was stationed on the aircraft carrier USS Coral Sea CV-43, which was homeported in Norfolk Virginia. The Coral Sea made frequent port calls in Europe where Keene became intrigued with the history of the continent.

The Heroes of Sainte-Mère-Église is Keene's first novel. Although initial ideas were set to paper in early 2018, it didn't come to life until he visited the village of Sainte-Mère-Église in Normandy France. While there, the story began to emerge in his imagination.

The success of *The Heroes of Sainte-Mère-Église* has inspired him to write other novels, including *Nino's Heart* and *Nino's War*. He currently has initial outlines drafted for several other novels relating to WW2.

www.ingramcontent.com/pod-product-compliance
Lightning Source LLC
Chambersburg PA
CBHW011933250425
25732CB00023B/80